LOTUS

JENNIFER HARTMANN

To the lost and the wandering—
You will find your way.

PROLOGUE

"**G**ET OUT OF THE ROAD, FREAK!"

I jump back. Vehicles speed past me, loud and obtrusive, flashes of colors and lights. Panicked breaths climb up my throat as I stumble along the side of the roadway.

This is a dream.

There are humans behind the wheels of these vehicles, some hanging out of their windows, pointing a device towards me. They are breathing the air. They are gawking and laughing and shouting clipped words into the dusky evening.

This can't be right.

I break out into a run, a shot of dizziness funneling through my veins. The sound of my heartbeats nearly detonating in my ears has my legs weakening with every urgent step. There is so much noise, so much chaos. I unzip my hazmat suit mid-run, my insides suffocating, and pull it off as I reach for my mask.

I falter.

The sound of a blaring horn startles me, and I almost trip on the plastic bunching around my ankles, revealing my blood-soaked chest and pants. The cold air shocks my skin.

Before I can think it through, I yank off my mask—my final barrier of protection.

I inhale giant gulps of oxygen, breathing in deep, letting the ice fill my lungs for the first time in decades. God, it is glorious. Unrivaled. I drink it in like water, like sustenance, basking in the earthy winter musk I had long since forgotten.

Then I smell what lies beneath—something astringent. Fumes of some sort. My heart rattles with dread.

Oh, God... fumes.

Bradford was right.

I have made a fatal mistake.

Clutching my neck, I wait for death. Chest tight, lungs wheezing, I fall atop the gravel when my knees give out, hitting hard. Vehicles continue to pass, spraying me with sludge and dirt. Through blurred vision, I see one of them decelerate beside me, feet appearing in my line of sight a few moments later. The feet grow closer, my breaths quickening.

"Sir? Are you all right, sir?" It's a male voice, similar to Bradford. "I think you're having a panic attack. I'll call 9-1-1."

The voice fades out as I fully collapse, struggling for air. The toxic fumes are consuming me, snuffing out my life. I curl my legs up into the fetal position and whisper raggedly as everything goes dark, "Lotus…"

The Black Lotus has been defeated.

CHAPTER ONE

SYDNEY

I DIDN'T MEAN TO FLASH THE NEIGHBOR.

I was only running out to grab the mail, so my robe seemed like an acceptable amount of coverage. My neighbors are used to seeing me in paint-smeared pajama pants, assorted beanies, mismatched socks, and oversized t-shirts with nineties prints on them. Usually, all at the same time.

So, the robe seemed like a step up. I felt good about it.

But then I slipped on a patch of ice and fell spread-eagle on my driveway, facing Lorna Gibson's house. I was wearing underwear at least, but the tie came undone, and a boob popped out, prompting the old woman to clutch her rosary and perform the sign of the cross a dozen times.

I tuck the girls back into place and climb to my feet, groaning at the throbbing ache in my tailbone. I wave to Lorna, who dropped her own mail and is staring up at the Heavens, surely praying for God himself to strike me down. "I'm okay!" I call out with forced cheerfulness. She ignores me, still chanting her Hail Marys. "The leopard print panties are on sale at Victoria's Secret if you were curious. Super breathable!"

Lorna gasps with a hand over her heart, shaking her head at me from across the yard. She looks like she wants to personally give me an exorcism. "Blasphemous child," she mutters before scooping up her mail and racing into the house.

Sydney Neville. The sacrilegious tramp of Briarwood Lane.

I chuckle under my breath, unfazed. Lorna has hated me ever since I politely declined her offer to join her Bible club a few years back. I'm assuming it's like a book club with only one book—the Bible.

Considering I like to read dark romances with lots of graphic sex and explicit language, I'm certain I would have been sitting there bored, wondering when Adam and Eve were finally going to get freaky.

"You okay, Sydney?"

I massage my backside, then tighten my robe, turning to face the house on the opposite side of mine. Gabe is poking his head out through the screen door with a worried frown.

I grin through my shrug. "Oh, you know, just pissing off old ladies before I've even had my morning coffee. The usual."

"Troublemaker," he winks, propping his elbow against the frame. "You hurt yourself?"

"Just my pride and sparkling reputation."

"So, you're good, then."

"Fantastic." I smile wide. "*Always Sunny* marathon tonight?"

He points a finger at me. "Make that taco dip and it's a date."

I give him an agreeable salute and watch as he disappears back inside.

Gabe Wellington is my best friend. We're like siblings, having grown up together over the past twenty-six years. I moved into this house with my parents when I was only three, then bought it from them last year when Dad retired and wanted to pursue his lifelong dream of living on a golf course. Gabe grew up in the house next door with his father and stepmother.

And Oliver.

But we don't talk about Oliver anymore.

Gabe's stepmom passed away over a decade ago, and his father, Travis Wellington, remarried and transferred the title of the house over to his son.

So, we're still neighbors, still friends, and still making terrible decisions together.

I wander into the house, flipping through my credit card statements and utility notices. I push my dark-rimmed eyeglasses up the bridge of my nose, reminiscing over the days I would look forward to getting mail —back when I was on the receiving end of a *Teen Beat* subscription and money-filled cards from Grammy.

My tabby cat, Alexis, purrs as she circles my ankles, and I tug at my messy bun before leaning down to scoop her up. I make my way into my office with the orange cat tucked under my arm, prepared to sort through e-mails and get to work. I'm primarily a graphic designer who focuses on building websites for clients. That's what pays my bills, anyway.

I also paint.

Painting is my true passion, and I'm grateful that it provides an additional financial cushion to help support my coffee habit and dirty book collection. I've had a few pieces shown in art galleries, as well as auctions. I attend craft fairs and vendor shows, and I take on personal requests through my Etsy shop.

It's a dream life in a lot of ways. I'm independent, and I work from home doing what I love. I even bartend on the occasional weekend so I can pretend I have a social life outside of Facebook and my cat.

But I won't lie and say it's perfect—loneliness creeps in more often than not. My parents live an hour away, and my sister, Clementine, has her own life with a young daughter as she battles through a messy divorce.

After powering up my laptop and settling in with my mug of coffee, I get to work, scrolling through e-mails and corresponding with one of my favorite romance authors who I have the privilege of designing a website for.

While I reach for my cell phone to turn on a *Lord Huron* playlist, I accidentally elbow Alexis, who jumps from the desk and knocks my coffee over in the process.

"Shit!" I curse, realizing my Arabian mocha has just toppled onto a stack of paintings I had carelessly placed beside my workstation. "No, no, no..." I act quick, grabbing a discarded t-shirt and rushing back over to the scene of the crime. My breath catches when I notice the painting that caught the brunt of the mess.

It's a painting of Oliver Lynch.

My childhood best friend.

Gabe's stepbrother.

The little boy who went missing on the Fourth of July almost twenty-two years ago, never to be seen again.

I frantically begin dabbing at the portrait, tears springing to my eyes.

Not this one. Please not this one.

I spent eight long months working on this painting. It was based off the computer-generated, age-progressed photo of Oliver released by the media. It's an image of what he may look like today if he were still alive.

The shirt soaks up the dark coffee, and I watch it seep into the cotton fabric before setting it aside to trail my finger down along his jawline. It's been over two decades, but the wound feels fresh. My heart still aches when I think about the boy with light brown hair and eyes like a burgundy sunset. I can still hear his laugh and picture his dirt-smudged overalls.

Sometimes, I swear I *feel* him or hear him whisper my name…

Syd.

Oliver's old bedroom is adjacent to my office, which used to be a playroom when my sister and I were kids. I have vivid memories of shouting knock-knock jokes from window to window, playing 'telephone' with a string and two tin cans, and telling ghost stories with flashlights underneath our chins. On that final day, July 4th, 1998, we made plans to go see *The Parent Trap* when it released later that month. Our mothers were best friends and loved taking us to the movies—we'd giggle through our popcorn and gummy candy, while my mom and his mom, Charlene, snuck wine into the theater and giggled more than we did.

I never did see *The Parent Trap.*

To this day, I still haven't seen it. It never felt right seeing it without him.

With a final glance over to Oliver's window, which is now dark and filled with boxes and junk, I finish drying off the portrait and move it to a safer location in the corner of the room. I choke down my emotions and try to refocus.

Before I can settle in again, my ringtone goes off. It's the *X-Files* opening credits music, which means it's my sister. I send her to voicemail, flustered that I've made zero progress with my deadlines and it's already almost ten A.M.

She shoots me a text instead.

Clem: *Answer me, hoochy*

I groan.

Me: *I'm working, skank*

Clem: *I need you to watch Poppy this weekend. Pretty please. No cherries on top because I ate them.*

A grin slips as I sigh and text her back.

Me: *I'm working at the bar this weekend, but I can bring her with me. We can make fabulous memories and learn about what choices not to make when she grows up. Plus, Brant is sure to teach her some colorful new words, AAAND there's a wet t-shirt contest going on. #auntniecebondingherewecome*

Clem: *I'll ask Regina.*

Clem follows up her text with an abundance of aggravated emojis, and

6

I can't help but laugh, silencing my phone and running downstairs to make another pot of coffee.

That asshole stood me up.

Gabe and I decided on seven o'clock for our *Always Sunny in Philadelphia* binge-fest, and it's almost eight. The taco dip is dwindling away with every scoop of my tortilla chip, while Alexis lies perched in my lap. I pluck off my glasses and reach for my cell, prepared to blow up Gabe's phone with David Hasselhoff memes. He probably found a hot girl to cozy up with tonight, which is perfectly fine, but he could have filled me in on his change of plans.

Instead, I see a missed text from Clementine.

Clem: *Sis. Turn on the news.*

I frown. She knows I don't have basic cable—only Netflix and Hulu like most millennials these days. I'm about to open Facebook, my preferred news source, when I notice flashing lights reflecting in my television screen. I pull myself up to my knees on the couch and peek through the curtain, my mouth going dry.

Gabe's house is surrounded by police cruisers.

What the hell?

At first, I wonder if he's having one of his parties, but there are no other cars in the driveway, and I didn't hear any music or loud noise.

Shit. Something's wrong.

Nausea sweeps through me like a windstorm, taking my breath away. I don't think twice before pulling on my winter boots and running out the front door in nothing but my sweatpants and *Rugrats* t-shirt. The crisp air is a welcome contrast to the heat prickling my skin.

My head twists to the right, spotting Lorna Gibson standing on her front porch, taking in the scene. One hand clasps her cross pendant while the other cups her mouth, and her eyes aren't filled with their usual scorn and judgment—they are filled with tears.

Heart racing and knees begging to buckle, I gather my courage and trudge through the thin layer of snow coating my lawn. The police lights are blurry as I make a clumsy trek over to Gabe's, realizing I forgot to put my glasses back on. When I reach his front stoop, I don't bother to knock. I yank open the screen and push inside, almost hitting an officer with the door. Three unfamiliar faces turn to look at me with pinched brows and tight lips.

"Are you a friend of the family?" one of them asks.

My voice trembles as I respond, "Where's Gabe? Is he hurt?"

But then I see him.

An officer steps aside, revealing my friend. Gabe is sitting on the edge of his couch, elbows to knees, his hands tented in front of his face. His eyes are red and bloodshot, rimmed with tears, and he gazes up at me with the most haunting expression I've ever seen.

My heart clenches through chaotic beats, confusion and fear battling it out inside of me. "Gabe... what the hell is going on?"

Gabe stands, scrubbing his face with his palms as he takes slow steps toward me. His dark blonde hair is stuck to the sweat glistening on his forehead. "Sydney."

I stare at him, waiting with wide eyes and quivering limbs.

"Sydney..." he continues, then heaves in a deep breath. "It's Oliver. They found Oliver."

The air leaves my lungs with a giant whoosh, and I teeter on both feet, wondering if I misheard him. My foggy vision becomes even more hindered as fresh tears coat my eyes. "Wh-what?" A strangled gasp escapes me, the words registering one at a time.

They found Oliver.

They. Found. Oliver.

I manage to get one more question out: "Where was his body?"

His body. His bones.

His dirty overalls with popsicles stains.

Gabe takes a few more steps forward, his throat bobbing as he swallows hard. He reaches out to squeeze my shoulders, and I'm grateful for that, I'm so grateful, because his next words rip the rug out from under me.

"He's alive."

I collapse.

CHAPTER TWO

SYDNEY

A POWDER BLUE HOSPITAL CURTAIN is the final barrier hovering between me and my childhood best friend—the man discovered on the side of a snowy highway thirty miles west of his hometown, shirtless and bloody, with a protective hazmat suit gathered around his ankles.

It's the only *physical* barrier, anyway.

My sneakers pegged to the sticky hospital floor provide an equally effective excuse to remain on the opposite side of that curtain, chewing on my fingernails. Hands shaking violently, eyes closed tight, the dense lump in my throat refuses to budge.

Much like my feet.

I'm not sure what I'm expecting to find when I walk through that curtain, and that's exactly why I'm stalling. That's why I'm scared shitless, near tears, tongue-tied and teetering. Part of me thinks I'll see that same little boy from twenty-two years ago with freckles on his nose and shaggy hair, bangs cloaking two curious eyes. We'll share a popsicle and a knock-knock joke, then everything will go back to the way it was before.

The way it's supposed to be.

Another part of me expects a ghost.

Oliver Lynch can't be real… he can't be *alive*, walking and talking, warm flesh, blood flowing. He can't be more than a pile of brittle bones and soil.

A beautiful memory.

The last twenty-four hours have overthrown everything I thought I knew, shattering the walls I've constructed over the years, dismantling each and every misaligned theory I force-fed myself, just so I could *cope*.

Just so I could move forward with my life without him.

But part of me knew—part of me fucking *knew* he was still out there, and I hate myself for not looking hard enough.

Gabe's hand floats to the small of my back, causing me to jump in place. "You okay?"

I forgot he was even standing beside me.

Nodding through a watery smile, my lie is as transparent as my nerves. My hands continue to tremble, nailbeds raw from my teeth, legs hardly holding up my weight.

God, what am I supposed to say to him?

Will he even remember me? I look nothing like the seven-year-old girl he left behind with sun-kissed pigtails and chubby cheeks. I'm a grown woman now.

And he's a man.

"What did he look like?" The question squeaks out as a whisper, my gaze fixed on the curtain as if my eyes might gift me with x-ray vision, allowing me to steal a peek at him.

I know all I need to do is pull back the drape and step inside, I *know* this... but if he doesn't remember me, if he doesn't look at me and see fireworks and oatmeal cookies and laughter beneath the summer sun, I swear my heart will shrivel up and die.

Gabe's hand travels up and down my spine with languid strokes, curling around my shoulder and offering a comforting squeeze. He replies in an equally strained whisper. "Lost. He looked... lost."

My insides twist and ache as I fight off tears. "They still don't know what happened to him?"

"Not yet. He's confused and not entirely coherent. The doctor wouldn't even let me see him right away because they didn't know if he was violent, or..." Gabe falters through a pained gulp, dipping his chin to his chest. "He didn't recognize me."

No.

I realize Gabe was only in preschool at the time of Oliver's disappearance, but Lord help me, I want him to remember *everything*. Every single detail from our magical childhood that has been carved inside me, permanently engraved.

"Do you want me to come with you?"

My dismissal is quick, despite the fact that my feet are still rooted in place, idle, refusing to press forward. "I got this."

"Yeah?" He quirks a grin amidst the emotional turmoil swimming between us. "Because I'm literally holding you up right now."

Gabe lets go of my shoulder to prove his point, and I stumble, almost plowing through that ugly curtain like a human wrecking ball. He catches me by the wrist before I make an overly dramatic entrance. "Ugh, point taken," I bite out, inhaling a giant breath of courage and slamming my eyes shut. "But I need to do this alone."

"I get it, Syd." Gabe taps his knuckles along my upper arm with a light punch before stepping backwards. "I'll be in the waiting room. Text me if you need me."

Gnawing my bottom lip between my teeth and resisting the urge to drag Gabe into the room with me as a security blanket, I bob my chin, seeing him off.

And then I inch towards the curtain, counting to ten, chanting words of encouragement under my breath as I try to zap away the rattling nerves.

I raise my hand, bunching the stiff, itchy fabric between my fingers to move it aside.

That's when I see him.

That's when my eyes land on Oliver Lynch for the first time in twenty-two long, devastating years. The curtain drops from my fingers as my hand shoots up to cup my mouth, preventing a strangled cry from escaping. I'm frozen in the entryway with Oliver directly in front of me, lying partially covered beneath a white blanket. He's hooked up to various cords and monitors, and I'm thankful they are beeping and buzzing, filling the air between us, otherwise all we would hear is the sound of my heart screaming and choking with the weight of each breath.

Oliver doesn't look at me. His eyes are trained on the popcorn ceiling, a slight frown marring his forehead. Maybe he doesn't realize I'm in the room, or maybe he's lost inside his head, but while his focus is elsewhere, I take a moment to drink him in, my gaze soaking up every incredible inch of this man—this stranger, in a way, and yet... *so much more.*

He is beautiful.

That same light brown hair falls at his shoulders, shaggy and untamed, infused with hints of amber. A shadow of scruff lines his sharp and masculine jaw, emphasizing sleek cheekbones and a sallow complexion.

My gaze slips lower, and I'm surprised to discover a man who seems to have been well-cared for. Despite whatever circumstances he's endured, Oliver is not overly thin or malnourished as I had anticipated—the opposite, in fact. Biceps peek out from his hospital gown encompassing broad shoulders and a strapping chest that heaves with his own weighty breaths.

Tentative feet carry me closer to his bedside, his name croaking out between my lips and addressing him for the first time in decades. "Oliver."

My God, those three syllables caressing my tongue force out a sob that finally catches his attention. Just barely.

Oliver blinks. Long eyelashes flit and flutter, his gaze still pinned on the ceiling, his fingers gripping the bed covers between tight fists.

Moving closer, I pull my lips between my teeth, unsure of what to say or do. I don't want to startle him. I don't want to spook him.

I just want him to look at me—to *see* me.

"Oliver," I repeat. My own hands move behind my back, wrists crossing as a way to prevent them from reaching for him. "I'm Sydney. Do you remember me?"

I monitor his micro-expressions carefully. The subtle twitch of his mouth. The tensing of his jaw. The muscle spasm in his right bicep.

The slight widening of his eyes—so quick, I wonder if I imagined it.

I continue forward, stepping closer until the front of my sweater grazes the guardrail and I can feel his body heat warming my skin. Curling my fingers around the rail, I mutter softly, "It's me, Oliver... it's Syd."

A flash of recognition washes over him; I swear it, I'm *convinced* of it.

My throat tightens on a sharp inhale, ribs vibrating with delirious beats. The side rail is the only thing keeping me from collapsing onto him, a mess of tears and heartbreaking joy.

Oliver cranes his neck as he finally pulls his focus off the ceiling, head shifting lazily towards me until our faces meet.

Eyes of blue incredulity meet his haunted, hollow pools of burgundy and brown. I can't express what the moment does to me. Emotions so raw and unbidden, so inconceivable, threaten to drown me. I want to weep and wail and hug him so tight, he won't be able to escape.

He can't leave me.

Not again. Not ever.

As his eyes search my face, both wandering and heavy, Oliver inhales a choppy breath. Gold flecks shimmer back at me, masking years of mystery, of unknown horrors that have whittled away the carefree, fun-loving boy I can recall with agonizing clarity.

When he speaks, his voice is laced with a touch of disbelief, a hint of awe, as if he can't believe what he's seeing. I think he's about to say my name, but instead, he rasps out, "Queen of the Lotus."

What?

The air between us thickens. I have no idea how to respond to the words that just broke free. A tear tracks down my cheek like a quiet reply, while the back of my wrist lifts to swipe it away. We hold our stare, and I watch as confliction etches itself into his features, pulling his brows together, narrowing his eyes with bloodshot bewilderment. Something new washes over him, something frightening, replacing that fleeting pocket of recognition with... *panic.*

Oliver shakes his head back and forth, his hands tightening around the covers as he twists away from me. "No, no, no... this isn't real."

I wet my lips as I determine what to do next, my nerve-endings tingling and frayed. I want to reach for him, to console him with my touch and heartbeats and words of solace, but I'm afraid I'll only make it worse. "It's okay, Oliver. You're safe."

"This is all wrong. I'm dreaming..." Oliver continues to chant under his breath, head swinging side to side, knuckles white from fisting the sheets. "You can't be real..."

Tears burn while my heart breaks for him. "I'm real. I'm—"

"You're fine, Oliver. It's all right."

A nurse enters the room, stealing away the rest of my words and causing me to flinch back from Oliver's bedside. I glance at her, visibly shaken, my palms clammy as I wring them together in front of me. "I-I'm sorry. I'm not sure what upset him."

The woman offers me a cheerless smile. "He's confused and easily agitated. There's no telling what may trigger him," she explains, tinkering with a long needle. "I'll give him a sedative to help him relax. He'll be okay."

My bottom lip catches between my teeth and I bite and nibble until it hurts. Gaze floating back to Oliver, my stomach pitches at the sight of him so broken, so unhinged, so *confused.* His eyes are squeezed shut, lips moving with jumbled, mixed-up blather.

He recognized me in some way, I'm sure of it, but did he truly *see* me?

Does he *remember* me?

"I think we should let him rest now."

I blink at the nurse's request, taking that as my cue to get lost.

Swallowing, I produce a small nod, pacing backwards from the room with my eyes fixated on the man who is now curled up onto his side, blanket to his chin, knees drawn up like he's trying to hide. The image is a swift punch to my gut, dizzying my feet until I find myself tangled up in that awful, goddamn blue curtain.

I break free and push through to the hospital hallway where I steady my ragged breaths, the heel of my palm pressed against my breastbone.

One question floods my mind as my shoulders heave up and down.

What happened to you, Oliver Lynch?

I know it's a question for another day, so I hold back a new onfall of tears and whisper softly, "Goodbye."

It's a goodbye for now.

Not forever.

Three weeks later, I'm watching through cracked curtains as Gabe opens the passenger's side door of his Challenger and waits for Oliver to step outside. I observe the hesitation, the fear, the uncertainty, as Oliver clutches his knees between tense fingers and stays implanted to the leather seat. He's wearing one of Gabe's plaid button-down shirts, along with jeans that appear too tight for his more muscled physique.

Oliver stares at the raised-ranch house made of honey-colored bricks and dark shutters, his jaw taut, his eyes flickering with unease.

I want to run to him.

I want to tell him it's okay, *it will be okay*, but Gabe and I decided it was best if I let Oliver get acclimated to his living arrangements before coming over. He's overly sensitive to new faces, new environments, and to stimulation in general.

Oliver slowly plants his shoes on the pavement and pulls himself out of the vehicle. He's exceedingly tall, well over six feet, towering over Gabe who is at least a few inches shorter. It's incredible staring at these two men, side-by-side, after twenty-two years. My last image of them together consists of sticky popsicle fingers, bowl cuts, and grass stains on their knees. Now they are grown men—both handsome and striking in appearance, though, vastly different.

And one of them looks utterly terrified.

Ashen.

I clutch the neckline of my shirt in a trembling fist, the other holding the drapes away from the window as my eyes stay locked on Oliver. He scratches at his overgrown hair, his gaze darting around the yard with suspicion. I can see that his own hands are shaking while he studies his surroundings, prepared to bolt at the slightest threat. Gabe reaches out with a cautious touch, placing his palm against his stepbrother's broad shoulder, and Oliver flinches back, startled.

My heart clenches.

After a few moments of indecision, Oliver finally moves his feet to follow Gabe up the cracked stone walkway towards the front of the house. As he presses forward, he pauses to glance around once again, still unsure, still noticeably hesitant. His eyes peruse the right, then the left, and before he drags his sights back to the house, they land on me through the bay window.

My breath catches as my hand squeezes the curtain so hard, I almost tug it right off the rod. Oliver narrows his eyes slightly, trying to read me or understand me somehow—as if he's attempting to fit me into the complexities of his mind, like a missing puzzle piece.

We are yards apart, separated by a pane of glass and twenty-two long years, but I feel something pass between us. A current. A frisson of wayward memories and new possibilities. I want to know what he's thinking as he stares at me, studying me with a rigid jaw and inquisitive eyes. I'm overwhelmed with not knowing what the hell to do or how to break this clutch, so I offer a small smile and lift my hand with an awkward wave.

Lame.

Oliver blinks away our hold while Gabe turns to face me from his driveway. He smiles at me, a sad, unsettled smile, and pulls Oliver from our stare-down.

I let out the air trapped in my lungs and loosen my grip on the curtain, watching as the two men continue their trek to the front door and disappear inside.

Does he remember me?

I still don't know.

Police and detectives are trying to piece together the details of Oliver's captivity. He hasn't given much information—in fact, he's hardly spoken at all.

Gabe visited Oliver a few times after he was transferred to an inpatient psychiatric unit for monitoring, but his ramblings mostly consisted of "lotus" and "Bradford" and "the end of the world". Nothing coherent. Nothing cohesive. If authorities have gotten more out of him, it hasn't been revealed to us yet. I have no insight into the reality of his life —I don't know the horrors he's faced or the obstacles he's had to overcome. I don't know if he's been abused, or chained up in some madman's basement, or God forbid, sexually assaulted.

My stomach twists at the thought, and I step back from the window, releasing a hard breath.

Lotus.

I wonder what it means to him. I want to know its significance.

Oliver called me "Queen of the Lotus" during our brief reunion, and the title has been haunting me ever since.

I make my way over to the living room couch, reaching for my journal lying atop the coffee table. Flipping through the lined paper, I open the notebook to my most recent page of scribblings and absorb the words:

*The **Lotus** flower is an emblem for rebirth in an assortment of cultures, as well as eastern religions. It has attributes that correlate perfectly to the human condition: the **Lotus** will bloom into the most magnificent flower, even when its roots are in the murkiest of waters.*

This was what I discovered when I researched the meaning of the word, and it took my breath away. I instantly copied it down, mulling over the meaning for weeks. Why is this flower important to Oliver?

Why does he associate it with *me*?

I prop my feet up on the coffee table, crisscrossing them at the ankles, then toss the notebook beside me on the cushion. My gaze skips over to the canvas portrait leaning against my far wall.

Familiar eyes stare back at me.

Eyes that are eerily accurate, and yet, at the same time, could not possibly portray the true depth and mystery of the real thing.

My painting of Oliver Lynch is still dappled in faded coffee residue, and I would give anything to fix him.

CHAPTER THREE

OLIVER

"CAN I GET YOU ANYTHING?"

I stare straight ahead, unblinking, hardly registering the words coming out of this man's mouth. This man who claims to be my brother. My stepbrother, specifically, tied to me by matrimony, now forced to take me in and help pick up the pieces of my shattered reality.

Legs sprawled out in front of me, back to the wall, I sit beneath the window of what I've been told is my old childhood bedroom. I don't recall it. I don't recognize the stickers on the ceiling or the chipped, blue paint. It smells musty and strange.

My vision settles on the cracked closet door across from me, and I consider crawling inside and holing up within the small, dark space. The thought brings me comfort as I close my eyes and retreat into the confinements of a familiar prison.

"I have some TV dinners and pop. Are you hungry?"

Gabe's voice penetrates my solitude and I force my eyes back open. He lingers in the doorway, fidgeting in my peripheral view.

I'm unsure what a television dinner consists of, and I'm honestly not hungry. I don't respond.

Gabe continues to scuff the toe of his shoe along the shag carpeting, his shoulder propped up against the doorframe. He lets out a sigh as he scratches the nape of his neck. "Well, if you get hungry, the kitchen is down the hall to the right. This is your house, too, so feel free to explore and make yourself at home. I'll help with anything you need."

I flick my attention to Gabe. He visited me multiple times over the last few weeks as I was poked and prodded, coddled by a myriad of unknown faces, and questioned until it felt like my brain was going to dribble out of my ears. It was determined that I wasn't a danger to myself or to society, so I was released back into the world—a world I thought had been destroyed and contaminated. I was sent on my way with little knowledge of how modern civilization worked, merely given a tiny paper card, detailing the information of a psychologist I have no intention of consulting anytime soon. It's difficult enough trying not to panic while my stepbrother converses with me from a few feet away.

I realize then that I am completely dependent on this man in front of me, this stranger, who is spearing me with his worry and pity… just like I was dependent on Bradford.

Still, I can't seem to muster any words, so I simply nod my head and resume staring at the wall.

I'm relieved when Gabe backs out of the room, leaving me alone. I'm used to being alone. I'm comfortable with it.

My thoughts travel to Bradford again, and I can't help but wonder if he's still alive. There was so much blood. I tried to explain my living arrangements to the police officers who drilled me with their interrogations, but my home beneath the earth was not easy to detail.

Cement flooring with a dark green rug. A maroon sleeping bag. A small television to play video tapes. Stacks of books and comics, a cupboard with snacks and nonperishable goods, and my art supplies that Bradford provided me with. It was a small haven—a modest living space that offered me everything I needed.

Everything I *thought* I needed.

The authorities looked at me as if I were crazy when I attempted to give them answers. I told them about the stalks of corn, the raccoon with wise eyes, and the little wooden home that housed my cell. But my responses were clipped, my descriptions vague. How does one accurately portray something when they have nothing to compare it to?

When one of the detectives, a man with an off-putting mustache, regarded me, his gaze was patronizing. He addressed me as if I were a frail, immature child. He spoke slow and used elementary words. He even made drawings on white paper, trying to get through to me—trying to make me understand.

But I did understand. I comprehended his words and queries and desperate need for answers.

What I didn't understand... was *why*.

Why the lies?

Why so many years of isolation and a false sense of fear?

Why *me*?

I suppose I'll never know. Bradford is likely dead from blood loss by now, and he was my only hope for closure.

My knees draw up to my chest and my socks skim across the carpet. It is soft and comforting beneath my feet—a sensation I've never felt before. Or one I don't remember, anyway.

And then I'm thinking about her, the woman in the window, her hair light and sunny like the carpeting and undoubtedly just as soft. She told me her name was Syd, and she reeked of familiarity... but how could it be? How could she be *my* Syd?

My Syd was a fabrication.

My Syd was an artificial companion brought to life by my insatiable need to quell the loneliness.

I created her with the lead from my pencil tip and my own imagination.

Queen of the Lotus.

I shake my head, overwhelmed and splintering at the seams. It's too much. It's all too much. I don't know how to function in a world so vast, so cluttered and loud. I can't decipher what's real, what *really* existed before Bradford took me beneath the soil and fed me lies. I can't differentiate between a memory, a dream, and a tall tale.

I trusted Bradford. I thought he was my caretaker. My protector.

My *hero*.

I feel betrayed in the worst way.

Resting my head against the wall, I try to wrangle my unsteady breaths and zone out. I go back to my cave and sit Indian-style on the green rug, munching on crackers, a newly sharpened pencil in my hand. My mind comes alive with colors, adventures, and thrilling villains to defeat.

I much prefer the monsters I create myself.

I prefer them because I always win.

"It's bad out there, Oliver. Real bad."

I'm chewing on a granola bar, watching as the man called Bradford climbs down the metal steps, wearing a strange yellow suit. It looks to be made of plastic and zippers. He looks like he's about to go trick-or-treating, but it can't be Halloween yet. I've only been down here for about a week... I think. Maybe I should start tallying the days on the stone wall beside the letters of my name.

Bradford sighs deeply. "There's been a nuclear attack. The air outside is toxic."

I'm not sure what nuclear means, but it doesn't sound so good.

"But you said I could go home soon. You said you just needed a few days to think about stuff. Does this mean I can't go home yet?"

Oh, no. My mom must be so worried about me.

"I'm afraid you won't be able to go home for a very long time, Oliver. It's not safe out there."

My bottom lip quivers. "How long? The whole summer?"

Bradford approaches with caution, his face hidden behind a weird mask that makes him breathe funny. "There's a war outside. There are hardly any survivors."

"Survivors?"

"They're dead, Oliver. Most of the population has been annihilated... everyone except the ones who prepared for this," he explains. "Like us."

My brain has trouble understanding, his words registering murky and slow. "When will the air be better?"

"I don't know... maybe never." He pulls his mask off and massages his chin. "I saved your life, kid. I had a feeling this day was coming. I just knew it."

A gulp.

Maybe never.

"I don't want to live down here forever, mister..." It's a whimper, a worried plea. "Maybe I can hold my breath outside and make it home okay."

"No," he snaps. "You can't go home. It's dangerous. From now on, you'll stay down here and I'll do what I can to make you as comfortable as possible. My own bunker is right next door, and I have a kitchen in mine. I'll bring you fresh food when I can."

I do miss eggs and bacon.

Bradford paces the cement floor, hands on his hips. "I'll be gone a lot. When my food supply runs out, I'll need to locate more. This could take days of dangerous travel."

"Can you bring me books to read? I'm learning to read in school, and it's really boring down here."

All I have is a cupboard with snacks, two buckets, a flashlight, and my sleeping bag.

He nods. "Yes. I have supplies in my bunker—lots of books and games. There's electricity down here, so I'll install a television and some better lighting."

My heart skips a beat at the prospect of new things to do.

Bradford pauses to look my way, his dark eyes softening, a flash of sadness filling them. "It's gonna be all right, kid. You're safe down here."

He puts his mask back on and makes his way up the ladder, leaving me all alone once again.

Safe.

I may be safe, but I don't feel happy. I want to go home.

Hopefully, it won't be too much longer because I miss my family.

I miss sunshine.

I miss her.

Three hours later, Gabe returns to the bedroom with a warm plate of food, and he finds me in the exact same place he left me, staring at the wall.

A day has passed, and I still have not moved from my perch beneath the window. My bladder feels heavy, and my throat is parched, but finding the will to move is an exhausting process. Gabe has come and gone, his attempts at conversation and hospitality ignored. I'm not trying to be rude or ungrateful—I am just lost.

When I finally gather the strength to pull myself to my feet, I stagger to the bathroom, pausing briefly to glance at Gabe resting across from me in the living room. He's sprawled out on the sofa, the back of his arm draped over his eyes, and a television flickering on the far wall. The mounted screen is much larger, more vivid and compelling, than the one I had in my underground cell. I squint my eyes at it, overwhelmed by the realistic images. It resembles the one I saw in Bradford's bedroom, as well as at the hospital.

Gabe doesn't hear my footsteps in the hallway, and I'm grateful he's asleep with a wire spilling from each ear, muted noise filtering through. Music, perhaps.

I pull my gaze from the monitor and make my way into the bathroom. I have a vague recollection of toilets, even though my living arrangements were not equipped for proper plumbing. Forgotten memories seeped inside me when I observed the lavatory at the hospital for the first time.

I was assaulted with flashes, recalling an ivory sink adorned with colorful toothbrushes.

A floral shower curtain.

The image of a little girl standing beneath the shower jets in mud-covered clothes and pigtails, squealing when I forced the temperature colder.

All I had in my hole in the ground were buckets that Bradford would wash and collect regularly—one for waste and one for bathing with a soapy sponge. The shower I was introduced to at the hospital felt uncomfortable at first, the hard jets of water biting my skin like barbed wire. But it soon became an enjoyable occurrence, cathartic even, and I realize now it's only one of the many experiences I've been missing out on.

I shake my head through a swallow, flipping on the lights, then wincing when I'm blinded by the harsh fluorescents. Everything is so bright in this new world.

As I case my surroundings, more fractured visions sweep through me, causing my knees to quiver. The ivory sink is still there, chipped and tarnished. The floral shower curtain has been replaced by one that is gray and sterile, and the little girl is long gone, but I can almost still hear her laughter echoing in my ears.

I do my business, then glance in the mirror before I exit.

I went twenty-two years without a mirror.

No reflection. No concept of my physical appearance. No knowledge of my eye color or bone structure or the curve of my mouth. I had my name, though. I carved it into the cement wall, so I'd never forget it.

I blink at the reflection staring back at me. This imposter. This unfamiliar man with irises like cinnamon and tawny hair falling over his forehead in chaotic waves.

A jaw encased in rough bristles, growing longer by the day.

Pale skin from lack of sun exposure.

Long, thick eyelashes and defined cheekbones.

A hollow, withdrawn look in his eyes, not even disguised by the dancing, golden flecks.

My fingers curl around the sink, gripping the porcelain as I heave out a long breath and look away.

And when I finally turn to open the door, she is there.

The woman in the window—the one who visited me, claiming to be Syd. She is here in my brother's house... well, *my* house, I suppose. She is standing right in front of me with wide, sapphire eyes hidden behind dark-rimmed spectacles. With her nose like a button and her full lips, she parts those lips to speak to me:

"Hi."

A frown unfurls between my brows as I glance at the stack of clothing clutched within her arms. Her hair spills over both shoulders in streams of white-gold, and she tilts her head to one side, analyzing me. Either with confusion or concern; I am uncertain. Both would be acceptable.

My voice evades me, and I remain silent.

"My dad left some boxes of old clothes in the attic. I think he's about your size. They might fit better than Gabe's... until you can purchase your own," she tells me, her teeth gnashing her bottom lip as she holds out the pile of button-down shirts and an assortment of slacks.

Before I can respond in some way, Gabe saunters over from the living room with a yawn, scratching his tousled hair.

"Don't you knock?"

His words sound crass as he addresses Sydney, but his eyes are soft, his grin brightening. She doesn't seem to be put off by his blunt query.

"Only as often as you do, which is never," she quips, her eyes flicking to Gabe, then back to me. "I was just dropping off some clothes for Oliver."

They seem to have a rapport—a friendship. I wonder what that's like. I look down at my feet with a stiff jaw, unsure of what to say.

Gabe steps in and reaches for the clothes, nodding his thanks. "Nice. We'll have to run out and grab some new things. Do you think Oliver is more of an Aeropostale kind of a guy, or something classier like Express?"

My eyes dart between them, trying to find a place for these unfamiliar words in my cluttered mind. I cannot pinpoint them.

Sydney seems to know this already. "We can find out what he likes, but these should do for now."

She smiles at me, and there's something warm and inviting about the expression. It's a little lopsided and framed with dimples. *Endearing.* I catch myself staring at her mouth, causing her to clear her throat and turn her head back to Gabe.

"Well, I can—"

Her words are cut short when I walk away.

Sydney stops mid-sentence, and I can sense both of their eyes trained on my back as I wander down the hallway and into the bedroom. I feel out of sorts standing between these two people—two people I was supposed to grow up with—unable to contribute anything of value to their conversation. I can't handle their pitying stares and awkward responses to my silence.

Instead, I pull away and confine myself to the solitude I've grown accustomed to, carrying my feet towards the bed adorned in navy blue blankets and two pillows. It squeaks when I sit.

I'm uncertain if I'll enjoy this new way of sleeping and contemplate pulling the blankets to the floor beside the bed, pretending I'm back in that basement, curled up on the hard ground.

I anticipate doing that very thing when tentative feet creak into the room and she makes her presence known.

A light cough infiltrates the silence. "Hi, Oliver. Can I come in?"

My entire body tenses at the prospect of more human interaction. I fist the bed covers, my eyes darting up to Sydney, who is standing in the doorway.

She doesn't wait for my reply and steps forward, approaching me on the bed, and I watch as she takes a seat to my left, her body heat emanating into me. My instincts are to look away, but I find myself soaking up her every move, intrigued and curious about this woman. I absorb each blink, twitch, and wayward expression. I observe the way her legs swing back and forth against the side of the bed in opposite time as she swipes her hands along her thighs. Our eyes meet.

And then I see her.

I can envision her sunny pigtails bouncing as she skips rope in the front lawn. I hear her laughter intermingle with the midsummer breeze.

"Last one to the park is a rotten egg!"

My throat tightens.

Sydney holds my gaze, something passing between us, something akin to the exchange through the tall window yesterday.

"I know you probably don't remember me," she says, folding her hands together in her lap, fingers intertwining. Her eyes are a captivating shade of blue as they implore me. They are twinkling, even. "But I remember you."

I'm inclined to look away, inhaling an uneven breath as I try so hard not to withdraw altogether.

"You would pull on my pigtails, telling me that I looked like Angelica from *Rugrats*. We would make mudpies in my driveway after a rainstorm. Our families would sit out back around the firepit roasting marshmallows, while you, me, Gabe, and Clem tried to outdo each other with the scariest ghost story. We would play 'telephone' from window to window, we'd set up lemonade stands at the edge of the road and use the money for the ice cream man, and we'd catch fireflies in glass jars." Sydney stops to collect herself, her eyes reflecting wet tears. "I remember everything about you, Oliver. You were real. Your life before what happened to you was real."

Sydney touches her hand to mine, and I jerk away on instinct.

I'm not used to human touch. Bradford never touched me. The doctors at the hospital had to use sedatives on me because I was inundated by the hands and fingers and faces so close to mine, that I panicked. I tried to fight and flee.

I am no expert on human emotion, but the look in Sydney's eyes at my reaction to her attempt at comfort tells me I have offended her. My insides twist with guilt.

"I'm sorry," she whispers softly, inching back and wrapping her arms around herself like a one-person hug. Sydney hesitates before rising to her feet. "It's too soon. I'm sorry..."

When she moves to make a quick escape, words tumble out of my mouth, surprising us both. "I remember a little girl," I say, my voice ragged and worn. I don't even recognize it. I watch as Sydney pauses her steps, turning to face me, her eyes a vibrant sea of awe and wonder. "That was you?"

She nods, a gesture that is slow and timid as she tucks a gilded strand of hair behind one ear. I'm unable to determine if her expression is pained or joyful. Her voice shakes when a query floats over to me from across the room. "You remember me?"

"I thought I created you."

Sydney's unease seems to wash away at my words and her body relaxes, a smile blooming to life. "I've always been here."

My teeth rattle and my chest hums as I remain rigid on the bed, everything inside me wanting to tear my gaze away from the look in her eyes. I see more life and vitality in those eyes than I've felt inside my soul in the last twenty-two years combined. I'm envious of such a sentiment. I want to reach out and touch it... steal a part of it for myself.

But I don't move. I finally dip my chin to my chest and listen as her footsteps walk out of the bedroom.

Sydney is gone, but she leaves a little spark behind.

I suppose she always has.

CHAPTER FOUR

SYDNEY

"Y OU DIDN'T TELL ME HOW HOT HE WAS. The news broadcasts haven't done him enough justice."

I scoff as I search the living room for my heels, poking my head up from behind the couch to glare at my nosy sister. Clementine has her face glued to the window, watching as Oliver sits on his front porch staring at the bird feeder.

He's just sitting there, motionless.

It's been three hours.

"He's my friend. I think. And he's traumatized," I huff back, craning my body to reach the rebel shoe that Alexis must have hidden. "Keep it in your pants, Clem."

"Well, your hot, traumatized friend is in better shape than my physical trainer," Clem breezes, finally stepping back from the window and pulling the curtains closed. "Captivity is a good look for him. After my divorce is finalized, I'll probably be over here a *lot* more."

I feel my jaw tense at my sister's flippant assessment. My feet find their way into the uncomfortable heels, one by one, while I adjust my tank top. "Don't be gross."

"Not gross. Just lonely and totally over my vibrator, and please, can you help me land a hottie tonight? I'm out of practice."

I'm on the clock tonight at The Black Box, a trendy bar and nightclub across town. Clementine is tagging along because she "needs to put herself out there again" after a long divorce battle from her ex, Nate.

Poppy, my niece, is with her father this weekend, so it's just like old times —me and Clem, heading out to the bar in our too-tight clothes, too-teased hair, and too-high expectations.

Only, I'll be slinging the shots tonight, and my sister will inevitably be barfing them up come sunrise.

I adjust my glasses, applying a dab of gloss to my coral lipstick. "Brant is working with me tonight. Pretty sure he's single." I frown in contemplation and zip my purse. "Pretty sure he's gay, though."

"What about your manager, that Italian stallion? Marco?"

"Definitely gay."

She groans. "Dammit. Do you have any co-workers that would go for a thirty-something single mom with trust issues, an only slightly obscene amount of credit card debt, and a frog obsession?"

I slip on a cropped leather jacket, blowing a piece of hair out of my face. I hate dressing up. I'm definitely a t-shirt and sweatpants kind of a girl. "Possibly Rebecca."

She narrows her eyes at me. Then she shrugs, tossing her purse over her shoulder. "That could work. Ready?"

My lips thin through my blink. "Yep."

"By the way, you look super sexy. I hardly ever see you all put together like this," Clem adds, heading for the door. "You look like a porn star."

"Gee, thanks. It's been an ambition of mine since I found Dad's nudie magazines in his underwear drawer when I was twelve."

We share a laugh, stepping out onto the porch. I've always had a nice body —petite waist, toned legs, and a generous C-cup. Lorna Gibson once called it a 'body made for sinning' in an off-handed conversation with the hot neighbor, Evan, who writes gritty thriller novels and lives one house over.

I was flattered. Truly.

It's afforded me my fair share amount of male attention over the years, though, no one male ever seems to stick. I've bounced around from casual relationship to unemotional fling most of my life, never really feeling that all-consuming spark people write books about. I used to envy Clementine and her charmed life, with her successful husband and adorable daughter.

That is, until her husband became more successful at screwing his intern than honoring his marital vows.

Clem's blonde bob, painted with electric blue streaks, bounces up and down as her heels click down my front walkway. After I turn to shut and lock the door behind me, we both slow our pace, our heads turning to the left to glance at Oliver sitting alone on his front stoop.

"Should we invite him out? Maybe the guy just needs to get laid," Clem shrugs, trying to keep her voice down.

And failing.

Oliver looks over at us as I ram my elbow into my sister's ribcage, swallowing down my embarrassment. "Stay here. I'm going to say hi really quick."

I wander across the lawn, my heels sinking into the spongy earth. It's late March, and the mild temperatures are poking through a treacherous winter, showering us with rainstorms and hints of spring. Oliver stiffens as I approach, his hands clamped around his knees. His eyes trail me, but not in the salacious way I'm accustomed to from men.

"Hi, Oliver." I hug myself, glancing towards the vacant bird feeder. "You like watching the birds?"

It's been two weeks since our emotional confrontation in his bedroom. I've stopped by to visit a few times, but Oliver has been quiet and reserved. I'm hoping our continued interactions will eventually bring him out of his shell. I want to know the rest of his story.

All we know so far is what he's told police: Oliver was held captive beneath the floor of some psycho's house, fed lies, and brainwashed into believing he was one of very few survivors left after an atomic bomb poisoned our air.

Unreal.

Oliver's eyes dip to my cleavage, but he glances away quickly. "I enjoy wildlife," he replies.

I smile wide. It's a happy, genuine smile, because Oliver is speaking to me. He's engaging. He's opening up. The sound of his voice is low and gravelly, rich and beautiful like my favorite song, and I want nothing more than to play it over and over again.

Part of me wishes I could call off work and water this little seed he has planted, but I really need the money. And my sister needs this night. I step closer, nodding my head. "Me, too. Sometimes the squirrels climb the feeder and steal the food away from the birds."

He looks back over at me, his gaze drifting lower once again, then shooting back up to meet mine. I realize then that he's probably never seen a woman's body in the flesh before.

He's likely still a virgin.

Shit. I don't even know how to handle that bomb of a revelation.

And I certainly don't know why I care.

I clear my throat, popping my thumb over my shoulder. "That's my sister, Clementine. I call her Clem. We all played together when we were kids."

Oliver peers around me, expressionless. There is no recognition there.

"I have to work at the bar tonight. She's tagging along. She's going through a divorce and could use the distraction, and..." I trail off, realizing he either doesn't understand or doesn't give a crap about my sister's marital woes. "Anyway, I just wanted to see how you were doing."

Our stare is heavy, as it always seems to be. I wonder if he's trying to make up for all the things he cannot say.

"Sydney! I'm freezing my ass off out here. Let's go." Clem's voice is shrill, sharply severing the mood. She clears her throat and softens her tone, shooting us a wave. "Hey, Oliver."

He squints his eyes through the dusky haze, the sun having just set behind the horizon. He is silent for a beat before muttering, "Her hair is blue."

Oliver says it with such a straight face, with such an air of whimsical confusion, I can't help but laugh. He looks back to me, startled, appearing as if I should be sharing in his perplexity. "It is blue. Sometimes. Hair color has evolved a bit since the nineties," I tell him gently, my grin still touching my lips. "Mine was pink last summer."

He blinks, then scans my hair, like he's trying to picture such a thing.

"Syd, come on!"

A groan escapes as I adjust my purse strap. "Sorry, but I should get going. Do you, um..." I peer down at the grass, nibbling my cheek. "Do you want me to stop by tomorrow? Maybe we can talk, or watch TV or something? You know... hang out?"

Cool. Like we're freakin' six-years-old. I flash back to knocking on his front door, asking Mrs. Lynch if he could "play".

Oliver's brow creases as he contemplates my offer. The golden glints in his eyes swirl and spin, echoing his racing thoughts. Then he says, simply: "No."

Oh.

Okay, then.

Slowly nodding, my teeth grind together to hold back a wave of emotion that feels an awful lot like rejection. I try not to take it personally. I try not to feel a total sense of loss over the baby steps I thought we'd been making. "Yeah... no problem. Maybe another time." I back away, forcing a strained smile, noting a puzzled, searching look in his eyes that I'm not quite sure how to decipher.

I don't dare to. I turn around fully, joining my sister on the walkway, and we hop into my Jeep.

It's a busy Saturday night as spring break week begins and people flock to the bars in droves to celebrate. I glide back and forth behind the counter with syrup stuck to my fingers and a rag over my shoulder, collecting orders and putting drinks together in record time.

"Looking fine tonight, Neville."

I don't bother to glance up at the voice I immediately recognize. Casper—an embarrassing one-night stand and serious lapse in judgment.

My co-worker, Brant, slides over to me and nudges my shoulder with his own. He's all too familiar with Casper. "I got these guys. Go take care of the Sanderson sisters at three o'clock."

I glance to my right, almost losing it when I spot a woman with buck teeth and red hair, snickering with her blonde and brunette friend.

"I wasn't lying," Brant teases, reaching for the bottle of Smirnoff and spinning it with expert ease, shooting a wink my way.

My eyes rove over the dance floor that's pulsing with techno-infused pop songs and strobe lights. I can see my sister dancing amongst a group of complete strangers, looking sexy and confident, like she isn't a thirty-two-year-old newly single mom. *Goals.*

I'm putting together a round of Lemon Drop shots when Casper makes his way to my end of the bar, leaning forward on his arms. My eye roll is so enthusiastic, I almost give myself an aneurism. "Not interested," I say with indifference, his presence not distracting me from my task.

"That's not the impression I got last summer."

I set the shots in front of a group of college kids, smiling my thanks when they hand me a generous tip. My eyes flick to Casper. "I was going through some stuff last summer. Someone said something mean to me on Facebook. My cat meowed weird—it could have been serious. Oh, and I think that's the day I ran out of *Schitt's Creek* episodes, and I didn't know what to do with my life."

"Funny."

I offer him a shoulder shrug, mixing another drink. Throwing it together swiftly, I pop some extra cherries through the toothpick and add one of those cute paper umbrellas. I set it in front of Casper, propping myself up on my hands with a sweet smile. "On the house."

He glares at the concoction. "What is this girly shit? I didn't order this."

"It's a Rum Runner." I blink at him, coyly. Then I wiggle my fingers in his face, like a send-off. "*Run* along."

Casper just stares at me.

"I'm *running* out of patience?" I try, cocking my head to the side.

He grumbles then, shaking his head, but he remains rooted to his bar stool.

"You're *running* on borrowed time before I wave down Brutus the Bouncer and have you escorted out of here."

"Yeah, right. On what grounds?"

I tap my chin with my forefinger. "Hmm. Stalking one of the staff members for three months might do it."

"Don't flatter yourself," Casper spits out, rising from his seat. "Stalking is a massive exaggeration."

"Fine. Stubborn pursual of an unwilling target."

He curses under his breath, abandoning the drink. "Whatever."

"And stay out of my bushes!" I call after him, watching as he retreats from the bar.

A smile forms at my small victory, just as Gabe saunters up with his arm wrapped around my sister. *Lord help us all.*

Clementine reaches for the cocktail, holding it up with gratitude through her wobbly posture. "Thanks, sis!"

She's impressively intoxicated.

I take another order before turning my attention to my sister and friend. "What are you doing here, Gabe? You left Oliver alone?"

He releases his hold on Clem and perches himself on the vacated bar stool. "Yeah, why? He's a grown man—he doesn't need a babysitter. Besides, I think the guy might be smarter than I am. It's a little creepy... and kind of emasculating."

"He's still adjusting. What if he hurts himself?" Anxiety bubbles in my gut at the prospect of Oliver being all alone.

"He likes being alone. And I have a life, Sydney," Gabe says, folding his hands as he watches me pop open a beer cap. "I'm lucky I've been able to work from home for the last few weeks, but I need to go back after break. Oliver will be fine."

"I just worry." I hand out the beers, my mood shifting. Oliver's brush-off filters through my mind as I ring up a tab. "I asked if I could stop by tomorrow to spend time with him, and he said no."

"No?"

"Yeah… just, *no*. That was it."

Gabe blows out a breath, running a hand through his wavy hair. "Bright side: you actually got him to talk. I've had shit luck in that department."

Handing Gabe a complimentary beer, I lean against my elbows and rest my chin on my knuckles. "What do you think happened to him?"

He stares into the spout of the beer as if it holds all the answers. "I don't have the slightest clue. I'm not sure I even want to know."

"Yeah…" I nod, a chill coursing through me. "You're probably right."

Clem sucks down the Rum Runner in a notable amount of time, then drapes her arm around Gabe, whispering something into his ear.

Weird. Just weird. My sister has been with Nate for almost all of her adult life, so seeing my two worlds collide is verging on awkward.

"You doing okay, Syd?"

Brant saunters over to me, wiping down the counter with a rag and nodding his head in greeting at Gabe and Clem.

My sister gives him "fuck me" eyes, and I let out a sigh. "Peachy. Casper made like a ghost and disappeared."

Brant almost doubles over with laughter "Shit, Neville. And here I thought you needed me to rescue you."

I grin, turning my attention to another patron. "Nah. I can take care of myself."

I lied. I need help.

My hand freezes when I insert the key into the keyhole.

My front door is unlocked, and I *know* I locked it behind me. I'm a stickler for safety ever since Casper started lurking in my bushes like a goddamn creeper last year.

Shit.

Is that asshole hung up on me again? Did I piss him off, and this is him trying to scare me?

I glance around, the only sound penetrating my thick fog of fear being the distant noise of traffic and my own erratic heartbeat. I debate calling

9-1-1 and hiding out at Lorna's house until the cops get here, but my dislike for Lorna trumps my terror, and I really don't want to bother Oliver if I'm just being paranoid. Pushing open the door, my feet make their way inside. "Hello?"

My voice is small and feeble, and I hate myself for it. I'm strong. I'm independent. I'm a fighter who takes shit from no one.

No one except for the ominous intruder who might be hiding under my bed.

Double shit.

I suck in a choppy breath, holding out one of the keys on my keychain like a makeshift weapon. My eyes scan my living room, checking for disturbances. Nothing seems out of place.

Maybe I *am* just being paranoid. Maybe I *didn't* lock the door behind me, having been distracted by my sister and our chatter about Oliver.

I know I locked that damn door.

Replacing my keychain with a steak knife from the kitchen, I traipse through the house, feeling like an idiotic damsel in one of those cheesy horror films.

Run. Get out of the house. Call the police.

No! Don't go up the stairs.

What a damn fool.

But I'm embarrassed to call the police when I have no real proof of a break-in.

When everything looks to be copacetic, I let out the breath I've been holding onto and make my way into my office. My laptop is powered on, which unnerves me. I'm almost positive I shut it down this afternoon after responding to my e-mails.

But I'm not certain.

I set the knife down on my desk, and I'm about to turn to leave, when something catches my eye. My attention fixates to the window, the blinds still open, giving me a perfect view into Oliver's illuminated bedroom.

I step forward and realize... he's drawing on the walls.

Characters and scenes come to life as he puts pencil to plaster and creates something that looks like a picture book. Oliver is propped up on his knees, his back to me, his face close to the wall as he concentrates on his art. I'm impressed by his talent—even from here, many feet away, I can appreciate his attention to detail. The shadowing, the facial features, the vivid scenery.

He's good. Very good.

I kneel down in front of the windowsill, pushing open the pane of glass and resting on my arms. I watch Oliver draw, create, release. I watch him work, and it fills me with something hopeful and sweet.

I'm not sure how much time goes by when he finally turns around, scratching his head and tossing the pencil to the floor. He's about to move out of frame, over to the bed, maybe... but he falters. His head pops up and he twists toward me, almost like he felt me, our eyes locking instantly.

The air traps in my throat, catching and holding.

He's caught me staring at him. Watching him. Invading his privacy. Part of me wants to close the blinds and pretend he never saw me—pretend I wasn't soaking up every pencil stroke, or the way the muscles in his back twitched and tensed as he focused on his mural.

But his eyes nail me down, securing me in place, giving me away. I'm transported back in time to when we'd look at each other through this same window, smiles on our faces, stories on our tongues, and mischief in our eyes. He's that same little boy, and I'm that same little girl, and we are untouchable.

We hold our gaze for a long time, unable to break the invisible tether. I drink him in, from his tired eyes to his messy hair, to the rumpled clothing from the boxes in my attic. I try to pretend how things would be if he hadn't disappeared for twenty-two years, if he hadn't suffered through horrors that we only read about in fiction novels. I wonder what Oliver Lynch would be like right now, on this very day, standing in his window, facing mine.

I muster up a smile, despite the pang of heartache I feel cinching my chest.

And then I close the blinds.

CHAPTER FIVE

OLIVER

"*I* BROUGHT YOU THESE."

I curl up into my sleeping bag beside the special lamp Bradford gave me. He said it will keep me healthy in the same way sunshine would. I'm learning a lot about health lately as I research exercise and nutrition, and I always remember to take the vitamins Bradford gives me with breakfast.

I was just about to practice my sit-ups when Bradford sets a stack of comics near the pile of books I've been devouring. "I love comic books," I say, my insides spiking with eager excitement. I've been down here for months, and the boredom has finally managed to fade. I've done so much reading. I've learned lots of new things. There's a word called 'collywobbles' that makes me giggle every time I think about it.

Collywobbles!

Bradford takes his mask off, crouching down beside me. "You look like you're in better spirits, kid," he tells me, scratching his cheek. "You like the books?"

I sit up straight. "I love them! I learned that a laser could get trapped inside water. Did you know that?"

"Sure did," he says, reaching into a backpack and pulling out more supplies. "I wanted to be a scientist when I grew up."

"You did?"

"Yep. I wanted to have a big science lab and make secret potions."

"Why didn't you?"

He averts his eyes. "Life took a different turn, I guess."

"Well, I hope you can still be a scientist someday. Maybe you can fix the air outside. That would be cool, huh?"

"Yeah, kid." A pause before Bradford hands me the items he pulled out of his bag. "I brought you this, too. I thought maybe you could draw or something."

My fingers curl around the spiral spine of the sketchpad. I'm not so good at drawing, I don't think. I haven't done it much.

"Thanks. Maybe I can draw my own stories, like the ones I've been reading about."

He nods at me, lingering for a few silent beats. "All right, well, I'll leave you alone now. Enjoy, Oliver."

When Bradford departs, the hatch locking shut above me, I look down at the blank pad of paper in my hands. Bradford left a box of colored pencils next to the stack of comic books—tools for my creations. Yes, I like this idea. It will keep my mind busy and growing until I make it out of here. I can design exciting new worlds and grand adventures.

Then I can show my mom and Syd. I know they're still alive, even though the deadly air destroyed a lot of people. My mom and Syd are the bravest people in the world, so they must be alive—they must be a part of the survivors who are holed up in a basement, just like Bradford and me. It's gotta be true, because sometimes I can almost feel Syd. I hear her call my name.

Oliver…

Settling against a pillow, I bite down on my bottom lip, deep in thought. I'll need a name for my comics. All great stories have great names.

But what?

My eyes dart around the dimly lit quarters, landing beside me on the stone wall.

A breath lodges in my throat.

Yes!

It's perfect…

I awake with a start, damp from sweat, my fingers twisted up in the blue comforter I took with me onto the carpeted floor. I prefer sleeping on the ground as opposed to the bed. The mattress feels unbalanced and precarious—a luxury I have yet to get used to.

The cotton shirt is stuck to my chest, a chest that is heaving with anguished breaths as the muddled images threaten my fragile thread of sanity. My dreams and flashbacks to the lonely basement fill me with equal parts anxiety and comfort. It's a peculiar thing.

With my palms to my face, I lean forward as I try to regain control of my breathing. It's dark in the bedroom, the sun fast asleep, telling me that it's still the middle of the night.

So, why do I hear talking and laughter?

I pull myself to unstable legs and pace over to the bedroom door, the voices becoming louder when I tug it open. It sounds like my brother and a mysterious female.

Sydney?

Creeping down the hallway, I stop in my tracks when a partially nude woman runs out of Gabe's room, giggling and saying something unintelligible over her shoulder. Her eyes go wide when she spots me.

"Oliver! I'm so sorry. I forgot you were here."

I frown, watching as she yanks the hem of Gabe's t-shirt down over her thighs. It's Sydney's sister—the woman with blue hair and a name that matches a fruit.

Tangerine, perhaps.

Gabe appears in the frame of the doorway, shirtless, his head ducked bashfully. "Sorry, man. We didn't mean to wake you."

Tangerine forces a smile as she runs past me and escapes into the hall bathroom. I look up at my brother.

He clears his throat. "We were just... playing a game. *Twister.* You know, with the colorful dots and weird yoga poses? Crazy fun."

"*Twister?*" My frown deepens. "I assumed you were having sex."

Gabe's mouth shapes into an 'O' as his eyebrows raise, his feet shuffling back and forth like he's uncomfortable. "Right. We did that, too. After *Twister.*" He coughs into his fist. "All that nervous energy, like, *'who's gonna win'?* It's a breeding ground for sexual tension, and—"

Tangerine slips out of the bathroom, tiptoeing by me as if she may go unnoticed. People are strange.

"Anyway, sorry to wake you up. We'll be quiet," Gabe finishes just as Tangerine sweeps past him and disappears into the darkened bedroom.

He throws me an awkward smile and closes the door.

I head back to my room with a sigh, glancing at a nearby clock and noting it is after three A.M. Being able to tell the time is a convenience I never knew I was missing.

I pause in front of my bedroom window, glancing out to the adjacent house and noting the window across from me is dark and motionless. Sydney is surely asleep, along with the majority of the world. My mind skips over our last few exchanges, settling on the look in her eyes when I told her not to come over. I offended her in some way.

I didn't mean to, of course, and her reaction made me feel uneasy inside. I'm not accustomed to such a feeling—the kind that resembles a little woven knot of dread blooming deep inside my gut. My emotions have always been fairly dependable. Nonexistent, mostly. The only time anxiety or remorse would trickle its way inside me was when I'd read a compelling novel, or when I watched *The Princess Bride* for the very first time. Human-inspired emotions are confusing and unexpected.

But I can't help but wonder if my blunt honesty gave Sydney that same dreadful feeling, and the thought alone only heightens that feeling for me.

I turn back around to face my far wall. It's partially covered in pencil etchings, creating a familiar world I wish I could escape into. Exciting characters, new adventures and conflict, a beautiful damsel in need of rescue.

I will save her; I always do.

My eyes drift higher, reading over the three words that kept me company for two long decades: *The Lotus Chronicles.*

I'm watching the birds again the following day from the cement stoop, reveling in the exquisite way their wings flutter and their heads bob with quick precision. I am fascinated.

After my eyesight adjusted to sunlight, I thought, surely, the sun was the most wondrous part of freedom. But as I continue to absorb nature, animals, and wildlife, the sounds and smells… I am inclined to change my mind.

I'm only outside for short while when Sydney steps onto her front lawn. At first, I think she's going to approach me, but she only sends me a quick smile before she begins to busy herself around the yard. I observe her. She perches herself on the side of the house with rubber gloves and tools, then starts to dig small holes. A vague, hazy vision flashes through me of a woman teaching me how to plant a garden. A kind, soft-spoken woman. Warm and familiar.

Perhaps she was in a dream once.

My attention is shared between the birds and Sydney as I sit on the front porch in quiet reflection. The birds are incredible, but my gaze keeps pulling to the right, fixating on the woman who feels important to me in the most unusual way. She swipes at a light sheen of sweat skating along her brow, kneeling in the soil, planting seeds and bulbs.

Sydney glances up at me, having felt my eyes on her, and I tear my sights away. But it's not long before my peripheral view catches her sauntering over to me, dappled in dirt stains. I stare straight ahead.

"Good morning," she greets softly, landing just a few feet away. "It's beautiful out. I thought I'd get an early start on my vegetable garden."

I clear my throat, bowing my head. Words are elusive, as they often seem to be.

"Look, I know you didn't want to see me, but—"

"I wanted to see you." I'm startled by the sound of my own voice as I turn to look at her through a jagged swallow. "I just didn't want to be seen."

The heaviness of my admission has her softening instantly, and she takes my words as an invitation to step closer. I rake my eyes over her, noting that she appears much different than she had the previous night. She's dressed in a t-shirt showcasing an unknown man's face, tied loosely at her slender hip with some sort of rubber band. Her flaxen hair is pulled up, her face no longer painted.

The previous night she wore tight, revealing clothes that planted a tickly feeling in the pit of my stomach.

Puzzling.

She smelled of something sweet and pleasant, a scent I could not place. I notice she still smells that way as she closes the gap between us and sits beside me on the stoop, our shoulders lightly touching before I inch away.

We sit in silence for a prolonged beat, both mesmerized by the birds pecking at the seeds. I glance her way every few seconds, curious, but I never hold my gaze too long.

"You're a very talented artist," Sydney says, breaking the quiet lull. "I saw your drawings on the wall. Did you teach yourself?"

I muster up a slow nod. "Yes."

"Impressive. I'm an artist, too… I paint, mostly. I took some classes when I was younger, but I think skill really comes down to practice and passion."

Her eyes are boring into me—I can feel them. Hot and imploring. She wants me to respond, to give her the tiniest insight into my haunted mind.

"It's clear you have both," she continues. "Can I ask what you were drawing?"

At first, I want to build more walls and keep her out, just like I keep everyone out. But Sydney has a presence about her—a strange, alluring aura that compels me to pull each brick out of place, one by one, until that wall comes crumbling down.

I squeeze my knees with my palms as I piece together a reply. "It's a comic book. I created it when I was a child," I tell her, offering this woman a part of me, a part I've never shared outside of my cell. "It subdued the loneliness. It almost become a... friend." I work up the courage to glance at her, discovering a look on her face that I cannot define.

A look of wonder, perhaps, with remnants of innate sadness. Just when I think she's about to speak, Sydney surprises me by standing.

"Stay here. I'll be right back," she says through a smile.

I watch her jog across both yards, disappearing inside her house. A few minutes pass before she returns to me with something clutched in her hands.

Her cheeks are still stretched with a bright grin as she holds out a gift, slightly winded. "Here. I thought you might get some use out of this."

It's a sketchpad and a box of sharpened pencils.

I take the items from her outstretched hands, my heart rate increasing. Excitement. Eagerness.

Gratitude.

"Might work better than the wall," she adds with a wink.

I savor the feel of the fresh paper, a brand-new canvas, heavy in my hands. I also savor the dazzling look in her eyes.

I decide that I much prefer this one to the look I saw yesterday.

"Thank you," I murmur, my voice low and thoughtful. "This is very kind of you."

Sydney stands over me, seemingly pleased by my response. She adjusts her glasses, cocking her head slightly as she says, "You're smart. I can tell."

I place the pencils and sketchpad on my lap, my thighs a makeshift table. Considering her assessment, I nod. "I'm educated, yes. Informed."

And yet, I feel so dim-witted most of the time. I don't understand modern technology, especially the robotic devices used to communicate— the same devices I recall upon my escape, pointed at me through cracked windows, capturing video footage that I later came to discover. Gabe is always playing with his device like it's his favorite toy.

"How did you learn?" Sydney wonders, folding her hands together. "Did you go to school?"

Stacks of books flash through my mind. Bradford brought me piles and piles of fiction novels, how-to guides, textbooks, and manuals. All I did was learn.

I'm about to respond when we are both caught off guard by an unfamiliar trespasser snapping photographs from the edge of the lawn. I rise to my feet, stepping back.

"Oh, hell no," Sydney declares, storming over to the man with a camera. "This is private property. You're not welcome here."

My eyes take in the scene from the porch as Sydney rushes the man, blocking me from his view. The stranger tries to dodge her, taking more photographs.

"Did you not hear me? Get lost."

"Oliver Lynch!" the man calls out. "We want to know your story. You can't hide away forever."

I can feel my limbs stiffening, my brick wall swiftly reassembling. I move backwards until I collide with the screen. Their voices sound farther away as I mentally retreat into my cell, reaching for the door handle and turning to slip inside.

To hide.

I don't dare glance at Sydney as I disappear through the threshold. I'm collecting her looks like little treasures, and I'm certain she's wearing one I'd rather not keep.

CHAPTER SIX

SYDNEY

CLEMENTINE DOES THE WALK OF SHAME right through my front door later that morning, looking disheveled and guilty. "I boinked the neighbor."

I figured.

My reply pushes through a mouthful of glazed donut. "Nobody says 'boinked' anymore."

"This is serious, Syd. I've known the guy since we were comparing our Super Mario undies in his bedroom while binging *Ren and Stimpy* episodes." She huffs with aggravation. "Now I know what his penis looks like. It's not okay."

"His penis?"

Clem glares at me. "No. The situation *involving* his penis."

"Okay, let's stop saying penis in connection with Gabe. It's too early for these kinds of mental images." I toss the half-eaten donut onto the kitchen counter and lean back, watching my sister pace in front of me. "I mean, was it good? Do you have regrets?"

She pauses, puckering her lips and avoiding my stare. "No regrets."

Well, I'll be damned.

I fill my cheeks with air and blow it out slowly. "This is really fucking interesting, I won't lie."

"It's weird, I know."

"Super weird."

Clem fiddles with her wrinkled blouse, mascara smudged beneath both eyes. She perches her hip against my kitchen island and glances over to me. "Speaking of weird, Oliver was sitting on the porch again when I made my awkward exit. We woke him up last night."

"Jesus, Clem. Like he needs to be anymore traumatized than he already is."

"I forgot he was there, okay? It's not like he saw any naked bits or anything." She pauses, her nose scrunching up with consideration. "Do you think he's ever seen a naked woman before?"

Flustered, I pretend to busy myself around the kitchen and turn my back to my sister. "Don't know, sis. It's not something I think about."

Lies. I've totally thought about it.

"What happened to you, by the way?" she asks, changing the subject. "Looks like you and Kurt got into a fight with a mud monster and got your asses whooped."

I look down at my dirt-covered Kurt Cobain t-shirt and shrug. "Gardening."

"You domesticated woman, you."

"Just don't ask me to cook."

We spend the next half-hour chit-chatting, sipping on orange juice and completely annihilating the box of doughnuts.

Clem sighs as she rises from the chair, plucking her purse from the table and heading for the door. "Well, I need to pick up Poppy from her insufferable father. I hope he notices my 'just been fucked' hair." She twirls around, muttering, "Bastard."

"Don't worry. You're glowing with sexually active radiance."

We elbow-bump each other and I see her out, then traipse up to my office to check my e-mails with Alexis following behind me.

Day turns to dusk, and I've successfully accomplished zip. Well, except for showering and devouring an entire frozen pizza all on my own. It's fine, though—only my cat was here to judge me.

I'm in the middle of debating if I should reach for a book or my vibrator when I hear a clatter from downstairs. I shake my head, wondering what kind of mess my cat just made for me. Last week, she knocked over a potted plant and tracked tiny soil-stained pawprints all throughout my carpeted living room. *Oy.*

Deciding on the book first, because I'll inevitably be motivated to spend time with my vibrator after a few chapters, I flip through to my bookmark and settle back into the pillows stacked against the headboard. I smile at Alexis, who is curled into a ball at the foot of the bed.

"I'm going to have to kick you out soon. I'll be doing things not meant for innocent kitty eyes."

Alexis lets out a sigh, and I snicker to myself.

Then my blood runs cold.

I sit up straight, my heart leaping from its comfortable confinements. *Shit. Crap. Fuckety-fuck.*

If Alexis is on my bed, I either have a ghost downstairs, or a raping, axe-wielding psychopath, eager to pull out my intestines and wear them as a scarf.

Points for drama *and* creativity.

I look for the closest weapon-like object, which is a toss-up between my vibrator and the crucifix I keep under my bed, despite the fact that I haven't been a practicing Catholic since I discovered Santa wasn't real.

But I keep the cross, just in case. Hell is a lot scarier than coal in my stocking.

Slipping out of the bedroom, my clammy fingers curled around the crucifix, I close the door behind me so Alexis remains safely inside. Then, I tiptoe down to the main floor of my tri-level, trying to remember the moves I learned in Taekwondo when I was seven.

"Why are you holding a cross?"

I spin around and almost stab Gabe through the heart.

"Shit," he exclaims, snatching my wrist before it collides with his chest. "Jesus Christ. Easy there, Buffy."

"What the hell, Gabe?" My chest is heaving, my legs all a-quiver. "You scared the shit out of me."

He yanks the crucifix out of my hand, narrowing his eyes at it. "*Literally* Jesus Christ. Again, I ask, why are you holding a cross? Were you about to attempt another séance to bring Kurt Cobain back from the dead?"

"Ugh. Damn you," I mutter, trying to derail my nerves. "What are you doing in my house?"

"Don't act so surprised. I always show up unannounced."

"Not when I'm in the middle of a home invasion!"

One of his eyebrows arches in bewilderment. "What are you talking about?"

Yanking back the cross, I toss it onto the sofa and shake out my arms like I'm trying to cleanse myself of the goosebumps. A deep breath follows. "I heard a noise. I thought it was my cat knocking something over, but she was in the bedroom with me. Cue masked-man lurking behind my ficus tree, waiting to molest me."

We both glance at the ficus tree, sighing when the coast is clear.

"It was probably just me," Gabe determines. "You're being paranoid."

"You try being a female living alone after dealing with a stalker for three months."

He holds his hands up. "Sorry. You're right." Gabe saunters over to the couch and flops down, draping his arms over the top. His dark green eyes flick up to me as he cocks his head to the right. "We never had that *Always Sunny* marathon."

Shrugging my shoulders, I tentatively approach him, still on edge. "Your brother basically coming back from the dead distracted us a bit," I say, taking a seat beside him and clearing my throat. "Besides, you're super busy now."

Gabe groans and holds up three fingers, counting them down.

"You know, screwing my sister and all."

"And there it is," he concludes, pointing his index finger at me with dramatic flair.

A smile slips, and I shake my head, pulling my knees up to my chest. "Whatever. I'm fine with it. At least someone is getting some action."

"What happened to Milton?"

"His name was *Milton*," I reply, as if... *duh*. "If his parents hate *him* that much, I didn't stand a chance."

Laughter escapes my friend as he stretches out his legs. "Touché."

"I don't do relationships, anyway. You know me—independent, messy, hard to hold."

"It's all those sex books you read. Your standards are too high."

I chuckle at that, reaching for the remote and powering up Netflix. Gabe has a point. Maybe I'm desensitized to real men. Maybe my expectations live between the pages of books involving heroes with ten-inch schlongs and magical tongues, performing grandeur gestures to sweep their heroines off their feet.

All I get are stalkers and guys named Milton.

Oh, well.

I'm totally cool living in my fantasy world, dying a crazy cat lady.

I shoot up in bed, not knowing what the hell just woke me up.

A dream? Another weird noise?

Gabe breaking and entering like a psycho?

Looking around the darkened room for my cat, I catch her glowing eyes staring at me from the doorway. She mewls when I spot her. Maybe she's thirsty—I fell asleep on Gabe's shoulder and forgot to check her water bowl before wandering up the stairs to bed like a zombie.

Alexis purrs again, and I rub my eyes, working up the motivation to crawl out of bed and tend to my cat. This must be what parents feel like. "Okay, okay, I'm coming. So needy."

I'm still a zombie as I make my way down the stairs, through the living room, and into the kitchen. The light above the sink is on, giving me just enough illumination to make sense of what I'm doing. Peering into Alexis' bowls, I notice her water is full and she even has some kibble leftover from dinner. I grumble through a yawn and glance at the clock. It's a little after midnight.

These are the moments I'm glad I work from home. My tired ass is sleeping in tomorrow.

"You tricked me, kitty. I'll never believ—"

I falter as I turn around, my gaze landing on my favorite vase on the floor, having somehow been knocked off the side table. The water has almost entirely evaporated, the spring bouquet scattered across the tiles.

The tingle of dread returns—that familiar prickling of fear.

I stare at the fallen flowers longer than necessary, trying to make sense of the mess. I'm frozen. Processing. Alexis was in my room when I startled awake, so this didn't just happen. And the flowers were perfectly in place, in an upright position, when I came upstairs earlier this evening to read.

This was the clatter.

This was the goddamn clatter, and I know Gabe would have mentioned it if he were the culprit.

I close my eyes, swallowing hard, as I try to decide on my next move. I think I need to call the police. I feel unsafe. I feel watched. I feel threatened.

Realizing I left my cell phone in my office while checking e-mails earlier, I jog on shaky legs over to the stairs, heartbeat thundering with heavy beats against my breastbone. My mouth turns to cotton as I inhale sharp, winded breaths.

And when I reach the top of the steps and round the small corner to my office, I push open the door and those breaths eclipse altogether. With feet pegged to the floor, stomach in my throat, my eyes pop when a man dressed in black whirls around and meets me face-to-face. He's holding my computer in his gloved hands, his identity shrouded by a ski mask. The intruder almost looks as startled to see me as I am to see him.

What the fuck?

For a moment, I'm utterly rooted to the floor, my body numb and unwilling to move, as if it's been struck still by an invisible force. The unknown figure sets down my laptop and approaches me with caution, his palms held up and facing forward, a silent request to remain calm and quiet. But that's when my instincts take over and I fucking *flee*. I whip around and book it towards the staircase, nearly tripping as I hop down two steps at a time, eyes on the exit. A sweet escape is on the other side of that wood frame.

Only, I don't make it to the front door because I feel him behind me, causing my skin to dance with terror, and a scream erupts from my lips before I can even think about reaching for the door handle. Two arms slink around my waist in a firm hold, lifting me right off my feet. One of those arms trails upward, a leather-encased hand clamping down around my mouth, successfully trapping my shriek. I'm only able to produce a low muffling sound as the stranger whisks me around and heads back to the staircase.

Holy fucking shit.

This *cannot* be happening.

I flail my legs with unproductive kicks, my nails clawing at the hand secured to my mouth. He's clasping my jaw so tight, I can hardly breathe. As I'm carried up the stairs, one of my hands grabs the railing, holding on for dear life, trying to prevent myself from being hauled into a bedroom and brutally raped. That's *surely* what's about to happen.

My grip is surprisingly strong, infused with adrenaline, and the man lets go of my mouth for just a moment to pull me away from the rail. I scream again, using the temporary distraction to kick the asshole in the crotch. He stumbles back with a growl, and I break free, racing up the steps to lock myself in the bedroom while I figure out an escape plan. My cell phone is in the office, but that room doesn't have a lock, and I won't have time to grab it first.

Shit.

The man snatches my ankle before I reach the top, and I slip face-forward, my chin hitting the edge of a step and knocking my teeth into my bottom lip. Blood oozes from the wound, filling my mouth with the coppery fluid as I feel myself being hoisted up once more.

I sling my head backwards, connecting with his jaw. The cracking sound rips through me, and I don't even care that it feels like I just gave myself a concussion, because he lets me go.

Karma, motherfucker.

I manage to run free this time, racing as fast as I can into my bedroom, already deciding that I'm more than willing to jump out the window to safety. I'd rather break every bone in my body than be raped and tortured by that sick fuck.

I plow through my bedroom door, blood dribbling down my chin and staining my tank top. When I turn to slam the door shut, he's *there*. He's fucking there already, pushing back against the wood, trying to force his way inside.

And he does, of course. *Of course.*

"No!" I cry out, falling backwards from the weight of the door flying at me.

The man is dressed head to toe in black clothing, his face hidden by the ski mask. Only his beady eyes show through, and I can hardly make them out in the dark. He snags a fistful of my hair in his palm and pulls me up, tossing me onto the bed like I weigh nothing at all. My body bounces against the mattress, and he climbs over me instantly, holding my wrists down as his knee glues my lower half to the bed.

He snarls against my face, "You little bitch. You just had to do this the hard way."

A scream shreds my throat, and he smacks me hard across the face in response, leaving a harsh sting along my cheek. "Who the hell are you? What do you want?" I hiss, tears coating my eyelids.

"Answers."

I'm writhing beneath him, my body twisting and contorting, trying to free one of my limbs. He leans in closer to my face, our noses almost touching, so I turn my head to the side and attempt to hold back a sob. His voice is low and gritty, possibly like he's trying to disguise it, and his breath smells odd... like eucalyptus.

The stranger growls against my ear as I continue to fight. "Tell me what he—"

The man's words are sliced short when I feel his weight being lifted off me with sudden force. I'm confused for a moment, stuck to the bed by a torrent of terror and disbelief. But then I lift up on my haunches to figure out what the fuck just happened.

My breath stops when I see Oliver Lynch in front of me, tossing my attacker to the ground, totally zoned out and throwing punches to the man's face.

Oh. My. God.

I don't know what else to do since my phone isn't within reach, so I run to the window and tug it open, then start screaming for help into the night. It only takes three screams for Lorna Gibson to poke her head out her front door. I shout in desperation, "Call 9-1-1!"

Racing back towards the scuffle, I grab my lamp along the way, yanking the cord from the wall and holding it over the two men when I approach. Just as the attacker gains the advantage, I thrust the lamp downward.

Only, the second I do, Oliver rolls them both over and ends up on top.

The lamp collides with his skull.

Shit!

Oliver clasps the back of his head with a howl of pain, falling to his side as the masked man scurries to his feet and makes a break for it.

He runs out of my bedroom like a fucking coward.

"Fuck. Shit-fucking-shit. I'm so sorry." I'm at Oliver's side, crouching down beside him, reaching out to touch his head wound.

I'm taken off guard when Oliver jumps up and grabs me, then pins me down to the ground by my wrists. His face hovers above me, drinking me in. It's dark, but I can see his features twist from blind rage to shock and horror when realization sinks in that I'm not the bad guy. He loosens his grip on my arms, his eyes darting across my face, making sure it's really me.

Oliver doesn't get up right away. With his eyebrows pinched in conflict, he looms over me, our chests and groins pressed together as we both intake heavy, volatile breaths. Our eyes are locked, our bodies trembling from the fight, an effusion of emotions scattering to the surface.

Police sirens cut through the moment, and Oliver shakes his head, quickly letting go of me as if my arms manifested into flames. He jumps up, scalded, landing beside me and scooting backwards until there's a considerable distance between us. I sit up, still breathing heavily, still a mess of anguish and fear and confoundment.

I was just attacked. I could have been raped. I'm caked in blood from my busted lip, and I can already feel a bruise welting on my jaw.

And Oliver Lynch rescued me. The man unable to even touch another human being just fought off my attacker without a second thought.

"You saved my life."

My words are a hoarse whisper, my voice ragged from the screams.

We sit across from each other on my bedroom floor, staring at one another through the cover of darkness, listening as the sirens grow closer.

Oliver responds so softly, I almost don't hear him.

"I always save you."

CHAPTER SEVEN

OLIVER

I CAN STILL HEAR HER SCREAM as I hold the ice cubes against my bruising knuckles.

The last few days have been a whirlwind of flashing lights, law enforcement, questions, probing, statements, and a showering of gratitude for my heroic actions.

It's all a blur—the days, hours, minutes, bleeding together into a giant, fuzzy fog.

But her scream stands out.

According to Gabe, Sydney has spent the last few nights with her sister, so her house sits dark and empty next door, brimming with the horrors that unfolded three nights ago. I can still see her staring up at me with frazzled breaths, her eyes wide, her hair a tangled mess, her bottom lip cracked open and oozing blood. I may have saved her, but it wasn't enough.

In my own stories, I am quicker. Stronger. Braver. She never looks at me with blood-tinged tears streaking her cheeks, frightened and shaking, permanently branded with an ugly stain.

I feel like I failed.

Gabe's voice penetrates my dark musings as he shuffles into the kitchen, mussing his hair with his fingers. "How's your hand healing up?" he inquires, opening the refrigerator, staring inside for a solid thirty-seconds, then closing the door.

"Favorably."

"Sweet. Keep icing it." He opens the door again, inspecting the contents, almost as if something may have magically appeared. Gabe sighs his disappointment and shuts the door again. "Want to grab breakfast?"

I frown, puzzled by the request. Gabe usually has cereal for breakfast, so I open the top cupboard and grab a box off the shelf.

He mimics my own bewilderment as he takes the *Lucky Charms* from my hand. Then a smile pulls at his mouth. "Shit, sorry. I meant, did you want to go out to eat? You know, like a restaurant?"

Oh. I toss the melting cubes of ice into the trashcan and slip my hands into the pockets of my blue jeans. Gabe ordered me new clothes all the way from the Amazon, and they fit remarkably well. And they arrived much quicker than one would anticipate for such a lengthy travel.

Pondering his suggestion, I clear my throat. "I don't know. That sounds... complex."

The only time I left this house was when I had to give a statement to police officers, detailing Sydney's attack and describing the villain who harmed her. He was a faceless man, just like the villain in my own comics. The whole process was harrowing and uncomfortable, and I much prefer staying inside and keeping to myself.

"Come on, it'll be great," my brother urges. "You need a good dose of the real world—one that doesn't involve police stations."

"I suppose it's inevitable, yes?"

"If you want to experience life, then, yeah. We all need to step outside our comfort zone if we want to grow and learn."

I find myself nodding, despite my hesitation. After years of grieving for a world I thought was lost, I should be celebrating the fact that it's not. "All right."

Gabe claps his hands together. "Awesome. Let me change really quick, then we can head out."

Twenty minutes later, we're sitting across from each other in a red booth with plastic menus on the table in front of us. It smells like bacon and eggs. Bradford would occasionally bring me hot plates of fresh food, and bacon and eggs was one of my favorites. It was always a treat when I could enjoy something other than the spaghetti-in-a-can or cold soups.

I feel Gabe's eyes on me as I peruse the menu. There are so many choices. My gaze flickers up to my brother, who is staring at me with his hands folded. "Did you wish to say something?" I wonder.

"No, I just... I didn't think you could read."

I draw my lips together and glance back down. "I can read. I can write. I can sketch."

"Can you sing?"

"Not well."

It wasn't meant to be humorous, but Gabe laughs, leaning back in his booth with an amused grin. "You're really something else, Oliver. I can't even imagine what happened to you..."

I try not to put myself back in that cellar. As the days push forward, I'm finding less and less solace in the memories of my previous accommodations. "It was quite lonely," is all I offer him.

Gabe doesn't press me for more information, and I'm grateful for that. Instead, he picks at the peeling plastic of his menu, his attention shared between me and his food selections. He breaks the silence a few moments later. "We looked for you, you know. We were all so sure you'd turn up eventually. Your mom, especially, she..." He trails off, ripples of emotion following. "She was a mess for years. But she never gave up hope you'd be found one day. It kills me she's not around to see you now."

A thick heaviness envelops our table, swirling between us, making my chest feel tight. I was told early on that my mother's name was Charlene Lynch and that she passed away a decade ago from lung cancer. My biological father died when I was merely seven-months old, and my stepfather, Travis, lives just over the border in Wisconsin.

I feel like I should miss my mother, but it's hard to conjure up genuine remorse for someone I can hardly recall. I'll occasionally get cloudy visions of a copper-haired woman with light brown eyes reading me a story or chasing butterflies by my side. She is always smiling. Always jubilant. The visions fill me with warmth, but I can never seem to fully grasp them. "I don't remember her much," I admit, my voice cracking on the last word. My hands squeeze the cloth napkin in my lap. "Everything is all mixed up. My memories feel tainted. Poisoned, in a way."

"You were brainwashed for twenty-two years, man. It's understandable."

I nod through the swell of anxiety washing over me. Tapping my feet in opposite time beneath the table, perspiration dampens my brow as I look around the crowded restaurant. I observe the large groups of people moving around, speaking loud and shrill, competing against the kitchen noise of clinking plates and falling glass. It's dizzying.

A little girl with sun-kissed pigtails catches my eye. She's running around her family's table in clumsy circles, holding a teddy bear in her arms. A quick flash punctures my mind, something vivid and almost painful.

"I have a secret, but I'm scared to tell you."

"You can tell it to my teddy bear. She's very good at keeping secrets."

I clutch my head in my hands, causing Gabe to lean forward and reach for my arm.

"Dude, you okay? What's wrong?"

The contact jolts me upright, and I pull my arm free, trying to shake away the shockwaves of some sort of buried memory bursting to life. I attempt to cling to the images, but they fade back into my subconscious, disintegrating with so many other lost recollections. Forcing myself to stay calm, I grit my teeth and dig my fingers into my thighs. "I just became overwhelmed by the environment. I'm not accustomed to so many people."

"Shit, I'm sorry. This was too soon." Gabe looks apologetic; forlorn. "Want to go home?"

It takes a moment for me to realize he's referring to the house on Briarwood Lane and not my hole beneath the ground.

Home. That is my home now.

A quick shake of my head dismisses his offer. "I would like to eat some eggs and bacon."

We pull into the driveway and discover Sydney sitting on Gabe's front porch.

My front porch.

A flurry of scattered feelings filters through me, and my heart seems to beat a little faster, my skin growing warm and itchy. Sydney's knees are pulled up to her chin, her arms hugging her legs, and she moves forward and back, like she's swaying to a silent melody.

When we exit the vehicle, she rises to her feet, swiping her hands along her pant legs. She sends us a smile that doesn't seem to light up her face in the way it usually does.

"Sydney... hell, I've been fuckin' worried about you."

Gabe races to her with an urgency I feel but can't seem to translate physically. I trail behind him, scratching the nape of my neck with my eyes averted.

Her voice brings my eyes back up. "I'm okay. Still a little shaken, but I'll survive. The cops searched my house this morning, but I was kind of freaked to go inside alone, so I dropped off my cat and waited it out here..." Sydney wraps her arms around herself, as if the thought sends a chill right through her. She fixes her gaze on me, her features etched with something soft and kind. "Oliver."

It's a simple greeting, but it sounds like more. I swallow. "Hello."

We hold our stare for a few powerful seconds before Gabe paces forward and picks Sydney up, squeezing her until she shrieks. It's a playful sound, light and cheery, and I wonder what it's like to feel so weightless and carefree, even for just a moment.

A pang of envy shoots through me. It's not a sentiment I'm familiar with, so I push it aside.

As I step closer, I notice purple bruising along Sydney's left cheek, as well as a healing wound marred into her bottom lip. That knot of dread reappears in my belly.

Sydney whispers something into Gabe's ear and he nods, backing away and allowing her to approach me. Her hands are clasped together in front of her, and she looks to be wrought with nerves, much like myself. She bites her lip before voicing her request. "Would you mind going inside with me?"

My eyes shift from Sydney to my brother, thinking he is far better suited for the task. But Gabe bobs his chin, a silent encouragement, so I return my attention to Sydney and give her a reluctant acquiescence. "All right." It appears she's about to reach for my hand, but she stops herself, and I'm uncertain if I'm grateful or disappointed.

Instead, she slips her fingertips into her back pockets and dips her head to her house—an invitation to follow. We walk wordless through her yard, side-by-side, her sweet scent drifting over to me. I haven't been able to pinpoint it, exactly, but I think she smells of spring... the fragrant, floral blooms I inhale when I sit outside and watch the birds.

Sydney glances up at me through long lashes, her eyeglasses missing today. A bruise travels up along the side of her face, almost touching her temple. She tucks a strand of hair behind her ear, revealing three small, silvery hoop earrings. "I, um, wanted to thank you for what you did that night. I can't imagine what would have happened if you hadn't..." She looks down at her swiftly moving feet as we approach the front door. "That took a lot of courage."

"You were still injured. I regret that I wasn't quicker."

My confession causes her to jerk her head up, eyes sharp and slanted, hand pausing as it reaches for the doorknob. "You saved my life, Oliver. I'll take a busted lip over a funeral."

Unsure of how to respond to that, I remain quiet as we finally enter through her doorway. A feline greets us in the foyer, meowing with enthusiasm.

"This is Alexis. I let her inside when my sister dropped me off, but she has no concept of time," Sydney chuckles, scooping up the feline and stroking its rust orange fur.

I wish I could relate to that—*no concept of time*.

Time was all I knew, and it was my greatest enemy.

"Do you want to pet her?"

"Oh…" My tongue pokes out to slick my lips as I step closer to the animal, intrigued by the virile creature. "I would, if that's all right."

Sydney smiles, and this time it's bright and familiar, forcing my heart to skip. "Of course. She likes people. I've had her for ten years, since she was just a tiny kitten."

My fingers lace through the soft, silky hair, and I feel the vibrations from her purrs warm my skin. It's soothing. Before I know it, the feline is climbing out of Sydney's arms and into mine, her claws piercing through the material of my button-down shirt.

"Shit, sorry." Sydney's cheeks are still stretched into a wide grin as she pries the little paws from the fabric. "Like I said, she's a people lover."

I stand there with an awkward stature, my arms stiff around the animal while it makes itself comfortable. Sydney steps in closer, a giggle slipping out when she repositions the cat in my embrace. Her hand brushes against mine, her body only inches away, and I feel tingles dance across my flesh in response to her proximity. A strange, yet compelling feeling.

Our eyes meet with a lingering hold, and Sydney says, "She really likes you."

My lips pull up into a small smile, an instinctual reaction to her statement.

I am liked.

Sydney releases a quick gasp of air, the indigo glow of her eyes intensifying with wonder. "I don't think I've seen you do that before," she murmurs softly, still standing impossibly close.

I clear my throat. "You're correct. This is the first time I've held a feline."

She blinks, a sharp laugh following. "Not that. I meant… *smile*. I don't think I've seen you smile yet. Not since we were kids."

I suppose she's right. I can't recall the last time I smiled.

Perhaps it was when I read *The Catcher in the Rye*.

Sydney eventually steps away, that same look of whimsy bathing me in blue. "I'm going to run to the bathroom. If you hear me screaming, it's either the murderer or a spider. Both will require immediate action." A wink travels over to me, indicating she's making a jest. "And I promise I'll stay away from lamps."

The back of my head pulses in recollection.

Sydney leaves me alone with Alexis, and I'm not sure how to proceed. I stand there like a statue for a few moments before my arms begin to tire, then I gently place the feline on the floor. She immediately curls around my ankles, humming and singing for more attention.

"Alexis, you're an appealing animal," I say, patting the top of the cat's head.

I'm startled when I hear a voice from the kitchen, my hackles going on high alert. I follow the sound that appears to be female, and I ponder if Sydney's sister is still present.

The cat follows, now pawing at my shoelaces like they are one of her toys. "Alexis, be careful. I do not wish to step on you."

The woman answers me, louder this time. I spot a black cylinder on the countertop, lighting up in response to my voice.

"Hmm. I don't know that."

Odd and concerning.

Sydney appears behind me, causing me to jolt. "Everything okay?" she questions.

I squint my eyes at the strange device before turning my attention to Sydney. "Every time I address your cat, the woman in the speaker talks to me."

Laughter is her response.

Loud, jovial belly laughter.

She glances to the speaker, providing it with a new order: "Alexa, play nineties music."

"Alexa" obeys, and music fills the air.

"It's one of the cooler things to come out of modern technology," Sydney declares, her grin holding in place as I process this. "Do you like music?"

"I'm not accustomed to it. Perhaps..." The rate of my heart increases with an unexpected request that lands on the tip of my tongue. "Perhaps you can introduce me to your favorite music."

Sydney's eyes widen, a rebellious strand of hair falling forward and tickling her temple. She combs it back, swallowing through an eager nod. "I'd love that."

I feel my walls cracking, my armor crumbling, my nerves and tension dissipating.

And I'm not sure if it's the pleasant melodies filtering out of the speaker, the cat settled on my shoes, warming my toes, or the look in Sydney's eyes right now.

All I know is this is certainly a look I'll be keeping.

CHAPTER EIGHT

SYDNEY

"WILL YOU BE MY FRIEND, OLIVER LYNCH?"

I approach the neighbor boy, sitting on the stoop of his front porch, shoveling cookies into his mouth. The crumbs disperse onto his lap as he glances at me, a mop of light brown hair sticking to his forehead from the summer sun.

He narrows his eyes through a mouthful of cookie. "Girls have cooties."

"No, they don't." I cross my arms over my denim jumper, hoping he shares his cookies with me. They look really good.

"Yes, they do. That's what Anthony told me."

"Anthony is a big, fat liar. Maybe he has cooties."

Oliver shrugs. "Maybe."

I decide to take a seat beside him on the cement stoop, and I'm glad he doesn't tell me to get lost. I really want a cookie—they smell like Mama's oatmeal. "Did your mom make these?"

"Yes."

"Can I have one?"

Oliver studies me, debating his answer. "Only if you promise you don't have cooties."

"I promise," I tell him. "Cross my heart. I haven't been sick since last Christmas."

My response seems to please him, so he picks up the plate and holds it up. "They're oatmeal. My favorite."

Yes!

"I love oatmeal!" I wipe my chalk-covered hand against my jumper, having spent the last few minutes writing my name along the driveway, and snatch up one of the treats. I waste no time before I devour it. "So good."

"How old are you?" Oliver asks, flicking a crumb off his knee.

"Five."

"I'm six."

"Cool," I smile. We sit in silence, side-by-side, shoulders to shoulder, watching kids ride by on their bicycles. It's a warm afternoon in June, and Mama finally let me go to the neighbor's house by myself. "So, do you think we can be friends?"

He doesn't take too long to reply, swatting at his tawny hair that almost covers his eyes. "I guess so. You're not as annoying as my little brother."

A high-pitched toddler scream filters through the screen door, and we both look at each other with a laugh.

"I have a big sister. She's annoying, too."

"Do you think they have cooties?" Oliver wonders, a goofy grin forming on his face.

"Definitely."

We giggle again, and Oliver plucks a stick from the ground and begins to trace the cement cracks. "Want to go in the backyard and jump on my trampoline?"

"Sure!" I exclaim, practically leaping off the stoop with excitement. "Let's go."

We race around the house, through the gate, and climb onto the trampoline, laughing and out of breath. We bounce for hours, until day turns to dusk and the summer sun sets behind the scattered clouds. We end the night gazing up at the star-filled sky, our shoulders pressed together, lightning bugs buzzing around us as we share stories and knock-knock jokes.

I have a feeling Oliver Lynch is going to become my new best friend.

Clementine and Poppy are helping me bake a batch of oatmeal cookies for Oliver as a "thanks for fighting off that psychopath the other day" gratitude gift. I have no idea what he likes anymore, and this was better than a fruit basket. Nobody likes a fruit basket.

Besides, Oliver's mom used to make the *best* oatmeal cookies. He loved them. I'm hoping the taste will help trigger memories from his childhood.

While I was proud of my choice of gift, the plot twist is that I can't bake a cookie that even my cat would consider—and she's eaten mice.

That's why I have back-up.

"Auntie Syd, look at me!"

I glance at Poppy, who is holding up her flour-dusted hands with a gigantic smile. My five-year-old niece does a little jig, spinning in a circle and making a silly face, her blonde ponytail spinning with her. "You look like you're making some pretty delicious cookies," I say, propping my fist against my waist and admiring her handywork.

The timer beeps, signaling that my first batch of cookies are finished. I race to the oven, eager to view my masterpieces, and whip open the door. A frown settles between my eyes. "What the heck? Why are they totally flat?"

Clem skips over to me, peering at the tray of cookie failures as I pull them out of the oven with two potholders. She blinks. "Did you remember the eggs?"

I scoff at her. "Of course I... did *not* remember the eggs. God! What is wrong with me?"

"They're kind of cute—like flat little pancakes."

"They are *not* cute! There is nothing cute about being twenty-nine years old and having zero baking skills. This, right here, is the reason I'm single."

"That's ridiculous," Clem counters, shaking her head. "You're single because your standards are higher than The Dude."

"Do not use my favorite movie against me during this traumatic time."

"Nobody fucks with the Jesus!" Poppy shouts from the kitchen island, totally oblivious, rolling little balls of dough between her hands.

Clem and I both go silent as I try really, *really* hard to turn invisible, while my sister faces me, slowly, with red cheeks and the death glare of all death glares.

Shit.

"I hate you so much right now."

"I'm sorry," I yell-whisper, my eyes darting to Poppy, bouncing innocently on her stool. "I didn't think she was paying attention."

"She's a *sponge*. And a parrot, apparently." Clem crosses her arms, huffing out a breath of frustration. "Great. Now I'm down to Regina as my only babysitter."

I gather up the parchment paper and eggless cookies with a sigh, disposing of them in the trash. "A little dramatic, sis. And I'm sure there are plenty of qualified babysitters out there."

"There's not."

"But—"

"There's *not*," she repeats, the tiny trace of amusement gone. "It's you and Regina. That's it."

Jeez. Clementine has always been picky about who she leaves Poppy with, but I've never seen her quite so snippy about it. "Fine. Whatever. Sorry about the *Lebowski* thing."

We finish our afternoon of cookie-baking with far less entertainment, and my second batch turns out surprisingly well. Eggs sure do make a noticeable difference. After giving my sister and niece a hug goodbye, I hop in the shower to wash the flour out of my hair, then put together a basket of homemade cookies for Oliver.

When I head next door looking like the Betty Crocker I'm surely *not*, Gabe answers the door in his khakis and work polo. He's a Project's Manager for a construction company, and this is his first week back to the office after working from home ever since Oliver returned. "Yo. You look delightfully dapper."

"I look like a tool. Just got home. And you…" Gabe raises an eyebrow as he gives me a once-over. "You look like you're off to Grandmother's house with cookies you bought at Target."

I swat his shoulder, shoving through the entryway. "I'll have you know, I made these myself."

"Bullshit."

"Ask Clem."

"So, Clem made them."

My eyes narrow as I slip out of my sneakers, then look up into the main living area. "Where's Oliver?"

Gabe links his fingers behind his head. "In his room. I said 'hey' when I got home from work—he's drawing or something." We both traipse up the steps of the split level, and Gabe pauses at the top of the staircase. "He's really damn good. Have you seen his shit yet?"

"Sort of. He was drawing on the walls before I gave him my sketchpad. He said it was a comic book."

"It's wicked. He's got talent."

Nodding, I glance down the hallway, my knee bobbing with anxiety. "You think he'll be cool with me dropping by? I know he likes his space."

The last thing I want to do is bother him or infringe on his privacy. It felt like we'd made progress yesterday when he came by my house and helped me check the rooms, closets, and even under my bed. I can't stop thinking about that smile, or how sweet he was with Alexis.

I'm craving more.

Gabe shrugs, scratching the back of his neck at his hairline. "He's hard to read. Worth a shot, though." Before I can slip away, Gabe calls out to me. "Hey… you're okay, right?"

My free hand instinctively raises to my lip, haunting memories sweeping through me like a terrible dream. Goosebumps prickle my skin as I recall the ragged, raspy sound of the stranger's voice. He sounded mean. *Evil.* I can still feel the way his hard body planted me to my mattress like I was insignificant. A toy he could play with.

The *nerve*—the goddamn nerve to beat and humiliate me in my own house, between the safety of my four walls, where I will never feel entirely at ease again.

Gabe is staring at me with those protective green eyes, dousing me in brotherly concern. Forcing a smile onto my face, I bob my head. "I'm good. It takes more than a raging, masked lunatic with superstrength wishing death upon me to shake me."

He gives me a wink and a smile, holding out his fist. "Liar."

We fist-bump, and I make my way down the hall to Oliver's bedroom, the basket of cookies dangling from my wrist. I knock gently, then crack open the door, peering inside to find him in deep concentration at a wooden desk that Gabe must have brought in from the guestroom.

Oliver glances up at me, slight confusion puckering his brow, not expecting the interruption. But then he stands, his features melting into something resembling relief. "Sydney," he greets, his eyes trailing me as I take hesitant steps inside the room.

I smooth my hair out with my fingers, smiling, my own relief shimmering back at him. He looks genuinely happy to see me, and that sends my already weakened heart into a fluttering mess. "Hey. I hope I'm not bothering you—I just wanted to bring these by." Holding up the basket of cookies, I monitor his expression as he takes in the treats, the scent of warm, comforting memories wafting around me.

Oliver moves in closer, his gaze settling on the cookies. "You made these for me? Why?"

"Because you saved my life like a freakin' badass. Heroes deserve cookies." I hold the basket higher. "Try one."

He plucks a cookie from the pile, his eyes flickering to me, a smile hinting at his lips. Oliver takes a bite, his grin widening.

Nailed it.

"Not too bad, huh? It only took me two attempts and a minimal amount of tears." Waggling my eyebrows, I reach for my own confection and place the basket down on the desk. "Your mom gave me this recipe. Oatmeal cookies were your favorite."

Oliver's joy wavers ever so slightly, and he pauses mid-chew, his gaze drifting to the floor. "I can't recall that memory."

"That's okay," I assure him, biting into the chewy dessert, a familiar ache pinching my heart. "Maybe you will someday. I'll just have to make you a lot of cookies to jog your memory."

"I think I'd enjoy that. These are quite good."

Our eyes hold, both of us chewing through enchanted smiles.

Hell, I'd bake all the damn cookies if it meant I'd get to see this expression on his face again. I'd become the cookie *queen*.

"I like when you do that," I murmur softly, pointing at his mouth.

"Consume food?"

Good Lord. I can't decide if his blunt intellect is more amusing or charming. I respond with a chuckle. "Smile."

"Oh." Oliver nods knowingly, then swallows down the rest of his bite. "I enjoy your smile as well. It makes me want to smile more."

Charming. One-hundred percent charming.

I swear to God I almost blush as I slip out of my cardigan, catching the way Oliver's gaze travels over me, taking in my tank top and skinny jeans when I remove the extra layer. He's probably shocked that I'm wearing something other than a t-shirt and black leggings. Folding my cardigan over his desk chair, I sweep my hair over to one side and watch his eyes drift back up to my face in a slow pull. They look darker, more ablaze, alight with a heated curiosity.

I think he likes what he sees.

The thought draws a gulp from my throat as my tongue juts out to wet my lips. Subject change, coming in hot. "So, what were you drawing? Can I see?"

Oliver blinks, hesitating briefly, then approaches his drawing desk and reaches for the sketchpad. There is noticeable doubt in his movements, a trace of something shy, maybe even embarrassed. I can only imagine how personal these comics are to him—he called them a *friend*.

My stance softens as I inch towards him. "I'll understand if you're not ready to share them yet. I'm sure they're very special to you."

"Yes, but that's not..." Oliver pauses, his eyes skimming across the paper, then cutting back to me. "You may find them juvenile. Childish."

We stand there facing each other, and I'm taken by the fact that he cares about what I think. He's worried that my opinion of his work would not be favorable, and somehow, that touches my heart. "Oliver... I've already seen your talent. It's exceptional."

There is nothing juvenile about Oliver Lynch. While he does have a profound innocence about him, he's not at all *childlike*. Oliver is all man, from the muscles peeking out beneath his cropped sleeves, to the rough stubble along his jawline, to the low, gravelly sound of his voice, to the brilliance of his mind.

My response seems to please him, and Oliver hands me the sketchpad, then patiently awaits my feedback.

Well, damn.

I'm not sure if I've ever used the word *sensational* before, but it's the first thing that comes to mind. I outline the sketches with the pads of my fingertips, his story brimming to life, the characters almost three-dimensional. It steals my breath. "Wow..." Absorbing the pictures, I zone in on an orange tabby cat with a billowing cape, trotting beside a young man.

Oliver clears his throat to explain. "That's Alexis, my new sidekick. I'm working on introducing her character in this scene."

His words tug my eyes up, eyes that are now glistening with emotions I can't seem to contain. "Wow."

Great. Now I've turned into an illiterate dolt.

"It's silly," Oliver counters, massaging the collar of his neck with his palm and scuffing a sock against the carpet.

"It's incredible. This looks just like her." I force my gaze back to the comics, scanning over the boxes filled with different vibrant scenes and landing on a little girl with golden pigtails. A worn teddy bear is clutched to her chest, while a faceless figure looms over her. "Who's this?"

Oliver's cheeks tinge pink as he fidgets in front of me. "The Queen of the Lotus," he replies. "And the Faceless Man. He's the villain in the comics."

The Queen of the Lotus.

Heart skipping, my insides fuzzy and warm, I inquire, "Is that supposed to be... *me*?"

He nods. "Yes... I suppose it is."

"Wow."

Okay, I really need a thesaurus.

Oliver removes the sketchpad from my hands, seemingly frazzled, and sets it back down on the desk. "It's not finished yet. Hopefully, it will be more polished."

My lips press together to keep the emotions at bay as I observe this man, processing the realization that I was never far from his mind during those years he was locked away, lost and afraid, just as he was never far from mine. We stayed connected. He turned me into something tangible, beautiful and real.

He brought me to life in the only way he knew how.

"I've upset you."

Oliver's voice punctures through my haze, and I realize I have tears gliding down my cheeks, pooling at my jaw. I swipe them away with a sniffle. "No... no, I'm sorry. I'm not upset."

"You're crying," he confirms with a probing frown.

"I'm happy. Amazed." My watery smile shows him just that. "People don't only cry when they're sad."

"They don't?"

I shake my head. "Emotions are a funny thing." Nibbling my lip, I tilt my head to the side with curiosity, watching him watch me. "So... why am I still a child in your comics?"

A thoughtful pause distracts him for a moment, then Oliver turns around and walks toward the bed, perching himself at the edge of the mattress. Contemplation beclouds his bronze stare as he studies me from across the bedroom. "I grew up, but you remained the same. I couldn't envision you any other way."

My smile lingers, broadening, as I saunter over to him on the bed. "That makes sense." I glance at the empty space beside him and ask, "Can I sit?"

"Yes."

Our thighs brush together when I settle in on his left, and he doesn't inch away this time. "Why 'lotus'? Why did you choose that name?"

The million-dollar question.

Hands resting on both knees, head bowed with musing, Oliver hums out a low breath. His eyes flick up to me. "It was written on my arm. I think... I don't remember, exactly. Possibly from Bradford." His brows pinch with thought as he tries desperately to pull the memories to the surface. "I carved it into the stone wall beside my name. The word felt important somehow. I didn't want to forget it."

"You can't pinpoint its relevance?"

"No," he mutters, head swaying in disappointment. "Everything is twisted in my mind. I just have a vague recollection of it on my arm, scribbled in ink."

Lotus. Why would his captor write that on his arm?

I wonder if it's a mystery that will ever be solved.

Oliver looks my way again, eyes like a summer sunset burning me, roving over my face and absorbing the greenish-purple bruising along my cheek and jaw. I spare a quick glance to his knuckles, dappled in a similar, painful coloring, and I'm overcome with the need to touch him. *Feel* him. Thank him with the gentle stroke of my buzzing, trembling fingers.

Swallowing my pride, I reach for his left hand fisted in his lap and prepare for an inevitable pullback.

Only, it never comes.

There is a slight flinch, the tiniest twitch, but he doesn't reject me. He doesn't jerk back or break away from the caress of my fingertips. He doesn't flee.

Oliver allows me to cradle his hand in mine while I dust my thumb over the divots of his marred knuckles, dragging him out of his comfort zone and encouraging him to trust another human. I inhale with a deep, shaky swallow, swept up in the powerful notion that this hand was what prevented a horrifying nightmare from unfolding.

And then I'm stunned, frozen to the navy comforter, when Oliver releases my hand and lifts his own to the side of my face.

I remain still, breathless and speechless, my eyes following his hand as it connects with my cheek, his index finger extending and drawing an invisible line along my bruise. His touch makes me shiver, mostly because I didn't expect it, but also for reasons I can't quite explain. Goosebumps tickle both arms, sheathing me in a flurry of new sensations and an unexpected feeling of... *contentment.*

Fulfillment. Belonging.

Home.

When his eyes find their way back to mine, I realize we are both breathing heavily, our faces inches apart. That same charged current I felt as we stared at each other through my bay window surges within me, only, now I feel it tenfold. I raise my own hand and place it atop his, cupping his fingers in my palm as our gazes remain locked in a cogent clutch.

I ask him softly, timidly, our hands still connected, "Will you be my friend, Oliver Lynch?"

And then I slip him a smile, lightening the moment.

There is a noticeable hitch in his demeanor, a brief, silent battle between his inherent fears and his desire to conquer them. A war between his years of isolation, the only thing he truly knows, and... *me.*

71

My heartbeat picks up as I await his response, my fingers crawling into the cracks of his own, pressing his hand further against my cheek.

Oliver releases a surrendering breath, and his lips draw up into a smile that matches mine. A weight lifts. "I would like that."

I guess I don't have cooties anymore.

CHAPTER NINE

OLIVER

I'VE DISCOVERED A STRANGE, NEW PASSION FOR COOKING over the past few months, much to Gabe's delight. Sometimes I wonder if he tolerates my company simply because of the dinners I have prepared when he gets home from work, along with my desire for tidiness. One thing I've noticed is that we don't have much in common, despite the fact that we get along quite well.

Well, except for Sydney.

Our mutual affection for the girl next door is one trait we certainly share.

"Shit, it smells fantastic in here. What are you cooking?"

Gabe traipses up the small staircase and into the kitchen, his eager eyes scanning the countertops for dinner clues. The clank of his car keys against the island reverberates through the kitchen as he untucks his dark polo from his trousers. I spare him a glance before returning my attention to the stove. "Lasagna," I tell him. "I'm making a béchamel sauce."

Peering over my shoulder at the white roux, he nods, impressed. "Don't know what the hell you just said, but I'm here for it." Gabe busies himself behind me, sorting through the mail I brought inside. "So, my dad wants to come by and visit after the holiday. He's been staying away to give you time to adjust, but he's really excited to finally see you."

Travis Wellington—my stepfather. One of the only remaining family members I have left.

"I suppose." To be truthful, meeting new people is taxing. While I've made substantial strides over the last three months, crowds and new faces still plant a tickle of anxiety in my gut. I've ventured out to the grocery store and a handful of restaurants, but otherwise, I limit my socializing to my brother and Sydney.

Sydney's parents, Aaron and Justine, came by one afternoon in May to visit me, and it was profoundly uncomfortable. I didn't remember them in the slightest, so the firm hugs and exuberant conversation exhausted me. Luckily, it was a quick visit. Sydney could sense my distress and cut their stay short before I did something disrespectful and locked myself in the bedroom.

I do find it odd, however, that the neighbor's parents have stopped over before my own stepfather. He must be a busy man.

"Yeah?" Gabe claps his hands together. "Sweet. I'll let him know. I'm throwing that Fourth of July shindig at the house tomorrow, but maybe the following weekend we can set something up."

Ah, yes. The social gathering he seems overly excited about.

I will definitely be locking myself in the bedroom for the duration of the evening.

"All right," I say, stirring the sauce and inhaling the fragrant aroma. "What is he like?"

Gabe slides up beside me, back to counter, his arms crossed. "Pops is pretty cool. He re-married eight years ago and has two other step-kids I've met a few times. They're okay. My dad is a business guy and owns a bunch of restaurants in Lake Geneva. They have a big ass house along the lake."

"He sounds successful," I conclude. "It must be a rewarding life."

My brother shrugs with indifference. "Not really my scene. We don't share the same values, I guess. He's all about money and status. My priorities are friends and fun."

"I can see where there may be a dissidence."

He makes an agreeable humming sound before pulling himself forward off the counter. "Anyway, I'm going to hop in the shower. You should ask Sydney to come over for dinner."

I take the sauce off the burner and begin to gather the rest of the ingredients so I can assemble the dish. "Yes. I'll stop by and invite her."

"Or you can text her," Gabe chuckles, scratching at his shaggy mop of hair.

Hmm. I suppose I *could* send her an electronic message on the cellular device Gabe purchased for me, but I've been struggling to fully comprehend it. There are far too many icons. Gabe added a harrowing assortment of colorful bubbles to the device and told me they were called 'apps'. Software applications, I discovered. All of them provide different functions—most for entertainment, like Bookface... which has nothing to do with books.

Disappointing.

"I prefer face-to-face communication," I tell him distractedly, as I transfer the sheets of pasta over to the ceramic casserole tray.

He shrugs again, then disappears down the hallway. "Suit yourself."

While the lasagna bakes, I decide to head next door. Stepping through the threshold into Sydney's foyer, I realize I have picked up the horribly rude habit of forgetting to knock when I visit her—much like my brother. But I don't retract my footing because shrill music is vibrating the walls, her own voice singing loud and proud over the vocals. She wouldn't be able to hear my knocking, anyway.

I follow the melodies up the staircase and find Sydney dancing wildly, her back to me, her ponytail whipping around in circles as she sings into a paintbrush. It's a bizarre and entertaining scene, something I'm unable to tear my eyes from as I linger in the doorway. I watch her body sway and move as she rolls her hips and flips her hair from side to side.

I recognize the band to be *Nirvana*—one of Sydney's favorites, and the first she introduced me to three months ago when we officially rekindled our long-lost friendship.

Sydney is still unaware of my presence, which makes me feel uncomfortable, like I'm infringing on her privacy. But now I'm afraid I'll startle her if I make myself known and ruin this carefree moment she seems to be enjoying. I allow another minute go by, hardly containing my amusement when she pulls the rubber band loose from her hair and begins flailing her head up and down, blonde locks flying in a thousand different directions.

Unsure of what else to do, I pull out my cellular device. I suppose I should get some use out of it. Scanning through the plethora of icons, I find the one that allows me to transmit messages. I locate Sydney's name and type out:

Hi, it's Oliver. Don't be alarmed, but I'm standing behind you.

I tap the 'send' button and watch as she reaches into her back pocket, pulling out the device that seems to be vibrating.

Fascinating.

For as much as I prefer less complicated means of communication, I can't deny how impressive this new advancement is.

Sydney whirls around after reading my message, her cheeks flushed, her hair utter chaos, then tells the 'Alexa' machine to silence the music. She stares at me with a heaving chest and wide eyes. "Fuck, Oliver. How long have you been standing there?"

Her voice is hoarse. She's out of breath. Sliding my hands into my pockets, I study her sheepishly. "Approximately three minutes."

Sydney blinks. "Excuse me. I need to go die."

"Please don't do that." I rush into the room before she can make any drastic decisions. "I apologize. I couldn't seem to look away from your performance."

"My performance..." Sydney plants her palms against both cheeks, and they look even redder than before. "How far do you think the ground is from the window? Rough estimate? Do you think I'll croak, or will I just break my legs and live out the rest of my humiliation in a wheelchair?"

"Um... I would speculate it's roughly a fifteen-foot drop, and you're more likely to break your legs than die. However, if you fall head-first, you're inclined to injure your neck, which would either kill or paralyze you."

"Great. See you on the flipside."

Sydney turns and races toward the open window, and I react by reaching out and slinking my fingers around her wrist to hold her back. She starts giggling hysterically, falling against my chest, then looking at me upside-down with a wink. The worried breath lodged in my lungs escapes through parted lips.

She spins around to face me, her grin still wide and teasing. She's wearing a cropped t-shirt, cut high enough that her belly-button peeks through, her bronzed stomach lightly sheened in sweat from exertion. "Kidding. Sorry."

I'm still adjusting to her sense of humor.

Realizing my hand is still loosely gripping her wrist, I release her, pacing backwards and forcing my eyes away from the exposed skin of her abdomen.

It's been three months since I opened up to Sydney on my bed, letting her in, allowing our friendship to organically unfold. She is, by far, the most perplexing, endearing, complicated, beautiful, and charming human

I've come across so far. I'm drawn to her in many ways, and I'm not sure if it's our past history that binds us, or if it's something else.

I enjoy spending time with Gabe, and even Sydney's sister is bearable to be around, but there is something different about the woman standing in front of me, hair wild, cheeks still pink like her upturned lips. She doesn't treat me like glass that will splinter and shatter. She doesn't talk down to me like the old woman down the street or strangers who recognize me in public.

Sydney has an essence about her, something intoxicating and pure. I find myself thinking about her when I'm not around her. I find myself staring at her far too long, much like I'm doing right now. She ducks her head, a bashful gesture, breaking eye contact. Something inside me warms in response. "I'm sorry for intruding," I apologize. Scratching at the collar of my neck, I nod towards her easel. "Were you painting?"

We both glance to the left side of the room, eyeing the unfinished canvas. Sydney nods, bending down to fetch her discarded hair band and pulling her tresses up into a messy mound. "Yep," she chirps. "Painting. Dancing like a psycho. Take your pick."

"It's beautiful."

"The psychotic dance moves or the painting?"

My eyes travel to hers and we share a smile. "Both are impressive."

Sydney scrunches up her nose, moving into me, giving my chest a playful swat. "I like having you around. You're good for my ego." She smooths back the stray hairs from her forehead, a deep sigh following. "I need to get ready for work. I'm bartending tonight."

"Oh. I came by to invite you to supper," I explain, unable to veil the disappointment in my tone. Then, when her words sink in, my gut pitches with unease. She's been working most weekends at the liquor establishment, and the prior Friday night she came home frazzled because a presuming customer had put his hands on her. "Are you sure you're safe there? Should I accompany you?"

Sydney worries her lip between her teeth, my eyes zoning in on the action. "I'll be fine. But you can help me pick out an outfit."

"I don't feel qualified..."

Her fingers curl around my wrist as she tugs me out of the office and towards her bedroom. "You're a guy. You're qualified."

I'm not certain how my gender correlates to her fashion selections, but I find myself standing beside her, facing her opened closet. It's brimful of colorful garments, ranging from sweaters to dresses to winter apparel. Sydney usually wears something close-fitting that accentuates her body when she works on the weekends. It's a stark contrast to her normal weekday attire.

"What do you think?" she wonders aloud, puckering her lips as she skims over the clothing assortments.

I'm not sure why, but my attention is pulled to the opposite end of the closet. "How about this little ensemble?" I suggest, reaching for one of the hangers. "Appealing, yet conservative."

Sydney gawks at me, one eyebrow arched with a flare of concern. "Oliver, that's a snowsuit."

"Well, it's pink and feminine. And it looks awfully comfortable."

"Maybe I was wrong about you being qualified..." she snickers, snatching the winter wear from my hands and stuffing it back into the closet. She peruses the other items and settles on a seductive black dress. "What about this?"

I eye the choice distastefully as she holds it up. "It's all wrong. But *this*..." I pull an oversized parka out from the mix.

Laughter invades my ears. "Okay, no. I'm not going skiing in the Aspens—I'm slinging cocktails for preppy college kids. Dress code calls for sleek and sexy."

She decides to go with the black dress, and I cross my arms with defeat, clearly not winning this debate. To be truthful, I'm uncertain why I even care so much. There's no doubt Sydney will look stunning in that dress. All eyes will be on her.

Perhaps I fear the *wrong* eyes will be on her.

"Are you sure you don't want me to accompany you?" The offer almost physically hurts me when the notion of being in such an overcrowded establishment registers. But Sydney's safety trumps my own discomfort. "I can join you after supper."

Her eyes seem to sparkle at the suggestion—pale blue eyes, the color of ice, yet always so warm.

A conundrum.

"That's really sweet of you, Oliver. I know you don't like crowds."

Sydney surprises me with a quick step forward, her hand reaching for my shoulder for balance. She leans up on her tiptoes to press a kiss along my jaw. Taken off guard by the gesture, I turn my head, just slightly, and her lips catch the corner of my mouth instead. We both freeze for a moment, eye to eye, my breath sticking to the back of my throat like syrup.

She flattens her feet, lowering herself back to the ground, her fingers twisting the sleeve of my shirt. "Sorry." A rosy blush stains the apples of her cheeks as she quickly lets go of the fabric and steps away. "Well, I'm going to freshen up. I appreciate the offer, but you don't need to subject yourself to that kind of torture. It's loud and crazy, flashing lights, an obnoxious DJ... women drunkenly throwing themselves at you. You'll hate it."

I swallow, my lips still tingling. "That does sound unpleasant."

"It's an acquired taste," she agrees. Nibbling her lip again, her eyes flicker across my face before she says, "Bummer about dinner, by the way. I literally daydream about your cooking."

I can't help but smile at the compliment. I'm a fast learner when I set my mind to something, and cooking has definitely piqued my interest recently. "Thank you. Perhaps I'll actually have something to teach *you*."

"Gasp." Sydney feigns offense, clinching her hands over her heart. "Are you dissing my culinary abilities?"

"Abilities is a bold word."

I hope she catches on to my sarcastic quip. I've learned from the best, after all, and well... as I said, I'm a fast learner.

Luckily, she doubles over with laughter, gripping her belly with both arms as if it aches. "Oliver Lynch," she scolds with mock audacity. Her wink softens her words. "You've been picking up some bad habits. Must be that blasphemous girl next door. Terrible influence."

I stuff my hands into my pockets, head ducking briefly before glancing back up at her with only my eyes. "Yes, well... I must admit, I'm rather fond of her."

My innocent accolade reads more like flirtation, and my lips tickle in remembrance of her botched kiss. Sydney's smile slips, just marginally, making me wonder if I've made her uncomfortable, or if she's pondering the same thing.

"I'm fond of you, too, Oliver." She breaks our hold after a potent beat, folding the black dress over one arm, then scurrying around the bedroom searching for accessories. "Wish me luck tonight. It's a holiday weekend, so it'll be madness. How are you feeling about Gabe's party tomorrow?"

I teeter on the heels of my feet. "Anxious. Fireworks and crowds of strangers both make me skittish—the combination of the two will likely have me holed up in my bedroom all evening."

Sydney pauses, hairbrush in hand. "Shit. I didn't even think..." Her eyes shift from me to the carpeting beneath her bare toes. "Fourth of July. God, it's the anniversary of your..."

Her words trail off into a void of 'things better left unsaid'.

"I didn't forget, Oliver," she continues, closing in on me once again.

"The whole reason Gabe started throwing parties every year was to celebrate you. We wanted to turn a tragic day into something positive and memorable. It's just… now that you're back, I didn't even consider how something like that might affect you."

I nod, my throat bobbing with a strained swallow. While I don't have a vivid recollection of my abduction, I do recall the fireworks that night. I remember the cracks and booms lighting up the sky with pretty colors—a deceptive sort of beauty. I sat in the backseat of a strange man's vehicle, my eyes fixated on the display outside the window, wondering why everyone else was watching the show on their front lawns with friends and family, while I was lost and confused, my arms roped behind my back.

The fireworks are the last thing I remember of that night before a blindfold was wrapped around my eyes and I was led into a new life of loneliness.

"One person's suffering shouldn't take the joy out of something others may find pleasure in," I tell her. "It would be a very sad world if that were the case."

Sydney's smile reappears, but this time it's accompanied with glossy eyes. "Your suffering matters more to me than the joy of fifty acquaintances and strangers. I hope you know that."

A solemn, yet poignant silence travels between us until Sydney lets out a long breath. She holds up her dress and hairbrush, indicating she needs to withdraw from the conversation. "I'll see you tomorrow. It won't be that bad. We can hang out in a dark corner together and silently judge everyone."

With a wink, she departs.

I linger for a moment, listening to the sound of the showerhead twist on, trying not to envision what Sydney may look like underneath that showerhead. When my skin heats at the image, I take that as an indication to head back home. The lasagna should be nearly finished.

Making my way down the stairs, I give Alexis a few pats on the head as she circles each one of my ankles—her way of trying to prevent me from leaving, I'm sure. My heart swells at the token. I spare a few moments to pet her fur, smiling at the way her rear and tail lift up at my languid strokes.

Crouched down to my knees, I watch as she scampers over to the far wall where a canvas sits perched, facing away from me. Alexis rubs her body against it as she strolls back and forth, and my curiosity stirs. I rise to my feet and pace the few steps over to the canvas, bending to read the markings etched in pencil along the backside.

Oliver Lynch — 01.22.17

My heart lurches inside my chest. The date is from years ago, long before my return. My hands tremble as I reach for the canvas and flip it around, closing my eyes for a simple second, then popping them back open.

Alexis lets out a soft meow, masking the gasp that surely passes through my lips. It's a portrait of myself—though, how she could determine my physical appearance as a grown adult is a mystery to me. The details are exquisite, the resemblance uncanny. I'm looking slightly upward, to the left, my hair overgrown and dappled in various browns, reds, and golds. My eyes seem to match the color of my hair, and there is an expression in them that I can't quite pinpoint.

Worried, whimsical... *haunted*, perhaps.

"We'll be best friends forever, right?"

"Yes. Until I die."

"Even then, I'll find a way to bring you back."

I teeter backwards, catching myself on my outstretched palms, the dream piercing me like a serrated knife. My chest aches and burns, my head throbbing as it fights to keep a firm hold on images that have been entombed for far too many years.

Was it a dream or a memory?

Everything is still so muddled and tangled, twisted in long, winding roots that travel deep.

Too deep.

Gathering my bearings, I pull myself up and suck in a wavering breath. I spare the portrait a final glance before giving Alexis another pet and walking out the door.

"I'll find a way to bring you back, too."

CHAPTER TEN

SYDNEY

I'M NEXT DOOR IN THE KITCHEN WITH GABE, trying to put some quality appetizers and desserts together before guests arrive for the party. I take a step back from the counter, admiring my handywork. *Not too shabby.*

Gabe glances over to me as he sorts through the alcohol, then does a double take. "What the fuck are those?"

"Cupcakes. Obviously." I shoot him a 'duh' glare. "What do they look like?"

"You don't want to know."

"What? Don't even mess with me right now. I stayed up until three A.M. making these." A scowl lands on my face as I try to figure out what Gabe sees. They are red, white, and blue cupcakes—white cake, red frosting, and a blueberry in the middle. I think they're cute.

Gabe scrubs a palm over his jaw, returning to his task. "It's fine. People will be too drunk to care that they look like weird nipple cakes. Hopefully, they taste good."

Nipple cakes?! I cock my head to the side, my features falling.

Shit. They sort of do.

"And the red is a little disturbing. Looks like blood or something."

"Oh, my God. I made bloody nipple cakes."

"Pretty much."

I throw myself onto the counter dramatically, my arms catching my forehead. "Clem should be here soon. She'll know what to do," I mumble.

Gabe doesn't respond, so I turn my head to glance at him, noting his furrowed brow and tense posture.

He finally clears his throat and opens a beer, chugging half of it before responding. "I doubt she's coming."

"Why?" I stand up straight, eyes narrowed with confusion. "I talked to her yesterday. She was pumped."

"That was before she ran out on me last night, right in the middle of sex. No fucking clue what I did."

"What the hell? She hasn't texted me or anything."

Gabe shrugs, his frustration evident, then downs the rest of his beer. "Things were going good. It was fun. I honestly don't get it."

That's strange. Clementine has seemed happy the last few months while spending time with Gabe. I was even starting to wonder if this "rebound" situation was going to turn into something more. "Yikes. What were you doing? What did you say?"

An eyebrow raises at me. "You want detailed bullet points, or the cliff note version?"

"Eww. I meant, does anything stand out?"

"Yeah. My blue balls."

I shake my head through an assortment of theatrical gagging sounds, then spin away from him. "Whatever. I'll talk to her."

The shower turns off from down the hall, and I hear the door creak open. Footsteps are soon plodding towards us, Oliver's voice following.

"Do you know where I can locate a fresh tube of deodorant?"

Gabe and I both turn around, and my mouth goes dry.

Oliver startles when he sees me, his eyes widening, his grip tightening on the towel around his waist.

The towel being the only thing he's wearing.

I can't help my traitorous eyes from scanning him head to foot like Thirsty McThirstin'. His skin is renewed with a healthy glow, glistening from beads of shower water, his hair damp and tousled, his muscles clenching in reaction to my brazen perusal.

His muscles.

Damn.

"I'm sorry for my indecency," Oliver forces out, a crack in his tone. "I wasn't aware there was a lady present."

Sorry that my whore eyes just drank you up like a tall glass of water.

Meanwhile, Gabe snorts at the term "lady", and I quickly elbow him in the ribs.

"You're fine," I squeak out, my voice sounding borderline pathetic. "I mean, you're fine, not...*fine.*"

Oliver's eye twitches, his mouth quirking into a perplexed smile.

"Under the sink," Gabe finally responds, answering Oliver's question and graciously putting me out of my misery. He turns to me when Oliver nods his appreciation and retreats back down the hallway. "Shameless."

My cheeks burn as I grab the bag of blueberries and start frantically tossing them onto the cupcakes in a panic. "Don't know what you're talking about."

"You were checking out my brother. Fucking weird."

"No, I wasn't."

"You're literally drooling on the nipple cakes."

I throw a handful of blueberries at him.

The music is loud, the chattering of voices louder.

Glass against glass, high-pitched squeals and laughter, the deep, rumbling bass of the most popular party songs nearly rattling the walls.

I'm shocked Oliver even came out of his room.

I watch as he ventures into the kitchen, hands stiff inside his pockets, keeping his gaze lowered to the floor as he fetches a bottle of water. Earlier in the evening, I attempted to keep him company in his bedroom, but my knocks went unanswered. I figured he must've gone to bed, or maybe he had earbuds in.

Now, he's here and he's lingering, his feet unsure as he fidgets with the plastic bottle in his hand. His eyes scan the crowd, drifting from face to face.

I think he's looking for me.

Before I can approach, I'm stopped in my tracks by one of Gabe's friends—some guy I hardly know.

"Syd, you look great. What have you been up to?"

Clearly, not remembering you, I want to say, but I force a smile, trying to keep an eye on Oliver as I figure out a way to end this conversation quickly.

Our gazes finally connect across the room, and I lift my hand in a wave. The relief on Oliver's face is evident when a smile blooms to life, tickling me from head to toe.

"Excuse me," I mutter, interrupting the guy in front of me and making a hasty retreat. Taking a swig of my beer, I sprint over to Oliver, grinning wide when he also starts moving towards me.

Only, this time *he* gets stopped.

He's halted by some tipsy chick, whose cocktail is splashing over the rim of her cup as she sways back and forth, either to the music or from her notable intoxication. I swerve through the mass of bodies, trying to hear some of the conversation.

"You're *him*, right? The missing boy?" she asks, twirling her hair with her unoccupied hand. It soon leaves her strawberry locks to fiddle with the collar of Oliver's striped button-down shirt. His eyes trail her administrations as he backs away, appearing uncomfortable. "You look amazing. I saw you on the news, but… wow. You're very attractive."

"Oh, I… appreciate the flattery."

She giggles, tossing her head back. "You talk funny." He backs away again, but she doesn't take the hint. "Can I make you a drink? Or maybe we can go somewhere to talk?"

That's my cue.

I barge over to the twosome, throwing my arm around Oliver's waist, then say, not so quietly, "How about that dark corner we talked about?"

"I'd enjoy that very much."

The woman offers an apologetic smile, accepting her fate. "Sorry. I didn't know he was taken."

When she disappears into the crowd, Oliver turns to me, my arm still loosely draped around his back. "Taken?" he wonders, eyebrows raised in question. "Was she alluding to my abduction?"

"She assumed we were sleeping together," I explain, a smile lifting.

"Oh." The question doesn't leave his face. "That's an odd conclusion to make."

A chuckle slips out when I realize he doesn't understand the context. "She thought we were having sex."

Blush stains his cheeks.

Damn, that's adorable.

Oliver tucks his chin to his chest and repeats, "Oh."

"Come on," I grin, lowering my arm to lace his fingers with mine. I lead him down the two flights of stairs to the den, where there are only a few small groups of people mingling and conversing. "I was serious about that dark corner."

My hand is still tucked in Oliver's large palm, and I'm briefly taken back in time to when we were kids, our hands often connected in a similar fashion as we chased fireflies and birds and dandelion wishes. The memories hold tight as I guide him to the unoccupied loveseat, and we both plop down, finally letting go of each other. My knees draw up on the cushion when I twist to face him, and my eyes twinkle into his over the spout of my beer. "What made you join in on the festivities? I didn't think I'd see you all night."

Oliver's gaze follows the beer bottle as it catches my mouth, his tongue poking out to slick his bottom lip. "I was listening to an assortment of songs you recommended, and it made me want to see you," he replies softly. His focus trails over me with tender appreciation, and he adds, "You look lovely."

I duck my head at the compliment, my belly buzzing at his words as I take in my periwinkle sundress and white sandals. My lips are cherry red, giving the ensemble a festive flare. "I clean up okay," I shrug modestly. "And so do you. I thought I was going to have to peel Strawberry Shortcake off of you."

"She was very friendly."

Part of me wonders if I overstepped by interfering. Maybe Oliver was enjoying the attention—maybe a little female flirtation is exactly what he needs to help bring him out of his shell more. He's made impressive progress over the last few months, but he's still extremely reserved and introverted.

Unless...

"So... awkward question time," I blurt, watching as his one knee bobs, his legs parted in front of him. "Are you attracted to women or men?" A gulp strains in my throat, my cheeks flushing warm and red. "Or both?"

He turns to me, his eyebrows creased, a muscle twitching in his jaw. "Women."

I nod, oddly relieved by his answer. "Okay. Well... do you have a type?" I cough as I shift on the couch. "You know, do you think of anyone in particular?"

Oliver's head tilts slightly through a quizzical frown, visibly processing my query. "Are you referring to masturbation?"

The heat engulfs me from toes to top.

Jesus. I was not expecting that reply.

At all.

"Oh, um, I mean..." Holy hell, I feel like a blushing schoolgirl in the middle of Sex Ed class. I clear my throat. "Sure. I guess."

His eyes are ablaze as they sink into me, coasting over my curves, and he answers easily, "Sometimes I think of you."

It takes an astounding amount of effort to keep from blacking out. I feel my mouth go dry as a ridiculous squeaky noise passes through my lips. Oliver's head is still cocked while he studies my reaction, and there is not an ounce of shame or embarrassment radiating from him. He's completely nonchalant, as if his response didn't just freeze my ass to the sofa cushion and suck the air from my lungs.

"Is that okay?" he wonders, his frown deepening. He's inquisitive—possibly a little worried he's upset me.

Collecting my bearings, I blow out a breath. "Yeah. That's... okay."

Oliver smiles. *Relief.* "What do you think about?"

Only sarcasm can save me now, so I stare right at him and deadpan, "Danny DeVito."

"Oh." His smile falls as he looks down between his knees. "I'm sure he's nice."

As I start flying through all the files in my head I've titled, *New Conversation Starters to Save Me from An Awkward Hell,* fireworks crack to life outside the window. We both jump, startled.

I lift myself to my knees, peering through the pane of glass above the loveseat. There's a miniature display right by the house, lighting up the sky, and I'm grinning like a little kid—I love fireworks. "Oliver, check it out—" My words are cut short when I turn just in time to see Oliver rise from the couch and hurry from the den, his feet pounding each stairstep in time with the worried beats of my heart.

That was weird. Maybe he's going to grab a drink or something.

I stare out the window a few minutes longer, realization surfacing that he's not coming back.

Shit.

Did the fireworks spook him?

Leaping off the couch, I run up the stairs and begin scouring the crowd for any sign of Oliver. Unfortunately, the only thing worth noting is Gabe macking on some random brunette on the living room couch. She is definitely not my sister.

Asshole!

I make a mental note to slug him later.

Deciding he must be in his bedroom, I make my way down the hall and tap my knuckles against the wood frame. "Oliver?"

No answer.

Two more knocks follow before I twist the knob, relieved to discover the door is unlocked. With my concern for Oliver's wellbeing overriding my concern for his privacy, I enter inside, scanning the bedroom. When I don't spot him after a solid onceover, I almost retreat, wondering if he went outside... but something pulls my attention to the left, my sights settling on the cracked closet door. Heart skipping, nerves dancing, I pace over to the closet and pull open the oak door with a sharp intake of air.

He's huddled up inside the dark, enclosed space, his head buried in his hands as he rocks forward and back.

Oh, God.

I rush to him. I don't think, I just run, collapsing to my knees before him and pushing my way between his legs until we're face-to-face. "Oliver. Talk to me." My tone is hushed and encouraging, my fingers trailing up the front of his chest until they curl around his neck. When he finally raises his eyes to me, my heart cracks into a thousand tiny fragments.

He's petrified. He's breaking.

He's someplace else.

"Hey, hey..." My hands travel higher until I'm cupping his jaw, keeping his gaze fixed on mine, refusing to let it slip. "Oliver, you're safe. I *promise* you're safe. You know that, right?"

Oliver stares at me with red-rimmed eyes, his skin blanched and layered in a light gloss of sweat. He nods mutely with a hard swallow, and I can feel his entire body shivering.

His own hands lift, clasping onto my wrists as I stroke my thumbs along his cheekbones. "I never want to go back there."

I shake my head, adamantly. "You won't. It's over, and you survived. Do you trust me?"

Another slow nod. "You're the only one I trust."

Oliver's voice is ragged and strained, but his words put my shattered heart right back together. "Good, because I won't lose you again."

We stay locked in that position for a prolonged, striking moment, my hands holding his face, his hands clamped around my wrists like he's too scared to let me go. Eyes on eyes, breaths intermingled, souls bound and twined like they were designed that way.

I break the tether by leaning back on my heels and letting my fingers slide down his face, then his chest, until they're resting on his thighs. He releases my wrists. "I'd like to take you somewhere. Would that be okay?"

At first, I think he's going to decline, and I'll understand his hesitation, his resistance, his implicit fear. I'll understand his desire for reclusion while he battles his demons in the comfort of his own room.

But he surprises me by standing instead, offering me his outstretched palm—a gesture of acceptance. A token of trust.

I take it, rising to my feet with a pacified smile, and we sneak out of the house, hand-in-hand.

Oliver and I sit atop the grassy ravine overlooking a lake, watching the sky ignite with an array of colors that reflect off the rippling water.

But that's not as captivating as the way the colors reflect in Oliver's eyes as he stares in cautious wonder.

I dragged him up the hill, both of us huffing and puffing, almost choking on our laughter. It's a tall hill, adjacent to an old, vacant playground, and it's one that I'm all too familiar with. Every year on the Fourth of July, once I became old enough to venture out on my own, I'd trek the short walk to this hill and watch the fireworks alone. I'd think of Oliver. I'd imagine him watching the very same display, somewhere safe and warm.

I'd pretend he was thinking of me, too.

The magic of this moment, of watching fireworks with the boy who's taken up the biggest piece of my heart, here on our secret hill we used to lie on side-by-side, takes my breath away. I assume the look in my eyes, as I gaze upon the boy-turned-man on my left, is astonishingly similar to the look in Oliver's eyes as he takes in the fireworks overhead. He's squeezing my hand so tight my fingers feel tingly, but I can't seem to care.

I know he's anxious.

And I know he's trying so hard not to be.

Leaning into him, I rest my temple on his broad shoulder, sighing deep. "I'm scared of spiders. Like, petrified," I mutter against his arm. "It's this irrational, stereotypical fear, but it's real. And it's powerful." A resounding crack makes Oliver jump, and I smoosh my cheek further into him. "One day, I spotted a huge garden spider outside near the side of my house. It was weaving a web. My instincts told me to scream or run, but somehow, I found an ounce of courage and stood there, watching. I watched this spider weave together the most intricate, breathtaking web I've ever seen. It amazed me."

Oliver pulls his attention from the fireworks to glance down at me. His breath moves the hairs on my head, as if they are caught in a delicate breeze. "It must have been beautiful."

"It was." My head bobs, brushing along his shirt sleeve, and I lift my chin, finding his eyes. "There is beauty to be found everywhere... even in the things that scare us."

I see the correlation wash over him before he looks back up to the vibrant sky, heaving in a choppy breath. "Sydney, I—"

Oliver is interrupted when a blaring ringtone penetrates our moment. Confusion replaces his look of awe, and he glances around, trying to locate the source of the noise. Peering down at himself, he frowns. "It appears my pants are singing."

Laughing, I take the liberty of sliding my fingers into his front pocket, pulling out his cell phone. "Something like that," I tease, dangling it in front of him.

"Oh." He plucks the phone from my hand with a bashful grin. "Thank you."

Oliver holds it up to his ear and waits, but it keeps ringing.

"You're such a goof. You have to press 'accept'." I'm still giggling when I swipe the phone back, noting that the caller is Gabe. I answer it myself. "Hey, asshole. Does my sister know you moved on in less than twenty-four hours?"

A beat passes, commotion stirring in the background. "Sydney? Where the fuck are you guys? The cops are here."

"What?" I stand from the hill and begin to pace, nerves surfacing. "Did Lorna make a noise complaint again?"

Gabe sighs wearily on the other end. "No, they're here for Oliver."

My chest cinches as I look down at the man in question, who's gazing up at me with an oblivious smile. "Is everything okay?" I ask Gabe.

"They found the guy, Syd. They found the bastard who took him."

"Oh, my God. Is he alive?"

A frown creases between Oliver's eyes as he rises to his feet. We stare at each other as Gabe replies, "No. They found him with his head bashed in."

CHAPTER ELEVEN

OLIVER

ZIIIPPPP.

It's a sound that has echoed in my ears thousands of times before, but never like this. It has never come straight from my own blood-soaked fingers.

The zipper slides up with ease, and I release the tiny clasp as my body shudders in nervous waves. My breaths are quick and muffled through the mask. I glance down at Bradford, who is unmoving, his head wound ghastly.

I need to get help. I'm his only hope.

There is brief hesitation as I look around my quarters, wondering if I should take my comics with me. They are all I have—my only solace.

But I know I'll be back. I just need to locate Bradford's allies and fetch a doctor. Bradford told me there are other survivors, just like us, scattered around the area, living in similar conditions. One of the allies provides our food source, so it's imperative I track him down in case Bradford doesn't survive—I'll need to stock up on sustenance if I'm going to make it.

I try not to trip over the body as I stumble towards the ladder, my hands curling around the metal stair steps, my legs trembling as I pull my weight.

Glancing up through blurry eyes, I squint while making my way closer to the top. Darkness looms above me, both frightening and ominous, causing me to pause on the rickety staircase.

I can do this.

I force myself up the steps, into the unknown—into the terrifying world I've been sheltered from for seven-thousand-eight-hundred-and-seventy-six days.

Bradford explained that his own safety shelter was right beside mine, but when I make it to the top of the ladder and poke my head out, I am immediately confused. It appears I've climbed out of a hole under the floorboards of someone's bedroom. There is a bed to my right and furniture to my left. There's a nightlight, and a stack of books, and a large black screen on the wall flashing with images. There is a half-eaten carton of food beside the bed.

This room looks lived in.

I find myself baffled. Who do these things belong to, and how has this been right above me for all this time? This is certainly not what I had anticipated waiting for me on the other side of this hatch door.

Looking around with further inspection, I spot a very familiar pair of boots residing near the bedside.

Bradford's boots.

This is... Bradford's bedroom?

Why did he reside in comfort, while I was cold and alone down in the cellar?

My stomach feels sick inside, my flesh itchy with bewilderment, but I cannot dwell on this right now. I need assistance. I need to find the others.

Pulling myself fully out of the hole, I climb to my feet. I nearly stumble when the hatch door slams shut—a door made of the same wood planks as the rest of the flooring. A brilliant disguise to trick an enemy. They would never know I was down there.

I try to quiet my racing heart as I approach the exit door of the bedroom, which will surely lead me out into a frightening, new world.

Oliver Lynch is petrified, but I cannot be him right now.

I am the Black Lotus.

The Black Lotus can do anything.

They found him.

They found Bradford.

Only... his full name was Raymond Bradley Ford—he'd fed me an alias, along with hundreds of other hideous lies.

How could I have been so foolish? So impressionable? I've always prided myself on my knowledge and intellect. It's been the one constant in my life; it's the only thing I've ever been good for.

I trusted him. I believed him.

I looked into his almond-shaped brown eyes, and I saw *truth*.

It seems I may be well-versed in literature and facts and futile information, but when it comes to the human condition, I am supremely ignorant.

My feet hit the pavement in opposite time, sweat trickling down from my hairline. I'm running because I can. I'm running because I was unable to run for twenty-two years. Instead, I exercised in my cell, focusing on push-ups, sit-ups, jumping jacks, and an assortment of strengthening routines I'd read about in books. I enjoyed working-out because it felt good, and because my body was one of the very few things I had control over.

So, I'm running because it's enjoyable and freeing, and perhaps, in some way, it feels like I'm running from all the things I cannot run from.

The detectives told me Bradford died from head trauma, and he was likely dead within moments of the injury. Part of me knew he was deceased when I left him there. His limbs were still, his pulse nonexistent. Maybe it was curiosity, the prospect of freedom, that guided me up those rickety steps and into a world I thought was lost.

The truth is, he fell—I didn't hurt him. I could never purposely cause harm to the one and only person I knew and trusted. Bradford tripped on the very first step of the metal rungs, landing headfirst onto the cement flooring, his skull cracking, blood misting me as I watched in silent horror. It was an accident.

It was a horrible accident.

It's been three days since I sat on that grassy hill with Sydney, since she took my hand in hers and led me home in thick, heavy silence, while my eyes watched her features wrinkle and crease with noticeable worry. I never asked her why we left so abruptly. I never questioned the concern radiating off her in palpable waves. All I did was hold her hand the entire walk home, until we approached the flashing police lights in my driveway and I was taken to the station for interrogation. *Again.*

Raymond Bradley Ford was a recluse, having lived alone in his secluded farmhouse ever since the death of his wife and only son in the late nineties. A family member reported him missing back in March, but due to the hidden state of his body and disguised hatch door, the initial quick sweep of his home did not produce his whereabouts.

The detective with the mustache, the one I dislike, grilled me once more. "Why do you think he singled *you* out? What made you special to him?"

They were attempting to piece together a motive, but the motive seemed clear, even to me. "Perhaps I reminded him of his deceased son."

The detective stroked his salt-and-pepper mustache, his eyes almost accusatory as they speared me. "Let's go over the details of the abduction again."

An anxious sigh dispensed.

I remembered the fireworks. I recalled bits and pieces of the lengthy car ride, like the way Bradford's hands squeezed the steering wheel until his knuckles turned opaque. There was a song on the radio, something upbeat and old-fashioned—a striking contrast to the dismal mood.

Bradford had been muttering to himself, appearing frazzled and out of sorts.

"It's all right, kid. It's gonna be all right."

His words contradicted the sweat pooled along his brow.

After that, memories are choppy. Timeline is disorganized. Befores and afters and in-betweens are blurred.

"You never once tried to escape?" Mustache Man inquired.

"I did in the beginning, but the hatch was always locked, and a young boy was no match for a man of his caliber. Then I began to trust him. I believed him when he told me that we were under attack—that the outside air was filled with poison." I swallowed down my grief and pangs of regret. "It seems silly now, but I thought he was protecting me. He was convincing in his demeanor... and the protective gear he'd always wear..."

A slow nod. "And he never touched you inappropriately?"

I had answered this question already. The notion sickened me. "No."

Mustache Man leaned back with crossed arms and a hum of frustration. "It doesn't make sense. Why would Mr. Ford go to all that trouble storing a kid in his basement for over two decades, without some kind of twisted perversion involved? Sexual predators might do this. Even cult members might do this. But a lonely farmer with no priors?" He shook his head, his dark eyes squinting at me. "It doesn't add up. Why doesn't it add up, Oliver?"

I couldn't hold back, and I blamed Sydney for it. "Pardon my forwardness, but I believe that's your job to figure out, sir."

Mustache Man did not appreciate my response.

Thankfully, I was released a few hours later, but I had one question before I stepped out of the interrogation room: "Did you locate my comics?"

Another detective stepped in, guiding me down the long hall. "We did, but they're in evidence right now. All personal belongings will be returned once the case is closed."

A hollowness swept through me, and it lingers still.

The case will never be closed. There will never be answers because the one person who holds them is dead.

I continue running until I become too out of breath to proceed any longer, and I partially collapse in the front entryway when I reach the house. I'm bent over, hands on my knees, chest burning and stinging. An unfamiliar voice startles me.

"Oliver?"

Pulling myself into an upright position, I glance up the staircase and into the living room. A bearded man with silver spectacles studies me over the rail, a glass of amber liquid in his right hand.

Gabe saunters out of the kitchen, popping the cap off of a beer bottle. "Oliver, hey. My dad came by to visit. He was in the area."

Travis Wellington, my elusive stepfather. "Oh," I manage in between sharp breaths. "Hello."

I'm drenched in sweat, my shaggy hair matted to my forehead and curling behind my ears. All I want to do is take a long shower, but I carry myself up the stairs and mentally prepare for this reunion.

Travis moves in when I reach the top, his gaze piercing as he stares at me. His face is expressionless, as if he's waiting for something. I find it a bit unsettling.

He lets out a small sigh. "You don't remember me, do you?"

I realize he was waiting for recognition, which I failed to deliver. My head swings back and forth, almost apologetically. "Don't take it personally, but I hardly remember anyone."

"It's quite all right. I know it's been a long time," Travis says, bringing the rim of the glass to his lips. "Besides, I'm an old man now."

Gabe steps over and smacks him on the back, squeezing his shoulder before he flops down onto the couch. "And you've got that beard going on. Can't say I'm a fan."

Travis releases a hearty chuckle as his fingers begin playing with said beard. "The wife likes it. She gets the final say."

"Down vote," Gabe quips. "And hey, you look good for fifty, Pops. Hardly old."

My eyes dance between father and son, taking in the effortless banter. Gabe is correct—my stepfather doesn't look old at all. He's in impeccable shape, his muscles outlined through his tight dress shirt. His hair is dark blonde like Gabe's, with only tiny hints of gray. He looks distinguished and smells of cigars.

Bradford smoked cigars. He even offered me one when I turned eighteen.

It was awful. I choked and sputtered and felt nauseated afterwards. "What do you think?"

I blink, glancing back up at my stepfather. It appears I've zoned out. "Sorry?"

"Dinner tonight. I hope I'm not intruding on any plans."

"You're not. My schedule isn't exactly flourishing at the moment."

Travis laughs again, his chest rumbling, his whiskey sloshing against the sides of the glass. "You've got a sense of humor. My son must be rubbing off on you."

A smile twitches, but never fully forms. "Yes, and Sydney."

"Ah, yes." He makes an agreeable sound and turns away, joining Gabe on the couch. "The neighbor girl. How are the Neville sisters these days? It's been a long time."

"Clem is ignoring me for unknown reasons, while Syd is avoiding me because Clem is ignoring me," Gabe interjects, taking an aggressive pull of his beer. "Women."

I stand off to the side, hands perched on my hips, watching as Travis spins his glass between his fingers. "Syd," he smiles fondly. "That kid was a firecracker. I always thought you two were well-suited."

My stomach coils, which I find to be an odd reaction.

"We're basically the same person," Gabe jokes, letting out a sharp laugh. "It doesn't work at all. We're better as friends."

My stomach uncoils.

But that doesn't stop my mind from racing, wondering if my brother and Sydney have ever been... *intimate* before. It seems like a natural progression, having been close friends and neighbors for so many years.

Then I wonder why I'm even wondering about it.

"Come sit, man. Stay a while."

Gabe is waving me into the living room, so I walk with tentative steps over to the opposite couch and take a seat. I feel awkward and out of place at first, but Gabe and Travis both include me in their discussions, laugh at my unintentional jokes, and ease my discomfort until I actually feel like I'm part of the family.

And then I realize... *I am.*

"Oliver?"

Sydney stands before me in a long t-shirt that barely skims her middle thigh, her hair untamed, her black eyeglasses perched on her scrunched-up nose. "I remembered to knock," I say, keeping my gaze straight ahead, refusing to let it slide down to her exposed legs. "I wanted to bring you some leftover dessert. I made brownies."

Her face lights up when she spots the plate of chocolate confections in my hands. "Shit. Come on in." Sydney holds the door open wide, giving me an exaggerated hand motion. "Chop, chop. I need sugar."

My smile expands as I step through the threshold. She's quick to snatch the plate of brownies, wasting no time in peeling back the plastic wrap and plucking one from the top. "Best neighbor ever," she mumbles through a mouthful. "Way better than Lorna."

Goodness, she's endearing.

Sydney pauses mid-chew, grinning around the bite she just took.

Oops. It appears I've voiced my internal dialogue.

"Endearing, huh?" She sets the plate down on the side table, licking each finger before she swallows. "I think you meant crude and off-putting."

"I did not." I slip my hands into my pockets and rock back on my heels. "Sorry to drop by unannounced. I hope I'm not interrupting anything."

"Just 'Pants-less Tuesday'. It's all good."

"Oh." I can't help it this time—my eyes drift downward on instinct, and I swallow. "Well, I'll leave you to it. I hope you enjoy the brownies."

Before I make it very far, Sydney has her fingers curled around my bicep, tugging me into the living area. "Sit and get comfy. I'll be back down in a minute."

"All right."

I watch her skip up the staircase to her bedroom, then drop down onto the couch. Merely seconds go by before Alexis hops up and settles contentedly in my lap. I'm growing quite fond of this feline.

"Look at you two," Sydney announces in a charmed voice, rounding the corner, wearing a pair of fresh leggings under her t-shirt. There's a strange character on the front of her shirt with a head shaped like a football.

Realizing I'm staring at her chest, I clear my throat and shift in my seat. "I like your blouse."

"It's *Hey Arnold!*," she explains, situating herself beside me. "Do you remember that show? We'd watch it when we were kids."

For some reason, her proximity makes my skin heat. She's sitting so close, our thighs are melded together, her stray hairs tickling my shoulder. Why is her presence suddenly affecting me so much? "Oh, uh... no. I'm afraid I don't."

Sydney puckers her lips. "We'll have to have a nineties cartoon marathon sometime."

"I'd like that. My favorite thing to watch is *The Princess Bride*."

"No, shit?" She cranes her neck back as she turns to look at me. "I love that movie."

I can't help the smile that instantly forms. "You do? We should watch it together."

She places her hands over her heart, voicing dramatically, "*As... you... wish...*" Her performance is followed by a bout of laughter as she collapses against my shoulder.

My eyes rove over her, drinking in her sweetness, her quirkiness— everything that makes her, *her*. And when her own gaze lifts to mine, her blue eyes creased with humor, her cheeks lightly flushed... I am struck by an overwhelming sensation. Something unprecedented and startlingly unfamiliar. I feel captivated, enchanted, in the most peculiar way.

"What?" she wonders, her eyes dancing with aqua flecks, her smile still in place. "You've got a funny look on your face."

"Yes... I suppose I do."

Sydney sticks out her tongue and crosses her eyes, and I think it's meant to make me laugh, but all I want to do is kiss her.

Oh.

My breath catches when I inhale an abrupt breath. "Fuck."

She sits up straight, her eyes widening. A beat passes—a horribly long, painful beat—and then, she's laughing again. "Did you just say 'fuck'?"

Did I?

My own laughter emerges, and I look away, ducking my chin to my chest. I stroke Alexis' soft head, right between her ears, distracting myself. "You and my brother say it all the time."

"We do," she acknowledges, oblivious to my unexpected revelation. "It just sounds different coming from you. You're so... articulate."

I shrug at her assessment. "Boring, you mean."

"No." Sydney is shaking her head, her hand reaching out to squeeze my forearm like she's trying to emphasize something. "You're the *least* boring person I know."

"Lies are unbecoming of you, Syd," I tease, still unable to meet her gaze.

Her warm palm is wrapped around my arm, transmitting little tremors to my heart. I think I hear her gasp.

"You called me 'Syd.'"

I finally find the courage to glance up, discovering a wondrous look on her face. "Is that all right?"

She nods, emphatically. "It's definitely all right."

"All right."

We share another smile, and it holds for far too long, causing a strange mix of confusion and thrill to sweep through me.

What is happening?

Deciding it would be in my best interest to change the subject, I avert my attention to anywhere but the intoxicating draw of her crystalline stare. "My stepfather came by to visit me. Travis. Do you remember him?"

Sydney shifts beside me, pulling her legs up until her toes tickle my pant leg. "Of course. We didn't see him much—he was literally always working. I felt so bad for your mom sometimes."

"Was she lonely?"

Sydney cocks her head to one side, debating her answer. "Your mom was very independent. I always looked up to her... maybe she influenced me, in a way. We shared a lot in common."

A sadness overtakes me when I think about the mother I never grew to know. "I wish I could recall more about her."

"Yeah..." She graces me with a wistful sigh. "But Travis was cool. When he was home, he'd take us out in the yard to play *Capture the Flag*."

My head nods with agreement. "He was likeable. He said he's been traveling for work, managing restaurants all across the country," I explain. "It's an admirable achievement."

"Admirable is a word for it. I prefer the lowkey lifestyle."

"Like my brother."

"Yep. We're basically..."

"... the same person," I finish, echoing her words.

Sydney flicks a finger in my face, clicking her tongue at me. "Nailed it."

An odd prickle of aversion sweeps through me, but I push it aside. "So... Travis told me I should start searching for a job. I have little qualification, but perhaps something entry-level for now." There's a feeling of insecurity that courses through me, knowing that I'm thirty-years-old and likely unable to secure any sort of notable occupation. I realize it's not my fault, but that stirring of lowliness sinks its teeth into me. I don't want Sydney to be unimpressed.

Her opinion matters.

She shows no signs of pity as she swats at my thigh in a playful manner. "That's great, Oliver. Want to stop by tomorrow and we can look at job listings? I'll help you with your resume," Sydney offers. "Then we can pig out on those brownies and watch *The Princess Bride.*"

As Alexis purrs softly in my lap, her eyes closed, I look over at Sydney with an agreeable smile. I can't think of a better way to spend my day. "As you wish."

CHAPTER TWELVE

OLIVER

GABE POURS HIMSELF A CUP OF COFFEE while I stand over the stove, folding an omelet in half and watching as the cheese oozes from the creases.

"Smells bomb," Gabe announces, floating through the kitchen in that hurried way he does when he's running late for work.

"It's a Denver omelet. I'm cooking it for you."

"Yeah?" He sips his coffee, wincing when it scalds his tongue. "Thanks, man. I'll take it to go—I snoozed my alarm one too many times this morning."

I fail to see the point in setting an alarm for a specific time, knowing you will not abide by the time you set it for.

A strange habit, indeed.

My eyes find Gabe as he blows into his ceramic mug, trying to cool the hot brew. "You do look a bit sluggish."

"I slept like shit." With a sigh, he smooths back a few pieces of hair that have come loose from his styling product. "Clem was texting me last night, apologizing for bolting last week. She said she just wants to be friends."

"What triggered the change of heart?" I wonder.

"Beats the fuck out of me. She wouldn't say. I guess I took it harder than I thought I would—we seemed good together."

"That's a shame."

Gabe makes an unidentifiable sound as he zones out, staring into his coffee cup. "Anyway, I'll get over it. What about you?" He nudges me with his elbow as I plate the breakfast. "Are you ready to jump into the dating pool?"

I stiffen at the suggestion, turning off the burner and averting my eyes. "I don't think so."

"Nah? I mean, I get it. It's a bitch out there," he explains with a sharp chuckle. "But if you change your mind, I could have a Tinder profile set up for you like that."

Gabe snaps his fingers in front of my face, causing me to frown. "A tender profile?"

"*Tinder*," he clarifies. "It's basically a website for getting laid. You'd have all the chicks swiping right."

I don't know what any of that means, so I just nod. "Sounds interesting."

He takes another sip of coffee before setting it down and reaching for the plated omelet. "That's one word for it. What are your plans today?"

The thought of my plans has a smile inadvertently spreading across my face. I lean back against the edge of the counter, watching as Gabe shoves forkfuls of eggs into his mouth, while simultaneously checking the clock. "I'm visiting Sydney at noon. She's going to help me locate a job. Travis was right—I should be making myself more productive, especially since my government assistance is nearly running out." Tightening my jaw, I glance down at my sock-covered feet, a hint of embarrassment flaring. I find no enjoyment in relying on others.

My brother is quick to quell my anxiety. "Well, I've got no issues with you being here if you're worried about that," he responds, his words almost indecipherable as he chews. "You keep shit clean and cook like a damn boss. Plus, I kinda dig having you around." Gabe glances at the clock again. "Speaking of boss, Howard is going to kick my ass. Gotta run."

My brother discards the half-eaten omelet and gives my shoulder a hearty smack, then hustles down the stairs and out the front door.

I find myself smiling again, my eyes also on the clock, as I wait for it to turn noon.

Sydney is leaning over my shoulder, her proximity so close, our cheeks are almost kissing one another. It's a bit distracting as I scroll through the occupation listings on the screen in front of me. I find that my attention is divided between hourly pay rates and the scent of Sydney's floral hair product tickling my senses.

"Ooh! This restaurant is looking for a line cook," Sydney declares with enthusiasm, clicking on the headline. Then she huffs with disappointment. *"Previous restaurant experience required."*

We've been running into quite a few hurdles. It appears most jobs require experience, and yet, how am I able to acquire any experience if no one will consider me?

A catch twenty-two.

I gave Sydney a rundown of the things I enjoy partaking in—cooking, drawing, reading, birds, nature, cleaning, and organizing. The list was fairly short as I continue to be introduced to new hobbies and interests.

"Reading!"

I'm staring at a freckle just below her temple when she lights up, turning to me with her sapphire eyes. It takes a moment for me to realize she's awaiting my reply—it wasn't a question, though. "I enjoy reading."

"I have the best idea ever," she says with an irresistible amount of fervor. "The library. Our local library is always looking for help."

I ponder her suggestion.

Yes… that *is* a fantastic idea. I've always wanted to visit a library, and I wonder why I haven't done it yet. "I think I'd like that. Should we stop in and speak to someone?"

Sydney nods, standing up straight and stretching her arms. "I took my niece there last week and saw some 'Help Wanted' flyers. A girl I went to high school with is a librarian. I'm sure she'd hook you up."

"That would be lovely."

This new prospect is exciting, but part of me can't help but wonder if it's also a bit… underwhelming. An entry-level position at a library doesn't seem very remarkable. I suppose I can't help my circumstances, though, it's a mystery how I'll ever advance in the professional sense. I worry about how I'll be able to provide for myself, or one day, possibly, provide for a family.

A *wife*.

Sydney looks almost amused as she peers down at me, one hand curled around the back of my chair and the other planted on her hip. "I kind of need to know what you're thinking right now," she prods me.

I don't mull it over and blurt exactly what's on my mind, a concerned frown in place. "If you saw that I worked at a library on the 'getting laid' database, would you swipe right?"

She immediately starts coughing, as if she's choking on her own air. "Wait, *what?*"

"Are you all right?" I rise from my seat to face her, assessing her condition. "Did I upset you?"

Sydney's coughing fit transforms into delirious laughter. She cups one hand over her mouth, her eyes watering with mirth. "Shit, Oliver. What the hell is Gabe teaching you?"

"The Tinder. Do you have one of those?"

She regains her composure, shifting her weight from one foot to the other and sucking her bottom lip between her teeth. "Um, yeah. I have one of those."

"For finding a suitable partner," I deduce.

"Well…"

My fingers muss through my hair as these strange new priorities begin to infiltrate me. "I would like a wife one day. Children, too. I fear I won't measure up in the eyes of a woman."

Sydney's amusement fades, her features twisting into something else. Something soft and empathetic, with glassy eyes and the slightest wrinkle of worry between her brows. "Oliver…" She reaches for my hand, interlocking our fingers together. "First of all, fuck what other people think. If a woman doesn't think you "measure up", then she's an idiot and not worth an ounce of your time. Secondly, I think you're jumping the gun a little. Right now, you should be focusing on learning and growing —*healing.* Finding yourself. Figuring out who *you* are."

All I can seem to focus on right now is the way her fingers feel laced with my own. "I know who I am," I mutter softly. "I've had twenty-two years with myself. I want to learn what makes people tick—what drives them. I want to experience raw emotion, inspired by other humans. Love, passion, companionship."

Sydney tightens her hold on my hand. "It's not so simple. Some of us wait our whole lives and never really get to experience those things."

That sounds absurd to me. "Why is that?"

"Because we're a fucked-up, complicated species prone to self-sabotage, baseless insecurities, and the notion that there's always something better around the corner. We're constantly chasing imaginary destinations, thinking we're missing out, wanting *more.* We're never truly present." She smiles, but it's a sad smile. A little hopeless—maybe even ashamed. "The truth is, sometimes I'm envious of you, Oliver. People haven't desensitized you. Relationships haven't broken you. Society hasn't poisoned you."

"Envious?" The notion is preposterous. "Of me?"

"Told you we're a fucked-up, complicated species." She lets go of me with a wink, diluting the somber mood that has settled in. "But just for the record... hell yeah, I'd swipe right."

Her face brightens with another glittering smile, her nose crinkling in that playful way it does, then she turns around and floats out of the room, her ponytail swinging behind her.

Oh.

I've concluded that 'swipe right' correlates directly to finding another human physically appealing.

My own smile spreads as I follow her out.

"Perhaps you can teach me."

We're sitting across from each other on Sydney's living room floor. Alexis is on her back between us, pawing at a toy that resembles a fishing pole. Sydney bounces it up and down, sometimes just out of reach, as the mouse-shaped trinket dances above the orange tabby.

My eyes lift to meet Sydney's as she pauses her motions, allowing Alexis to successfully nab the toy between her paws.

"You're really adamant about this, huh?" she determines, leaning back on her palms, Indian-style. "You don't think it's too soon? Too much at once?"

Alexis scampers away with the toy, and I stretch out my legs. We returned home from the library a short while ago. I filled out an employment application, while introducing myself to the female librarian Sydney is friendly with. It went over quite well. The visit has given me a newfound confidence to pursue other avenues that have ignited my curiosity lately.

Or, perhaps, *she* is the reason for my spike in confidence.

"I did too little for too long," I reason, catching her gaze again.

"That's fair." Sydney's tongue pokes out to wet her lips as she nods. "Why me, though? I don't exactly have the best track record or qualifications for this sort of thing."

"Because I trust you."

It's an obvious conclusion. There is no one else.

She swallows. "Okay. I guess I can help as much as I can. Just know... dating is subjective. One woman may like certain things, while another will want something entirely different."

"I understand. What do you like?"

A head tilt and pursed lips show me she is thinking about my question. "Food. Laughs. Movies on my couch."

"I can do that. I'll cook for you," I offer, pleased at her response. I was frazzled by the notion she may prefer upscale restaurants, limousine rides, and lavish gifts. But as my eyes case Sydney in her grungy tank top, a black beanie hiding her wild hair, and a crusted paint stain still spotting her collarbone... I know she is not that kind of woman.

Sydney holds up her index finger, as if a brilliant idea has sprung to her mind. "And I'll *help* you cook. That's where the laughs come in."

We ended up making chicken cordon bleu, only we used mozzarella instead of Swiss cheese—Sydney claimed that Swiss cheese was the equivalent of stepping on a Lego in wet socks.

The analogy was lost on me, but it sounded unpleasant.

Sydney had the task of placing the frozen bag of broccoli in the microwave to defrost, garnering a dramatic bow as she took mock pride in her contribution to supper. Laughter poured out of me all evening, particularly, when a song came out of the speaker that had Sydney turning up the volume, dragging me away from the stove, and forcing me into a series of clumsy, highly uncoordinated dance moves.

"I know every freakin' word to this song!" she chirped over the vocals, swinging our arms about and stepping on my toes. "What is a Chinese chicken? No one knows. But we're all here for it."

Sydney pulled back to break out an impressive solo, echoing every word, not missing a beat. She even used a spatula as her impromptu microphone. Hair flying, limbs animated, smile as wide as the feeling of enchantment that had punctured its way inside my heart.

She was still out of breath when the timer beeped, alerting us that supper was ready. "*One Week* by *The Barenaked Ladies*," Sydney informed me, a sheen of sweat reflecting off her face as I pulled the casserole dish from the oven. "A nineties classic. I'm totally teaching you all the words."

"I'm not confident I could memorize that. It was fairly intense."

"Practice, Oliver. I believe in you."

Thirty minutes later, we are finishing our meal on Sydney's oyster-toned sofa with a mewling cat to my left and a swooning woman to my right. The swooning is derived from a mix of the chicken dish and Westley's character in *The Princess Bride*.

"My God, when he hands her the bucket," Sydney says dreamily, her eyes glued to the screen, a sigh following.

A joke crawls up my throat. "If I had known you were so easy to please..."

"Oliver!" She snaps her head my way, giggles bursting out of her, and then she's collapsing backwards onto my lap. More laughter rumbles through her, causing her entire body to vibrate atop my thighs. "Funny, charming, *and* you can cook like nobody's business. Is there anything you can't do?"

"Sing. Specifically, that strange song."

Her amused grin remains, and my hand finds its way to the contour of her hip, holding her almost possessively. Something flashes in her eyes like blue lightning, stealing her smile, replacing it with an unfamiliar expression. While she doesn't remove my hand, she does twist onto her side until she's facing the television, and my hand slides up to her opposite hip. "You don't ever get tired of watching this?" Sydney remarks after a comfortable silence envelops us.

"I am not fatigued." Her ensuing snicker has me reevaluating the context of her question. *Oh.* "No, I do not get bored with it."

"How many times have you seen it?" she inquires.

"Approximately six-hundred times."

"Holy crap."

"It was my favorite," I tell her, my palm applying a gentle pressure to her hip. "I had an assortment of tapes I would enjoy to pass the time, but this was the one I watched most frequently. I would get lost in the fantastical world and the grand love story."

Sydney shifts against me, a soft breath escaping her and warming my knee. She lifts one finger and starts tracing indistinguishable patterns across that same knee, sending a tickle through my veins. I hardly notice the film anymore. It is a muted backdrop to the woman in my lap, her hair splayed out in delicate waves across my upper thighs.

And then I'm struck with an insatiable request.

"If we were on a real date, and things were progressing well..." I begin, my nerves frayed, both hands now clenched into tight fists at my sides. "Would it be appropriate for me to kiss you right now?"

Fluttering eyelashes glance up at me, her pupils dilated, her irises the brightest blue. "Oh, um, I think that depends on the girl," Sydney explains, her voice catching slightly.

"Let's assume that girl is you."

A slow nod accompanies her sudden fidgeting. "In that case, yes. It would be appropriate."

My mouth twitches into a nervous smile as I attempt to keep a rein on my courage before it disintegrates. I look down at her and state, with as much bravery as I can muster, "I believe things are progressing well. Don't you?"

It takes a moment for my subtlety to sink in. She blinks, then her eyes widen, her brows arching to her hairline as she sits upright from my lap. "What are you implying, Oliver?"

She knows what I'm implying. It's written in the way a light blush shades her cheekbones. "I would like to kiss you. If it's part of the dating process, I should know how, yes?"

Sydney's whole body shifts towards me, a perplexed look dancing across her doe-like features. "You don't think it would be weird?"

"No. I need to do it eventually—I'd prefer to learn from someone I trust and care about."

"Well, shit. I need more wine." Sydney plucks her eyeglasses from her nose, setting them beside her on the sofa cushion, then reaches for her beverage. After gulping down a few enthusiastic swallows, she blows out a hard breath and discards the empty glass. "Are you sure about this? I don't want to make things..." Her finger flicks back and forth between us. "Awkward."

"I don't anticipate that," I tell her. "I find you visually pleasing. I don't see how it could become problematic."

She scratches the side of her face with ebony-tipped fingers, a chuckle skimming her lips.

"Do you feel the same?"

"Do I find you visually pleasing?" she asks through a teasing smile. "Of course. You're hot, Oliver."

My skin does feel rather flushed. "All right. Show me what to do."

Her smile fades when her teeth begin tugging on her bottom lip. Wavering eyes drift to my mouth before she ducks her head. "Fuck, I've never felt nervous doing this before." Sydney shakes out her arms, as if she's trying to physically rid herself of the nerves and lets out a prolonged sigh.

And then she's climbing into my lap, straddling my thighs with both legs.

I inhale sharply, my hands squeezing the denim material of my pant legs, not expecting the gesture. I'm at eye-level with the swell of her breasts, causing me to grit my teeth together, almost painfully, as I await instruction.

"First off," Sydney says, our groins much too close. She sweeps three fingers through my bangs, moving them aside to place a kiss on my forehead. "Relax."

"I'm certainly trying to," I force out, finally able to pull my gaze from her chest and meet her baby blues. "I've never been this close to a woman before."

Her grin returns, soft and sweet. Reassuring. "It means a lot that you're entrusting me with this moment. You promise it won't be weird between us?"

All I can manage is a quick bob of my head. My jaw aches as my molars continue to clench and grind.

Sydney places both palms against my cheeks, her touch delicate and kind, and instructs me in a husky voice, "Close your eyes."

I obey.

And then I wait.

Th-thump. Th-thump. Th-thump.

My senses are heightened, overly sensitive, my heartbeat drumming in my ears and the feel of her breath against my parted lips sending shivers up my spine. Sydney takes my hands and guides them upwards until they are settled on her hips. My fingers instinctively curl around her waist, causing her to inch herself forward until the peaks of her taut nipples, bra-less beneath the thin cotton, graze my chest.

The blood rushes south, and my nether regions begin to swell and stiffen in response.

I hope she doesn't notice.

This can't be weird.

Before I can open my eyes, I feel her lips touch mine. It's feather-light, like the mildest breeze in early springtime, or the way a flower petal feels pressed between my fingertips. Sydney's hair begins to curtain us, smelling of honey and floral blooms, as she leans in further, deepening contact.

My mouth parts on instinct, and when it does, her tongue gently sweeps inside. I'm taken aback by the sensation, by the profound physical effect I feel when her tongue touches mine. It's enough to pull a groan from the back of my throat as my hands cling to the curves of her body.

Impulse overtakes me, and my tongue begins to engage with hers, stroking and caressing, as if I've done it a thousand times before.

Sydney's hands find my neck, her grip on me tightening as the seconds tick by. Her pelvis is flush against mine, and surely she feels the effect she's having on me. I can't help but wonder if she feels it, too, as satisfying sounds escape her and she becomes more deliberate, bolder, with her ministrations.

This doesn't feel like an act or a lesson. This feels primal; animalistic.

Meant to be.

When she pulls back for air, I hardly let her take a breath. My right hand curves around to her back and glides up her spine, landing at the nape of her neck and tangling in her hair. I pull her to me once more, our mouths crashing together with fierce potency, my body ablaze. Our tongues continue to mingle and twine as Sydney fists the collar of my shirt, our chests melded together. More squeaks, more hands, more thrusts, more moans.

More, more, more.

She nicks my bottom lip between her teeth, and my hips jerk up, seeking friction.

"Oliver…" Sydney pulls back again, just enough to whisper my name against my lips. We are breathing heavily, the weight of the moment nearly tangible. "We should stop now."

I almost don't hear her. I'm inclined to taste her further, deeper, *entirely*. But the request finally registers, trickling into my ears, overriding my racing heart. "Yes," I croak out, and it sounds more like a pained gasp. "All right."

Nothing inside me wants to stop, but I loosen my hold around her neck, until my hand slides down her back and rests on my knee.

Our eyes meet, and I can see the amorous glaze shining back at me, reflecting my own.

Sydney's fingers trail down my chest, then her forehead falls against mine. "Damn, Oliver." A smile curves her swollen lips, puckered and pink. "You're a natural."

"I am?"

"Uh, yeah. You sure you haven't done that before?" she teases, scrunching up her button nose. Her eyes are now twinkling, replacing the lust.

Had I only imagined it?

I drop my left hand from her waist because I fear if I don't let go, I never will. "I wasn't aware it could feel like that."

"What did it feel like to you?"

My mind is still spinning, my thoughts dizzy and blurred. I've never felt anything like that before, so I have little to compare it to, but I try to explain it the best I can. "Like every star in the galaxy tumbled to Earth and crawled beneath my skin."

A resounding silence settles between us, and I wonder if I've misspoken.

But then Sydney's smile broadens further, lighting up her face like a radiant moonbeam—as if she plucked those stars from my lips and kept them for herself. She leans into me, placing one last kiss to my forehead before removing herself from my lap.

I miss her warmth like I missed sunshine.

Sydney settles beside me on the sofa and tucks my trembling hand between both of her palms. She rests her cheek against my shoulder and whispers, "Those are the best kind."

CHAPTER THIRTEEN

SYDNEY

I FUCKED UP.

I shouldn't have kissed him.

Almost forty-eight hours have passed since I straddled my childhood best friend on my living room sofa, and I still remember every wanton second of it.

Specifically, my vagina remembers.

I'm so screwed.

After spending the day catching up on deadlines and organizing my closet, both welcome distractions to the memory of Oliver's oddly skilled tongue, it's time to shower and figure out my evening plans, considering I'm not working at the club tonight.

My cell phone buzzes from atop my dresser, and I snatch it up before pulling my paint-smeared tank top over my head.

Clem: *Hey, hoochy*

Me: *'Sup, skank*

Clem: *Poppy is with Nate tonight. You working?*

Perfect.

Me: *Nada. Rum Runners and regret?*

Clem: *YESSS. Let's decide right now what shitty life problems we'll be drinking away tonight. You go first.*

Me: *I kissed Oliver.*

There's a long, dramatic pause, causing my insides to spiral with anxiety.

Clem: *Processing*

Dammit. I glare at the phone screen as I collapse backwards onto my bed in my bra and athletic shorts, awaiting the inevitable lecture.

Clem: *Ok, can't process. Please elaborate.*

Me: *Dude, it's self-explanatory. Our lips and tongues made contact. And I liked it way more than I thought I would. He asked me to teach him how to kiss, but he sure AF didn't need much guidance. Now I'm worried it's going to be weird between us :(*

Clem: *Shit. That's so hot.*

Me: *You're no help.*

Clem: *We'll discuss more tonight. I'm leaving to drop off Poppy now. Love yoooou*

I shoot her a kissy-face emoji just as the doorbell rings.

Oy. The tank top goes back on over my head, and I jog down the staircase, smoothing out my fly-aways in the process. I'm not exactly shocked to discover Oliver standing on the other side of the door, but I *am* a little taken aback by the way my heart skips more than one beat at the sight of him in dark running shorts and a crisp, white t-shirt that accentuates his pectorals.

And then my heart almost spontaneously combusts when I spot the singular flower in his hand, stem rolling between his thumb and forefinger.

"Hello," he greets, an adorable, dimpled grin on his face.

I blink. "Ugh... fuck me."

Oliver's eyebrows lift to his hairline, his cheeks coloring a demure shade of pink. "Pardon?"

Shaking my head and cursing my inept choice of words, I usher him inside the house, blowing a strand of hair out of my eyes. "Sorry, I didn't mean... hell, what are you doing here? More importantly, why do you have a flower?"

"It's for you. I took a run down to the lake where we saw the fireworks, and there were an abundance of American Lotus flowers. I thought it was fitting." He hands me the lush flower with soft-hued yellow petals. "Do you like it?"

Of course I like it. It's the sweetest goddamn thing I've ever seen in my life, and I might actually burst into tears.

Mustering a nod, I accept the gift, twirling the stem in lazy circles. My conflicted gaze hooks on Oliver, who is watching my reaction intently. "Oliver... why are you here?"

"I was hoping I could kiss you again."

My heart erupts. Ruptures and explodes, fireworks and embers.

So long, heart.

A sound squeaks past my lips, then I exhale another sharp breath. "That's not how this works. And you can't just say stuff like that."

"Why not?" he wonders innocently.

I almost say it's because my loins can't take it, but instead, I muster, "Because we're friends. That was... *practice*, remember? A one-time thing, for research purposes only."

"But I enjoyed it immensely."

All of the skin on my body flushes in agreement. "Good." I clear my throat. "Then I guess I taught you well."

"Did you enjoy it?"

I choose to be honest. Oliver is always honest, and it's one of my favorite qualities about him. "Um... yeah, I did."

I enjoyed it even more later that night when I was under my covers with my...

"I'm glad."

His smile is alight with pride and relief, making the ashes of my heart ache. "But that doesn't mean we should do it again. We're not *actually* dating, remember?"

A beat. One soul-sucking beat, and that precious smile crumbles, his gaze dipping to the floor. Oliver forces a new smile, produces a nod, fakes his way through his words like he's an expert at it—like he's *one of us*. "Yes, you're right. I apologize for being presumptuous. I'll leave you alone now."

My fingers reach out and curl around his wrist, catching him before he drifts too far. "Oliver..." Our eyes meet, blue on brown, both a little wounded. "Listen, you mean a lot to me. Our friendship means a hell of a lot to me. Stuff like that—kissing, sex, romance—it complicates everything. It tears people apart, and I refuse to lose you again. What we have right now is *good*. Let's not shake it up."

Oliver's attention is fixed to the way my hand slides down his wrist until our fingers intertwine. His mouth twitches into the faintest smile before he gives my hand a tender squeeze and glances up at me. "I understand, Sydney."

"Do you?"

I need to *know*. I can't lose him.

"Yes." The word escapes him like a strained whisper, laced with acceptance and defeat. Before he walks out, his gaze flashes with something curious, something searching. "Can I ask you a question?"

"Sure," I answer, my hesitation evident. I already know I can't lie to him.

Please don't ask me what I did after you left that night...

Oliver averts his eyes, then releases my hand to sift his own through his mop of overgrown hair, a look I find to be as sexy as it is boyishly charming. His hair is shorter than it was upon his discovery, but it's still shaggy, a little wavy, and just long enough to grab onto when...

Stop, Sydney!

"Have you and my brother ever been romantically involved?"

Oliver's voice slices through my inappropriate thoughts, and I'm temporarily thrown by his question, not expecting it. "God, no. It's not like that between us. I mean, we kissed a few times years ago, but it was always when we were drunk, and we always regretted it."

Oliver studies me, his eyes glinting with gold. "I have a hard time believing that."

I can't help but feel offended as my arms cross defensively. "Why is that?"

"I have a hard time believing someone could kiss you and regret it."

My tension dissipates in a flash, my walls collapsing at my feet, landing right beside the remnants of my heart. I don't know how to respond.

"Have a good evening, Sydney."

Oliver nods a farewell, and it feels like a *farewell*, and I panic when he steps out the front door. My voice betrays me as one hand clamps around the doorframe, holding me back. "We're okay, right?"

He promised.

Oliver spins toward me as he walks down my stony pathway, still pacing backwards across the lawn. "Of course."

My desperate smile is matched with his smile of concession.

And as I clutch the lotus flower to my chest, I have no idea why that hurts so much.

Four painfully high stilettos saunter up to the familiar bar counter, our arms linked, our bodies sheened in the sexy kind of sweat you can only produce while dancing to Justin Timberlake.

Brant sends a wink our way as he multitasks like champ. "Neville. I thought that was you shakin' your shit out there." A nod to my sister follows. "Good to see you again, Clem."

Clementine leans into me, her lips grazing my ear. "Are you sure he's gay?"

Hazel eyes travel over me for a split second before my co-worker hands out a round of shots to the group of girls beside us. *Hmm.* "To be determined," I whisper back.

"Howdy!" Rebecca is working the bar with Brant tonight, her neon-green pixie cut and pierced eyebrows a striking statement to her punk rock style. Her petite frame and dainty features make her look like a badass Tinkerbell who will fuck you up. "It's nice seeing you on the other side for once. What can I get you girls?"

I'm leaning forward on the counter, debating our poison for the evening, when Brant sweeps in and slides two shots in front of us, accompanied by another wink and a quick glance at my cleavage. *Double hmm.* My 'thanks' meets his back as he retreats to the opposite side, servicing a different group.

"Eww, God, what is this?" Clem's nose puckers as she sniffs the mystery shot, squeezing in beside me and another patron. "It smells like citrus and battery acid."

Mine is down the hatch in no time, my wince only slight. "Kamikaze."

"I'll need a chaser. I think I'm too old for shots." Clem deflates, a pitying look washing over her face before she swallows down the cocktail. "Shit, that's depressing. More shots, please."

Rebecca grins amidst her Jägerbomb creations. "I got you, girl."

An hour later, we're huddled over a high-top table, our mutual intoxication spurring an emotionally-charged discussion about frogs.

Clementine's eyes are glazed with unshed tears. "You don't understand, sis." She squeezes my forearms over the table. "I'll never know what happened to them. *Never.*"

"You did everything you could," I say with adamancy.

My sister is reliving the traumatic story from her childhood when she captured a bucket of tadpoles from a local pond. She tended to them daily for weeks, having named all nine of them: Tad one-through-nine. So clever.

One dreary summer morning, Clem ventured out to check on her reptilian children, and they had all disappeared. Just gone. For some reason, this memory still stands out seventeen years later and almost always comes up during our drunken conversations.

Clem releases my arms with a melancholy sigh. "I hate not knowing."

"They probably grew little legs and hopped away to a murky swamp made of froggy dreams."

"Or they were eaten by an asshole fox."

"Certainly the more likely scenario."

We both sigh then, reaching for our near-empty beverages. My gaze cases her, taking in her side-swept hair, still streaked blue and partially matted to her forehead. "Speaking of not knowing…" I begin, twirling my glass between my fingers. "Are you ever going to tell me what happened with Gabe?"

A flinch, and then a shoulder shrug. "Meh. It's not a big deal, honestly."

"He said you bolted mid-sex, then no-showed his party. Sounds like a big deal to me."

There's a flicker in her eyes, a flash of something earnest hidden behind her cobalt blues. "I'm still adjusting. I thought I was ready, but he just reminds me of…" Clem's words trail off into the sea of club noise, her attention now fixed on her watered-down Rum Runner. "Never mind."

I frown. Nate is *nothing* like Gabe with his never-wrinkled-suits and country club attitude. "Gabe wouldn't intentionally hurt you, sis. He's the best guy I know."

"And Oliver."

My turn to flinch. "Yeah," I reply in a subdued breath. "And Oliver."

"You know I've been waiting all night to get the scoop on your make-out sesh. Time to spill, Syd."

Her penciled-in eyebrows waggle at me, causing me to inch down in my chair. "Nice redirection."

Clem clicks her tongue. "Details. Now, please."

"He wanted to practice," I mutter, chugging down my lasts few sips of sugar-infused rum. My dark nails drum against the tabletop as the memories sweep through me like a forest fire. "I obliged."

"And you enjoyed," she confirms, eyes narrowed and interested.

"Maybe." I clear the catch in my throat and sit up straight. "But seriously, it's not what you're thinking. Oliver is a very attractive guy. You'd have to be blind and broken to *not* enjoy kissing him."

Clem's grin is wide, her intent teasing. "Do you think he needs more practice?"

"Don't even think about it."

A gasp. "You're catching feelings for him, aren't you?"

My own gasp follows close behind. "No."

Her lips pucker to the side, eyes even more squinted than before. She's reading me from the inside out. "Defensive. Blushing. Fidgeting with your straw." Clem collapses against the seatback with a breath of satisfaction. "You've got a crush."

I do *not* have a crush.

I don't crush. I don't get attached. I don't *catch feelings.*

My sister knows this.

Everyone knows this.

I date around. I enjoy the occasional one-night stand. Sometimes one turns into two or three, but it never develops beyond casual sex, and I prefer it that way. I'm not void of emotions; I'm just guarded. Relationships breed heartbreak, and there is no dignity in heartbreak.

I like my dignity.

And I like Oliver Lynch far too much to break his beautiful heart.

"Earth to sissy," Clem says, snapping her fingers in front of my face. "You're zoning out thinking about how you're going to steal that boy's virginity, aren't you?"

"Hardly," I snort.

But now I am.

"I mean, why *not* you?" she continues, like we're discussing who's up for a damn job promotion at the mini-mart. "It's not like you're a prude. I'm sure he'd want to give his V-card to someone who has his best interest in mind."

"I never should have told you about the kiss," I grumble, literally despising this turn in conversation. My buzz is fading faster than my interest in Lorna Gibson's Bible Club. "It's not like that between Oliver and me. He's... fucking perfect in every way, and there's no way in hell I'm going to be the one to corrupt him."

"Better you than some hussy who *doesn't* have his best interest in mind. You know women are going to start lining up on his front porch—they don't make guys like Oliver."

She's right about that. My teeth clench in spite of myself when I think about Oliver dating random girls, or sleeping with a woman who doesn't know him, doesn't *understand* him the way I do.

It's a ridiculous, unwarranted thought that has no business poking around inside my brain.

Oliver is a grown man, becoming stronger and more confident every day. He'll get a job, he'll settle down, he'll fly free like the birds he watches in fascination from his front stoop.

He'll *flourish.* He'll probably change the world one day.

And I can't hinder that.

"I'm not going to sleep with him," I say softly but firmly, transfixed on a spot of sticky syrup glued to the wood table. "It would ruin everything we've rebuilt over the last few months."

Clem spears me with a cynical stare, swinging her shoulder-length hair from side to side. "You see ruin where I see potential," she states with poignancy. "But I'll accept your backwards way of thinking. I won't bring it up again." Clementine stands from her chair, straightening her miniskirt and signaling towards the bar with a head bob. "More drinks?"

God, yes. I follow her lead, ignoring the barb, and we situate ourselves at an opening at the counter. Rebecca sends us a wave from the opposite end, and I mouth '*no rush*'. But she slaps Brant on the shoulder and points in our direction, earning us a wink and an easy grin.

Thirty seconds later, we're sipping on fresh cocktails, preparing for another round on the dance floor. But before the flashing DJ lights can beckon us over, Clem's cell phone starts ringing in her purse. Her subsequent eye roll leads me to believe it's Nate.

"Make it quick. It's loud in here," Clem clips as she accepts the call. She holds the phone to her ear and listens intently, her features twisting into something chilling. "*What?*"

My attention is piqued, my eyes peeled to my ashen sister. Clem runs tense fingers through her hair, tugging back the roots, absorbing whatever Nate is telling her.

"Okay, I'm on my way. Jesus... take her in. I'll meet you at the hospital."

Shit.

"What the hell was that?" I wonder, rattled. "Is Poppy okay?"

Clem stuffs the cell phone back into her purse and digs through her wallet for cash. Her hands are shaking. "She fell and hit her head at the park tonight, but Nate said she seemed fine after a few tears. Now she's throwing up and complaining of a headache. I think she has a concussion."

"Oh, my God."

"I'm so sorry, sis. Here's some money for an Uber." Clem tries to shove the money at me, but I dismiss it. "Please take it. I feel terrible for ditching you here."

"No way, I'll be fine. Go take care of your baby."

Brant is in front of us, leaning forward on his palms. "I'll give her a ride home," he offers. "It's not a problem. My shift is up in an hour."

"You're the best," Clem says quickly, already moving away from the counter, fear radiating off her in waves. "Love you, hoochy."

"Love you more, skank. Keep me posted."

A nod, and she's gone.

I twist back towards Brant, gifting him a sincere smile. "You're sure you don't mind hauling me around? Don't you live on the other side of town?"

"I'm good. It's not a big deal. Drink up and have fun." He taps his knuckles on the counter before getting back to work, his tight t-shirt emphasizing every taut muscle.

I could have sworn he was gay.

Funny story...

Brant's not gay.

I know this because our lips are locked together as we stumble up my pebbled walkway with frisky hands and clumsy feet.

I pull back for a breath. "I totally thought you were gay," I mutter through a strained laugh as Brant fists my hair and grins.

"Why did you think that?"

"You were flirting with some preppy college guy when I first got hired."

He presses a kiss to my mouth, his amusement evident. "Tips, Neville. You've got to learn to read the room."

Point.

We're back at it, and he spins me around until I'm pressed up against the brick siding. I'm enjoying it at first. Brant is sexy, totally my type, and his mouth is hot and capable. He tastes like spearmint and a damn good time.

But when his hands grip my hips, I'm transported back to my living room couch forty-eight hours prior, and it's Oliver's hands on me in the same position. Holding me the exact same way. It's *his* eyes drinking me in, alight with red and gold flecks, glowing like a molten sunset.

And the moment that memory traipses through my mind, stomping all over my perfectly good evening, I choke. I freeze. I turn my head away, and Brant's lips collide with my cheek.

He keeps kissing me for a short while, trailing his fevered tongue down my neck, but I'm already checked out. And Brant realizes this when my arms fall limp at my sides and a defeated breath escapes me.

He pauses with his fingers stalled beneath my top. "I lost you, didn't I?"

The hard swallow burns my throat. "No, I... I mean, I think I'm just tired. I'm sorry."

Dammit. Fuck. Shit-fuck.

Brant pulls away, finding my eyes, the truth shining back at him in pools of light blue. He ducks his head, releasing me with a self-deprecating chuckle. "Shit. And here I'm preaching about reading the room..."

"Brant, you read the room right. I was totally planning on climbing you like a tree tonight."

He takes a step back, and I miss the warmth, but I'm not sure if it's *his* warmth I miss.

Gliding his fingertips through his jet black hair, he puffs his cheeks with a hollow breath and lets it out hard. "It's cool, Neville. No hard feelings."

"God, I suck. I'm really sorry," I spit out, confusion mingling with alcohol and guilt. My palm wraps around his forearm, applying enough pressure to physically transmit my apology. "I swear it's not you. I'm tired and worried about my niece. Maybe we can do a rain check?"

Brant places a finger beneath my chin, his thumb grazing my jawline as his gaze digs into me, trying to see the bigger picture. A faint smile crosses his lips. "Don't apologize, Syd. You wear your heart in your eyes, and it's clearly taken."

"What? No—"

He presses a kiss to my forehead. "See you next week?"

All I manage is a nod.

Brant shoots me his trademark wink and walks away, tossing his keys in the air and catching them before disappearing into his Highlander.

My feet are stuck to the woodchips that line my house, my jaw aching with tension and words I never got to say.

My heart is taken? What kind of sappy bullshit is that?

Maybe he does suck at reading the room.

Finding my bearings, I push off the bricks and resign myself to a lonely night of junk food and reading as I await updates about Poppy.

That's fine. Alexis is good company.

Before I make it to the porch, my peripheral vision catches movement to my right. My head swings in the same direction, and my body goes rigid when I spot Oliver sitting on his front stoop, his head bowed, staring down between his knees.

Shit.

We shared an epic kiss, and two days later he sees me making out with my co-worker on my front lawn like a giant sleazeball. I'm the *worst.*

Oliver isn't looking at me, but I know he saw. And I know the kiss we shared wasn't supposed to mean anything, but it clearly meant something to him.

It meant something to me.

Biting down on my bottom lip, I inhale a flimsy breath. "Hey," I call out, watching his head perk up to find me in the dark. "You're up late."

Part of me expects to see animosity. Jealousy. Anger.

But Oliver smiles. He fucking *smiles,* and that feels so much worse.

"I couldn't sleep. I enjoy listening to the crickets and cicadas when my mind is restless."

I glance down at my painted toes peeking out of my too-tight stilettos, my arms tucking around myself like armor. "Summer nights are my favorites," I reply across the adjoined yards. "The cool humidity. The sticky breeze. The sounds of nature, vibrant and alive."

I'm rambling. I'm talking nonsense at almost midnight, trying to pretend Oliver didn't witness my tongue in some other guy's mouth. And I don't know why, I don't understand why I feel this bitter coil of guilt weaving itself around my fragile insides, but I *do.*

I just fucking do.

"It's calming," Oliver agrees, his voice barely audible as it catches on a slight draft that travels over to me. Then he stands, slipping both hands into his pockets and meeting my penitent gaze through the starry night.

"What did it feel like to you?"

"Like every star in the galaxy tumbled to Earth and crawled beneath my skin."

I gulp. "Goodnight, Oliver."

"Goodnight, Syd."

He smiles again, knowing but warm, and turns to head inside.

I do the same.

Tossing my purse to the floor and kicking off my ridiculous heels, I let out the breath I feel like I've been holding in all night.

I didn't do anything wrong. Oliver wasn't mad.

Everything is fine. It's just the alcohol emotions rearing their ugly head.

Satisfied with my assessment, I head upstairs and begin peeling off my clothes, leaving a trail of leather and cheap perfume behind me. When I step into my bedroom, Alexis is sleeping soundly at the edge of my mattress. The image tickles my heart.

And as I squint my eyes through the dim lighting, trying to get a better look, that tickle grows into a heady palpitation when I spot her curled up beside the wilting lotus flower.

CHAPTER FOURTEEN

SYDNEY

"I CALLED HER 'BABYGIRL'."

Gabe and I are fighting over chips and guac at our favorite hole-in-the-wall Mexican place, and I swat his hand away when he tries to reach for the extra scoop-y chip—the kind he *knows* I prefer. My eyes lift to him across the burnt orange tabletop as I gather an obscene amount of guacamole on my tortilla chip. "Who? What?"

He strokes the light stubble along his chin, distracted, staring just beyond my shoulder.

"Hi," I chirp, waving the chip under his nose. When he meets my gaze, I smile. "Welcome back."

"Shit, sorry. Just thinking."

"New girl?" I wonder, taking a bite.

"Clem," he clarifies. "I've been wracking my brain, trying to figure out what triggered her to leave so suddenly, and that's the only thing that comes to mind. I called her *babygirl*, and she just kind of froze, then bolted."

Eyebrows dipping to my nose, I process his words, slowing down my chews. "That's weird."

"Yeah, it is. But it's the only thing I can think of."

"Maybe she thought you had a Daddy-kink and panicked."

"I don't have a Daddy-kink."

I throw my hands up, palms facing him. "I'm not one to kink-shame. Just an observation."

"Dude." Gabe's gaze is irritated as he glares at me. "I don't have a Daddy-kink. It just came out in the heat of the moment. I don't fucking know."

The truth is, I don't know either. Clem has never been forthcoming with her sex life in regard to Nate, and I know she hasn't had much experience beyond her ex-husband.

"I'm stumped." I pop another chip into my mouth and lean back against the booth, studying my friend as he appears to zone out again. "Maybe just give her some time. She's still adjusting to the divorce and doing the single mom thing. You probably got ahead of yourselves."

"Yeah." Gabe says it with little believability before shaking his head, sighing, and diving back into the chip basket. "Anyway, it's for the best. I mean, can you see me being a pseudo-dad to Poppy? That would have been a shit-show waiting to happen."

His playful smile sparks my own as I envision Gabe taking on the father figure role—a concept that is equally frightening and adorable. "I love you, but you're not wrong. Poppy already has to deal with me and my instability."

"Exactly. So, picture *two* of you shaping that kid's future."

We share a laugh.

Frightening, indeed.

Clem texted me early this morning, assuring me that Poppy was fine. My niece suffered a mild concussion, but her cat scan showed no serious trauma or any potential worries. She was already feeling better by sunrise, *thank God.*

I don't know how parents do it—the constant worry, the late-night ER visits, the fevers that could be the common cold or a brain-eating infectious disease. I panic when Alexis sneezes.

Our plates are finally brought over, each adorned with enchiladas smothered in ranchero sauce. Gabe gets chicken, I get beef. Taking a bite, I address him with a mouthful of food like the classy lady I am. "How's Oliver doing?"

Gabe sips his water through a red straw, eyes flickering from me to the dancing ice cubes in his glass. He responds with a shoulder shrug. "Fine, I guess. He nailed down that library position, so he's pretty psyched about it." He slurps more water, then pauses. "Well, as psyched as Oliver gets. He said something along the lines of, *'This is very desirable news'.*"

A giggle slips out before my smile falls.

He didn't tell me he got the job.

It's been a week since I've spent any quality time with Oliver, and I can't lie—it's killing me. We haven't exactly been avoiding each other, considering he's regularly outside watching the birds or going for runs, and I can often be found tending to the yard in my free time. There have been quick conversations, warm waves, genuine smiles.

Casual. Easy. Carefree.

Yesterday, he caught me gawking at him as he jogged down our tree-lined street, sweating through his heather gray tank top, his muscles flexing gloriously as each foot pounded the pavement. When he spotted me perched between my bushes, he threw me an amiable wave, despite the fact that I was watching him like a Peeping Tom.

I waved back with the hedge shears, also looking like a serial killer.

It's a miracle I've ever had sex.

Gabe mixes his rice and beans together, shooting me a curious glance. "You went to a place. Anywhere I want to be?"

"Doubtful," I huff, deflating against the table on my crossed arms. "Why didn't Oliver tell me about the library position?"

"How would I know? He's not really big on small talk." Gabe swallows a bite of food, then sets his fork down on his plate with a clatter. "Did you guys have a fight or something?"

"More like... a battle."

A frown settles between his eyes. "Of wills?"

"Of tongues."

"Jesus Christ, Sydney..."

"What?" I counter, my defenses flaring as I throw my hands up. "He asked me to teach him how to kiss. He promised it wouldn't be weird. And now it's weird."

"Ya think?"

"I knew you wouldn't understand..."

Gabe pinches the bridge of his nose with a shake of his head. "Oliver is super vulnerable right now. He's impressionable. He's like a damn kid."

"He is *not* a kid."

"I'm referring to the way his brain works. He was locked away in a cement hole for twenty-two fucking years, Syd. He doesn't need your tongue complicating shit for him when he's trying to get on his feet."

My neck cranes backwards, offended and a little bit outraged. "First of all..."

Gabe groans, his eyes rolling up when I whip out the finger list.

"... Oliver is the smartest person I know."

"He's book smart. He's not street smart."

"Two," I continue, ignoring him. "The only way Oliver is going to learn and 'get on his feet' is to have experiences. He *asked* me to kiss him, Gabe."

"Sydney..."

"And three," I bark, pressing my index finger to my opposite ring finger, venom spilling from my eyes. "Don't talk about my tongue like that."

Gabe's arms are crossed as he leans back in his booth, his jaw tight, one eyebrow raised. "Are you done?"

I stab my enchilada, pretending it's Gabe's stupid face. "Yes."

"I wasn't trying to be a dick," he insists, a sigh of surrender escaping him. "You have a nice tongue."

"Don't be gross."

Stab.

A smile flickers, then dissolves. "Listen, I *know* you, Sydney... you have walls up. You don't get attached, and that's great, more power to you, but..." He lowers his eyes, as if he's afraid to see my reaction. "Oliver's walls are a lot thinner than yours. It won't take much to break through them."

My fist squeezes the end of my fork as I pin my steely gaze across the table. "What does that mean?"

A sharp look, and then, "It means... you hold the sledgehammer, Syd. One wrong swing and he's going to fall."

A lump forms in the back of my throat, causing my voice to crack. "You're overreacting. I don't have that much power."

"I've seen the way he looks at you. You have *all* the power."

My fork hits the table, and I start sifting through my wallet, pulling out a twenty-dollar bill. I toss it at Gabe. "Thanks for the vote of confidence. It's great to know where I stand."

"Come on, don't take this personally. I'm just looking out for my brother."

I heave my purse strap over my shoulder and rise from the booth. "So am I."

"Sydney..."

"Don't!" I spin around, garnering the attention of patrons and wait staff, but I don't even care. "Don't tell me you're looking out for him now, when I was the only one *still looking* for him after everybody else had given up."

Gabe's jade eyes, normally bright and good-natured, turn to stone. "That's a low blow."

My heart clenches, a touch of regret piercing through my shield, little by little. I want to take it back, but I don't. I'm too pissed to lower my flag. "Enjoy your lunch, Gabe."

I storm out of the restaurant.

Screw this.

I waited twenty-two years to get Oliver Lynch back, and I refuse to go another day with awkward interactions and superficial conversation. We've come too far.

He's come too far.

Gabe's car isn't in the driveway when I head next door, and I'm grateful for that. I'm still reeling from our argument this afternoon. We *never* fight. We bicker and tease and give each other shit, but we never fight dirty like that.

My anxiety is spiking to dangerous levels, so it's time to tidy up one of these messes.

I tap my knuckles against the familiar mahogany door, my insides twisting with nerves when I hear footsteps approach a few moments later. Oliver cracks the door open, peering out, like he's hesitant to find out who's on the other side.

Just good ol' Sydney Neville with her sledgehammer and complicated tongue.

The relief is evident when Oliver pulls the door open further, his features relaxing. A smile follows, lighting up his handsome face. "Sydney."

He says my name with such warmth, such affection, I can't help but flash back to the words Gabe hurled at me over Mexican food:

You have all the power.

A gulp sticks to the back of my throat. "Hi."

"Hello."

His smile remains, steadfast and sweet.

Dammit.

I waste no more time and push through the threshold, almost knocking Oliver off his feet when I throw my arms around his neck and bury my cheek against his hard chest. The words tumble out before I can stop them. "I missed you."

Oliver's arms find their way around my waist, uncertain at first, careful and delicate. But then his grip tightens, pulling me close, closer than he probably should. His breath beats against the top of my head, tickling my scalp and heating my skin.

His right hand travels up my spine in a way that's too familiar. I think about how it felt when he gripped the back of my neck, my hair braiding between the cracks in his fingers, his mouth hot and demanding on mine.

Down, girl.

"You missed me?" he wonders into the disheveled wisps of my messy bun.

I nod into his chest. "Yes."

"But…" Oliver falters, debating his choice of words. Then he finishes, "It's been… one week."

A pause.

A temporary silence.

Absorbing, absorbing…

My laughter hits me like a slug to the gut when his joke registers. I collapse further into him, my body shaking with mirth, my feet barely holding my weight. This only causes Oliver's arms to clutch me tighter, his own amusement mingling with mine.

"Holy shit, Oliver. Did you just *Barenaked Ladies* me?"

"It appears so."

Chin to his chest, my head lifts up to find his eyes, and they are dancing with humor.

One week.

One week without his closeness, his quirks, his charm, his beautiful soul radiating into me, and it felt like a part of me had withered away.

I have no idea how I survived twenty-two years.

Oliver's foot slams on the brake, and I lurch forward so hard, my forehead almost collides with the dashboard.

"Oliver!"

"There was a tiny mammal."

When my breath dislodges from my throat, I glance out the windshield and spot a squirrel scampering up a neighbor's tree. "It was just a squirrel. Squirrels are suicidal."

"Beg your pardon?"

Smoothing my hair back, I urge my heart to slow down. "It's fine... you don't need to brake so hard. Go easy on the pedal."

"It was an unexpected interference. I panicked." Oliver's chest expands with each hard breath, his fingers curling around the steering wheel like he's holding on for dear life. "Perhaps we should turn back."

"I mean, it *is* illegal and incredibly dangerous..." I chuckle at the wide eyes pointed in my direction. "Oliver, we're only driving down our neighborhood street at seven miles per hour. It's totally fine. My dad practiced with me and my sister when we were fifteen on this same stretch of road."

Oliver's complexion has turned chalky, his nerves visible. Two days after our mini-reunion, I offered to take him out for driving practice. He starts his new job next week, and he'll need to figure out transportation at some point. I volunteered to drive him to and from the library for now, but it's not a permanent arrangement—and not because I *wouldn't*. I'd do anything for the man beside me, clutching the wheel with sweaty palms, his bangs grazing his eyelashes, his body tense with apprehension.

It's because he needs this.

Oliver signed up for a driver's education course that starts in two weeks, but I figured there was no harm in taking him around the block for a trial run.

"You kids are going to run down my mailbox and Dwarf Hollies!"

That is, unless Lorna Gibson starts besieging us with her pruning saw.

"Shit," I mutter with an embittered moan, ducking lower in my seat, as if the old woman hadn't already cast her eyes of scorn upon me. My window is partially rolled down, an unintended invitation for Lorna to stalk over to my vehicle in her floral nightgown. "Good morning, Ms. Gibson," I say, my tone sounding unnaturally pleasant.

"*Mrs.*," she huffs as she approaches. "I'm widowed. God rest his soul."

Edgar. The neighborhood hornball. Even as a child, I remember Lorna's husband being a total creep—leering at the bikini-clad teenagers, making vulgar remarks, cracking inappropriate jokes. Mom wouldn't even let us out of the house when he was doing yardwork.

Lorna does the sign of the cross, then pokes her head inside the car to scope out the very illegal driver.

Oliver looks like he's going to vomit. "Good day, ma'am."

"Oh, Oliver!" Lorna's entire demeanor shifts into sunshine and puppy dogs and a choir of heavenly angels. "I thought you were your hooligan brother."

I clear my throat. "I was taking Oliver for a test drive. He's studying for his learner's permit."

A sneer in my direction, then she's back to swooning over the man on my left. "You're looking very well lately. Your mother would be so proud."

"I almost hit a squirrel."

A snort-chuckle escapes me.

"Yes, well, they are pests—always stealing my bird seed from the feeder. Run them all over if you must," Lorna replies, her drawn-on eyebrows pinched into her wrinkled forehead. "If you ever need anything, I'm only a short walk away. I'd love to make you a home-cooked meal."

"Oliver is actually a really good cook—"

"And if you need money, I'd be happy to hire you for chores and yard projects. My knees aren't what they used to be."

"He's starting a new job at the libr—"

"I'm sure it's been a nightmare trying to locate work with your unsavory history. Is the government providing you with financial disability?"

I lean back against the headrest with a sigh, holding back a vulgar retort.

Oliver struggles with his response, shifting uncomfortably. "I appreciate your kindness. Thank you."

Lorna's smile is beaming. "Such a polite young man." That same smile vanishes when she turns her eyes to me. "Keep in mind the company you keep, Oliver. I'd hate to see you venture down an unseemly path…"

Her bony hand lifts into a wave as she steps away from the car, singing *All You Need Is Love* by The Beatles and wobbling back towards her house.

"She's not very fond of you, is she?" Oliver inquires, his eyes squinted with bemusement as he watches Lorna retreat. "I can't imagine what you've done to upset her."

"I'd love to know that answer," I shrug, indifferent. "Ready to go?"

"Um…"

"Hey, Sydney."

Oy. I wonder if we'll ever make it farther than one driveway. Glancing up, I spot a fellow neighbor, Evan, walking with his daughter, Summer. He's probably taking notes for his new novel: *The Blasphemous Adventures of Sydney Neville.* "Hi. Your daughter is getting so big."

Summer spins around, her ear buds in place, her oversized t-shirt twirling with her as she dances.

My spirit animal.

"She really is," Evan remarks, scratching at his dark hair. "Hey, I was actually wondering if you could babysit this Saturday night. I'm going to a concert and my usual girl is busy."

"Yeah, of course." I work at the club on Friday, but the rest of my weekend is free. "But only if you put in a good word to Lorna about me."

Evan chuckles, his sparkling smile and Paul Newman eyes leaving no mystery as to why Lorna gushes over the man. "She only likes me because I mow her lawn."

Yeah, okay.

"Hey, man," Evan greets, bending down and lowering his hands to his knees, nodding through the open window at Oliver.

Oliver looks beyond lost. "Hello."

We smile our goodbyes when Summer skips ahead of her father, and I can't help but laugh as I roll the window up. Oliver and I share an amused glance. "Joyrides are not usually this eventful," I assure him.

Oliver fiddles with the gears, a small grin brightening his face. "Everything is eventful with you."

Swoon.

An hour later, we're lounging on the couch, needing a break from the scorching midsummer heat. But despite the welcomed draft from the air conditioner, the heat doesn't leave me entirely as I snuggle up beside Oliver, my knees pressed into the side of his thigh, our shoulders fused together.

He's tense, his hands folded tightly in his lap, and part of me wonders if I'm giving him mixed signals by touching him, by being so close. That's just me, though—I've always been a hugger, a feeler, an invader of personal space. I'm like a tidal wave, crashing onto a sandy shoreline, even on the days it wants to stay dry.

And maybe I'm just eager to soak him up as much I can.

The TV drones on from across the room, some reality show drama providing background noise to our otherwise quiet moment. Oliver's eyes drift to me every so often. I feel them in the same way that I felt *him* for two long decades—a sixth sense. An inherent tingle beneath my skin that would trigger my nerve endings to dance to life every so often, unannounced.

I glance up, seizing his curious gaze with my own, watching an assortment of emotions darken his cinnamon-tinged eyes.

I've seen the way he looks at you.

God, me too.

Before the moment can lapse into something heavier, the front door springs open and Gabe's voice greets us from the foyer below.

"Honey, I'm home. Best Monday ever. I—" His footsteps cease when he spots me cozied up beside Oliver on the sofa. "Oh. Hey."

I twist my neck around in time to see him pull his eyes from me, pacing into the kitchen and tossing his car keys onto the counter. "Hey."

Even Oliver can sense the tension that just boiled to the surface. He frowns down at me in question.

A sigh passes through my lips as I commit to damage control. I give Oliver's thigh a squeeze before standing, noting the way his whole body stiffens at the gesture. "I'll be right back. I need to talk to Gabe about something."

His nod sees me off, and I traipse into the kitchen, swinging my arms back and forth like some futile attempt to quell the awkwardness. Gabe spares me a brief glance before rummaging through a cabinet—looking for nothing, I'm sure.

"Can we talk?" I ask him, stuffing my fingers into my back pockets in order to stop them from aimlessly swinging.

Gabe pauses his unproductive perusal, his chest puffing out with a resigned sigh. "Yeah, sure."

I tilt my head towards the hall, encouraging him to follow, and soon we're standing face-to-face behind his closed bedroom door. I'm quick to slice the silence. "Can we be done? This sucks."

He studies me with folded arms, his expression stoic.

My eyes are pleading and sorry as I pucker out my bottom lip, my lashes fluttering, begging for his submission. "You know you can't stay mad at me."

"You underestimate me."

Another pathetic eyelash flutter, my lip jutting out with impressive effort.

"Dammit, Sydney." His resolve falls like a lone meteor, crashing and burning at our feet. My subsequent wink pulls a smile from the rubble. "Come here."

I'm yanked into a firm hug, Gabe's chin resting on the top of my head as he wraps his arms around me. My anxiety dissipates, knowing I have my friend back. "I'm sorry," I murmur into his pink polo.

"Me, too," he sighs. "You're my ride-or-die, Syd. We're not allowed to fight."

Agreeing with a nod, I pull back, relief brimming in my eyes. "So, you don't hate my tongue?"

136

He chuckles through his eye roll. "Your tongue is fantastic. But that's what I'm worried about..." Gabe pops his thumb over his shoulder at the door, his implication clear. "Just tread with caution, okay? I know you're both adults. I know you care about each other and always have. I just worry something will break him apart before he's even fully put back together."

Even though my defenses spark to life, sharp words creeping up my throat, I understand why Gabe is concerned... and I *know* I never should have kissed Oliver in the first place.

Oliver *is* impressionable. He *is* vulnerable. He *is* susceptible to raw, human emotions, and I had no business toying with them, despite my noble intentions.

I swallow my pride and lift my chin. "I won't hurt him, Gabe."

Gabe gives my shoulder a light nudge with his fist, his smile wistful as he reaches for the door handle. "I know you won't mean to."

CHAPTER FIFTEEN

OLIVER

THERE IS A RACCOON.

It's a baby—that much I can tell.

It is alive and staring at me between the stalks of corn, its eyes curious, but no more curious than mine. I stand stiff and still, processing this discovery after taking an exorbitant amount of time adjusting my eyes to the hazy midday glow. How is this raccoon alive, breathing in these toxins? Are animals immune to the chemicals in the air?

It has a friendly face with a black mask colored across its onyx eyes—like Westley in The Princess Bride. Its paws are clasping a piece of food, nibbling on the treat as it studies me. I must look like quite the sight in my hazmat suit, and my own peculiar mask.

But it does not appear afraid.

I share a moment with the creature, brief but poignant. This raccoon has been the only living being I've encountered in nearly twenty-two years, aside from Bradford. If I make it through this, I surely won't forget this precocious friend with beady eyes and a tail made of stripes. Its paw lifts, almost like a wave, while I continue on my journey.

As I glance up at the flock of birds soaring overhead, a discerning feeling pinches me. Something feels wrong. That lived-in bedroom. The little wooden house with plumbing, fresh food, and miscellaneous luxuries. My heart hasn't stopped thundering inside my chest since I climbed up that ladder, a mix of fear and doubt coiling in my gut.

But I need to press on. These corn stalks appear to be endless, and I have no knowledge of what I'm doing or where my travels will lead me.

When I continue forward, pushing through the tall stalks, breathing heavily through my mask, an unusual sound drifts into my ears from behind me, and I turn around. I can't see much. My mask is full of fog and my nerves are making me feel dizzy, but there seems to be a steady stream of motion in the opposite direction, in the far off distance. I think I heard a beep, or a siren, or a shrill horn. A signal to alert the others, potentially. The movement is connected to a winding, gravel trail—a long driveway. Perhaps this is a maze.

I feel compelled to follow it.

There's activity ahead, and that must be where I can find the others. My mind made up, my hopes higher than before, I turn around and begin my trek into the strange unknown.

When I glance back to wish the raccoon farewell, I realize it has vanished.

I am alone.

Summer fades to fall as the months press on, and it's a delightful transition. The air turns crisp, the leaves golden, the smell of bonfires lingering amidst every subtle breeze. My morning runs have become far more enjoyable as the sticky heat dissolves into milder temperatures. I even keep the window open in my bedroom, especially when I work on my comics. The drafts that spill through are mollifying, and they quiet the thoughts in my head, assisting my focus.

"Knock-knock!"

My smile is instant when her voice captures my ears.

There may be alternative reasons for keeping my window open.

Spinning around in my desk chair, I spot her leaning forward on her arms as she grins at me from her office window. Her hair hangs over her shoulders in tangled waves, dancing to the silent song of the autumn wind. I approach my own window, my skin already buzzing with warmth when we face each other—the way it always does when she smiles at me.

"Who's there?" I call back.

"Yoda lady."

"Yoda lady, who?"

Her index finger shoots out to point in my direction. "I didn't know you could yodel, Oliver Lynch."

Oh, dear.

Sydney laughs at her own joke, lassoing my heart in the process.

"Wait, wait… one more," she giggles, removing the windswept strands of hair from her eyeglasses with her fingers. "Knock-knock."

"Who's there?" I reply.

"Suspense."

"Suspense, who?"

Sydney goes quiet, staring at me, her eyes twinkling mysteriously.

"Suspense, who?" I repeat through a frown.

She continues to stare, the suspense buildi—

Oh.

I massage the nape of my neck with a hearty chuckle, shaking my head at her. "You're becoming quite good at these jokes."

"Yep. I'm very proficient at Google," she winks back. "So, what are you working on today? Did Alexis sweep in to save me when the Faceless Man had you held up in the abandoned warehouse?"

Sydney is referring to my comics and her interest has me ducking my head, timidity sweeping in. I'm not embarrassed of them, per se, but I went so long keeping them to myself that it's still exceedingly vulnerable sharing them with another.

Gabe has caught glimpses of my comics, but I have yet to go into detail. Only Sydney is privy to the stories that come to life on those pages.

"Alexis has been captured with me," I explain, chewing on the inside of my cheek. "I'm planning on introducing a new character that will rescue us. Potentially, a redemptive character that is often up to no good, but generally sides with the heroes when it counts."

Sydney beams at me from a few feet away, the sparkle in her eyes showcasing genuine enthusiasm. "Shit, I love that idea. Redemptive arcs are the best. I'm always rooting for the anti-hero," she proclaims, tilting forward until her top dips down two inches too far.

I pull my eyes away when the peaks of her breasts tease me, bathed beneath the October sun. The effect she has on me, both physically and emotionally, has grown to a confusing level over the past few months.

We spend an extensive amount of time together. *Inseparable* is the term Gabe used, and I'm apt to agree. We go for walks, play with her cat, watch movies as we sit much too close together on the sofa. We listen to her favorite nineties' music, sometimes lying on my bed, looking up at the glow-in-the-dark stars that are still stuck to the ceiling from a different life. I've finally grown accustomed to sleeping in my bed, all thanks to Sydney and her request to take a nap together one late-summer afternoon. The prospect of falling into slumber with Sydney beside me, her body heat near, her scent close and potent, her distinct aura calming me, made the transition so much easier. Now I associate the mattress and sheets and box spring with *Sydney*, and the floor doesn't seem so appealing anymore.

We joke and tease and tell stories, and I often catch her watching me, studying me, the look in her eyes flickering like blue flames. Those are the looks that singe me, scalding straight to the bone, leaving smoke and burn marks in their wake.

But when I return that same look with an eager curiosity, she always pulls back. She retreats into cooler climates, as if she's afraid we'll overheat.

It's apparent that my affection for the girl next door has taken on far more sexual undertones lately. And while I've always found Sydney physically appealing, to the point where she's often made appearances in my less wholesome reveries, those lustful feelings are escalating as more time goes by. They started stewing the moment her mouth met mine, our bodies locked together by forces unseen, only felt, the fire in her eyes consuming us both.

But Sydney got out. She ran from that burning building, while I remained trapped inside, hardly able to catch my breath. I'm still there, waiting to see if she'll ever return for me, so we can face the flames together.

"Can I stop by later? *Pulp Fiction/Fight Club* movie night?" Sydney hollers over, straightening her posture in the window. "I need to finish up this website, but then I'm all yours."

Oh, how I wish that were true.

I send her a nod, grateful for any time spent in her company. "I can pencil you in," I call back, holding up the drawing pencil still clutched in my hand.

She gives a two-fingered salute, then disappears from the window.

"You two are honestly sickening."

Twisting around in my rolling chair, my eyes land on Gabe, who is perched against my doorframe with his arms crossed, a decidedly amused grin on his face. I clear the tickle from my throat. "I'm a bit enamored by her," I admit, though, the revelation is far from shocking.

On a Saturday evening, roughly one month ago, Gabe had a new woman in his bed. He's had an assortment of females come and go ever since Sydney's sister ended their courtship, but this particular female was quite... *vocal*. The pounding headboard mingled with her boisterous pleasure noises had Gabe apologizing later that night after the mystery woman had departed.

"Sorry, man," he told me, still buzzed on spirits and inebriated from the marijuana he'd been smoking throughout the evening. "That was probably super awkward. I'm still getting used to not living alone."

He stood in my doorway, in a similar fashion to the way he is right now, and I squeezed the pencil in my hand, glancing up from my drawings. "I'm glad you're enjoying yourself. No need to apologize—it's your home."

"It's *our* home. I should be more considerate," he countered with a quick ruffling of his golden hair. "You know... you should, uh, try that sometime."

I blinked, alarmed by the suggestion. "Sex with a person I hardly know?"

"Well, you can get to know them first." A foot shuffle, followed by a cough into his arm sleeve. "I can help if you want. I know a lot of single ladies."

"So it seems."

"It doesn't have to be this big thing, Oliver. Maybe you should just rip the Band-Aid off."

My eyes narrowed as I processed this. "That's a fairly crass way of describing it."

"Maybe," he shrugged. "But it's not always like you see in the movies, with the grand love stories and the dramatic musical scores. Sometimes it's just... *fun*. I think you need fun."

"I have fun," I told him.

"A *distraction*."

Gabe's eyes flashed with implication, as if he were referring to something specific. I understood then, leaning back in my chair with a sigh. "You think Sydney is distracting me from potential admirers."

He swallowed, his focus averting to his *Simpsons* socks. "I think you're going to get hurt if you keep pursuing that particular avenue," he confirmed in his roundabout way.

My gaze traveled over my stepbrother with his baggy t-shirt and sweatpants, his boyish features and tousled hair. He was a good-looking person who certainly had no trouble with sexual conquests. The proof was in the numerous holes carved into his bedroom wall from that overused headboard.

But the playful spark in his eyes seemed fabricated—a well-crafted veil for everything stored behind the ruse. Gabe was happy-go-lucky, but I didn't believe he was truly *happy*. The women, the alcohol, the drugs... they were all vices to temper his loneliness.

Therefore, his opinion felt invalid to me.

"I'll think about it," I told him, having no real intention of doing so.

It may have been the first lie I ever told.

Gabe looks at me now with that same sprightly stare, teetering on the balls of his feet. He's dressed casually on this sunny Saturday, preparing for golf with his father. They invited me to come along, but the sport did not appeal to me. Travis encouraged me to watch a few videos of it being played on the YouTube application, but I ended up falling asleep.

"Enamored is a word for it," Gabe quips with knowing eyes, looking between me and the open window. "Sydney certainly has a way about her."

This catches my interest as I stand from the chair, pacing to my desk to set the pencil down. "Do you have romantic feelings for her?"

"Fuck, no. Hell... she's like a sister to me—a discovery I made *after* I had my tongue down her throat, unfortunately." Gabe physically cringes. "She's hot, obviously, but we don't click like that. I'm just saying, I've seen far too many guys fall head over heels for that girl, only to get their hearts ripped out when she throws her walls up. She doesn't mean it, but she's allergic to relationships."

"That's an odd allergy to possess." I try not to let his words bother me as I busy myself at my workstation, collecting my sketches and placing them into a manilla folder. "I appreciate your concern, but I'm not like you. I can't turn my feelings on and off."

"That's because you're constantly around each other. Maybe take a breather. Do you have friends at the library you can socialize with?"

I pause as I place the folder into my desk drawer. The truth is, I don't have many friends at my place of work because I keep to myself. Everyone is kind and friendly, attempting to integrate me into their social circles, but I'm still acclimating. I keep my distance. While the environment is quiet and peaceful, and I enjoy the work itself, there are still so many people. So much bustling around, the clacking of keys, children crying, a myriad of whispers.

My schedule is only part time for now, just twenty hours per week, which doesn't give me an enormous amount of opportunity to make connections, even if I wanted to. And I don't. "Not really. I'm fairly reserved."

Gabe purses his lips together, nodding at me. "Yeah, no rush. Just a suggestion." He taps at his thighs with the pads of his fingers. "You sure you don't want to go golfing with me and the old man? Get some fresh air?"

My dismissal is quick. "No, thank you. I plan to go for a run and watch the birds shortly. Enjoy your afternoon."

My brother takes the hint and turns to leave, his footsteps creaking down the hallway. His *'see you later'* fades out as he disappears into the living room.

Before I slip into my running clothes, I pull the folder out from the drawer, flipping through the loose sketches until I land on the one of a woman being held captive by the Faceless Man. My index finger traces over her outline, etched in pencil and colorful shading, and I smile at this updated version of her character.

The Queen of the Lotus is no longer a little girl with pigtails, clutching a tattered teddy bear to her overalls. She's a full grown woman with wild sun-kissed hair, black spectacles, and a *Nirvana* t-shirt tied at her hip with a rubber band. Her eyes are shaded in the bluest colored pencil I could find, and her nose is small, her lips plump, her frame slim, yet busty. Her humor shines through in her dialogue, along with an assortment of curse words and witty retorts.

She is fierce.

She is goofy.

She is beautiful.

She is Syd.

There is a raccoon.

I watch as it scurries from a neighbor's yard to mine, then veers behind the house while I try to catch my breath after a five-mile run. My brows knit together, perspiration lining my hairline, when I notice the animal stumble into the backyard with a limp.

Then my eyes trail to the blood spatter left behind, little red droplets seeping into the gravel driveway.

Oh, no. The animal is injured.

Without thinking it through, I follow the creature, jogging swiftly into my backyard as worry courses through me. I see the raccoon collapse beside a Cypress tree just as I begin to slow my steps and approach with caution. As I close in, the animal's head tilts up towards me, our eyes locking from a few feet away.

It's young, likely still a kit. Those dark eyes feel familiar, and yet, it's a preposterous notion to think this is the same raccoon I encountered upon my escape. There are tens of thousands of these mammals in the county alone. It's nonsensical.

But I can't help but feel a draw—an odd connection, an overwhelming desire to help.

I'm no doctor, but I've read countless books on the matter.

Crouching down, I observe the animal for signs of distress beyond the flesh wound. Raccoons are nocturnal, so the fact that it is active during daylight hours could potentially be a sign of rabies or disease.

I don't come to that conclusion, though, and take my chances by moving forward, slow and kind. "Hello, friend. My name is Oliver."

My voice remains low. Soft and inviting. This wild animal should be running afraid, or even attacking me under stress, but it just lies there, its tiny claws scratching at the dirt.

"I'm here to help you." I inch closer on my knees, pressing my luck. "Have we met before?"

I'm aware I'm being foolish—asking questions to a wild mammal, as if it might respond. But I'm nearly certain I see an answer in its ebony eyes. It's possible I've imagined the brief flash of recognition, the flicker of invitation to continue my efforts, however, I'm willing to take my chances. I'm going to help this raccoon.

Contemplating my options, I decide I'll need gloves and a towel to safely capture the creature. While my instincts tell me it won't hurt me, I can't be sure, and safety comes first. "Stay right here, little one. I'll be right back."

A few minutes later, I've returned with Gabe's winter gloves and a bath towel I swiped from the linen closet. The raccoon hasn't relocated, causing me to believe it was awaiting my return. Silly, perhaps, but it has wise eyes. This animal trusts me; I'm certain of it.

Inching closer, I continue to speak in a placated tone, cursing the bulky gloves on my hands. I'd prefer for the raccoon to smell my scent, but I can't risk a bite or a scratch. "I'm going to fix you, little raccoon. You're going to be just fine." Leaning in, I watch as the animal flinches, just slightly, before splaying its hands and feet to the earth as it anticipates contact.

In one fell swoop, I collect the animal in the alabaster towel, only its head peeking out as I hold it to my chest. Its breaths are quick and heavy, a combination of nerves and the injury. With one arm around the raccoon, my left hand reaches out to stroke its head, the silky fur tickling my fingers. "You'll be all right. I'll help you."

I'm positive the animal's breaths begin to soften from my touch.

Carrying the raccoon inside, I make my way into my bedroom and close the door, eager to assess the wound. Only, I've hardly settled in before my door barges open and Sydney barrels inside like a tempest.

"Oliver?"

The raccoon struggles against me as I turn to Sydney and order, "Shut the door. Hurry."

My tone of voice seems to startle her, and she hesitates for a moment before doing what I asked. "Sorry… I was on my way over and saw you carrying something in a towel. Do you want me to call someone? Is it an animal?"

"A raccoon, yes. It's hurt."

Sydney approaches me with tentative feet, her lip caught between her teeth. "I didn't mean to interrupt. Should I go?"

"No, no… stay. You're fine." I pet the animal, soothing it with whispers and hushes. "It's been injured."

"Should I call a vet? Or a wildlife sanctuary?"

"No, I've got it." I lower the raccoon to my carpeted floor and carefully unravel the covering. I immediately notice two puncture wounds along its abdomen as I lay it on its side, discarding the blood-stained towel. "It has a bite mark. A coyote, perhaps."

"Stitches?" Sydney wonders, kneeling down beside us, her hands placed atop her denim thighs as she watches with guarded curiosity.

"No. Puncture wounds cannot be stitched. The risk of infection is too great."

"Oh…"

I glance at her, wondering if she can help. "Do you happen to have a crate or a carrier? One that Alexis may have used?"

Sydney nods, already rising to her feet. "I do. I'll be right back."

"Thank you."

While she's gone, I carry the raccoon into the bathroom and tend to the injury, applying a gentle pressure to the puncture marks to halt the blood with a clean, damp towel, then rinsing the wound under warm water. The animal does not try to escape as we climb into the bathtub and I lie back against the fawn tiles, holding her to my chest. She's a female, I've determined.

She squeaks out curious noises as I stroke her fur, her arms wrapping around my bicep as she tries to climb me. Her nails poke through my running shirt, her little hands stretched and trembling mildly.

"It's all right. You're going to be just fine," I say in a muted tone, the rumble of my chest calming the animal until she stills in contentment.

There's a knock at the bathroom door, and I usher Sydney inside. I can't help but smile at the look of amazement sweeping over her features when her eyes meet mine inside the porcelain tub. The raccoon is snuggled to my chest, her charcoal nose jabbed into the crook of my armpit. It must be a bizarre sight to see.

"Um, the crate is all set up in your bedroom," Sydney explains, sliding her fingertips into her back pockets. Her gaze roves over me with silent questions, her footsteps uncertain as she approaches. "Is there anything I can do? This is a little outside my expertise, but I'd like to help..." she offers.

A nod towards the medicine cabinet has her following my signal. "There's a first aid kit in the mirrored cupboard. Would you mind bringing it to me?"

Sydney is quick to assist, carrying it over, then kneeling beside the bathtub. She opens the top and sifts through the contents when I request an antiseptic and a bandage. Applying a thin layer of antibiotic cream with my right hand, the raccoon held tightly in my left, the animal only squirms for a moment before quieting her movements and nuzzling back into my chest. Sydney adheres the bandage a few moments later, her fingers quivering as she works. It's strange to see her nervous, while I'm so calm—it feels backwards.

Sydney finishes the task and moves away, her hands falling to the edge of the tub while she stares down in wonder at the contented raccoon lying peacefully against me like a small child.

"This is incredible. You're like a raccoon whisperer," she breathes out, enchantment lacing every word. "Aren't you afraid it could have rabies?"

A quick shake of my head dismisses that theory. "No. She's showing no signs of disease."

"It's a 'she'?"

"Yes. We should think of a name for her, don't you think?"

We share a glance and Sydney removes a rogue wisp of hair from her eyes, tucking it behind her ear. She looks back to the raccoon, her smile whimsical. "She looks smart," Sydney decides, her head tilting a little to the right. "She has wise eyes. Like you."

Her compliment dances across my heart, prompting my own smile to spread. *Wise eyes.* I thought the same thing. "Athena," I say. "The Goddess of Wisdom."

Sydney's eyes twinkle in agreement, her hand lifting from the tub towards the animal in my arms. She falters, peeking over at me for permission. "Can I pet her?"

I note the touch of pink in her cheeks, the nibble to her bottom lip, the tips of her hair grazing the top of my shoulder. I swallow through my consent. "Yes. She's very docile."

Her features brighten, accentuating her dimples and the tiny divot below her lip. When the pads of her fingers make contact with the fur behind Athena's ear, Sydney lets out a breathy gasp, as if the moment is profound to her.

She turns to me, our faces so close I'm afraid to pull my eyes to hers. The magnetism is too strong, the distance between us too slight. If I look at her now, I'll be lost.

But I do. And I am.

The beats of my heart flounder when we catch and hold, and not because I'm lying in a bathtub with a wild mammal in my arms—no, it's because Sydney's heated stare is burning a hole right through me, her eyes blue embers, her charmed smile slipping into something else.

Her gaze flicks to my mouth, the gesture fleeting, and yet it clamps around my heart and pins me in place while I fight the urge to kiss her. *Raccoon be damned.*

That urge only intensifies when Sydney's hand moves from the animal's head to mine, gliding a piece of hair off my forehead and curling it around her finger before she draws back. Her touch has my skin buzzing, my eyes fluttering closed, and I know I can't be imagining this heady charge in the air, wafting around us like magic. Even Athena is wiggling about, her limbs restless.

Sydney's lips connect with the top of my head in a sweet kiss, her palm pressing to the side of my face, her floral scent, like rosebuds and wildflowers, devouring me.

"You're an amazing man, Oliver Lynch," she breathes into my hair.

The swell of her breasts is entirely too close to my face, to my mouth, and my inhibitions feel scattered. On instinct, I lift my chin in an attempt to capture her lips with mine, when Athena crawls up my chest, onto my shoulder, and encircles her little arms around my neck.

This essentially severs the mood, causing Sydney to jump back, startled, and I wince when Athena's claws pierce my skin. *Rascal.*

A timid laugh releases beside me as Sydney rises from the hard floor.

Her jittery cough, fidgeting hands, and the way her eyes refuse to focus on me, leads me to believe she was aware of my intentions.

It's the flush of her skin that tells me our intentions may have been aligned.

"I'm going to grab a blanket from your room," Sydney says, her voice shaky. "Athena looks cold."

She's out of the bathroom before I can respond, and I let out a long, splintered breath. I redirect the paws from my neck, lowering them until the animal is clutching the center of my shirt instead of my skin. My fingers trail down her soft fur as my head falls back against the tiled wall. "I need your wisdom, Athena. What is happening between myself and the girl next door?"

The raccoon replies by pressing a sharp claw, a nail like a dagger, right to my heart.

Touché.

CHAPTER SIXTEEN

OLIVER

"EXCUSE ME, CAN YOU HELP ME FIND A BOOK?"

A sweet, lilting voice captures my attention, and I lift my head from the stacks, connecting with eyes like chocolate. Her hair falls over her shoulders in sheaths of dark satin, her expression sincere. "Oh, hello. Yes, of course."

We stare at each other for a few beats, her smile blooming. "Do you need the title?"

I blink, then duck my head, wondering why I'm acting so foolish. Usually, I try to avoid the patrons and keep myself busy amongst the shelves, sorting and alphabetizing. "Please," I respond through an embarrassed chuckle. Her hands are curled around a stroller bar, housing a baby who appears to be fast asleep.

"*Of Mice and Men*," she replies with a soft grin. "My friend insists I need to read it, and she gave her copy to someone else."

My gaze shifts to the left, spotting a petite blonde, her hair a similar color to Gabe's, with her nose in a book. I glance back to the woman in front of me. "I've read that one. It's quite depressing," I say, folding my arms, attempting to make conversation.

"Pain pays the income of each precious thing," replies the blonde friend, her gaze friendly as it sweeps up to me.

A knowing chuckle slips out. "Shakespeare buff?"

She snaps the book closed and sets it back on the shelf, sauntering over to us with a wink. "English teacher."

"That's very admirable." I look back and forth between the two women, both captivating in their own right. There is something about each of them that speaks to me on a different level, a level that goes beyond their physical beauty. Their eyes hold stories, tortured and raw, and I've seen those eyes before.

I see them every day, reflecting back at me in the bathroom mirror.

Fearing the silence is bordering on uncomfortable, I clear the tickle in my throat and nod my head over my shoulder. "This way."

The women follow, baby stroller in tow, and I try not to eavesdrop on their whispered chatter behind me. We arrive at the appropriate shelving unit, and I pluck a copy of her requested book from the sea of novels. She takes it, a pleasant smile still fixed across her face. "Here you are. You can check out with Melanie at the main counter," I explain, pointing over her shoulder.

"Thank you. I really appreciate your help, Oliver."

Frowning, I glance down at my invisible nametag that does not exist. "Pardon?"

She tucks a section of shiny hair behind one ear, bashfulness coloring her cheeks. "Sorry. That sounded a little foreboding."

The friend snickers, her ponytail bobbing as she shakes her head. "Faulty delivery. Definitely creepy."

"I'm sorry, but I'm not following. Have we met before?" I wonder, my eyebrows pinched and quizzical.

The lighthearted mood wanes, and the smiles fall. The raven-haired female holds out her hand to me. "I'm Tabitha. Tabitha Brighton. This is my friend, Cora."

I hesitate for just a moment, absorbing the introductions, then take her hand in mine. "It's a pleasure to meet you both. You've seen me on the news, I take it?" It's the only conclusion that makes sense. My gaze drifts back and forth between the women, noting the way they stiffen at the query. "I don't get out too much, and I'm certain I'd remember you."

Realizing my statement comes off as flirtatious, I drop her hand and shuffle my feet, scratching at the back of my head.

Tabitha's smile returns, her grip on the stroller bar tightening. "I'm aware of your story," she confirms, studying me fondly. "I visit the library once a week with my daughter, Hope, and we look at the picture books and play with the wooden puzzles. I recognized you right away, but I wasn't sure if it was my place to introduce myself."

"Oh. I'm glad you did."

Oddly enough, that's true.

"Good," Tabitha says, her relief escaping as a soft sigh. "I, um... well, I went through something similar. I was also abducted, but my circumstances were very different from yours, from what I've seen. Cora and I both suffered at the hands of an evil man, and we know what it's like to come out on the other side. It can be just as scary, just as harrowing, as the ordeal itself."

The words process slowly, then hit me like a dull knife. I nearly choke on the lump in my throat as my skin grows clammy, my mouth dry like sand. Unsure of how to respond, I lick my lips and glance at the linoleum flooring beneath my tennis shoes, prompting a warm palm to reach out and squeeze my wrist.

"I'm so sorry if I upset you," Tabitha says softly, the sweetness of her tone overwrought with apology. "I just wanted you to know that you're not alone. Cora and I connected through our shared tragedy, and now she's a dear friend. Good things can be found everywhere... even in our worst nightmares."

I swallow down the lump, forcing a nod. "Yes, I... thank you. I appreciate the sentiment."

She releases me just as her baby stirs awake, little feet bouncing beneath a lavender blanket. Tabitha tickles the child's toes. "Hope is a testament to that," she murmurs, her words so hushed I almost don't hear them. "Anyway, I'm sorry to bother you while you're working. But if you ever need someone to talk to, I'm here every Tuesday at eleven."

"That's kind of you," I reply. My gaze meets Cora's, pulling a smile from her, the look in her eyes echoing Tabitha's words. "It was very nice to meet the both of you. Perhaps we can talk over coffee sometime."

The offer tumbles out of me, unexpected, and I realize too late that it sounds like I'm suggesting a romantic rendezvous.

Gabe would be proud.

I attempt to backpedal, just as Tabitha lights up with affirmation.

"I didn't mean—"

"I'd love to."

A gulp. "All right. We can reassess next week."

Reassess. Terrible choice of word. I am most certainly bungling this.

Both women exchange a laugh as Cora glances at her cell phone, then turns to Tabitha. "Dean's about to call me on his lunch break. We're figuring out our Thanksgiving plans for this week since everything is kind of new and complicated. Mind if I dip out for a sec?"

"I'll come with you. I can tell Hope is getting hungry," Tabitha says to her friend. She glances up at me before retreating, her warm, mocha eyes a striking contrast against her white-as-snow complexion. "I'll see you next week, Oliver."

"Yes, I'll be here," I confirm, stuffing my hands into my khaki pockets as a nervous smile twitches on my mouth. "Have a good day. Enjoy the book."

They wave their goodbyes, leaving me standing between the stacks of literature, wondering if anyone has written a story that mimics my complex life.

I could certainly use some direction.

When I return home from my shift that afternoon, still reeling from the encounter with the two women, I pull off my fleece jacket and amble into the bedroom where Athena anxiously awaits my return.

The raccoon has healed up nicely over the past three weeks, allowing me to clean the wound and apply fresh bandages daily, and thankfully, avoiding infection. She is a curious little thing, affectionate and mischievous. Gabe wasn't thrilled with the idea of me keeping her around for quite so long, insisting the creature would escape and wreck the home, but I've managed to keep her entertained for the time being. She only stays crated when I'm at work or at Sydney's, otherwise she has free reign of the bedroom.

I know it's time I release her back into the wild, but I'm having a bit of trouble letting go. Attachment may very well be the most detrimental human emotion, and I'm beginning to realize this in more ways than one.

Approaching the medium-sized carrier, I'm greeted with little hands poking through the grates, eager to play and feed. I refill her bowl with raspberries, eggs, baby carrots, and cashews, replace the water dish, then spend some time interacting with her on the floor. Athena sprawls out on my chest as I lie back, her barbed claws prickling me, her squeaks and sounds causing me to erupt with charmed laughs.

I have a date with Sydney tonight—apparently, we are watching a movie called *The Parent Trap* and she is overly delighted to view this particular film with me. She hasn't told me why, but she said she's making an abundance of oatmeal cookies to consume while we watch together.

As the hours roll by, I take a quick shower and change my clothes as I prepare to head next door. Before I depart, I pause to look back at Athena, her dark, pleading eyes gleaming at me from between the thin metal bars. Her arm slips through and reaches out, and I know, without a doubt, that I am severely lacking in the willpower department.

"All right, Athena," I sigh with defeat, unlocking her crate and silently begging for the animal to behave. "I'll return in a few hours. Don't cause trouble."

I make sure the door closes and latches behind me, pushing against it just to be sure. Athena is already showing signs of domestication—I'm fairly certain she'll be on good behavior.

A few minutes later, I'm letting myself into Sydney's home, observing the sound of the showerhead turned on from one floor above me. Peeking at my cellular device, I note that I'm a bit early and decide to pass the time in Sydney's bedroom while she finishes her shower. Her bed is made up, designed with a mandala print, colored in dark gray and robin's egg blue. The room is adorned with funky posters showcasing her tastes, a light mint wall color, pillar candles, and various knick-knacks and quirky décor, everything coming together in a way that is perfectly *Sydney*.

Taking a seat along the side of the bed, I fold my hands in my lap and wait, glancing absently around the room. My eyes land on her bedside table, distracted for a moment by the hypnotizing lava lamp, then shift to a novel with a bookmark peeking out halfway through. There's an oddly shaped device sitting atop the book that has me furrowing my brows with curiosity.

That curiosity gets the better of me, and I reach for the object, studying it with a mix of intrigue and bewilderment. My thumb hits a button and the contraption bursts to life, buzzing and vibrating in my hands. I let go, startled, and it clatters to her hardwood floor, causing a ruckus. It must be some kind of electronic massager.

Fascinating.

I lean down to capture the device, fumbling to turn it off, then quickly discard it into the drawer of her nightstand. The adjacent book catches my eye, so I snatch it up and begin flipping through the pages, eager to uncover the kinds of stories Sydney enjoys.

It's not long before the truth is revealed, and I'm torn between hiding the book along with the vibrating gadget, pretending to have never seen it, or continuing to read.

Goodness.

I have an assortment of burning questions to match the burning of my cheeks, but one, in particular, stands out:

What is a moist muffin?

I'm so absorbed in the erotic prose, I don't even hear the shower turn off, nor the subsequent footsteps. However, I do hear the gasp of surprise from the bedroom doorway.

My head snaps up to find a wide-eyed Sydney standing a few feet away in only a t-shirt, her hair still damp, the water blotching the cotton fabric and dripping to the wood planks below.

I clear my throat, sitting up against the decorative pillows. "My apologies... I let myself in."

She blinks, feet glued in place. "I could have walked in naked."

"Yes, that would have been intensely awkward, I'd imagine." I try hard not to imagine that very thing. "I saw your book and it looked compelling."

Mouth twisting to the side, she heaves in a rattled breath. "I see that."

"Your taste in literature is... unanticipated." I'm afraid she's going to scold me, but Sydney's posture begins to soften, her chin dipping to her chest, soft laughter spilling from her lips. Book still in hand, I glance down at the open pages and begin to read a passage out loud: "*She cups his warm balls in her trembling hand...*"

The blush instantly appears as Sydney stalks over to me, her wet strands of hair leaving tiny droplets in their wake.

She tries to swipe the book from my clutches as she approaches, but I dodge her. "Why is the temperature relevant?" I inquire, a smile hinting.

A huff of exasperation, and possibly a semblance of embarrassment, is drawn from her lips. "It's a description, Oliver. It pulls the reader into the scene."

She reaches. I dodge. Holding the book high above my head, too high for her smaller stature, I clear my throat and tease, "They were a balmy seventy-two degrees."

"Oliver!" Sydney leaps up onto her tiptoes, her laughter a bewitching contrast to the flush staining her cheeks, and tries, in vain, to retrieve the novel.

My own laughter competes with hers as I attempt to elude her flailing hands, and then she's climbing on top of me, straddling my thighs. I lean back further, stretching my arm as far as it will go. "What is a moist muffin?"

"Stop!" Giggles rip through her body as she presses into me, her chest flush with my face, and she bounces up from my lap in a final effort to reclaim her book. "You are *terrible*," she says with playful admonishment, her chilled hair whipping against my cheek as she collapses back down, empty-handed.

And then I realize my body seems to have registered the fact that her bottom half is covered in only a thin layer of underwear before my brain did. It's when the apex of her thighs collides with the stiff bulge beneath my slacks, that I inhale a sharp gasp, a strained moan, and we both forget about the book.

Sydney freezes, the smile leaving her face in a way that's slow and captivating, like how the sun sets behind the horizon after a glorious summer day. Her hands are settled on my shoulders, her fingers fisting into the fabric of my shirt sleeves, as if she's trying to hold on tight to the easy, jaunty mood that has been snuffed out. It has fallen, just as the book falls from my grip and hits the mattress beside us, giving my hands the opportunity to grasp her hips instead. It's a hold that is tantalizingly familiar.

It's Sydney's turn to release a shaky exhale; a lust-filled squeak. The sound is a shot of arousal straight to my groin. I decide in that moment, that if I could recreate even one of those scenes from her book, I would die a happy man.

Her eyes are closed, masking the truth she knows I'll see in her dark pupils. "Syd..." I croak out, sliding my hands up her hips, her waist, until she catches them just as I reach her breasts.

Sydney's eyes flutter open, her body trembling on top of me, the chemicals buzzing and crackling, desperate to ignite. "We should get the movie started." Her words are forced, false... *fearful*. With clammy palms clutching mine, she leans in to place a kiss to the side of my jaw. "We're friends, Oliver."

Her hair is like ice as it dances across my heated skin, causing me to shiver. Squeezing her hands in mine, I tug her back before she retreats, my lips reaching around to her ear and whispering, "I want to be more."

The hesitation is evident in the way her thighs tighten around mine, the way her breath hitches, a quivering puff of air warming my neck, the way she melts into me for just a moment, just a magical, prolonged moment that I want to freeze in time.

But her resolve wins out and she pulls away like I just scorched her. "We can't," she says, the words coiled tight, almost painful. Sydney scoots off my legs, off the bed, pulling herself to unsteady feet. And then she changes the subject. "I made cookies."

Pushing up until my back is level with her headboard, I grind my molars and lower my head, zoning out into the intricate pattern of the mandala bedspread. I promised her it wouldn't be weird, that I wouldn't want *more*, but it's getting increasingly difficult to keep that promise. Everything she wants is in the way she looks at me, in the way she holds my hand when we go for walks, in the way she falls asleep on my shoulder as the *Rugrats* play across the television screen. It's in her laughter, her jokes, the way her skin heats and pinks when I'm close. It's in the way she's standing beside me as I glance up to meet her eyes, her limbs still shaky, her breathing ragged, her lips parted and demanding to be kissed.

"I'm going to get dressed and head downstairs," she chokes out, instead of saying all the things I know she's hiding. "I'll meet you down there."

As she turns away, I call out, unsure of why these words break through, "I met a woman today. At the library."

Sydney pauses with her back to me, head bowed.

This fact is completely irrelevant to our situation, but I feel compelled to share. "She was very pretty. Soft-spoken and kind. Her name was Tabitha—she was an abductee, like me."

She spins in a slow circle, her irises glittering with an unknown emotion. "Tabitha Brighton?"

"Yes." We stare at each other, and I realize I'm yearning for a reaction. *Something.* I don't know why. "Are you familiar with her?"

A short nod. *The Matchmaker.* He butchered eleven people, not far from here. Three survived and she was one of them. Cora Lawson and Dean Asher were the others. Clementine actually went to the same college as Dean. It was a horrible thing." Sydney scratches at her upper arm, her jaw set. "There was a time I wondered if he was the same man who kidnapped you, but the MO didn't add up. I'm grateful he wasn't, considering the stories I've heard…"

The information courses through me, making me fidget and itch. My captor was never cruel or violent. I can't even imagine what those people went through. "We're going to have coffee next week. It will be nice to connect with someone who can relate."

Sydney's eyes swell, just slightly, gleaming with something resembling anguish. It flashes, then dissipates, as if it were never there at all. "That's great, Oliver. I'm happy for you."

I'm almost certain she's lying.

And I can't help but wonder if what I saw in her eyes just now was the same thing *I* felt when I watched Sydney's mouth on another man's that summer evening. I never did tell her how my heart constricted with painful, sluggish beats, or how my throat closed up, my skin tingling with something strange and unpleasant. I'd discovered a new emotion that night on my front porch and it made me miss my sheltered existence, alone beneath the earth. "Yes, I'll have to let you know how it goes," I finally respond, unable to pull my gaze from hers. "I'm not so good at these things."

The anguish returns to her eyes, tortured and turquoise, and I recognize the double meaning in my statement. But I don't backpedal, and I don't correct myself.

"I'm sure you'll do just fine."

Sydney recedes with those parting words, pacing out of the room and leaving me alone on her bed. My head drops back against the headboard, my stomach unsettled and swirling with anxiety, my heart feeling worn and tired.

She just wants to be friends.

And I suppose, if this is how it feels to yearn for more, to desire, to become *attached*... perhaps Sydney has been right all along.

It tears people apart.

I already feel shredded, and it's only been one kiss.

A few hours later, I'm walking up to my front door after watching a movie that was not *The Parent Trap*. Sydney had a change of heart, so we watched *The Big Lebowski* instead. It was amusing, however, our minds were elsewhere. I could feel the distance between us, the distraction, the confusion swimming in the air.

We didn't eat cookies. We didn't cuddle close on the sofa. We didn't laugh or tease or dance to her favorite music. We sat in silence until the credits rolled across the screen, and then I left.

It tears people apart.

Moving forward, my disheartened sigh trailing me, I place the key into the lock and push the door open. Traipsing up the stairs, I flip on a light switch and go utterly still, paling when my eyes case the room.

Destruction. Mass destruction.

Tattered sofa cushions, stuffing everywhere, chewed wood, scratched walls, streams of garbage, cereal scattered over the tiles, torn pillows, broken glass...

And sitting atop the kitchen counter is Athena, without a care in the world, chewing on a banana.

I think it's an appropriate time to use the word *fuck*.

"Fuck."

Gabe is going to kill me.

CHAPTER SEVENTEEN

SYDNEY

H E'S STANDING ATOP THE FROST-TIPPED GRASS with Athena snuggled against his chest, facing the line of trees that fence in his backyard. I'm standing at my office window.

Watching him.

Gabe told me about the 'Raccoon Debacle' that happened four days ago after Oliver left my house looking like I'd knocked him to the ground, then kicked him for good measure. It was the first time in my life I found little enjoyment in watching *The Big Lebowski* as we sat in silence on opposite ends of the couch, the only reel playing in my mind being what transpired in my bedroom.

I want to be more.

Those blunt, undiluted words have kept me up every night since, sinking deeper and deeper into untapped parts of me. I'm used to people skirting around their feelings, dancing around truths. I'm accustomed to picking apart riddles and rhymes. Peeling back the lies.

But Oliver Lynch doesn't know how to lie.

And I'm fairly certain my own truths were revealed in the way my body reacted when our groins connected on my bed, his arousal pressing into me, his hands roving and curious. But my mouth betrayed me, my fear won out, and I told him we were *just friends*.

Lying is a learned art, and I'm teaching him well.

My eyes glaze as I stare at him through the ice-crusted glass. The temperatures have plummeted over the last few days, adding to the chill that has already been lingering on my skin. Oliver is dressed in a russet-colored fleece coat, Athena's little head poking out through the zipper as he pets her fondly. His tall, broad frame is an endearing contrast to his delicate manner, and it's just one of the many things that attract me to him.

Attraction.

It's a deadly word—one I've been adamantly trying to avoid for the past few months as my feelings for Oliver continue to heighten and swell. There's a decipherable difference between *attractive* and *attraction*, and I've been straddling that line every time I straddle *him*.

There's no denying the pull between us, or the sparks that flicker and scald like tiny embers when our eyes collide, ocean on sunset. While he *is* my friend—my best friend—he's also so much more. He always has been, even as a memory.

That same month he was taken from me, I told him I was going to marry him one day. I planned our wedding, documenting it in my *Lisa Frank* journal, from the dress I'd wear, to the floral arrangements, to the beachside honeymoon in Maui.

Leaning out my window on a sweltering summer morning, I asked him if he wanted to marry me, too. Oliver replied, "Who else would I marry?"

Our future was set in stone. Life was *good.*

And then he was gone.

In a flash, in a blink, without warning, Oliver was ripped from my hands. As the fireworks burst to life overhead, something inside me died that night. I *felt* it. The loss was crawling all over my skin like little fire ants, stinging and biting, leaving scars that would forever brand me. And even though he's back now, so perfect and beautiful, I'm not convinced I've ever fully recovered from that loss.

Oliver wasn't the only victim that day.

My ribs ache, my heart stretching twice its size as I bore holes into him. Oliver still stands in his yard, holding that raccoon in the same tender fashion he holds every piece of me.

I decide to join him. I'm far from presentable in my wrinkled *Cranberries* t-shirt and sweatpants, makeup-less, my hair in the messiest of messy buns, but I throw on my puffer coat and boots and make a quick exit out the front door. My breath is visible as it hits the frosty air, and I stuff my hands into the warm pockets of my coat, approaching Oliver while the grass crunches beneath my soles.

Maybe he hears me. Or maybe he *feels* me the way I feel him.

"It's a hell of a thing," he says, still facing away from me as I come up behind him. His breath escapes in icy puffs.

I'm at his side, our shoulders kissing. *For warmth.* "What is?" I wonder.

Oliver strokes Athena right between the ears, his gaze twisted with sorrow as he watches the animal's claws latch onto the front of his shirt. "Letting go."

A swallow builds and stretches my throat. Those same eyes drift to me, the sorrow still visible, glittering with multiple meanings. I reach for his free hand and lace our fingers together, as if I'm trying to physically counter his words. "Will she be okay? It's so cold."

"She's a wild animal. She'll adapt to the elements." Oliver lowers his gaze to the ground. "We all learn to adapt."

I squeeze his hand. "Adapting and thriving are two very different things."

This time I look away, unprepared for him to see the vulnerability spewing out of me. I feel his fingers twitch, threaded with mine, our heated proximity somehow rivaling the frigid temperature.

Oliver releases me then, grasping the raccoon between both palms and holding her up, her tiny arms and legs splaying outward. "Goodbye, Athena. Safe travels." He places the animal onto the ground and takes a small step back. "Run free, now."

Athena paces toward Oliver and circles her arms around his calf, standing up on her hind legs, as if she's trying to climb him.

"I think she wants to stay," I chuckle, touched by their bond.

Oliver doesn't seem to share my reaction. He lets out a breath of frustration mixed with grief and tugs her arms away from his leg. She clutches him again instantly. "Athena, you must go. You can't stay where you don't belong."

Why is my heart suffocating every time he speaks? Why am I reading into his words?

If the shoe fits.

We haven't spent much time together over the last few days, and the holiday was a welcome distraction for us both. Thanksgiving was spent with our respective families, save for some late night pumpkin pie with my two favorite men next door. I stopped by that evening, after I returned home from my parents' house, and situated myself between Gabe and Oliver on the living room couch while we inhaled whipped cream-doused pie. It's been a yearly tradition between me and Gabe: gorging on pie and watching *The Santa Clause* to welcome in the

Christmas season. I was so thankful Oliver took part in our tradition this year, even though we didn't talk much or cuddle up together like we usually do. The gratitude was simply in his presence. His second chance.

His survival.

But that distance between us is killing me, sucking me dry, and I know it's my fault.

If only he understood this was for his own good.

"Maybe I can talk Gabe into letting you keep her," I offer, my insides cinching at the display. Gabe was *not* happy to come home and find the house destroyed. The main couch, the one I recall picking out with my mother and Charlene many years ago, fared better than some of the other furniture. The loveseat needed replacing, along with the dining room chairs. Luckily, Travis chipped in and helped with the unforeseen costs. Oliver felt terrible.

He's quick to dismiss the suggestion. "No, this is the right thing to do. Athena needs to be on her own. I can't be her crux forever."

Okay. This is hitting way too close to home. "Hey…" I snatch his hand back up, the raccoon still curled around his leg. "Is there anything you want to talk about?"

Oliver falters, his eyes making a languid shift from Athena to myself. A slow dance. His jaw tightens with words he refuses to let out. "Thank you, but I'm all right."

I force a nod through the sting, releasing his hand. "Okay. But I hope you know, I'm here. I'll always be here."

"I appreciate that, Sydney." Oliver returns his attention to the raccoon, bending down to pluck the limbs from his ankle. "Go now, Athena. I insist."

The animal hesitates, then turns away and darts toward the trees. She only pauses once, twisting around and lifting her little hands like a send-off, before disappearing beyond the brush.

I can't help my eyes from welling. "She really loves you."

"Yes," Oliver says softly, his gaze still fixed ahead. "But not all love is meant to stay. Sometimes it only serves a temporary purpose."

My eyelids flutter closed, a few rebel tears leaking through. I swipe them away, shivering at the chill they leave behind.

"Have a nice weekend, Syd."

Oliver moves to leave, and my instincts reach for him, my hand curling around his wrist before he can get too far. "Please don't hate me. I won't survive it."

My words catch him, pulling him back to me with pinched brows, a look of horror etched across his face. "Hate you? God, I could never... why would you think that?"

"I..." His pained eyes seize the words from my lips, making me feel like a fool. *Pathetic.* Shaking my head through a self-deprecating laugh, I glance away, still holding onto him. "Sorry. I think my hormones are out of whack."

A twitch of his mouth, and then, "There's nothing you could do that would ever make me hate you, Syd. *Nothing.*" Oliver trails his knuckles along my jaw, pulling a sigh from us both. "Please know that."

My whole body lights up like a Christmas tree. A goddamn heat wave. *Polar vortex be damned.* Gaze floating back to his, I shuffle my feet against the grass, inching closer. His cheeks are stained in light pink, kissed from the cold, his eyes searching me for something. His hair is a delicious display of bedhead, and I want nothing more than to run my fingers through the copper-streaked strands. I clench my hands into fists to avoid doing that very thing, inadvertently tugging him closer. "Oliver..."

"Go inside and warm up. It's quite cold out."

His hand drops from my cheek and I let go of his wrist, undecided if it's better this way or if I want him to warm me up himself. "Yeah... okay."

Oliver gifts me his knee-weakening smile, dimpled and bright.

Before he walks away, I call out one more time. "My parents host an annual Christmas party the weekend after Thanksgiving. It's kind of this big event with family, co-workers, and close friends." I watch the way Oliver's eyes glint as he waits for me to finish. "I'd love for you to come with me this year."

"Oh." His thoughts scatter with the breeze that sweeps through, stealing our breath, and he's silent for two beats too long. I'm about to take back the offer, wondering if I overstepped, when he finally responds. "Yes. I'd like that."

"Really?"

A subdued grin. "Really."

"Great." I can't help my own smile from stretching my cheeks as anticipation blooms in my belly. "Stop by around four P.M. next Saturday. Clem and Poppy will ride with us."

"I look forward to it. Thank you for the invitation."

Oliver spares a final glance to the woods edging his backyard, then sends me a nod.

I smile my goodbye, my own gaze pulling to the trees behind me after he's rounded the corner. I squint my eyes through the hazy morning, a quick breath escaping me.

Athena sits beside a Cypress tree, watching from a distance.

And when I blink, she is gone.

CHAPTER EIGHTEEN

SYDNEY

I'M APPLYING MY FINAL STROKE OF MASCARA when Poppy shouts from below, "Your nice man-friend is here!"

Screwing the cap back on the tube and spritzing myself with a candy cane body mist to match the red and white stripes on my dress, I give myself a final onceover in the mirror. I decided to dress up more than I usually do this year, forgoing my ugly Christmas sweater tradition and opting for a holiday dress with a sweetheart neckline and flared skirt, fifties-style. My hair is curled to match the smile on my bright red mouth as I appreciate the final product.

I can't help the little buzz that soars through me when I hear Oliver downstairs, engaging with my niece. They've only interacted one other time when I was babysitting the neighbor girl, Summer, and Oliver stopped by to watch them so I could run out and grab cat food. I'd returned to find all three of them reading in a circle in the middle of the living room, each girl leaned into him, completely engrossed in his storytelling. Alexis was perched on his lap, oblivious to my return, which was unlike her.

Oliver has a special presence about him, one that is both captivating and addicting.

And when I exit the bathroom and proceed down the staircase, my ruby-tipped fingers gliding down the railing, I can't help but wonder if my own presence has a similar effect on him.

Oliver cuts off mid-sentence, his conversation with my sister long forgotten as his eyes trail up to me, drinking in my appearance as each white pump descends the steps. My fingers squeeze the wood rail to keep my balance steady as my belly flips and coils in response to his reaction.

I've seen him look at me in a thousand different ways, but this is something new. I'm being bathed in a lethal mix of adoration, awe, and knee-buckling *desire*. My air waves tighten, my white-knuckled grip on the railing the only thing keeping me upright.

Our eyes stay locked across the room, and the silence that has settled over us is so resounding, Clementine twists around on the couch to investigate why Oliver has simultaneously gone mute and paralyzed in a flash.

"Damn, sissy," she announces, a dramatic whistle following, her gaze skimming me from bottom to top. "I didn't get the memo we were getting all cute. I look homeless compared to you."

It takes more effort than I anticipate to tear my eyes from Oliver and regard my sister, her one arm draped over the back of my sofa. "Last minute decision. I had this dress lying around and figured I should get some use out of it."

I'm a dirty, little liar. I panic-bought it online and paid an embarrassing amount of money for two-day shipping.

"You look beautiful, Syd."

Oliver's voice pulls me back, a smile blossoming onto my crimson-tinged lips. "Why thank you, Mr. Lynch. You look quite dashing, yourself," I reply in my most sophisticated tone, trying desperately to diffuse the crackling electricity in the air.

And it's the damn truth.

He looks *sinfully* dashing in a forest green sweater nearly painted onto him, his pecs and biceps taunting me, dark gray denim tapering his legs. The curls in his hair are tamed slightly with a styling product, while stubble lines his strong jaw. His eyes are like chestnuts and steel firing into me as I finally leave my unsteady perch on the stairstep.

Whew.

"Can you spin like a princess, Auntie Syd?" Poppy chirps, her own emerald dress swishing side to side.

"Of course, dear niece. It would be my pleasure." Apparently, I'm still talking like I just shared tea and crumpets with the Queen of England. This dressing-up thing is going to my head. Doing a quick twirl, the skirt of my dress flaring impressively, Poppy claps with approval from her knees on the couch. I take a formal bow.

Okay, I'm done being fancy. Time for booze and vulgarity.

"Ready?" I quip, reaching for my winter coat, while everyone scatters to do the same. As my arms slip into the sleeves, Oliver slides up beside me, hands in his pockets. He smells like every sexual fantasy I've ever had, mixed with a trace of pine. My lips quirk into a nervous smile. "I'm glad you're coming tonight. If my relatives start bombarding you with questions, we can go hide out in one of the bedrooms."

Oliver's throat bobs, his eyes lingering on my lips for a beat before meeting with mine. "I'm not certain that would be wise."

The meaning behind his words seduces me instantly, causing my legs to start shaking like they have a mind of their own. My mouth dry, my underwear far from dry, all I can manage is a slow blink before he turns away with his own timid smile tipping his lips.

Clem appears behind me with an elbow to my arm. "Cold? You're shaking."

Stupid legs!

Collecting myself, I dismiss her. "I'm fine. Let's go."

As we pile out the front door, my sister whispers in my ear, her tone taunting, "Potential."

"Ruin," I snap back, pulling my car keys from my purse. I glance at Oliver, pacing beside me. "Oliver gets shotgun."

A frown appears while his brain processes. "I'm not proficient with firearms."

Our giggles are collective as we approach my Jeep.

"That just means you get to ride in the front seat with Auntie Syd," Poppy proclaims, darting out in front of us and diving into the back.

Oliver and I share a humorous grin before entering the vehicle and getting situated, preparing for the one-hour drive to the Neville household. It goes by quickly, the atmosphere light and playful as we swap stories and jokes, while Christmas music serenades us from the speakers. Even Oliver is talkative, asking questions and sharing in the cumulative laughter. His walls are being stripped away, little by little, day by day. I wonder if I've played a role in that, and the notion sends a series of flutters to my heart.

When we pull onto the familiar street and park, I reach for Oliver's hand as we walk through the front yard that is bedazzled in twinkle lights. Giving his fingers a light squeeze, a silent promise that he'll be okay, we reach the front door and I force myself to let go.

Clementine's voice is already in my ear. "Potential."

"Dude. I'm going to ruin *you*," I reply in a strained whisper.

Her laughter is interrupted when the door flies open, my father already three sheets to the wind in his Rudolph sweater and light-up antlers. "My beautiful daughters have arrived," he beams, his eyes glazed over with entirely too much rum. Then he turns around to holler, "Honey! Our beautiful daughters have arrived!"

Mom appears, ushering us all inside and scooping Poppy up into a giant hug.

I'm tempted to reach for Oliver's hand again, a gesture of reassurance, but I don't want to be the source of whispers and gossip all evening. Instead, I give his forearm a quick squeeze, just as my mother pounces on him with another fierce hug, her perfume nearly toxic.

"Oh, Oliver. I didn't think you'd tag along. We're so happy you could make it," she tells him as Oliver's stiff limbs raise to return the embrace.

"I'm humbled to be invited. Thank you for the kindness."

My mother is grinning brightly as she pulls back, her short, flaxen bob only slightly streaked with silver. She scans our group. "No Gabe this year?"

Clementine clears her throat, snatching Poppy's wrist and leading her inside the bustling house to mingle with friends and family.

I shake my head. "Clem and Gabe had a thing. Now they don't."

Mom nods, the implication registering. "No worries. Why don't you two make yourselves some drinks? Sydney, I'm sure Oliver would love to meet Uncle Rory."

"Uncle Rory is terrifying."

There's no way in hell I'm subjecting Oliver to Uncle Rory's never-ending stories of life in the Bronx, back when he was a drug-dealing gangbanger turned Christian minister. *Oy.*

But drinks sound fantastic.

"We'll be around, Mom. Appetizers and eggnog are calling."

"Enjoy!" she calls to our backs as I drag Oliver away.

Taking his coat and removing mine, I drape them over an empty chair and eyeball the drink cart. As I saunter over, I get a whiff of an off-putting smell that sends a quick shiver up my spine: *eucalyptus.* Keeping the flashbacks at bay, I glare at the bushel of dried leaves and swallow back the traumatic memory. "Eggnog?" I ask Oliver, collecting myself, while noting his restless legs and roving eyes. He's clearly uncomfortable, and I don't blame him—even *I'm* uncomfortable amongst my crazy-ass relatives, and that's saying a lot, considering I'm... *me.*

Oliver licks his lips, finally giving a reluctant nod. "All right."

I scoop two generous glasses, handing him one of them. "Cheers."

"Yes. Cheers." He forces a smile as we clink our glasses together, then takes a big sip.

He spits it right back out into the glass.

"You don't like it?" I ask, a laugh slipping through.

Oliver glances up at me with wide eyes. "I think the beverage has been tampered with. We should alert the others."

More laughter, accompanied by a snort. "Oliver, that's just the rum. It's an alcohol-based eggnog." *God*, the look on his face as he processes my response. Relief, humor, a hint of embarrassment. Nothing, *no one*, touches my heart the way Oliver Lynch does. "But if you don't like it, I can get you a Pepsi or something."

He scratches the nape of his neck, gaze floating up to me. "This is fine. Now that I'm aware it's not going to kill me."

Our smiles match, causing my skin to heat.

Sensing our hold, my sister ambles up and smacks me on the behind, pulling a yelp from my throat. She waggles her eyebrows. "Step a little to the left and look up. I can give you a push if you want."

My glare is deadly. "Mistletoe. Cool. I'm not fifteen, Clem."

"Missile's toe?" Oliver inquires, spinning his glass between long fingers, then taking another sip. He winces through his gulp.

"It's a Christmas-kissing thing. Ignore her, she's a child."

"Oh." Another slow sip. More processing. "I'm unsure what a projectile with feet has to do with kissing. Or Christmas, for that matter."

Clem laughs beside us, sipping on a can of soda since she volunteered to drive us home. "It's a plant—if you're caught standing under the mistletoe, you have to kiss. It's *tradition*," she insists, eyes narrowing. "If you fail to uphold tradition, Syd, I'll have to call Cousin Hattie over here to take your place, and you *know* how her tongue gets when she drinks Schnapps."

"You're evil," I say through my teeth, compiling all the ways I can get her back for this. I return my attention to Oliver, who is watching me with interest, brows slightly furrowed, lips parted like a silent query. "Fine."

I don't think it over too much and lean up on my tiptoes to plant a chaste kiss against his stubbled jaw. I linger briefly, just long enough for Oliver to twist his head and capture my lips, his own kiss equally soft and sweet, hardly applying any pressure at all.

But I feel the pressure as it winds tightly down below. My senses go into overdrive, and he's all I can smell, taste, touch. I swear I can hear his heartbeat in my ears.

Or maybe it's mine.

Maybe it's both of our heartbeats, beating in perfect rhythm, together as one, and maybe they always have been.

When I lower myself back to the floor, Oliver's eyes are closed, his lips still parted and lightly smudged with red lipstick. I lift my thumb to his bottom lip in an attempt to remove the small stain. His eyes flare open, words written in his blazing irises, telling me everything he meant to say with that kiss.

But I heard him, loud and clear.

My thumb tingles as I draw back, and Clem is quick to interrupt our fusion. "'Atta girl," she quips, her shoulder nudging mine as she winks. She whispers the word while gliding out of the kitchen, "Potential."

Oliver stares at me, his longing evident, and I feel myself crumbling.

Ruin.

Watching Oliver transition into tipsy territory has been an amusing development that has kept my smile in place all evening. I had been reluctant to leave his side, but once the eggnog kicked in, Oliver found his footing *and* his confidence… and Uncle Rory.

Luckily, Oliver looks glued in on the tale I've heard recapped approximately eight-million times throughout my life. I don't pick up on any distress signals, so I give him his space, observing from afar and sipping on my own cocktail, letting the alcohol warm me.

That warmth turns into white-hot heat when Oliver meets my gaze from across the room. He sensed me. He felt my eyes on him.

Uncle Rory keeps blathering away, not noticing the fact that Oliver has zoned out of the conversation and is having an entirely separate one with me from ten feet away. It's silent and wordless, our eyes doing the talking. I have no idea what mine are saying, but I sure as hell know what *his* are saying, and it causes me to clamp my thighs together as my center throbs and tingles in response.

Oliver takes a slow sip of his beverage, his stare still hot and unwavering. The alcohol is making him bolder—this much is obvious. He's never held my gaze so long; so unabashed. So unapologetic.

Fuck, I need a breather.

Pulling a small smile onto my lips, I quickly turn away and head up the stairs to hide out in the spare bedroom while I collect my bearings. Confusion and alarms are fusing with a potent attraction I can't seem to ignore any longer, and I'm being torn in two different directions. Logic and reason beg me to retreat, terrified to taint our friendship and turn it into something we can never come back from.

Casual sex is one thing, but my relationship with Oliver is anything but casual.

It's *everything*.

The risk of permanent damage is too great, and I refuse to cross that line.

Closing the door behind me, I pace over to the dresser and lean forward, palms down, trying to slow my heartbeats to a more manageable rate. I press one hand to my chest and close my eyes, centering my breathing until it settles and a calm washes over me.

The click of a door latch pops my head up, causing my heart to dance erratically once again when I spot Oliver standing in the doorway with those same flame-filled eyes I saw downstairs. "Hi," I croak out, clearing the hitch in my throat.

He shuts the door behind him and moves toward me, his steps heavy with purpose. "Hello."

Turning to fully face him, hip propped against the dresser, I slick my tongue across my lips. "Sorry to abandon you. I just needed a minute."

"Are you all right?"

Concern twists at his features, melting me. "I'm fine. The crowd was getting to me."

"I haven't upset you, have I?"

My tender smile and quick shake of my head has Oliver softening with relief, his proximity closing in on me. "Of course not."

"Good." He returns the smile, just as tender, maybe even a little timid. But the eggnog pushes him closer until we're toe to toe, the lip of the dresser digging into my lower back. His hands twitch at his sides, as if he's aching to touch me. "I brought something," he says in a low voice.

His scent wafts around me, pine needles and cedarwood, enveloping me in a thick cloud that blurs every line I've ever drawn. My fingers curl around the dresser as I lean against it. "What did you bring?" I give myself an internal slap for the tremble in my tone, then follow with a joke to make up for it. "Hopefully, no stories from Uncle Rory."

Oliver slips a chuckle as he reaches into his pocket, pulling out a tiny bouquet of green leaves tied at the stems with a red bow.

Fucking mistletoe.

173

My eyes trail slowly from the greenery up to his face, chest heaving, grip tightening on the edge of the dresser. His expression is a deep, penetrative stare, laced with a singular question that has rendered me silent.

Oliver takes my silence as an invitation and places the mistletoe right above my head, on top of the bookshelf beside us. When his arm draws back down, his hand lands on my jaw, cupping it in his palm, his thumb grazing my cheek with gentle strokes. "You hypnotize me," he whispers in a ragged, fervent breath, the words touching my lips like a prelude to the kiss I crave.

"Oliver..."

A pathetic attempt at restraint that even *he* can see right through.

Oliver moves in until our noses touch, and I wet my lips, noting how they quiver with anticipation.

God, I shouldn't.

God, I really fucking want to.

Memories of our last kiss sweep through me like a carnal typhoon, and I tilt my chin up on instinct—the final permission he needs.

The gap between us dissolves to ash as his lips find mine, and I'm not sure whose moan filters through my ears, or whose hands reach out first, but in a flash, I'm lifted onto the dresser, my legs wrapping around his middle. His tongue is in my mouth, tasting every dip and divot, tangling with mine until we can't breathe. But I don't care about breathing when I'm wrapped around him like a spider monkey, one hand clawing at his scalp, the other fisting the front of his sweater to keep him close.

Oliver's hands cradle my face, his fingers threading through my hair as he devours me, teeth clacking together, breaths intertwined. He groans when I pull back, his bottom lip caught in a love bite. I release him, and his forehead falls to mine with a heavy gasp, his hands trailing down my body and cinching around my waist. His mouth moves to my neck, my favorite place to be kissed, and I arch into him, the back of my head colliding with the dresser mirror. I hold him in place as he kisses and nicks my throat, sending shockwaves through my system.

"Sydney..." he exhales against my sensitive skin, then inhales deep. "God, you smell like peonies and peppermint."

Smiling through a moan when he nips my earlobe, I reply, "That's because I ate my weight in candy canes tonight."

His laughter near my ear rumbles through me, causing my legs to tighten around his midsection, hard arousal pressed right between my thighs. Oliver lifts his head until we're face-to-face, my hands resting clasped at his nape. His eyes are glassy, reflecting lust and reverence and weakness and passion—everything I'm feeling from the inside out. Our smiles still linger when he leans in once more, crushing his perfect mouth to mine. My lips part to let him in, and when our tongues meet again, I melt, I wilt, I surrender. Our pace is less hurried this time, a delicious slow burn, and Oliver's fingers grip my waist so tight, it's like he's physically trying to hold himself back from losing control.

There is something wildly sexy about that notion.

Just as our kiss deepens further, a groan passing from one mouth to the other, the wetness between my legs rubbing against his erection and causing him to tremble in my arms, there's a light knocking at the bedroom door.

We break apart just as Poppy's small voice can be heard on the other side. "Auntie Syd, are you in there? Grandma is looking for you. She needs help getting dessert ready."

I almost choke on a gulp, my words trickling out frazzled and rushed. "O-Okay! Be right there," I call back, my hands sliding down Oliver's arms, our moment snuffed out.

It's for the best.

Oliver loosens his hold on my waist, his forehead dropping to mine again when Poppy's footsteps disappear down the hallway. He exhales a flurry of thoughts and feelings I can't even begin to decipher. "Are you all right?" he asks again, careful and kind.

I respond with a nod, my chin lifting to place a kiss against his hairline.

Oliver sighs when he pulls back, and I unlock my ankles to free him from my hold. He runs his fingers through mussed hair, his skin flushed bright as he glances away with the faintest of grins. "I rather like mistletoe," he says.

My laughter triggers his grin to grow, and our eyes connect for a powerful beat, brimming with more emotion than I can handle.

As I lead him out of the bedroom with bee stung lips and soaked panties, hoping to God my family members don't notice anything amiss, I can't help but wonder where we go from here. I'd like to say *this* was when everything changed... but I know that's not true.

Everything changed the moment he came back.

CHAPTER NINETEEN

OLIVER

A LITTLE AFTER TEN P.M. we make our way back home, Clementine in the driver's seat and Sydney in the back with a sleeping Poppy. My head twists around to catch Sydney's gaze every so often, my fingers itching to reach out and hold her hand. The alcoholic beverage has worn off, effectively subduing me, while leaving me with more questions than my tired brain can process at this late hour.

When I spare Sydney another glance, there's a reassuring smile in her eyes that quiets my disheveled thoughts for the time being.

"Poppy seemed very taken with you today, Oliver," Clementine states over the low hum of radio music. "You have a sweet disposition with the little ones."

The compliment touches me. For a good portion of the evening, I was in high demand amongst the assortment of young cousins and the two Labrador Retrievers that resided in the home. It was a pleasant feeling to be favored. "Thank you," I say. "She's lovely. We had a nice time reading together during our last visit."

Clem hesitates before responding, "You've met her before today?"

"Yes. Sydney was providing childcare for Poppy and another neighborhood girl, and I stopped by."

"Oh, I didn't realize."

"Sydney needed to retrieve cat food, so I stayed with the children while she was gone."

Sydney chimes in through a yawn. "Oliver was so good with them. A total natural."

A silence settles in, and it's the heavy kind of silence—the kind I've discovered to be venomous. I look to my left, awaiting Clementine's response, but she appears to be deep in thought. Distressing thoughts, it seems. Her hands grip the steering wheel a little tighter, the lines in her face hard and taut. After another moment of tension passes, she aims her reply at Sydney. "You left Poppy alone with him?"

We are both taken aback by the hostility in her voice, and Sydney and I share a startled look. I can't help but feel a bit offended by the inquiry.

Sydney falters, as if she's trying to piece together her words. "It was only for ten minutes. The girls were perfectly fine."

"I left Poppy in *your* care. Not Oliver's." Her tone is pointed and clipped. "What were you thinking?"

"I was thinking I needed cat food," Sydney snaps back. "What's the big deal? I trust Oliver. He was amazing with them. All they did was read some books together."

Clementine releases a brittle laugh, shaking her head. "And I trusted *you.*"

I'm feeling very lost and slightly uncomfortable. Shifting in my seat, I clear my throat to intervene. "I assure you they were both well-cared for. We enjoyed our time together."

She glares at me through a tight jaw, enhancing my confusion.

Sydney is now leaning forward between the two front seats, one hand gently squeezing my shoulder. "Clem, you're being super disrespectful to Oliver. He's sitting right here. I promise Poppy was in good hands."

"Whatever. I'll just need to reevaluate my childcare arrangements."

"What the hell? Are you threatening to keep me from my niece?"

"I'm not threatening anything. *You're* the one threatening my child's safety."

A horrified gasp. "Excuse me?"

My protective instincts poke through, causing me to speak in Sydney's defense. "Maybe it's not my place, but Sydney is wonderful with Poppy. She would never jeopardize her safety."

Clementine's caustic eyes are pinned on me. "You're right, it's not your place. You know nothing."

"Okay, we need to table this for now," Sydney declares, collapsing back against her seat. Her voice cracks, clearly rattled. "It's not fair to Oliver. We'll discuss tomorrow."

"Fine," is Clementine's curt reply.

And then the venomous silence infiltrates once again, lasting for the duration of the drive home. It's a relief when we pull into Sydney's driveway and exit the vehicle—like a breath of fresh air. An essential reprieve.

Clementine transfers a groggy Poppy to her own vehicle, not saying a word to me or Sydney, nor sparing us a parting glance. She slams her car door and disappears into the night, leaving us both standing in the driveway, confused and sucker-punched.

Sydney's eyes are glistening with the tears she held in for forty long minutes, her arms crossed, her feet fidgety. She looks up at me with a quivering chin. "I'm so sorry, Oliver. I have no idea what that was all about. Please don't take any of it to heart."

While the implication stung, I'm far more concerned about Sydney right now. I move in to tuck a loose strand of hair behind her ear, watching as her eyes flutter closed, a tear slipping through. "I can't pretend to know what it's like to a be a parent. We are protective of the ones we love."

Her eyes open slowly, meeting mine, as she reaches up to clasp my hand, giving it a tender squeeze. "Yes, we are."

Our prolonged stare scalds me, and I'm forced to look away. As much as I want to continue what we started in that bedroom, I realize now is not the time. "Well, goodnight," I whisper, learning forward and pressing a kiss to her temple. "We'll talk soon. Get some rest."

I flash her a smile before I turn away, but she stops me. My name meets my back, as if it escaped through her lips unplanned.

"Oliver."

Our eyes meet again, the flame still lit. "Yes?"

"I, um..." She glances away, scratching at her collarbone, then returns her focus to me. "I probably won't be able to fall asleep for a little while. Did you... did you want to come inside with me? We can watch a movie while I wind down?"

"Oh." I was not expecting the offer, but I'm certainly not opposed. Nerves dance across her pretty face beneath the moonlight as she squeezes her upper arms, blood red nails digging into her coat sleeves. Sydney's breath hits the air like plumes of smoke, a fitting parallel to the fire in her eyes. "All right. A movie sounds wonderful."

The anxiety in her eyes flitters away like a blue bird, a relieved smile taking its place. "Great."

Her house is dark as we make our way inside, Alexis greeting us at the door per usual. I provide her with some well-deserved ear scratches, while Sydney discards her coat and shoes, shivering slightly as she flips on the light switch.

"I'm still on edge whenever the house is dark," she says, running her hands up and down along her biceps and blowing out a quick breath. "It happened months ago, but I still always feel like he's in my house, hiding, waiting for me to let my guard down. I can't believe he was never caught."

Her attacker, I presume. "You know I would never let anything happen to you."

A bold promise, and one I couldn't possibly uphold. Life is far too unpredictable.

However, the sentiment has her lips tipping upward, her gaze filled with gratitude. "I'm going to change out of this dress. I'll be back in a few minutes."

My nod meets her slow retreat, as if she's reluctant to leave me. Then her words register, and I have to force myself to push away thoughts of her changing out of her dress.

God, that dress.

The only thing preferable to Sydney wearing that dress, is Sydney *not* wearing that dress. It's an image that has me shuffling over to the couch with my breath in my throat and the blood rushing south. Luckily, Alexis curls up beside my thigh with a contented mew, and I'm temporarily distracted until Sydney returns, adorned in her typical t-shirt that almost entirely covers her cotton shorts. Her long, bare legs approach, and she plops down beside me on the sofa, our shoulders touching. She gifts me a quick glance with the shyest of smiles before fumbling for the remote control that is stuck between the cushions.

"Movie," Sydney voices, like she needs the reminder. "Anything you want to watch?"

Eyes on the woman beside me, I can't think of anything else I'd prefer to watch. I don't think I can tell her that, so I turn my attention to the television screen, lit up with the Netflix application. "I suppose we could watch *The Parent Trap*," I suggest. "I was a bit disappointed we didn't view it last week. You appeared to be excited."

Sydney shifts beside me, pulling her feet up by the ankles. "It wasn't the right time. The movie is special to me."

"How so?" I wonder, curiously.

She picks at her polka-dotted sock, her demeanor shifting. "It was the movie we never got to see."

I blink, processing her statement. Sydney is focused on her sock, black with white dots, her fingernail snagging on a piece of fuzz. She's avoiding my stare, the mood heavy and suffocating. Scooting towards her even more, our bodies pressed together, I reach for her occupied hand, cradling her fingers in my palm. "We had plans to see it before I was... taken?"

A quick nod, followed by a shaky inhale. "We talked about it that morning, window to window, without a care in the world. We had no idea everything was about to change."

"Syd..."

"I refused to watch it over the years," she tells me. "It's just a silly kid movie, but... it reminded me so much of everything that never came to be."

I stroke my thumb over her knuckles, feeling the tension dissipate. "We can watch it now."

Sydney turns to me, eyes shimmering like crystals, and bobs her head. "I'd like that."

The movie bursts to life on the screen as Sydney's head falls against my shoulder, our hands intertwining. It's an entertaining film that holds my interest, but it's hard to be entirely focused when the woman I adore is melted into me like she simply belongs there. We don't speak about the kiss at her parents' house, nor the implication of such an act, and I'm comfortable with the silence for now. I don't need answers or titles when Sydney is curled into me, warm and buzzing—she is enough.

Halfway through our viewing, Sydney straightens beside me, rolling her neck and massaging the nape with her palm.

I glance her way, watching as her muscles twitch and tense. "Do you need a release?" I wonder aloud.

Sydney jerks her head towards me, eyes widening. "What?"

I must have used the wrong word, so I clear my throat. "The tension in your neck. You look uncomfortable. I can... help. If you'd like."

"Oh." Her lips part, still glossy from the lip balm she applied a short while ago. "Sure."

"Come between my legs."

Sydney coughs into her fist, a flush creeping into the apples of her cheeks. It appears I've misspoken—*again*. But she doesn't question me this time and stands from the couch, resituating herself between my thighs. She's tentative in her movements, peeking over her shoulder as her bottom lands on the very edge of the sofa cushion. Her heat and proximity prompt a lump to form in my throat, a tingle washing over me. My hands are fisting the fabric of my jeans as I shift back, putting a little more space between us.

"I've had this kink in my neck ever since I woke up this morning," Sydney mutters, tipping her head forward slightly. "I think it's from the painting I'm working on. I get so stiff and focused."

"That could be," I nod, lifting my hands from my hips and bringing them to her shoulders. I splay my fingers, my thumbs pressing firmly into the stem of her neck, circling the area that's bothering her. "Is this enough pressure?"

Sydney makes a soft squeaky sound, her body relaxing. "That's wonderful."

The noise she makes, coupled with her closeness, has a noticeable, physical effect on me. My heartbeat is increasing, my body warming. I skim my hands a bit lower, massaging the muscles in her back, watching her head loll from side to side. My hands case up her spine, my thumbs tending to her with circular motions as she sags against me.

"Feels so good," she whispers.

My jaw is tense from gnashing my teeth together. The scent of her hair, like a fragrant meadow, is tickling my nose while she leans into my chest. This is supposed to feel good for her—so, why do I seem to be enjoying it? It's an innocent massage.

I curl my fingers around her upper arms, squeezing gently, sliding them back up to her shoulders, then her neck. "I like the way you feel in my hands," I mutter, unsure if that's something I should say. My words kiss her ear, and a few wispy strands of hair dance along her temple.

She squirms between my legs, her hip caressing the quickly forming bulge in my pants. If she notices, she's unbothered. "I like the way your hands feel on me."

Her words come out in a single breath. There is a charge between us, a current of heat, erotic and unabashed. My body has never surrendered to another human before—not quite like this. Our kiss filters through my memories, gasoline on fire.

Sydney continues to move, either on instinct or on purpose. I am unsure, but I'm far too tethered to this moment, to these feelings, to question her motives.

Instead, I move my hands over her back, her arms, her neck, and even dip down her chest until my fingertips graze the swell of her breasts. I glance over her shoulder, realizing I can see down her loose fitting, V-neck t-shirt. I swallow, quickly averting my eyes, deciding that is not a sight meant for me. "Syd," I murmur. I'm about to tell her that perhaps I should stop touching her, perhaps this is becoming inappropriate, perhaps I'm feeling things I shouldn't be feeling from a mere neck rub...

But Sydney twirls her hips against my erection, causing my own hips to jerk forward as a groan passes through my lips.

I'm convinced that was deliberate.

My grip on her tightens, and her head falls back to my right shoulder. I watch as her eyelids drift closed, her body still moving, still writhing against me. The more she moves, the more the coil of heat grows low in my abdomen, funneling downward. I can hardly concentrate on her massage, and my hands are basically just squeezing her now, holding on for support.

Sydney's eyes remain shut, but her movements don't cease. "You can touch me if you'd like."

I inhale her flowery scent with my lips pressed against her hair. I'm already touching her, so I'm confused at first, but then I think I understand.

She wants me to *touch* her—like a man touches a woman.

If Sydney weren't currently wriggling her backside against my throbbing arousal, I'd probably flee. I'd panic. But logic seems to have slipped away and my inhibitions are lost to me. I allow my hands to respond on their own, curving over her shoulders and sliding down beneath the fabric of her shirt. I watch as my palms cup her breasts beneath the cotton, soft and supple, and she arches into my touch with a wanton sigh.

My lip catches between my teeth and I bite hard, sweat creasing my brow, my body beginning to tremble with a need I've never known. I slip my hands out from her shirt and trail them down her sides until I reach her hips. One glides back up her t-shirt from the bottom, while the other teases the hem of her pajama shorts. Hesitation sinks in, mingling with my lust, and I don't know if she wants me to touch her *there*.

But Sydney clasps my hand in hers and tugs it down further, offering permission while she grinds against me. "It's okay," she rasps, her voice husky and tight, shaking lightly with her own desire.

God. I never knew these feelings existed. I've experienced carnal thoughts before, sure, and I've pleasured myself with my own hand. But *this...* this is something else entirely. The sensation of another human being so intimately entwined—the palpable connection, thick and heady. It's more than physical. It's more than surface-deep.

It's unparalleled.

With one hand palming her breast, the other sneaks into her shorts, then inside her underwear. An ounce of fear and uncertainty pokes at me, but it's devoured by my insatiable curiosity and my body's own internal instincts. Her heat invades my fingertips, slick and smooth, and a sound erupts from both of our throats, my dark growl fused with her whimper. Sydney's hips move faster, still stroking my hard length through my jeans, bowing up to meet my hand as my fingers begin to move between her wetness.

She gasps. "Oh…"

I pull her closer to my chest, a primal and possessive feeling trickling through me. Her breast is in one hand, her sex in the other, her body hot and thrashing between my thighs. Everything in me is screaming to unbuckle my pants and yank them down, then to sheathe myself inside of her. I'm blinded by the craving—nearly dizzy from it.

Should I? Can I?

Is that where this is headed?

"Syd, I…" I don't know how to express my thoughts. My yearnings. I'm overcome with lust and confusion and blurred lines and crippling need. Sydney keeps moving, keeps grinding, keeps torturing me in the most exquisite way. "I want to…"

I try to pinpoint the correct word. Copulate. Fornicate. Intercourse. Sex.

All accurate, but nothing sounds quite right.

So, I blurt the only thing that does: "I want to make love to you."

She stills for a moment, her eyes opening slowly, seemingly in a fog. Our gazes lock with her head tipped back, her mouth parting with a small sigh.

I bite down on my lip again, still touching her in the most intimate way. Have I upset her? Offended her? Does she want the same thing?

Sydney swallows, not breaking our stare.

Then she begins to move again. She doesn't respond with words, and for a moment, I'm perplexed. But all thoughts slip away when she angles her hip against my groin, gyrating with purposeful motion, with the perfect amount of pressure. Her eyes are still on me, my hands are all over *her*, and the tension swelling in my core begins to climb.

I insert one of my fingers inside her and begin to pump, letting her breathy moan drag me closer to the pleasure moment. Her back is arched, her head resting on my shoulder, and we are cheek to cheek. Sydney's eyes close as she continues to use her body as a tool to guide me to ecstasy. I palm her breast, tweaking the hardened nipple, and groan into the curve of her neck.

I feel myself spiraling, peaking, chasing the feeling I'm absolutely desperate for. I cup her sex in my hand, pressing her backside firm against my groin as she rides me.

And then I explode.

An orgasm sweeps through me, hitting me like a tidal wave, stars flickering behind my eyes, and my head drops back against the couch as I shudder beneath her weight. I feel my pants flood with warmth, my hips jerking up against Sydney. She slows her movements, and I come down from my high, shocks still rippling through me. My limbs are heavy, my breathing heavier.

Her wetness is still slicking my fingers and I'm not sure what to do now—do I keep going? I want to, and it seems only fair.

I thrust my finger inside her, inserting one more, forcing her to squeak in surprise. Sydney reaches for my hand, twisting her head to look at me. "It's okay, Oliver."

While her words sound like permission to keep going, the tone of her voice says otherwise.

I think she wants me to stop.

My jaw tenses as I raise my head from the couch, finding her eyes. I pull my hand out from her shorts, my other falling from her breast, and swallow. "I'm sorry. Am I doing it wrong?"

Sydney lifts off me, revealing the wet spot that has seeped into my denim-clad thigh. She smiles, shaking her head as she takes her place beside me. "You're perfect."

I'm perfect, but she wants me to stop.

I'm not understanding.

She must notice the confusion and rejection pinching my brow, because she touches her hand to my cheek with hazy eyes. "This was just for you," she adds.

"For me?" I tilt my head, puzzled. Does her sexual gratification turn this into something else? Something different than what she wants it to be? "I don't want this to be one-sided—it doesn't feel right. You can teach me what you like."

My voice is raspy, still laden with lust. The thought of her "teaching" me things, allowing me to explore her body, taking this further... it's exhilarating. I find myself becoming aroused again.

Sydney trails her fingers down my jaw, pressing the tips to my bottom lip. She eyes my mouth before pulling back. "You should go home and get cleaned up."

A dismissal.

Frustration and a hint of anger burns me. "Sydney, this isn't what I want. I don't require favors or kindnesses."

"I didn't mean..." Her throat strains with a swallow, trembling fingers trailing down my chest and gripping the material of my sweater. "You wanted to learn."

"This isn't about learning anymore," I argue, my chest tight, my emotions scattered. "This is about how I feel for you."

"I feel for you, too, Oliver," she grits out, avoiding my searching gaze. "So much."

"But not the same?" I don't hesitate, despite the way my heart skips a frazzled beat. My need to know where she stands overrides my fear that her response may not be what I want it to be. "Please be truthful."

Sydney doesn't hesitate either, placing my hand, palm forward, against her chest. "You know the truth. It's right here."

"Sydney..." I press my palm further into the hurried beats that vibrate through my fingertips. "Do you feel the same?"

Eyes are aligned, holding hard. Skin flushed. Breaths woven and wound. A silent eternity passes before she shakes her head. "I don't."

I crumble.

She catches me. "There's no way you could possibly feel what I'm feeling, what I've *felt*, from the moment Gabe told me they found you. That you were alive. You have no idea what it was like to be haunted by you for twenty-two years, then to hold you in my hands, flesh and bone, like you were back from the dead. You couldn't understand any of that." Sydney's fingers curl tighter around my wool sweater, her gaze tormented. "So, no, Oliver... we don't feel the same. It would be impossible."

I drink in her words, feeling them soak into my skin. I realize in that moment that Sydney also wears a mask, much like my brother. She hides behind her humor and sarcasm, a defense mechanism, a strategy to cope with all the ghosts she keeps inside.

Cupping her face between my hands, I feel her turmoil with every blink, every tremor, every jaded heartbeat trapped inside her throat, choking her. "I'm here now, Sydney. I'm right here."

Another fervent head shake. "The only thing worse than *not* having you, is having you and breaking you apart all over again."

"I'm not made of glass. You won't break me."

"You don't know that..."

A defeated breath spills out as I duck my head, dropping my hands from her face that is now reflecting wet streaks. I'm not sure how to breach her fears. I'm not equipped to tackle her ghosts. I haven't acquired the proper tools.

I move to stand as Sydney slips off of me, pausing to reel in my emotions before rising to my feet. She remains seated, nearly shaking with remorse and indecision. "I'm going to head home and get cleaned up," I say softly, echoing her previous proposal. I need to cleanse my body *and* my mind. "Thank you for the lovely evening."

Her grief-ridden voice seizes me as I reach for my jacket. "I don't want to lose you."

Sydney wraps her arms around herself, breath hitching, gaze tortured. I worry my lip between my teeth, piecing together my response. "You're going to lose me by trying too hard *not* to lose me, Syd." A quivering gasp echoes in my ears. "Goodnight."

Before I turn to leave, dejected and bewildered, I spare Sydney a final glance.

There's a hurricane in her eyes, and it's either going to swallow me whole or leave me crippled, on my knees, lost and alone amongst the wreckage.

CHAPTER TWENTY

OLIVER

P ART OF ME EXPECTS—HOPES, EVEN—TO DISCOVER SYDNEY on the other side of my front door when incessant knocking rumbles through the house a few days later.

I'm not entirely delighted to find Lorna Gibson, instead.

"Good day, Oliver," she greets, holding out a few envelopes and advertisements she must have collected from the mailbox. "I brought you your mail. I wanted to thank you for shoveling my driveway yesterday—that was very kind of you. I know Charlene is looking down, beaming with pride at what a wonderful young man you've turned out to be."

I reach for the mail in a robotic fashion, mustering a smile. "I, uh, didn't shovel your driveway, Mrs. Gibson. That was Sydney."

Images of Sydney bundled up with wind-burned cheeks are still fresh in my mind as I caught her finishing up the good deed for the crotchety neighbor woman the prior afternoon. By the time I'd gathered my winter gear and zipped my jacket, she was already headed back inside.

"Come again?" Lorna wonders, her tone portraying her disbelief. "That can't be right."

"I assure you, it is. I would have assisted, but I didn't notice until she was already done."

Lorna's wrinkles move and furrow as she processes this revelation. The old woman glances to her left, towards Sydney's house, her darkly shaded eyebrows pinched in contemplation. "Well, I'll be," she says in a low breath, as if she can't even fathom such a thing. The haze lifts from her tempered glass eyes and she returns her attention to me, a partially toothless smile growing. "Anyway, have a lovely day, Oliver. Tell your dreadful stepbrother to keep his noise down."

"His music?" I blink.

"Noise." She shuffles down the salted walkway, wobbly and unsteady. "Good day."

I watch her leave before closing the door, the cold draft prickling my skin. Sifting through the letters as I pace back up the staircase, Gabe saunters out of the bathroom, towel-drying his mop of hair. Before I'm able to greet him, a return address stamp catches my eye.

It's from the police department.

"Who was at the door?" Gabe wonders, sans shirt, his polyester shorts hanging low on his lean hips. "Sydney?"

"She would never knock," I reply absently, my attention focused on tearing open the envelope. "Lorna fetched the mail for us."

"Aw, shucks. That old bat has a beating heart in there, after all." Gabe's humorous grin fades when he notices my heavy distraction. "Anything interesting?"

Yes. Yes, indeed.

I can't help the smile that spreads when I read the letter. "My comics. I'm able to go pick them up at the police station."

"Shit. That's excellent. They don't need them for evidence anymore?"

A swift shake of my head. "They are closing the case," I respond.

"Oh. Is that... *good?*" Gabe inquires with caution, flicking the damp towel over his left shoulder. "Doesn't that mean you'll probably never get any real answers?"

"I suppose it does."

My tone is neutral like my thoughts on the matter. I was desperate for answers during those first few weeks, months even, but now I'm settled. I'm content. I'm finally accepting that what happened to me... *happened* to me. It is no longer a part of my present—a present I am growing quite fond of, save for my romantic interest in a woman who desperately confuses me.

I see no point in revisiting the past. Answers won't change anything. They will only hinder my healing.

It's better this way.

Gabe chews his cheek as he studies me, fingers aimlessly fiddling with the end of the bath towel. "Well, I was going to head up to Lake Geneva after work and grab dinner with Pops, but I can reschedule if you want. I'll take you to the station instead."

The generous offer pulls my gaze up from the letter that I've reread twice now, touched. "That's not necessary, as much as I appreciate the sentiment. Perhaps we can go tomorrow."

"That works. Otherwise, I'm sure Sydney would take you."

My skin heats, and my reaction must be noticeable as I shift from one foot to the other, stepping away to set the mail on the coffee table.

Gabe makes a hissing sound. "Ouch. Something happened, didn't it?"

"Something, yes."

"Goddammit," he curses, swinging the towel against the corner of the wall, where kitchen meets hallway. He makes a growling sound, frustration pouring off of him. "I told her not to go there with you. I could wring her neck."

"I'd prefer that you didn't," I sigh, collapsing back onto the sofa.

"She promised she wouldn't hurt you."

I feel Gabe come up behind me, leaning forward on the arm rest, his features taut. His concern is evident, and it's a good feeling, knowing that he cares for my wellbeing. "I don't believe she means to. Her intentions are pure, but her execution leaves a little to be desired."

A chuckle greets me as Gabe paces the few steps over to where I'm seated, plopping down with a heavy breath. "That's a classy way of saying she's a hot mess." I can see him trying to get a read on me out of my peripheral. "So, what happened? Did you guys... hook up?"

"If that's an intercourse reference, no. Not exactly."

"What, then?"

Flashes of Sydney writhing between my thighs, my fingers inside of her, moans and gasps and explosions, all slam into me, causing my neck to burn. "It's private," I force out.

Gabe raises one eyebrow, a question and a complaint. "Shit, fine. But I'm going to assume it's sexual because that's Sydney."

"How do you mean?"

"I mean, she's a sexual person. She doesn't exactly lack confidence in that department. It's all the other stuff that has her running the other way."

"Commitment," I gather.

"Commitment. Emotional attachment. All that mushy love stuff."

I wonder why that is. Did someone hurt her? Break her trust? It appears Sydney has a deep-rooted emotional complex when it comes to matters of the heart, and I don't know how to fix that. I lean back into the cushions, one hand on each knee. "We haven't spoken in four days. It's a troublesome feeling."

Gabe commiserates next to me with a long sigh. "Well, now that you realize I was overflowing with really good advice, maybe you'll use some of it—*find a distraction*. Out of sight, out of mind, you know?"

"She is always on my mind."

"Not when you've got another pretty face in your bed. Hell, it doesn't even have to be about sex. Go on a date. Talk and laugh over fucking Italian food or something," he tells me, his words almost pleading. "You need to, Oliver. This thing with Syd... it's not going anywhere. You'll be in this soul-crushing, back-and-forth limbo forever. Get out there and enjoy yourself."

My instincts want to resist his words, tell him to mind his own business, argue that I enjoy myself the *most* when I'm with Sydney.

But I don't because his words ring true.

Heaving in another sigh, I nod my head. "You may be right. There is someone... a woman I met at the library recently. She's quite lovely."

"No shit, really?" Gabe slaps me on the back so hard, I wince. "There you go, buddy. What's her name? She hot?"

"Tabitha. She's very beautiful and good-natured. She was one of the surviving victims of a serial killer investigation that occurred not long ago," I explain.

Gabe is immediately fishing through the pockets of his shorts for his cellular phone, pulling up the search application. "I know who you're talking about..." he says as his thumbs swipe away at the digital keypad. "Tabitha Brighton. Yeah, this chick."

Glancing over his shoulder, I nod. "Yes, that's her."

"Goddamn. Where can I get one of these?" he jokes, eyeing the photograph with approval.

"The library, apparently."

A sharp laugh. "She's a knock-out. Well done, man."

I clear my throat of the uncomfortable tickle. "We had coffee together on my work break last week. It was mildly cumbersome, considering what we share in common isn't exactly lighthearted coffee discussion, but I did enjoy her company."

"I have no idea what cumbersome means, but it was a damn good song," Gabe responds offhandedly, still staring at Tabitha's picture on the screen. He blinks himself out of the trance, stuffing his phone back into his pocket. "Take her out. You can even borrow my car since you can legally drive now."

That much is true. I passed my driver's test at the end of the summer, but I haven't been able to put my license to good use yet. Gabe allows me to use his vehicle for grocery store runs, however, I don't have the funds to purchase my own means of transportation. It's just another stressor weighing me down.

"Thank you," I mutter, rising to my feet. "I made pancakes, by the way, if you're hungry."

"Ah, fuck, work." Gabe jumps from the couch like I lit a match underneath him. "I'm still fuckin' half-naked. I'll snag some pancakes for the road."

He points two index fingers at me, a signal of gratitude I presume, then races down the hallway to his bedroom.

I do the same.

My intentions were to lose myself in my comics—my favorite source of distraction—but I make my way over to the bed instead, pulling a book from the nightstand drawer.

It's one of Sydney's romantic novels, brimming with explicit sexual content and debauchery. She let me borrow a whole stack of them, more so as a joke after our teasing altercation, but I find that I'm learning a lot about her through these stories.

I'm learning about what kind of attributes she appreciates in a male counterpart.

The heroes between these pages are not noble or kind. They are dark, twisted men, sometimes cruel and violent. They take, they hurt, they punish.

Is that what Sydney prefers? Is that the kind of man she desires?

I am nothing like her fantasy heroes.

But perhaps I can be.

An hour goes by and I close the book, my mind restless and agitated. Without thinking it through, I reach for my cellular device and start typing out an electronic message.

Me: *Hello, it's Oliver. I'm finding myself thinking about you and was wondering if you'd like to have dinner with me so we can talk.*

The phone pings to life from the bedspread.

Tabitha: *I'd love to.*

Forty-eight hours later, there is knocking on the front door once again. Only, this time, I know exactly who it is.

I'm fastening my burgundy button-down when I hear Gabe call out, "I'll get it!"

He *also* knows exactly who it is. A chuckle escapes me.

When I make my way out of the bedroom, Gabe is standing in the foyer, gawking at my date for the evening. He manages to find the courtesy to let her inside, his eyes trailing her as she passes through the threshold with a bemused smile. They share an endearing greeting before Tabitha spots me standing at the top of the steps.

"Hello," I say.

Her smile broadens as Gabe steps away, hands in his pockets. "Hi, Oliver. It's great to see you."

Tabitha looks stunning in a black, long-sleeved dress with the hem just skimming her knees. Her peacoat hangs open, her hair flowing over both shoulders like obsidian waterfalls. My fingers sweep through my own lightly styled hair as I clear my throat. "You found a caretaker for little Hope?"

"Luckily, yes. My cousin came through at the last minute."

Gabe interrupts, his eyes going wide. "You have a kid?"

"I do," she responds sweetly, not taking offense to the blunt question. Her gaze shifts to Gabe, irises glittering like shiny pennies. "She's turning one next month."

"Shit, that's cool."

My stepbrother appears nervous, or "off his game" as he's referenced in the past. Perhaps he's taken a liking to this woman. Her beauty is quite striking, I have to admit.

Making my way down the short staircase, I wait for Tabitha's eyes to drift back to me. It takes a moment, which is a curious thing. "Are you ready to go?"

"I'm ready," she nods brightly.

Tabitha offered to pick me up, despite my resistance. It feels strange having a woman pick me up for a date—*backwards*. I can't help but feel insecure about the very notion. But she insisted, seemingly unfazed. "All right," I say through a small smile. "Thank you for the ride."

"Of course. It's no problem at all."

I catch her eyes meeting with Gabe's for a lingering moment before they say a quick goodbye, and Tabitha and I step outside. It's ice cold, the sky shedding light flurries. The moon casts an ambient glow upon Tabitha, illuminating her milky skin as we walk towards her vehicle.

A jarring scraping sound grabs my attention, and I glance to my right to discover Sydney chipping away the ice chunks from her windshield, her legs bare and shivering beneath her long winter coat. Hesitation grips me as I call out to Tabitha, "One moment, please. My apologies."

Tabitha eyes the source of my distraction and nods a smile before slipping into the driver's seat. "No worries. I'll warm up the car for you."

Sydney glances up through her task, ash blonde hair spilling out from her pink beanie, her gloveless hands nearly matching the hat. A forced smile greets me as I approach.

"You look frozen to the bone," I say, coming up beside her and reaching for the ice scraper. "Let me. Get inside to warm yourself."

She falters at first, then concedes, gaze darting to mine before dancing away. "All I want for Christmas this year is remote start," she breathes out, her chuckle a ghost against the cold air. "Thank you."

Smiling back, I watch as she slides into the car and I finish what she started, shaving the thin layer of frost from the window. When it's complete and the heat from the vehicle melts the rest, I move to the driver's side and hand her the tool through the open window.

"I really appreciate that. I forgot to warm the car up, and I'm running late for work."

"It's not a problem," I respond, my tone subdued, if not laced with a tinge of longing. I urge my legs to retreat, and yet, they disobey. Our eyes pull together like a magnet, the heat between us almost enough to make me forget I'm standing amidst a Midwest tundra. "Well, enjoy your shift tonight. Be safe."

"You have a date?" she blurts before I turn away. Her eyes flicker with distress beneath her oversized spectacles, her fingers coiling around the steering wheel in a fierce grip.

I'm unsure why a stab of guilt pokes me in the gut. Sydney has made it clear she's not interested in pursuing romantic involvement with me. "Yes, with Tabitha. We will be eating Italian food."

Her features are pinched, tight with anguish, but she tries to disguise her reaction by flashing me her teeth, a smile straining. "That's wonderful. Have a good time."

I reply with an agreeable nod before I duck my head, hands gliding into my pockets. "All right, well, goodnight."

"Goodnight." Sydney's jaw goes rigid, her eyes glistening as she stares straight ahead, still clutching the wheel. She addresses me one more time before I head back to my driveway. "Oliver…"

I pause. "Yes?"

The words dance along the back of her throat, burning, searing, aching for release. But she swallows them down, her watery smile a send-off. "Nothing. I'll see you around."

Sydney backs out of the driveway, rolling the window up, leaving me standing there with questions in my heart and snowflakes in my hair.

"Favorite color?" she asks me, cutting her chicken into small bits.

I twirl the linguine around the tines of my fork five times too many, my appetite hindered by my nerves. Tabitha sits across from me in a cozy booth, our conversation easy, our questions easier. She's delightful company, always smiling and never making me feel uncomfortable or out of place. And yet, my stomach is still twisted into knots as I play with my pasta. "Red, I think. I've never really thought about that."

Tabitha gifts me a wide grin. "That generally implies that you're courageous, confident, bold, and outgoing."

"Oh." Those are not adjectives I'd use to describe myself. "That doesn't sound like me."

"No?" She pops a piece of chicken into her mouth, eyes twinkling. "Maybe that's who you are deep inside, and those traits were simply buried due to circumstances."

I blink, absorbing her words. "Perhaps."

"And you're definitely courageous. Anyone who can survive what you survived and come out on the other side with such grace is extremely brave."

My smiles meets hers over the table. "What's your favorite color?"

"Blue. I'm a peacemaker."

"That strikes me as very accurate. Do you enjoy psychology?"

She nods, sipping on her ice water. "It's my major. The human mind fascinates me, especially after…" A brief pause, accompanied by a wistful look my way. "Especially after my ordeal. My mind was my only weapon in that basement, and it saved my life."

A poignant grief tugs at me when I think back to the details I read about her case. Tabitha watched the man she loved die right before her eyes as she looked on, helpless, unknowingly pregnant with his child. The thought alone sickens me, causing me to wonder how this woman is so poised and kind. She referred to *me* as having grace, but she is the epitome of it. "I very much admire your tenacity and eloquence. Your daughter is lucky to have you as a guidance."

"That's sweet of you, Oliver. I hope I can make her proud. Being a single mom is a daily struggle, and I hardly even get out these days on my own. Tonight is a rare treat."

"I'm honored you've chosen to spend it with me."

Tabitha tucks her chin to her chest with a timid smile, moving her rice pilaf around on her plate. "This is actually my first date since my abduction. It's been almost two years."

"Oh, I see." While it makes sense, I'm still a bit surprised by her claim. Tabitha has such a bright, enchanting aura about her, and her beauty is clearly worn on the inside *and* out. "I can imagine it hasn't been an easy transition, given your past. Moving on from a lost love sounds like a horrendous endeavor. Impossible, even."

God, I can't envision such a thing. I cannot fathom losing Sydney in that way, much less *at all*. The idea has my heart in my throat.

Tabitha seems to drift away for a moment, swept up in her memories, before returning her attention to me with a small nod. "I'll never fully move on. He'll always be a part of me and our daughter," she whispers, twisting a cloth napkin between her fingers. "You don't ever forget. That ache never goes away. You just... *adjust*. You adjust to the void and rebuild your life around that missing piece, hoping something will come along one day and distract you *just enough*, that your pain abates... even if it's only for a little while."

Her words feel like a heavy weight upon my chest, and I'm thinking of Sydney again—thinking about her own words that eclipsed my heart: *You have no idea what it was like to be haunted by you for twenty-two years.* Did she feel how Tabitha feels? Was *I* that void?

I don't even realize I've zoned out when Tabitha's hand clasps mine on the tabletop, her soft gaze pulling me back to the present. "Who do you love, Oliver?"

"Pardon?"

Tabitha gives my hand a gentle squeeze before releasing me. "That look in your eyes—I recognize it. I stared into eyes like that every single day for weeks."

Another crushing weight as I swallow back a hard lump. "I care for someone deeply, yes. But I fear she doesn't feel the same."

"The neighbor girl?"

A curious nod. "Yes. How did you know?"

"I'm very intuitive," she grins, taking another bite of food, then adding, "Blue."

We share a small laugh and I tease, "So, you must have been aware of my brother's interest in you. He called you a 'knock-out'."

"Oh, did he?" The blush that pinkens her cheeks cannot be denied. "I'm very flattered. He seemed nice. Gabe, right?"

"Yes. He's been an enormous ally to me throughout all of this."

"It's important to have people in our corner, rooting for our successes," she agrees. Tabitha's head tilts slightly to the right as she finishes chewing her chicken. "And sometimes we need to be our own cheerleaders."

My eyes case her thoughtful expression. "How so?"

"We need to fight for what's in our hearts. No one else can do that for us," she tells me pointedly. "And if there is anything on this earth worth fighting for, it's love."

Love.

Warmth spreads through me as Sydney's face captures my mind and I lose myself in her smile, her laugh, her spunk, her humor, her art, her abominable dance moves. I replay our kisses, bursting with magic and possibilities. I melt at every knock-knock joke, every tender hug, every movie night on her couch with her sprawled across my lap like I am precious to her.

Like I *am* hers.

I nearly choke on the flurry of thoughts and emotions as I gaze across the booth at Tabitha. "I'm not sure what to do," I admit solemnly, fearfully.

Tabitha's encouraging smile shines back at me. "Be courageous. Be confident. Be bold," she says, her voice brimming with sincerity as she reaches for my hand once more. "Be red."

CHAPTER TWENTY-ONE

SYDNEY

I DRY-HUMPED MY BEST FRIEND on my couch and then I broke his heart.

Not even this entire can of dry shampoo on my head can save me from the dark hole of depression I've managed to dive into, headfirst, as I stare at my bedroom wall eating fun-size Snickers bars in an *X-Files* onesie. It took all of my effort to pull myself together for work yesterday, and even then, Brant and Rebecca were breathing down my neck, wondering why I looked like my cat croaked.

Great. I probably just manifested that horror into fruition, given the week I've been having.

I snuggle Alexis closer to my waist as I toss an empty candy wrapper across the room with my opposite hand, letting out a self-deprecating sigh.

To make matters worse, Clementine has hardly spoken to me since her massive overreaction the previous weekend. Her responses to my text messages are brief and detached. She even responded with a *'K'* when I informed her that I bought Poppy tickets for *Disney on Ice*. My head hurts and my heart hurts.

And now my stomach hurts.

Groaning, I toss off the covers and pull myself out of bed, deciding that a shower would serve me well. Of course, this is when the doorbell rings. I groan again, giving my messy bun a tug and adjusting my glasses, hoping they hide the dark circles under my eyes.

Pulling open the door, I'm greeted by Lorna Gibson.

Best. Week. Ever.

"Charming fashion choice, dear," she says, only mildly scathing, her see-through eyes casing me from head to toe. "At least you're properly covered for once."

One eyebrow arches with disdain. I can't even pretend to entertain her insults today. "Can I help you? I'm in the middle of something."

Berry lipstick smudges just above her mouth when Lorna purses her thin lips together. "I see that I've interrupted something riveting," she snickers, ignoring my eye roll. "Anyway, I was informed that you shoveled my driveway this past week and I've come to issue my thanks."

"Oh…" I'm taken aback by the offering of gratitude, considering I didn't realize she even knew, and well, it's *Lorna Gibson.* "You're welcome."

"Oliver told me in case you were wondering. His good morals and manners seem to be rubbing off on you." She adds as an afterthought, "Praise the Lord."

A huff. "Well, it's not a problem. I ran out of sinning to do that day and got bored. I mean, there's only a limited amount of unprotected sex and satanic rituals a girl can partake in before she needs to switch it up, you know?"

"Ever the comedian," Lorna says snidely, eyes still gliding over me with distaste. She's about to step away when she pauses, an unfamiliar look washing over her. Clearing her throat, she reaches into the front pocket of her blouse and pulls out a handful of photographs. "One more thing. I found these at the bottom of my jewelry box and thought you might have more use for them. Edgar enjoyed taking photos of you kids on his old film camera… looking at these Polaroids brought back some very special memories."

At first, I want to ask her what *else* he was taking pictures of on his old film camera, but there's a softness poking through her harsh exterior, and I'm not sure how to respond to it. I scuff my toes against the welcome mat, then reach out to take the photographs from her hand. "I appreciate that. Thank you."

Another pause before she departs. "You know, Charlene was always quite fond of you," Lorna tells me through a squint, a trace of candor seeping into her voice. "I think she'd be happy to know you found your way back to each other."

I'm unable to hold back the emotion-laced gasp that bursts through my lips.

"Good day, child."

Lorna hobbles away with her cane, not looking back, leaving me with tear stains and more memories than I can handle.

Evening turns to dusk, and I managed to shower and change before finding my way to the couch with a glass of wine and pictures of a past life. I've skimmed through the photographs countless times since Lorna dropped them off, unable to shake the melancholy feeling that has settled into my bones. Staring at a photo of Oliver and me, I hold my grief in the back of my throat like a burning ball of *could have beens*. I recall this photo being taken clear as day.

Oliver adorns his usual pair of overalls, a plaid shirt residing beneath the dirt-stained denim. His arm is around my shoulders, pulling me close, while I clutch a teddy bear in my arms. He's kissing my cheek and I'm resisting, but only partly, because I'm also drowning in joy and laughter, evident by the huge, toothy grin spread across my sunburned face.

When I zone in on that raggedy brown bear, a memory crosses my mind.

"I have a secret, but I'm scared to tell you."

"You can tell it to my teddy bear. She's very good at keeping secrets."

"Okay. You promise?"

"Promise. Pinky-swear, even."

With our pinky fingers linked together, Oliver leans into the well-loved bear, whispering something against her fuzzy ear...

Gnashing my teeth together, I make a mental note to ask Oliver if he remembers what that secret was. I had been curious at the time, but that curiosity vanished into thin air the moment Oliver Lynch did.

Flipping through the pictures again, I smile at the group photo of the four of us kids with our parents. Mom has her arm around Charlene, while Charlene has her hands on Gabe's shoulders, his goofy grin a testament to the man he would become.

Oliver and I are in the middle, wrapped in a giant hug, smiling brighter than the stars, and Clementine is on the far end with Travis standing behind her and Dad off to the side with a beer.

Clem looks the most miserable out of all of us—she was such a sullen, moody kid.

A knock at the front door startles me, and I jolt in place, always on edge lately… especially when the sun sets. Glancing down at my attire to confirm that I actually *did* change out of my embarrassing onesie, I skip to the front of the house with Alexis trailing my ankles.

I crack the door and peek out.

Oliver.

The crack widens when I spot him standing on my porch, shoulder propped against the frame as his eyes canvass me—from my neon fuzzy socks to my freshly washed hair. His expression is darker than normal, his presence radiating something entirely unfamiliar. Something very *un-*Oliver. "Hey," I greet softly, stepping back so he can step inside.

"Hello."

Even his movements are different. More deliberate, less apprehensive.

And his eyes haven't left me as they occasionally flicker south, landing on my cleavage that peeks out from my halter top. My skin heats. "Everything okay?" I wonder, a timid hitch in my voice.

"Yes," he responds simply.

Oliver presses inside, hands in his pockets, smelling of evergreens and pinecones, and his scent warms me. He leans down to pet Alexis before sauntering into the living room, his gaze drifting to the Polaroids laid out upon the coffee table. I follow. "Lorna brought them over. I don't have many pictures from those days—Mom threw most of that stuff out when they moved. I've been lost in memories all day," I tell him with a whimsical chuckle, my arms crossed.

He picks up one of the photos, assessing it carefully. "This is us," he states.

"And Coco."

A blink.

"My teddy bear," I grin, moving in closer to study the picture in his hands.

Oliver's smile twitches to life, a trace of his usual nature poking through, when he suddenly brings two fingertips to his temple, eyes closing like he's in pain.

"Oliver?" My protective instincts kick in and I squeeze his upper arm, worry coursing through me. "Is something wrong?"

He dismisses me with a shake of his head, flipping through the pictures. "I'm… fine." Oliver pauses on a photograph of us playing *Capture the Flag* in the front yard. He massages his temple, as if trying to physically pull a memory to the surface. "Something happened on this day."

"It did?" Confusion furrows between my eyes. I lean in and pluck the picture from his fingers, turning it around to glance at the date: *7-2-98.* I can't remember anything significant happening on that day, but then again, everything from the week Oliver disappeared is such a blur. I recall Gabe feeling sick, so he stayed inside with Oliver's mother while Travis took the rest of us out to play. My dad stopped by and they shared a beverage on the porch.

There was nothing but laughter and silliness as we hid the little American flag stake around the yard. Oliver and I always had to be on the same team. Returning the photo to him, I swing my head back and forth. "Nothing stands out."

Oliver pinches the bridge of his nose as he blows out a breath of frustration. "I know so many things—facts, faces, feelings. Dates and times. People I loved. But they are all trapped and buried inside of this *coffin.*" He jabs his index finger against the side of his head. "I get flashes here and there. Blurry images, voices, familiar sensations. Certain things will trigger pieces of conversations and interactions. But... I can't reach it, Syd. I can't hang on. It's too deep."

"Hey..." I pull his hand from his face, watching his breathing climb and his skin perspire. "It's okay. Have you thought about seeing a psychologist? Maybe even trying hypnosis?"

Oliver tugs his hand free and tosses the pictures to the couch, turning away. "No. I don't know. I was given the information of a psychologist upon my hospital release, but I haven't pursued it. Part of me is afraid to remember, I suppose."

Trying not to take offense to his pullback, I avert my eyes. "I can understand that."

"You don't understand. Nobody understands."

My eyes bore into his back as he sweeps angry fingers through his hair. "What's gotten into you? You seem... *off.*"

Oliver circles around slowly, that alarming look returning to his eyes. His gaze dips to my chest, then flicks back up. "Do I?"

I frown. "You're not acting like yourself."

"But that's what you prefer, yes?"

"What?" I cross my arms tighter as he paces toward me. "What are you talking about? Did something happen on your date?"

"It was a lovely date," he says with surety.

Oh, God, did he...?

Hardly able to squeak the words out, I mutter, "Did you sleep with her?"

"There was no sleeping involved."

Bile stings the back of my throat as my face flames with white-hot jealousy, the heat spreading to my neck and chest. It's a reaction I have *no business* feeling—I had my chance; I turned it down. Oliver has every right to move on. But that doesn't stop my stomach from churning with nausea as bitter tears spring to my eyes. "Oh."

There's a crack in his façade when he drinks in my pitiful reaction. "I've upset you."

I can't help but nod as the tears fall freely. Swiping them away, I reply with a quivering chin, "Yes, but it's okay. I'm fine."

"I didn't have sex with her, Syd." Whatever game he was playing crumbles at the sight of my pain. "We talked. We had a nice supper. We parted ways as friends because there's only one woman I want, and it's not her."

The ache in my chest dissolves, replaced with relief and a hint of confusion. "Y-You didn't have sex?"

"No."

"God, I thought…" I'm pathetic. Absolutely *pathetic*, acting like his virginity belongs to me, after he's already offered it and I dismissed him out of fear of hurting him. But all I'm doing is hurting us both by holding him in a loose grip, pulling and pushing, because I don't know what the fuck I'm doing. "I'm sorry, that was not an appropriate reaction. I have no right."

He glances away with a set jaw. "I'm inclined to agree with that."

My teeth grind together, seeing that he's put the mask back on—and I don't like it. "Oliver, please drop this act. It's not you."

"Good." Oliver finds my eyes again, taking a few steps forward until we're only inches apart. "I prefer it that way, and so do you."

"What? No… I like you just the way you are. I don't understand where this is coming from."

He huffs out a frazzled breath. "You've been sexually intimate with other men—a fair amount from what Gabe has implied—but you refuse to with me. Why is that?"

That shower of anxiety rains down again, drowning me. "Because you're different, Oliver." He lurches back, as if physically slapped. Offended and hurt. My eyes go wide, and I quickly backpedal. "No, wait… no, I didn't mean it like that. You're *special*. You're special to me. Sex… *complicates* things. You wouldn't understand."

"Because I'm so simple-minded."

"No, God… that's also not what I mean." I inhale a rickety breath, wondering what happened, what shifted. "No other man has ever come close to what you mean to me."

"And yet, you still want them. You still bring them to your bed." Oliver's eyes darken with a thick, ugly swell of jealousy as he advances on me. "You're worried I can't fuck you like they can."

An audible gasp escapes me. "Excuse me?"

"Frail, inexperienced Oliver Lynch. The boy who never grew up."

"Stop it," I demand, biting my lip to keep the sob from ripping through me. "That's not at all how I see you. You're perfect in every way."

"Not in *every* way, it seems."

All I can do is shake my head, stunned into silence, terrified that I have somehow ruined this man after trying so hard to keep him safe.

Ruin.

"You don't think I can satisfy you." Oliver continues, stalking towards me like I'm his prey. "You don't think I can make you writhe in pleasure and scream my name, just like you read about in your books."

Is this about the damn books? He thinks that's what I want?

We keep moving backwards until I'm pressed up against the far wall, the top of my breasts heaving with every labored breath, grazing the front of his shirt. In a quick swoop, he snatches my wrists with one hand, pinning them above my head, and a squeak of surprise breaks through my lips. I watch as his other hand raises to my cheek, his knuckles tracing my jawline as he fixates on my parted mouth.

"Maybe I do lack experience… but there's something you forget, Syd," Oliver says, his tone rough like grit. He leans down to whisper in my ear, my baby hairs tickling his nose. "I'm a very fast learner."

"No," I tell him, struggling to pull my wrists free. Flashes of my attacker pinning me to my mattress filter through my mind, sending my body into a panic. "I don't want it like this. I don't want *you* like this."

Oliver moves in for a kiss, but I yank my arms free and shove him away from me. The adrenaline spike heightens my strength, and I accidently push him too hard, with too much force. He crashes into my decorative side table, toppling over the picture frames, causing me to cup my mouth in horror.

Horror from inadvertently hurting him.

Horror from whatever the hell just transpired.

Horror from the look in his eyes when his guise disintegrates and *my* Oliver returns, his chest heaving, his guilty gaze pinned on me as his head swings from side to side.

"Sydney… I didn't mean…" He lifts off the table and covers his face with his palm, as if trying to hide from what he's just done. "Please forgive me. *Please.*"

I'm glued in place with tears rushing down my cheeks like tiny waterfalls, my heart beating a mile a minute. I'm rattled, confused, *hurt*.

Oliver slides his hand down his face, holding his jaw as his own tears shine back at me. "I thought that's what you wanted. Your books, I..." He exhales a sharp breath of pain that stabs like a dagger. "Your books are filled with men who take and push, who are selfish and unkind—who are *nothing* like me. I mistakenly assumed you preferred a man like that."

I need to dig through the growing surge of heartache in my throat to locate words. "Those are stories, Oliver. Fantasies. *Fiction*."

"I just..." He's wide-eyed and broken. "I'm trying to understand you, Syd. I'm trying to learn why you pull away from me—why I can't fully reach you. Why you *run*."

"Because I'm petrified of stripping away your progress and sending you back down into that hole!" I blurt, sorrow leaking out of my eyes, my throat stinging. "Feelings come with expectation, Oliver. I'm no good at that."

"You *heal* me. Every day you put another piece of me back together," he insists, crossing the room, cautiously approaching. "Why do you associate attachment with suffering and loss?"

I'm openly crying into my palm, shaking my head.

"God, who hurt you, Sydney?"

"*You* did!" I shriek, unplanned and untethered, my hysteria bubbling over. "Something inside of me fucking *died* the day I lost you!"

Oliver freezes in place, his eyes flaring, his limbs going completely still. He stares at me, slack-jawed, with the most wounded, bewildered look upon his face.

"I started building walls at only seven-years-old," I continue, my voice ragged from the grief spilling out, a tsunami of bottled-up ghosts. I ambush him with my graveyard. "Day by day, those walls went up, made of stone and brick and steel and *you*. I couldn't let anyone in because I couldn't *bear* to feel the way I felt after you disappeared. Not again... not ever. You have no idea what you meant to me. What you *mean* to me." The heel of my palm slams against my chest with clenched teeth.

"Syd, I..." He trails off, lost for words.

I keep going. "I've spent my whole life keeping people at arm's length because it's how I cope, how I protect myself. And yes, I've been with men, that's no secret... but it's never meant *anything*." I find his eyes, and they are just as tear-filled as mine. "With you, it would mean *everything* and that scares the shit out of me."

Oliver drinks in my words, studying me, trying so hard to understand.

He looks down at the floor, scattered with glass and debris from the fallen frames. Then he whispers so softly, "A wise woman once told me that there is beauty to be found everywhere. Even in the things that scare us."

Chin quivering, I suck in a sharp breath and swallow down his words, tasting his truth. "Oliver, I'm sorry. I'm so sorry I've confused and hurt you when all I've tried to do is protect your beautiful heart," I say, stepping towards him.

He moves back, away from me. "I... I should go."

"You don't want to talk about this?"

"No, I fear I've done enough damage." Oliver glances down at the mess near his feet. "Forgive me, Sydney. I never meant to frighten you."

"Wait, it's okay—"

He spins around towards the doorway.

"Oliver, I understand," I call out. "I know you didn't mean it."

Hand on the doorknob, he pauses to peer at me over his shoulder as he deflates with defeat. "It appears we continue to hurt one another, despite our greatest efforts not to. It's a paradox." Oliver's gaze drifts past me, his forehead wrinkling with contemplation. He lets out a remorseful sigh and opens the door. "Love is a paradox."

Oliver leaves me with those words, with his confession, as I collapse onto the shards of glass, bringing my legs up and sobbing into the valley between my knees. At some point, I drag myself to the couch and curl up beside my cat, clutching the photo of Oliver and me to my aching chest.

All these years, I've never given my heart to anyone. I told myself it was because I was too picky, too independent, my standards were too high... but that's not the truth.

The truth is, I didn't have a heart to give.

My heart was with a ghost.

CHAPTER TWENTY-TWO

OLIVER

O NE WEEK LATER, I'm lying on an unfamiliar sea-green sofa, my head resting upon a downy pillow. I'm staring up at a ceiling of white while a middled-aged woman sits beside me with a voice like a gentle lullaby, her hair wound into a loose knot. She makes me feel at ease, despite my jitters.

"Hello, Oliver. As you know, I'm Dr. Malloy and I'm a certified hypnotherapist. I'm here to help you with your memory loss," she tells me, soft and lilting, almost mesmerizing.

"Yes. Thank you," I reply, my fingers linked across my stomach.

After months and months of putting it off, I finally decided to seek out therapy. While Sydney and Gabe were enormous contributions to my mental and emotional recovery, I still feel like something is missing. I'm hopeful these sessions will unlock buried memories that will assist with my healing journey.

A smile greets me when I turn my head to the left. "I want you to relax, focus, and cast any fears aside. Hypnosis is perfectly safe, and the majority of my patients are hypnotizable, finding immense healing in the process. Roughly ten percent of those patients are *highly* hypnotizable, and they walk away with extreme breakthroughs."

A nod accompanies my swallow.

"Every experience on this couch is different and personal. You can walk me through your goals and specific issues, and we'll work together to ensure the most fulfilling outcome possible. How does that sound?"

"Lovely," I reply in a whisper.

"That's great, Oliver. Can you provide me with more details as to what you're hoping to achieve today?"

I breathe in deeply, inhaling a pleasant lavender musk. It calms me. "I was abducted at eight-years-old by a man who held me captive in his basement for nearly twenty-two years. During that time, I was fed lies—lies I'll never understand. The lies have blurred my memories with dreams and fantasies, and some I have no access to at all. I'll experience glimpses into past events when something triggers me, but it disappears before I can truly relive it."

Dr. Malloy makes a soft humming sound, pencil to paper. "That must be incredibly frustrating for you. Are there specific memories you are trying to uncover?"

"Yes, and no," I respond. Then I choke out, "I'd like to see my mother again."

"She has since passed away, I presume?"

"Ten years now, I'm told."

"I'm very sorry to hear. I hope I can help you with that," she tells me, her tone convincing. Dr. Malloy crosses one leg over her opposite knee, shifting in her recliner. "Hypnosis is a bit like reprograming your subconscious mind. An infiltration if you will. We want to move things around a little, try to shake up the way you think and react. And in your case, remember."

"All right."

"The process is similar to meditation in the sense that you will enter an element of increased awareness. You'll be fully awake, but your mind will be hard at work—focused," she explains thoughtfully. "Almost like a trance-like state."

My eyes close slowly, then flutter back open. "I won't be unconscious?"

"No, not at all. You'll be in a state of profound concentration, but you'll also be aware of what's going on right here in this room. You'll be entirely present." She scribbles down a few more notes before continuing, "Are you ready to get started?"

"Yes, I think so."

"Very well." A silence settles into the room, the only sound being my heavy breaths and the slight whoosh of the ceiling fan. "Oliver, I'd like you focus on your breathing as you raise your right hand just above your head."

Perplexed, I do as she tells me, holding up my arm. I breathe in and out, concentrating on the way my chest rises and falls with each deep breath.

"Now, hold up your index finger and look at it. Concentrate on that finger, but don't lower your arm."

I stare at my finger.

"The longer you stare, it may seem like your other fingers are fading out, becoming a blur. You'll feel your arm getting heavier and heavier."

My arm begins to feel like it's been tied with bricks as my gaze centers on that lone finger, my breathing still controlled and steady.

"Keep focusing on your finger, Oliver. Feel your arm drifting down as it gets heavier," she says, her voice caught on an ocean wave. "Heavier..."

I'm drifting, weightless and light.

"Close your eyes now. Your arm is coming down, slowly... very slowly..."

My arm starts to slip, my mind fuzzy, eyes closing.

"Once your arm is fully relaxed, the rest of you will enter an intense state of relaxation. Let your arm continue to fall slowly. Let your mind fall with it, deeper and deeper...

I feel myself fading away.

"Deeper, deeper... deeper..."

"Why can't I be on your team, Syd?"

"Because Oliver and Sydney are always on the same team. You know this."

"Because I like him more than you!"

A flash.

I'm looking around the front yard and it's all a blur of motion and sound, laughter and squeals.

Mr. Neville and Travis are sharing a beer on the front porch.

Lorna Gibson is laughing with my mother.

Lorna's husband, Edgar, is circling the lawn with an old camera, taking photographs.

Something happened this day. I feel uncomfortable. My skin prickles with dread.

Dr. Malloy's soothing voice bleeds into my subconscious. "You've had a protective shield up, but now you have total recall at will. Reach in and peel away every block, every layer, everything that is keeping you from these important memories. When you feel the block returning, inhale a deep, slow breath, and that block will begin to fade."

I breathe in deep, but the moment slips. "I-I lost it..."

"Shh. Remembering is your only priority right now. There is no more struggle."

Suddenly, I'm standing in my kitchen. A different memory comes to life.

I'm crying. I'm sad. I'm screaming.

My mother tries to console me.

Her eyes are light brown, chestnut and copper.

Her eyes are like mine.

She's speaking, but I can't hear her words. I'm crying too hard.

I'm frantic.

"I'm scared."

"Sweetheart, tell me what's wrong. Tell me what happened."

I don't know. I don't know.

"You are retrieving new information. You have total recall at will. Everything you have seen or experienced is available to you. Everything you've heard or felt—it's right there," Dr. Malloy says.

I'm at the park with Sydney.

She's so beautiful, like sunshine and watermelon on a hot day.

I love watermelon.

I love her.

"I have a secret, but I'm scared to tell you."

"You can tell it to my teddy bear. She's very good at keeping secrets."

"Okay. You promise?"

"Promise. Pinky-swear, even."

Our pinkies connect, her smile bright like the little flecks of light in her eyes. I bring the teddy bear close to my lips and whisper, "He saw me. He saw me. He saw me."

The Faceless Man.

I shoot upright into a sitting position, clutching my head with both palms.

"It's okay, Oliver, it's okay. Take a deep breath," the doctor tells me, leaning forward with an outstretched hand. "Everything you just experienced is now available to you. You can retrieve this information at any time. It's a part of you now, and it always has been."

"I can't," I choke out, throwing my legs over the side of the sofa. "I... I must go now."

"Oliver, I promise you're okay," she insists gently. "If you need to stop, that is perfectly fine. I don't want you to be uncomfortable. Just know this is a safe place."

My body feels flush, my limbs tremoring. I glance at her before I reach for my jacket and make a clumsy escape to the exit door. "I don't think it is."

I'm looking through hundreds and hundreds of old comic book drawings from my years in captivity, my imagination my only companion, when Gabe pokes his head into the room. His eyes find me sitting on the floor, back pressed up to the foot of the bed.

"Hey, man. How did your appointment go today? Any breakthroughs?" he wonders with interest, hands set loosely on his hips.

My gaze lifts as I set the enormous stack of comics beside me on the carpet. "It was fairly intense. I'm not certain I want to remember everything," I admit, pulling my bottom lip between my teeth. I've been consumed with nerves and trepidation since I returned home a short while ago. "Gabe, do you recall anything harrowing occurring when we were children? An unsavory man lurking around the neighborhood, perhaps?"

A frown appears. "Shit, not that I remember. We had a good childhood."

My sigh meets his look of worry.

"What happened? Was it Bradford?" Gabe takes a few careful paces into the room, concern creasing the corners of his eyes. "You think he was stalking you before the abduction?"

"It's possible."

"The police seemed to think it was random and *not* premeditated. They couldn't link that fucker to you or your family in any way, shape, or form—there were zero connections."

"Yes, I know. They concluded that he spotted me at the park that evening and I reminded him of his deceased son, so he acted recklessly," I concur, recalling their statement with perfect clarity as my eyes avert to the wall across from me.

"But you're not so sure now…"

"I'm not sure of anything, I suppose. My mind is a maze."

And that is the sad truth. My hypnotherapy produced more questions than answers, leaving me frazzled and uncertain of anything. Some things are better left untouched, untampered with.

"Damn, Oliver. I can't imagine what you're feeling, having those memories trapped in there like that. Maybe a few more sessions will help pull more things to the surface," Gabe suggests, scratching at his overgrown hair while he fidgets a few feet away.

He's uncomfortable with genuine emotion, much like Sydney. But he tries with me, and I appreciate that. "Perhaps. I'm not entirely sure I want to revisit it, though."

He nods. "Understood. What we don't know, can't hurt us, right?"

"Indeed."

Another beat passes before Gabe clears his throat. "So, uh, Pops is stopping by for dinner tonight. You cool with that?"

"I'm certainly not opposed. I'll cook steaks," I offer. Gabe had mentioned that Travis might be stopping by at some point this weekend, so I picked up extra at the supermarket. "I'll start preparing."

"Dude, we can order pizza. That wasn't a backhanded request," he chuckles, watching as I stand from my place on the floor.

"It's no trouble. I need the distraction."

My gaze shifts to my bedroom window at the term *distraction*. Sydney's office is dark and unoccupied, pulling a sigh from my lips.

Gabe notices the gesture and clicks his tongue, knowingly. "Still trouble in paradise?"

"Yes, as there should be," I reply, shame woven into every syllable. "I nearly attacked her and frightened her half to death. She'll never trust me again."

The excruciating silence leads me to believe that Gabe has not been informed of our most recent predicament. I thought for certain Sydney would have confided in him.

I turn to my stepbrother, who is staring at me, wordless. "You didn't know?"

"No fucking clue what you're talking about."

"Oh."

Gabe's eyes narrow, trying to draw his own conclusions. "What do you mean you almost attacked her? You don't have a violent bone in your body, Oliver."

Linking my fingers behind my head, I begin pacing the room, anxiety overtaking me as I think back to the prior Saturday. I heave in a breath of regret. "I came to a very erroneous conclusion and reacted foolishly. I'll never forgive myself."

"What conclusion?"

My jaw tenses as my molars gnash together. "I started reading her provocative novels and thought, perhaps, she enjoyed being treated in a similar fashion."

He blinks. "Ah."

"Yes. I said some foul things that I can never take back."

"Like what?"

The memory sickens me and my stomach flips. "I told her she didn't want me sexually because she was afraid I couldn't... fuck her properly." My face heats, ashamed. "And then I pinned her up against a wall, like I've read about in quite a few of her stories and tried to kiss her."

Gabe's mouth hangs open as he absorbs my mortifying confession. "Well, shit. That's sort of hot. She wasn't into it?"

"Of course not." I send him a deep frown, appalled by his response. "I acted like a barbarian."

"You're probably overreacting. I mean, a lot of women love that shit."

"She was not at all impressed."

Gabe pushes his tongue against the side of his cheek, attempting to put together a masterful piece of advice that will ease my mind, I'm sure. "I guess there's always Tabitha."

He fails quite miserably.

My glare sinks into him as I release a groan. "Tabitha and I enjoyed our date, but we're better suited as friends. I can't pursue another female when my loyalty is with Sydney."

"Dude, there's no loyalty," Gabe insists, moving towards me. "You're not in a relationship. You can both fuck whoever you want."

"I don't want to be intimate with anyone else."

"Whatever, man," Gabe sighs, walking backwards, throwing his hands up. He's about to leave the room when he pauses in the entryway. "So, this is totally tacky, but... since you're not interested in Tabitha, can I be?"

"What?"

He wiggles his eyebrows at me, a sly grin in place. "She's a solid ten. I will send her a friend request *right now* if you give me permission. I'm a dick, I'm sorry, but that girl is incredible."

"How will you transmit a request for friendship?" I realize technology has advanced a great deal since my return, but relaying mind signals seems out of the realm of possibility.

"Facebook, Oliver. You'd know what I'm talking about if you logged in more than once. All you've posted is an off-centered picture of a blurry raccoon."

"I'm still getting acclimated to the camera feature."

"You also only have two friends, and they're both fake accounts."

"They told me I had funds available in a deceased relative's account that they would help me retrieve. It sounded promising."

A sharp laugh hits me. "You didn't even accept *my* friend request."

"You weren't offering me two-million dollars."

Another laugh that prompts my own.

Gabe is still smiling, waiting—impatiently hoping I'll give him some sort of permission to pursue a woman who does not belong to me. "Gabe, you are welcome to contact Tabitha. She seemed a bit smitten with you, anyway."

"Are you shitting me?"

"No. I saw her looking at you fondly, and then she blushed at the dinner table when I spoke of you."

He claps his hands together, palms scrubbing up and down, the smile never leaving his face. He points at me before retreating from the bedroom. "You're the man."

Poor Tabitha.

"This is fantastic, Oliver. Just phenomenal." Travis pulls a napkin from his shirt collar, using it to blot his mouth as he groans with satisfaction. "Did you make this garlic-butter marinade from scratch?"

"Yes, thank you. It's a fairly simple recipe."

Another sound of pleasure. "Fantastic," he repeats.

Clearing the dinner table as Gabe and Travis discuss an upcoming golf retreat, I feel a vibration within my front pocket. I startle, almost dropping a dish. I hardly receive phone calls or text messages unless it's the media attempting to set up an interview that I'm still unprepared for, or Sydney—but even she has been silent lately.

I understand, of course, but the aching void inside of me yearns to hear her voice, hold her hand, and watch her eyes light up like blue skies on ocean waves.

An electronic message greets me as I glance at the screen, and I fumble for a breath when her name stares back at me.

Sydney: *I miss you. So much. I'm not mad at you, not at all, not ever. Please, let's talk. I'm working at the club tonight, but hopefully you have some free time tomorrow. xoxo, Syd*

My mouth feels dry as my eyes case the digital message about a dozen times. Tongue stuck to the roof of my mouth, air trapped in my lungs, heart swelling with hope, I turn to Gabe, who is still conversing with his father over the table. "Are you busy tonight?"

Twisting in his seat, Gabe meets my flustered stance in the center of the kitchen. He blinks twice, processing my question, his elbow hanging over the back of the chair. "Busy, as in, you want to hang out? Catch a movie or something?"

"Not exactly. I was considering venturing out to that social establishment Sydney works at..."

His eyebrows lift to his hairline. "No shit? Ready to mingle with some foxy ladies?"

I fidget at his cheeky wink. "Just one, actually."

"She's working tonight, isn't she?" Gabe sighs.

"Yes."

Travis pops a piece of chewing gum into his mouth as he rises from the dining room chair, making his way to the liquor cabinet. A baritone chuckles rumbles between us. "You know, Oliver, you're a handsome young man. Gabe tells me you've been a bit gaga over that Neville girl and he's worried you're going to get your heart broken. There's a whole lot of fish in the sea—maybe you should swim a little farther than the house next door."

I'm unable to prevent the scowl I throw in Gabe's direction, knowing he's been discussing my romantic entanglements with his father. Gabe swirls back around in his chair, tail between his legs. With a quick clear of my throat, I finally set the dirty dishware into the sink and address my stepfather. "I appreciate your concern, but I'm very fond of this one fish in particular."

Clinking glass sounds behind me as I switch on the faucet to rinse the plates and Travis hums a jaunty tune whilst preparing his beverage. "I understand the appeal, son."

Son. He's never called me that before.

"However, I'm inclined to agree with my boy on this one. That girl has always been spirited, and I worry she's going to shake you up and leave you rattled."

"I'm uncertain why everyone considers me to be so breakable. I survived in a basement for over two decades with not much more than a sleeping bag, a bucket, and a lifetime supply of *Chef Boyardee.*" My back is all that faces the two men across the room, so I don't see their expressions when I deliver the bold statement. "I'm not nearly as fragile as you all seem to think I am."

The ensuing silence runs in time with the water filling up the sink.

Gabe cuts in after a few heavy beats. "You know, you're absolutely right. You're a grown ass man and a survivor to boot. We just worry about you, bud."

217

Twisting off the faucet and drying my hands on a holiday dish towel, I finally spin to face them. Travis is leaning back against the counter, rim of a whiskey glass pressed to his lips, his posture rigid. Gabe greets me with a flash of white teeth, his demeanor matching his words. "I appreciate that. Thank you."

"And hell yeah, let's hit the club tonight. Maybe I can convince Tabitha to be my date for the evening," Gabe declares with a playful waggle of his dark blonde brows. "We're already messaging back and forth. There's mad chemistry."

"You do recall she has a child, yes?"

His face blanches slightly as his eyes pin just over my shoulder, his mind likely envisioning all the ways that could end in disaster.

Travis intervenes, tipping his glass back and finishing the liquor with an easy swallow. "Well, I'll head out and allow you boys to make your questionable life choices."

"Thanks for your unwavering confidence," Gabe jabs back, though, his tone is light.

They share a grin. Travis paces through the kitchen to set his glass in the soapy sink, turning to me before he moves away. A strong hand plants against my shoulder with a squeeze. "You know my door is always open, son. If you need a place to stay to get back on your feet, we have plenty of room, as well as the financial means to assist you. Maybe a change of scenery would be good for you."

I'm not sure why I flinch back, but the thought of leaving my comfortable routine here with Gabe, leaving *Sydney*, is a notion I can't bear to fathom. Travis is family, yes, but we hardly know each other. My stomach feels unsettled. "That's kind of you. I'll think about it."

A tight smile meets my weary expression, his hand falling. "And your comics, Oliver... that's money right there. You should think about selling them."

"Beg your pardon?"

"People would pay top dollar for those. You're national news—your story is still trending all over social media and it's been ten months since you escaped. Not to mention, they're incredible. Gabe sent me a few pictures of them."

I take a step back, lowering my eyes to the kitchen tiles. "I could never sell them. They're a part of me."

"They *were* a part of you. Letting go and moving on is a necessary step in the healing process," Travis explains, his whiskey breath wafting around us. "Please think about my offer. I'm a businessman, Oliver. If anyone can help you reach your goals and get out of this rut, it's me."

A slap against my bicep has me wincing again as Travis pulls back, his smile leaving with him.

Live with Travis.

Preposterous.

He may have had some points in terms of financial benefit—after all, my library pay is hardly going to support me forever, much less allow me to purchase a vehicle or think about moving out and providing for myself.

And I'm certain, despite his claims otherwise, Gabe is looking forward to the day he has his privacy and space again. He'll likely want to settle down with a woman soon—possibly with Tabitha, who has a small child —and my presence here will only complicate matters.

I suppose a temporary stay wouldn't be the end of the world if it means securing myself a more comfortable future.

Live with Travis.

Preposterous... *right?*

CHAPTER TWENTY-THREE

SYDNEY

CLEM: *I LOVE YOU, SIS. I'm sorry. Tell Oliver I'm so sorry... I promise my reaction had nothing to do with him personally. Call me soon. :o)*

The relief that flows through me when my sister's message pops up on my cell phone has me fumbling with a shot glass, unable to maintain my grip as it smashes beneath the bar counter. "Shit," I mutter, earning a worried frown from both Brant and Rebecca.

All three of us were put on the schedule tonight in anticipation of a pre-Christmas rush, but the snowstorm must have scared potential patrons away. We aren't nearly as busy as Marco predicted.

"You okay over there, Neville?" Brant hollers as he mixes a Whiskey Sour. Amber eyes drift over to the broom I just snatched up. He glances back down at the cocktail, nailing the ratio as always. "You seem jumpy."

Emptying the shards glass into a trashcan, I spare him a quick look. "Just a lot going on. You know me—I'm always a mess."

Rebecca chimes in, reaching for the bottle of Blue Label worth more than my car payment. "A cute mess."

"If by cute you mean it took me three days to finally shower, not to mention, my eyes are still swollen from crying over *Boy Meets World* reruns, then cool."

"Shit," she sniggers, her green-haired head swinging back and forth. "You pregnant?"

A snort meets her amused expression. "Yeah, right."

That would be impossible. I haven't even had sex since...

Wow, how long *has* it been? Months? A hell of a lot of months? I haven't been keeping track, but it feels like forever.

And then my belly flutters when I realize exactly how long it's been.

Ten months.

Since he came back.

As soon as the realization dawns, a feeling sweeps over me—a strange tickle, a whisper on my swiftly heating skin, like someone is breathing down the back of my neck. It pulls my chin up from my chest, my gaze landing straight ahead to where Oliver Lynch is standing, hands in his pockets, hair an untamed mess of waves and curls, his eyes fixed on me.

I fucking *felt* him.

It takes an embarrassing amount of time to notice Gabe standing beside him, waving stupidly, a familiar-looking brunette attached to his hip. My hand lifts in a lazy wave as I watch the three of them approach the bar, Oliver's sunset stare never drifting from my slack-jawed face.

A pinch to my hip interrupts my trance and Brant chuckles as he passes me to fetch a rag. "I repeat: *jumpy.*"

"I prefer *aware of my surroundings.*"

He shoots me a humored side-eye. "Looks like your surroundings are equally aware of you."

I tug my lip between my teeth, biting down hard as Oliver slides up in front of me, a tender smile stretching on his mouth. His dimples bloom to life, his gaze glittering, his nearness alone wrapping me up in the warm hug I've been craving all week.

Drinking him in with zero apologies, I can't help but appreciate his too-tight slate gray t-shirt with three little buttons popped open to reveal a light dusting of chest hair. The muscles in his arms flex, his eyes flaring with gold flames as he reacts to my blatant awareness of him. It feels like a shot of adrenaline and whiskey to my blood. I reach deep inside to find my missing voice. "Oliver..." I say in the most pathetic, longing breath. "What are you doing here?"

Those dimples blossom even more as he situates himself on a bar stool, eyes darting around curiously before focusing on me. "I couldn't wait until tomorrow."

I'm swooning. And it's so obvious I'm swooning, I swear everyone in the club is staring at me, pointing, laughing at the swooning girl who forgot how to talk again.

"Stop swooning." Rebecca's words are whispered jokingly into my ear, so only I can hear them.

Dammit.

Gabe finally catches my eyes, one eyebrow arched with a gallon of judgment, his arm draped around his date. She's astoundingly pretty with delicate features, shampoo-commercial hair, and alabaster skin. Her smile flashes brighter than the DJ lights.

"This is Tabitha," Gabe introduces, removing his arm from her off-the-shoulder mustard sweater and leaning forward on his elbows. "She doesn't know this yet, but I'm planning on proposing. The wedding is all planned out, a total fairytale, but I'm stumped on what kind of ring to get her. Does she seem like a princess-cut kind of a girl? Or maybe one of those rose-gold diamonds? Rose-gold is trending, right?"

Tabitha's face is buried between her palms, her body shaking with laughter.

"You see, this is only our first date, so I don't know her all that well yet. But we have our whole lives ahead of us, you know?" he finishes with a wink, giving her arm a playful nudge.

My chin is propped up on my palm, my own giggles mingling with Tabitha's. "You're such a dork," I tease, watching as a rosy flush stains the apples of the woman's cheeks when she lowers her hands. I realize then that she's the girl from *The Matchmaker* case, as well as Oliver's date from the week before. She looks shy, a little guarded, and her eyes hide more secrets than I'll ever want to know, but I can tell she's smitten.

The two of them share a sweet look, Gabe's megawatt grin meeting Tabitha's big, brown eyes, her lashes fluttering with bashful adoration. There's definitely something there, and it makes my heart twist with hope. Gabe deserves this.

This may be their first date, but I'm confident it won't be their last.

Meanwhile, poor Oliver is studying the drink menu like he's reading an introduction into brain surgery. I glide down the bar, deciding I should start actually working before my boss sees me slacking off and scolds me. "What can I get for you, Oliver?"

He sets the menu down, eyes lifting until he finds my baby blues. They seem to steal his breath for one blissful moment. "Oh, um, this strawberry creation looks rather good. It comes with a little fruit medley."

His eyes twinkle with authentic joy.

Over a fruit skewer.

"God, I love you."

The three words tumble off my tongue, unexpected, spontaneous—a potent proclamation. A weight that sinks me, *sinks me*, until I'm swallowed whole, struggling for air.

A gasp follows, his and mine, and for a moment I forget we're staring at each other in a crowded nightclub. The music dies out, the laughter, the voices, the noise; it's drowning, right along with me, and then I'm lying on that grassy hill with Oliver and we are gazing up at the starry night sky, watching the fireworks.

"Should I make a wish?" I wonder, my voice sprinkled with magic.

"You make wishes on falling stars, Syd. Not fireworks."

"Says who?"

"I dunno. No one, I guess."

I pucker my lips, deep in thought. "I make wishes on birthday candles and dandelion seeds. Fireworks can reach higher than those."

We're shoulder to shoulder, our faces alight with radiant colors as the fireworks burst to life above us.

"What do you mean, higher?"

"You know, for the man who grants our wishes. He lives in the sky."

Oliver appears dumbfounded. "Really?"

"Maybe."

"You should make a wish, then."

Our heads twist at the same time, and we're face-to-face.

"Okay."

His eyes are glowing with reds and blues and purples. "What's your wish?"

"I should write it down. Then it will definitely come true."

"So write it down."

I blink myself back to reality, shutting the lid on my box of reveries.

There's no need to reminisce the past, or get swept up in another life, or stress about the *what might have beens*, because the look in Oliver's eyes tells me all I need to know.

My wish came true.

"Come on, Neville, spill it. You're distracted and unfocused," Brant says to me an hour later as I'm struggling to ring up a complicated order. He's not angry or annoyed—he's concerned.

I blow out a breath, my hair dancing along with it, and pause to gather my bearings. I've been trying to stay professional all evening, but Oliver hasn't left the bar, despite Gabe's admirable efforts to get him on the dance floor or pull him over to a table. He's waiting for me to get off work so we can talk, and then I'll be forced to elaborate on those three friendship-changing words, and all my feelings will bubble over, and I won't know what to do.

My eyes scan the crowd, envious of the way Gabe and Tabitha make it look so *easy*. They're dancing like fools without a care in the world, and they clearly have the worst moves out of everyone on the dance floor—but they also have the biggest smiles, and that's what counts.

With a final sigh, slamming the cash register closed, I glance towards Brant. "Remember when you said I wore my heart in my eyes?"

He flashes me a knowing smirk. "Let me guess. Your heart is sitting two stools to the left on his third Strawberry Daiquiri, looking like he's working up the courage to ask you to Prom."

I blush through a slow blink. "You are freakishly observant."

"Told you I'm good at reading the room." Brant crosses his arms, a grin lifting as he deliberates his next move. It doesn't take long for him to add, "Get out of here, Syd. The heart is waiting."

"What?" I'm puzzled by his order, my brows pulling together. "I'm scheduled until eleven."

"You're scheduled until now. I rank you."

Not that I'm complaining, but, "What grounds?"

"Seniority. Also, I make a way better Long Island than you."

Mock horror. "Heinous lies."

"Go," he grins, giving my shoulder a friendly punch. "It's dead tonight, anyway. Rebecca and I are more than capable."

Reaching out to squeeze his forearm, I mouth 'thank you' as I back away, eyes shining bright with glimmering gratitude. Spinning around, my heart climbing its way into my throat and setting up shop, I discover Oliver slurping the last few sips of his Daiquiri through the straw.

He's so cute.

"Hey, handsome. I have good news," I say, leaning forward on folded arms, not missing the way his gaze hovers on the peaks of my breasts before trailing upward.

Slowly. Very slowly.

"You think I'm handsome?" he beams.

His goofy grin and sluggish stare carry me to one conclusion: he's buzzed.

So goddamn cute.

"I do," I tell him, unable to scrub the flirtatious inflection from my tone. "Very handsome. You're also sweet, generous, smart, loyal, and brave, amongst a thousand other things."

"I'm quite good at *Boggle*."

A laugh clears my lips, mixed with an unfeminine snort, and my arms take the brunt of my forehead. When I raise my head, Oliver is dimpled and doe-eyed. I look around for his Cupid's arrow, but I can't seem to find it—it's probably already lodged inside my heart. "You're also good at sucking down alcohol-infused strawberry slush."

"It's delicious, and I enjoyed the fruit salad garnish quite a bit," he tells me, slouching forward ever so slightly, our noses almost touching across the counter. "You have an impressive knack for food art, Sydney Neville."

"Shit. I found my calling."

"I would certainly support that creative endeavor."

Four inches. Four inches is all it would take to feel his lips on mine.

I shake the thought away. "So, my good news is that I'm off the clock. Brant sent me home early."

"You can depart?"

"I can depart." Standing up straight, I grab my purse from beneath the bar and sling it over my shoulder. I'm around the counter in no time, waving my goodbyes to Brant and Rebecca and reaching for Oliver's hand. "Ready?"

A mischievous sparkle inhabits his eyes. "One thing, first," he drawls, taking my outstretched palm in his and pulling me in the opposite direction. "A dance."

"Oliver, no, that's the rum talking." A comical squeal erupts from my lips as he ignores my protests and drags me onto the floor, which is bathed in strobe lights and writhing bodies. "You've seen me dance, right? It's not okay."

"And you've certainly seen my two left feet. We can look foolish together," he says, his smile never leaving, only growing.

Gabe sidles up beside us, glazed in sweat, Tabitha pressed against him with heated cheeks, both of them wrapped up in each other and drunk on pure happiness. "Fuck yeah, Oliver," he calls over, cupping his hands around his mouth and giving us a whoop. He pumps his fist into the air, then follows it up with a whistle, garnering the attention of fellow patrons.

All four of us laugh, candid, without constraint, and I know this moment will stand out in my mind for the rest of my life. Me and my boys—my sweet, beautiful men, smiling and alive, *together*, vibrating with genuine joy. The last two decades wash away like a message in a bottle; the one that housed a desperate plea from inside my heart, a letter to the man in the sky, holding my wishes in his capable hands.

Wishes that all boiled down to *one* wish, written a thousand different ways.

When Oliver's arms encircle me, boldly pulling me to his chest, I lose the fight I had no intention of winning. I collapse against him, my own happiness invading every little piece I've purposely left empty and hollow for far too many years. Those pieces were left for him.

Only him.

I hug him fiercely, hands linking behind his back as I inhale his woodsy, cedar cologne and the soap on his skin, clean and invigorating. Everyone is dancing around us, flailing and laughing to the upbeat song, and we are sinking, swaying, slow-sailing, swallowed up in the mere existence of one another.

I glance up at him, chin to his chest, already knowing I'd find him staring down at me with those chestnut-spun eyes. "Oliver..."

"Don't, Syd." Oliver threads his fingers through my hair, his nails lightly skimming my scalp. We undulate to the music, but it's our own kind of music—the kind we make together. The smile he casts down on me is the beautiful crescendo. "Just let me hold you."

A whispery breath leaves me on unsteady legs, my arms and heart clinging tighter than ever before. "I'm hard to hold," I confess, my words pulled from the coil of fear inside of me.

But Oliver's smile only swells as he lowers my cheek to his chest, his palm still cradling the back of my head like I am cherished—like I am *his* missing piece. "Nothing worth holding is ever too hard."

It's not long before we're stumbling through Oliver's front door, both buzzing—him on Daiquiris, me on *him*—peeling off our snow-covered coats and making our way upstairs. I know we won't be able to talk tonight. It's late, we're tired, and Oliver is tipsy, having spent the entire drive home educating me with random, useless facts, such as: *"Did you know the word 'set' contains the most definitions in the English dictionary?"*

He then began to list them all. I had to stop him at one-hundred-something.

Oliver collapses onto his bed when we find our way to his room, and I linger in the doorway, wondering if I should leave or lie down with him. In the one minute it takes for me to decide to stay, Oliver already looks fast asleep, resting peacefully beneath his comforter.

I take the liberty of changing into one of his t-shirts for comfort purposes, folding my clubwear into a neat pile on his dresser, plucking off my earrings, and cautiously climbing into bed beside him. He doesn't flinch when I scoot closer, my back to his chest, curled into him with my knees drawn up. His steady breaths and the heat from his skin warms me as I drift away.

Before sleep fully takes me over, I feel his arm encircle my waist, tugging me towards him until we're shamelessly spooning. Oliver's mouth meets the nape of my neck, the shivers running rampant as he whispers goodnight, snuggling me closer.

Holding me.

I'm not sure what wakes me, but it sounds an awful lot like Gabe's voice. Blinking away my dreamland, it takes a moment for me to process the fact that I'm not in my own bed—I'm in Oliver's bed, and it *was* Gabe I heard.

His voice trails off down the hallway on the opposite side of the door, seemingly having just returned home from the club. Then I realize that a reassuring weight has been removed from me, and I jerk around, looking for Oliver.

Our eyes meet through the hazy cloak of darkness. He's sitting up, his back against the headboard. "Oliver?" My voice is raspy, groggy, curious, as I pull myself up on my haunches. "You're awake?"

I can just make out his smile. "Yes. A dream startled me, and I wasn't able to fall back to sleep. I decided to sit here and think, instead."

Glancing at my cell phone through squinted eyes, I note that it's almost two A.M. Oliver's t-shirt is riding up my hips, so I tug it down, turning back towards him. "What were you thinking about?"

"Athena," he answers easily.

I'm charmed. "You miss her, huh?"

"Yes. She was a good friend to me."

Sliding further across the bed, I sit up along with him, so we're eye-to-eye. My glasses are discarded on his nightstand, but the closer I get, the better I can see him. His smile still lingers, his body stiffening slightly as I lessen our gap. "Thank you for coming to see me tonight. I know large crowds and noise make you anxious, so it means a lot that you were there."

A pause before he nods, gaze drifting away from me. "I wasn't sure if you wanted to see me after..." His Adam's apple bobs with worry. "After my behavior last week."

"Oliver, I'm not upset with you. I was just startled because I knew that wasn't *you*," I tell him with urgency, moving in even closer, my hand reaching for his. "I don't want you to ever feel like you need to change—not for me, not for anyone. You're perfect the way you are."

His fingers curl around mine, and I think I'm being drawn to him, pulled in closer, either by him or myself or an invisible force that turned us into magnets. Oliver grazes a hand up my arm, so delicately, causing goosebumps to flourish.

"For so long, I was just a name carved into a stone wall. I was a picture on paper, created by my own muddled mind," he confesses, and there's anguish woven into his words, evidence of his years of loneliness. But then his eyes find their way back to mine, and I see a shift. I see hope. "You make me feel like I'm... *someone*."

"You *are* someone, Oliver. You always have been." The tears hit hard, and there is no shame in them. Only love, so much goddamn love, a love I've been holding inside me for nearly all of my life. I choke on the words that spill out of me. "When I was five-years-old, I gave you my heart on your front porch, and you gave me an oatmeal cookie, and I've thought about that moment every single day for over two decades. Even when you were gone, you still held my heart."

"I'm not gone anymore, Syd." His palms find my face, clasping my cheeks, tears slipping through his fingers. "I'm right here, with you, and I'm still holding onto your heart. Please don't ask me to give it back."

A tiny sob breaks free, and I kiss him.

I kiss him because I *have* to, because it's the only choice, because it's the only thing left to do. I'm on my knees, clutching his t-shirt as I melt into him, his hands still cupping my jaw as our mouths lock. I feel his groan, I taste it, our lips parting to let the other inside. His tongue sweeps across my own, a trace of strawberries fused with passion, and that passion begins to mount and climb when one hand lowers to palm my breast through the thin layer of cotton. The heartfelt moment turns into a lust-filled haze, my body arching into him on instinct, our tongues starved.

I pull back to breathe, my body trembling as I kneel beside him, my fingers white-knuckled, gripping his shirt. "Oliver..." A familiar fear trickles in while I gaze into his eyes that are crackling with fevered flames, knowing this will change everything. *Terrified* this will change everything.

Our beautiful dynamic. Our precious friendship.

When I hold him at arm's length, it's so much easier to keep his heart safe and protected.

"Oliver, I'm scared," I admit, baring my weakness as I drop my forehead to his.

"I'm not." He brings me closer until my leg lifts on its own accord, and I'm in his lap. "I *ache* for you, Sydney," Oliver rasps, one hand curling behind my head, fisting my hair. "I crave to be inside you more than I craved freedom in all of those twenty-two years combined."

Holy hell. I feel my ovaries spontaneously fertilizing.

"God…" I whimper, wrought with need, our groins melded together as I straddle him. I can't help my hips from swiveling, grinding, begging for friction. "You can't say things like that."

"Why not?"

Our lips touch, just barely, and I breathe more words against them. "Because… my willpower is hanging by a flimsy thread, and I swear I'm only one longing look, one touch, one more fucked-up, glorious truth away from throwing logic out the window and never looking back."

"There is no logic in the way our hearts beat, Sydney. Only magic."

"Oliver…"

"Tell me how to break that thread."

My willpower turns to dust when his tongue pokes out to trace my lips, lips that are nearly quivering, a seductive request for entry.

I open, I accept, I squash my fears and doubts and insecurities and kiss him hard.

I break the goddamn thread.

He feels my surrender when our tongues meet again with renewed fervor. I sense it in the way his body trembles, his hands going rogue and casing my curves, desperate to explore the unknown. I hear it in the moan he releases into my mouth when the heat between my thighs presses into his rock-hard erection.

Our mouths part so I can yank his shirt up over his head, fingers splaying over his chest as I fall back down, his mouth catching me. I'm grinding, scratching, mewling, his hands dipping beneath the hem of my shirt until they find my bare breasts. He cups them, palming with urgency, his thumbs circling the tight nipples. I'm making sounds I've never heard before as Oliver touches me, and I reach down to pull my own shirt off, hair falling down in waves, my body finally exposed to him. His eyes blaze with something primal, a wildfire, and it spreads between us fast and furious. Instantly, he leans in, taking my breast in his mouth, then the other, his tongue swirling each nipple and making my underwear flood with my need for him.

And then it's a desperate race to discard our final barriers. I move back to fumble with his belt buckle, fingers shaking with blind lust as Oliver tangles his hands in my hair like he's unable to let me go for even a second. When I unlatch the belt and unzip him, I start pulling down his pants and boxers, bunching them at his knees as he lifts his hips to assist me.

His cock springs free, and my *God*, he's beautiful. Big, thick, fully hard and *aching* for me. I can't help but wrap my hand around his length, giving him a tug as I graze my thumb along the wet tip. Oliver's head drops back against the headboard, his groan mingling with mine, and while there are so many things I want to do to him right now, I can't go another minute without feeling him inside me.

I release him, yanking off my panties and scooting forward until I'm centered right above the tip of his cock. It teases my core, an exquisite torture, as our eyes meet through a fog of fire and frenzy. Oliver's hand curves around my neck, pulling our lips back together, while my own hands sift through his mess of hair.

Hips twirling, I rub my clit against his erection, the desire coiling low and deep, causing his own hips to jerk up, his grip on me tightening. "God, Sydney... please."

"You're sure?" I murmur, words intertwining with my needy gasps, my lips trailing kisses along his jaw.

Oliver responds by lining himself up with my entrance, slipping inside just barely, only an agonizing inch, ripping a shameless whimper from my throat. He hesitates, though, his eyes flaring. "I... I don't have a contraceptive," he says, his voice low and strained, his urge to thrust all the way in hardly controlled.

"I'm on the pill," I reply, my voice no different. "I'm safe. It's okay."

A hiss pushes past his clenched teeth when I reach between us to grip his cock, gliding it over my wetness before lowering myself onto him. We both watch as I sink down, taking him inside me, stealing his virtue inch by inch. The image is the most erotic thing I've ever seen, and I fucking almost come undone right then and there, with Oliver's drawn-out groan carrying me to the finish line. But I hold it back, biting my lip as our pelvises finally meet and he's buried to the hilt. "Fuck..." I whisper, strangled and unhinged.

This seems to trigger something in him, and his hands are instantly clutching my waist, fingers digging into me as he begins to pump his hips.

Lifting up, I slide back down, harder than before, then do it again. And again. Faster, needier, driven by all-consuming hunger. A lifetime of longing and yearning and *missing him*. I need him closer, closer than ever, desperate to feel every single piece he's willing to give. Every inch of skin that's warm and alive, beating heart, blood pumping.

Tugging his face to my chest, I increase my pace, feeling his cock filling me, stretching me, as his arms wrap around my back and cling tight. I know I should be gentle; I should go slow. We need to savor this moment, but *God*, I can't... I *can't*. There's no foreplay, no sweet caresses, no thought to the fact that I'm taking his virginity, and with that, should come tender restraint.

But I can't hold back, and neither can he.

We both start spinning, drowning, our bodies crashing together, flesh against flesh, and we aren't quiet—*at all*.

One hand fisting his hair, the other clutching the bedpost for leverage, I ride him hard, fast, and unrelenting. His face is buried between my breasts, stifling his moans, as the headboard slams into the wall over and over again.

Oliver's hand slides up my spine, landing in my sweat-soaked hair, and he lifts his chin to find me amidst this poetic mayhem. He wants to make sure I'm still here—that I'm *with* him.

And I am, I am, I am.

"Tell me again," he chokes out, mustering a breath amongst our thrusts and moans, skin slicked, air scarce. "Please."

Eyes joined in a poignant clutch, I already know what he's asking for. I know exactly what he wants to hear, and I say the words without hesitation, without a single second thought. "I love you," I whisper against his lips.

Oliver crushes his mouth to mine, as if he's trying to inhale those words, suck them down, so they live inside of him forever—so he's never lonely again. My hips slow, just a bit, our tongues moving in time with languid strokes. I feel the sparks igniting in my core, begging to burst, and it's at that moment Oliver pulls back from my mouth, his eyes closed tight.

"Syd, I... I want you to..." He squeezes me, one hand clasping my hipbone, the other knotted in my hair. "I'm not certain how much longer I can..."

"Me, too." I grind my pelvis into him, bringing myself closer, both of our bodies shuddering, right on the edge. It's when he tugs me down and buries his face into my neck, nicking and sucking, hardly hanging on, I shatter. "God, Oliver..."

My shameless moaning stimulates his own release, and Oliver tenses up, pulsating inside me, clutching me as close as he possibly can. His throaty groan meets the curve of my neck, and I tug his hair between my fingers, holding on while I buck against him, riding out the waves of ecstasy.

We come down at the same time, breathless. Hearts beating fast, lungs burning, limbs weightless. I soften my grip on his curls, sweeping my fingers through the damp strands and kissing the top of his head. As we process our feelings, thoughts, the heavy weight of our lovemaking, I inch back to find his eyes.

They are glazed over, burning bright, and smiling into mine.

"I love you, Oliver Lynch."

I say his name, I say it loud and clear, because he *is* real—he *is* someone.

He is everything to me.

CHAPTER TWENTY-FOUR

OLIVER

W HEN THE SUN TICKLES MY EYELIDS the following morning, I'm startled to find myself in bed, entangled with another warm body. I nuzzle closer, my lips grazing against champagne hair smelling of orchids and springtime, blending with the heady musk of sweat and... *me*.

Blinking, my body stirs to life, my senses firing as memories flood me.

Sydney.

My arm is draped around her middle, her skin exposed and bathed in a sparkling sunbeam leaking in through the curtains. One of my legs is caught between hers, her backside pressed into my pelvis, her left hand cradling mine as the other rests beneath her cheek. We are perfectly entwined, content, and connected on a wavelength that surpasses physicality.

I can't believe I had sex.

I can't believe I had sex with *her*—this beautiful woman, vivacious and free. She gave herself to me, mind, body, and soul. She told me she loved me.

Sydney *loves* me.

And I love her, so entirely, so painfully... I always have. I tell her in the way I hold her, in the way I look at her, in the way I say her name. She is my favorite part of me.

Not wanting to rouse her as she sleeps so peacefully, I carefully unravel myself and slip from the bed undetected. Before I step out to make her breakfast, I lift the bedsheet over her slumbering form, covering her, my skin warming as I think back to the prior evening.

The words said, the way she felt, the love we made.

After freshening up, Sydney climbed back into bed beside me in only her underwear, her breasts flush with my chest, making it very difficult to fall back to sleep. All I wanted to do was explore her, revisit every curve of her body, every moan that slipped from between her lips.

But she dozed off instantly, having never looked so content. Her head was perched within the crook of my shoulder, her steady puffs of breath a solace to my heart, and I know it was a night I will not soon forget.

It was the best night of my life.

Pacing softly from the bedroom, I close the door with caution and venture into the kitchen to prepare Sydney breakfast. I don't have much to offer in terms of spoiling her, but I know she enjoys my cooking. When I approach the refrigerator to peruse the ingredients on hand, I sense a presence from behind me.

Turning around, I'm greeted by both Gabe and Tabitha, staring at me with knowing smiles, sitting at the dining table eating doughnuts while sipping on coffee. "Oh, I'm sorry to interrupt. Good morning."

"Morning," Gabe says, his voice much more chipper than it normally is in the early hours. He winks at me mid-chew.

Tabitha's cheeks redden as she ducks her head, picking at the little cardboard heat protectant around the coffee cup. "Hi, Oliver. Gabe and I were up all night talking," she tells me through a modest laugh. "We didn't, um... you know..."

"I see," I nod, wondering why she feels the need to reassure me. Possibly due to our talk over supper—or, more specifically, how she told me she's taking her time with new courtships. But I am not one to judge. Clearing my throat through the awkwardness, I respond, "Sydney and I... well, we..."

They reply in unison: "We know."

Oh.

My own cheeks surely color at the insinuation. Sydney and I did not exactly hold back with our indulgence, nor did we consider the other occupants in the house. I understand now why Gabe and his lady friends were always so vocal. "My apologies for our rudeness," I mutter sheepishly, twisting back around to the refrigerator in an attempt to hide.

I go about fixing breakfast, a heart-shaped omelet with a side of fresh strawberries and bananas, and a serving of hash browns. Bits and pieces of Gabe and Tabitha's conversation filter through my ears while I plate the food, mostly of her explaining to him that she needs to get home to Hope, who is with her parents—apparently, they drove in from Utah to stay for the holidays. Gabe thanks her for the wonderful evening, and there is genuine longing in his voice, something I recognize more than I can say. He likes her, truly. She is different from all the others, and that makes me intensely happy for the both of them.

I don't miss the taunting eyebrow wiggle Gabe throws at me when I exit the kitchen with two full plates, and I'm certain he'll be pressing me for details later once both women have departed.

Pushing quietly into the bedroom, I find Sydney still curled beneath the comforter, only now, she's wearing my t-shirt. She rolls over to face me when the door creaks open, a smile blossoming as our eyes meet. "You're awake," I grin back, closing the door with my heel.

Sydney stretches out her limbs, kicking off the blanket to reveal her exposed legs. "Yep. I figured you either ditched me or got up to make breakfast. I was leaning towards the latter when I smelled eggs." Her eyes sparkle with amusement as she pats the mattress beside her. "Come. Feed me."

"Which part first?"

She stares at me, processing the question. Then she laughs with a snort, cupping her hand over her mouth and shaking her head at my folly. I'm relieved to discover that our easy humor has not been lost, despite the lines we bridged.

I climb across the bed on my knees, handing her one of the plates. "You're more covered than I had hoped," I tease, my gaze giving her a full sweep. Her hair is a tangled mess, her under eyes smudged with makeup, her one knee elevating and causing the t-shirt to ride up her thighs. I swallow, recalling how it felt to be right in between those thighs. "You're beautiful, Syd."

Sydney grips the plate between her hands, breath catching at my words. "You're not so bad yourself, Oliver. I wish I could look like you first thing in the morning." Her blue stare rakes over me with appreciation.

I blink. "Like a man?"

"No!" Her laughter bubbles over and she throws her head back against the headboard. "God, stop making me laugh. I have to pee. I mean, you still look hot as hell, where I look like I just battled my way through *The Ten Plagues of Egypt.*"

"You wear your boils rather well."

A hand swats at my shoulder, more laughter invading my ears before she glances down at the food she's holding. She pauses, momentarily entranced by the breakfast. "It's shaped like a heart."

"Yes," I concur, inching my way closer until we're shoulder to shoulder. "Do you like it?"

In a flash, her plate is set aside, her arms encasing my neck with an eager embrace, and we both fall to the mattress as she buries her face into my neck. "You're the sweetest man. I don't deserve you."

Lying back on the bed, Sydney sprawled out on top of me, I cup her face between my hands and lift her gaze to mine. "You always deserve what is meant for you, and if anything is meant to be, it's us," I tell her earnestly, with whispered passion, my thumbs drifting over her cheekbones.

"You're too good to me," she croaks back.

In a bold move, not allowing myself to think, I flip us over until Sydney is caught beneath me, hair splayed across the blue blanket, sunshine on water. Her eyes pop open at the maneuver, her lips following with a gasping sigh when my fingers graze down her abdomen to slip inside her underwear. Lowering my mouth to her ear, I whisper, "I want you to teach me everything. How to touch you, taste you, worship you." My fingers sweep over her wet heat, two of them entering her while my thumb circles her most sensitive area. Sydney arches off the bed, hands latching onto my hair, her eyes closed tight. Her reaction has my nether regions tenting my sweatpants, throbbing and yearning to replace my fingers. "You enjoy this?"

"Yes… God, yes." She bucks against my hand, begging for more. "Right there…"

I'm not an expert on sexual foreplay, nor on the female anatomy in general, but I've read books. I've looked at magazines.

When I entered my teenaged years, Bradford brought me stacks of magazines to look at, telling me that I would know what to do. My body responded appropriately, intrigued and curious as I flipped through the explicit photographs. And when I discovered video reenactments on Gabe's computer after my return, much like those pictures in the magazines, my curiosity only heightened. My sexual appetite began to grow. I envisioned Sydney often when I explored my own body, imagining *her* as the women in the footage.

I never expected those fantasies to come to life.

Nipping her earlobe with my teeth, I pump my fingers faster, circling my thumb with further pressure. My breath is hot against her ear, my arousal almost painful. Watching her buckle and writhe underneath me, *because* of me, is the most sensual thing I have ever experienced.

"You're incredible, Syd..." I breathe into her neck, trying to remain focused on pleasuring her, instead of on the aching erection between my legs. She is moaning, thrashing, wanton and ready to break. I fist her hair with my opposite hand. "Do you like the way I touch you?"

An undecipherable groan is her response, and I lift my chin to watch as she unravels. Her knees start to quake, her skin pink and flushed as the heel of my hand takes over for my thumb and palms her with fevered strokes, my fingers buried deep and thrusting hard.

"Oliver... shit, *fuck*... fucking kiss me," she rasps out, her entire body teetering on the edge. Sydney tugs me down by the roots of my hair, her mouth open and needy, and when our tongues crash together with demanding urgency, she crumbles.

Sydney climaxes against my hand, nails digging into my scalp, her moans trapped inside my mouth, crawling down my throat as I plunge my tongue into hers. She is quivering, blissfully breaking, clutching onto me for dear life.

And I savor every moment of it, a smile spreading against her open mouth with the knowledge that I am responsible for her ecstasy—with the realization that I want to be the *only* one responsible for her ecstasy... *forever.*

When Sydney is breathing heavily below me, body still shaking with the aftermath of her release, I remove my hand from her underwear, our mouths parting for air. I look into her glazed-over eyes, my own heated stare fanning the flames. And just before I kiss her again, she reaches for my hand—the hand that is slicked and glistening with *her*—and guides it to my lips.

She wants me to taste her.

Eyes holding with hers, I dip those two fingers into my mouth, tasting the evidence of her pleasure. I lick and suck, never breaking our powerful hold, and it's a raw, intoxicating moment, watching her watch me, noting the way her own tongue pokes out to wet her lips. She is aroused by the image.

When I lean back down to capture those lips, Sydney is already tugging down my sweatpants, and a tremor of anticipation and thrill courses through me.

It's not long before I'm sheathed inside of her once again, our hands interlocked above her head, mattress squeaking, moans overlapping, hearts bound and branded with the beats of one another's.

And soon, the morning has passed us by, and we both realize we completely forgot about our breakfast.

Sydney naps in my bed, exhausted from our morning of lovemaking, and I find my own eyes drifting closed when Gabe collapses beside me on the sofa, startling me.

Shifting into the present moment, I heave in a tired sigh, unprepared for the lecture I'm about to receive. "You don't have to say anything. I already know your thoughts on the matter," I tell him, swiping my palms against my thighs.

Glancing to my left, Gabe runs his tongue along his teeth, eyes narrowed. A smile follows. "I'm done hassling you about it, man. You two are like fuckin' magnets, apparently." He leans back, head dropping to the cushion with a heavy exhale. "Besides, I'd be a giant hypocrite at this point."

"How so?" I wonder.

"One date… one *goddamn* date, and I'm already crazy for this girl. I'm basically Syd, and she's kinda the chick version of you, but I can't seem to heed any of my own advice. I can't possibly be the right guy for her, you know? I'm a mess… like Sydney."

"Neither of you are a mess. You are both amazingly kind, generous, funny—I'm enamored with Sydney in the same fashion Tabitha is enamored with you, I'd imagine."

"I'm absolutely terrified I'll break her after she's overcome so much. And fuck, man… she's overcome *so much*. The shit she confided in me last night…"

I quirk a half-smile in understanding. "It's hard to break someone who has already experienced the worst out of life. We tend to be fairly resilient."

Gabe eyes me with something akin to respect, his features relaxed, gaze soft. "You know, I'm really glad you made it out of there. I'm glad…" His lips twitch, rattled by his own vulnerability. "I'm really glad we're brothers again."

I return the sentiment. "You and Sydney have certainly been my guiding light amidst all of the challenges I've faced. I'm very thankful to have you in my corner."

Gabe nods, clearly touched, his chin dipping downward. "I'm not good with this sappy shit," he chuckles, scuffing a hand through his hair as he fidgets in place. "So, I'm changing the subject to something more relatable: sex. Details, dude."

It's my turn to fidget. "I'm not comfortable discussing our intimate moments, Gabe."

"Come on, Oliver, it was your first time. How was it? Was your mind blown?"

Heat creeps up my neck, but I can't help the small grin that pulls at my lips. "It was... quite pleasant."

"*Quite pleasant?*" he mocks with finger quotations. That familiar eyebrow raises with the curve of his mouth. "You've got to give me something."

"I will not."

"Brother to brother, man to man." Gabe places a hand over his heart. "On my mother's grave, I won't tell a soul. Just *one* detail from last night."

"Your mother lives in Delaware."

"Dude. Metaphorical."

I sigh through a laugh. *Relentless.* "All right, one thing..." I turn to him, head cocked, grin in place. I draw out the silence for dramatic effect, then reply, "Sydney Neville makes a remarkable Strawberry Daiquiri."

He stares at me for three whole seconds, my response registering like sludge. Then we both break out into laughter, shoulders shaking, the affection between us palpable. For the very first time, I am truly and exceptionally *happy*. I have a family. I have freedom and possibilities and fresh air and sunshine. I have hope. I have meaning.

I have *her*.

As we fall into a comfortable silence, Gabe broaches another change of subject, propping his feet up on the coffee table and crossing them at the ankles. "So, have you given any thought to shacking up with the old man? Not that I want you gone, but I can't deny the appeal there... this adulting shit is stressful. If he offered me a rent-free space at his lake house with financial assistance, I'd probably be all over that. I might never have sex again, but fuck it," he laughs, folding his arms.

"I have considered it," I admit, recalling the way I've played out the scenario over and over in my mind, finding great difficulty in turning down such a generous offer. It would be a temporary burden in exchange for a *real* future. While Sydney does not appear to be the materialistic type, she will surely desire gifts, vacations, and dates that don't involve her living room sofa at some point in time. Our friendship and attraction will only take us so far before stressors begin to seep in like poison—my lack of career, vehicle, and sustainable income being the primary concerns. "You think I should accept?"

A thoughtful pause before Gabe shrugs. "I mean, I'll miss the hell out of you, but it might be in your best interest. It's not easy starting from scratch at thirty-years-old. Sometimes we need that push, and most people don't have a push as good as what's on the table for you, you know?"

I nod, seeing his point. "Yes. It seems like a smart move. I'll discuss with Sydney and—"

"You're leaving?"

Her voice has me twisting around on the sofa, and I'm met with stormy eyes, glistening like puddles after a rain shower. "Sydney... you're awake," I smile, overjoyed to see her because that will always be my reaction to seeing her.

Sydney hugs herself, still dressed in my t-shirt, along with her leather bottoms from the night before. She sucks her bottom lip between her teeth. "Are you leaving, Oliver?"

"I... I don't know. I was hoping we could discuss."

A slow nod greets me, matched with a tight jaw. "I didn't realize there was anything to discuss."

"I'm sorry, this was a sudden development." She's angry. She's hurt. I can feel the heavy emotions radiating off of her, nearly suffocating me. "Syd, I'm just trying to evaluate what's best for me. For *us*."

Gabe remains silent, distracting himself with his cellular phone, while Sydney begins a quest for her shoes. She sniffs, traipsing down the staircase to fetch them. "It's fine. I'm going to head out... I need to check on Alexis."

"Sydney." I'm on my feet, following her down the steps with worry piercing my heart. "Syd, please. It's not my intention to hurt you."

She shuffles into her shoes, ignoring me.

"Please don't shut me out. I'd like to talk about this."

Sydney throws me a wounded glance as she reaches for her coat. "There's nothing to talk about. We're not on the same page, and that's on me."

"That's not true at all," I try to reason, my anxiety swelling. "Lake Geneva is less than an hour from here—we can make it work. It would be temporary."

"And, what, spend the weekend fucking in Travis' spare bedroom, then go back to our separate lives?" Sydney swipes a piece of loose hair from her eyes, her cheeks flushed with indignation. "No thanks. That's not what I signed up for."

"I didn't realize there was a dotted line!" For the first time that I can recall, a feeling of outrage prickles my skin. My blood boils with anger, desperation, a sickly sense of dissolution. She's misunderstanding everything. "I would be doing this for *you*, Sydney. I'm trying to become a better man—a man you can be proud of. A man who has the means to take care of you."

Sydney zips up her jacket, pausing to drink in my words, her eyes averted just beyond me. Her chin is quivering as she deliberates her response. Swallowing, she finally replies, "You know me, Oliver. I don't need anyone taking care of me." Her voice has dipped into a quiet contemplation, her gaze drifting back to me with poignancy. "All I want is you. All I've ever wanted is *you*."

My heart clenches when she turns to walk out the front door. How, after the sixteen hours we shared together, can she just walk out like this? She hasn't even given me a chance to discuss the circumstances. I call out to her, pushing through the screen, sans my shoes and coat. "Sydney!"

"I just need some space, Oliver," she replies over her shoulder, stomping through the yard towards her house. "I just need to think."

I stare at her retreating back, eyes stinging, my skin blasted with a winter draft. She says nothing else as she disappears through the front door, prompting me to collapse onto the porch step, my head in my hands. Frustration eats away at me, uncertain on how to proceed. I did not expect this reaction from her. I did not expect any of this, given the intimacy we just shared.

As I sit and stew with strange, new emotions worming their way inside of me, I tent my hands in front of my face, tapping my fingertips against my lips.

Sydney wants space. I can give her space.

I'll give her anything she asks for.

Before I pull myself to my feet, a flicker of movement catches my eye from the left side of the yard. I frown, gaze casing my surroundings, searching for the source.

I don't anticipate what I see.

Athena.

My little friend is perched a few yards away, nibbling something between her two front paws. She faces me, her dark, beady eyes fixed on mine, as if she's waiting for me to summon her over.

It's most certainly Athena. I can feel it in my bones. Not many raccoons are active during daylight hours, and hardly any would be so bold as to engage with me.

"Athena," I whisper, my voice laced with invitation. "You've come back."

The raccoon approaches, slowly at first, and then prances the rest of the way until she's latched onto my leg. My sour mood disintegrates in her company.

"I've missed you, Athena," I tell her, petting her furry head and watching as she nuzzles against my shin. "I've been so worried."

She climbs onto the cement stoop, sitting beside me like a person would. I'm in awe of her intelligence, as well as her ability to connect with a human being. It's not particularly normal, and it's certainly not common. She is an enigma.

My cellular phone begins to vibrate in my front pocket, and I fish it out, glancing at the screen. I'm surprised to see her name, wondering why she wouldn't just speak to me in the flesh. I'm right outside her window.

Sydney: *You didn't say it back.*

A frown pinches between my eyes as I read over her words, my hand still combing the space amid Athena's ears.

I didn't say *what* back?

These riddles and ambiguous messages are confusing to me, causing me to scratch my head and sift through all of our prior conversations. Athena noses my ribs, and I can't help but smile as my mind wanders. She does it again, and for some reason, I'm compelled to look up.

Sydney stands at her office window, staring down at me, fingertips pressed up against the glass.

And somehow, right then, her implication dawns on me. My stomach twists into knots.

Love.

I never told her I loved her.

CHAPTER TWENTY-FIVE

OLIVER

L*OTUS*
        *The word is scrawled across my arm in black marker. I don't know
why it's there or what it means. This memory is buried too deep.*
"Did you write it on your arm, Oliver?"
Dr. Malloy questions me gently as flashes of the basement course
through my mind. "I don't... I can't recall."
"Is this an important word? Does this flower represent a piece of your
childhood or a defining moment in your life?"
Lotus, lotus, lotus...
"You're gonna be all right, kid. I just need to figure this out."
*It's my first night in that underground cell. Feelings of terror and confusion
ripple through me as I scoot back on my butt until I'm pressed into a dark corner.
I wrap my arms around my knees, then bury my face between the valley they
form. "I'm scared, sir. When can I go home?"*
The man paces back and forth over the stone floor.
Back and forth. Back and forth.
*He's pulling at his hair, his skin glistening with sweat. "This is a mess. This is
a goddamn mess..." he mutters to himself. "What the hell have I done?"*
"I want my mom. I want Syd," I plead.
"You gotta stop talking. I'm trying to think."
Tears begin to leak down my face. "What's your name?"
He pauses his feet, turning towards me as he runs a dirty hand down his jaw.

He's a tall man, maybe a giant, with a large forehead and jet black hair. "Call me Bradford."

"Where are you right now, Oliver?"

The doctor's voice pokes through. "I'm in the basement… the very first night. Bradford looks frightened. We're both frightened."

"Does he want to hurt you?"

"No."

A pause. "Look down at your arm, Oliver."

"lotus"

It means something.

I can't forget, I can't forget.

There's a penny in my pocket, so I pull it out after Bradford has left me alone with a sleeping bag and a black bucket. It's cold down here. I miss the sunshine.

With the penny held between my shaking fingers, I begin to carve letters into the stone wall beside my sleeping area. I start with my name.

Oliver Lynch.

I can't forget, I can't forget.

It takes a long time to write my name. The penny doesn't dig deep enough.

Then I write "lotus" beneath my name.

What does it mean?

I say the word aloud, whispering it into the lonely cell that is illuminated by only a flashlight: "Lotus."

The word sounds strange on my tongue; unfamiliar.

I don't know what it means, but I think…

I think it means everything.

I squeeze my eyelids shut, my mind reaching for the memories.

Only, this memory feels different somehow. It doesn't feel buried, it feels… *nonexistent.*

Finding my voice, I rasp out, "I don't think I ever knew what that word meant, not even then."

"That's okay, Oliver," Dr. Malloy says gently. "Maybe your captor was involved in something very serious, and it was some kind of code word. What do you think?"

"Perhaps."

"Did he ever reference something along those lines?"

"No."

Pen scratches against paper. "Let's get out of that basement for a moment," she says. "Let's go back a little bit further."

An image bursts to life…

My mother.

"There you go. That's perfect."

My mother's kind voice and encouraging words bring a smile to my face. We are sitting in the garden, covered in dirt, while she teaches me how to plant vegetables.

"Will I have to eat the tomatoes that grow?" I ask worriedly.

Her laughter sweeps over to me with the summer breeze. "No. But you'll have to eat the cucumbers!"

She tickles me, and I giggle. "Gross! Syd doesn't like cucumbers, so neither do I."

"Well, maybe you will both like these *cucumbers. They are extra special, after all."*

"Why, Mama?"

"Because they are planted by you, of course."

I look at my mother, memorizing her caramel-colored hair, always tied up in a pretty knot. Her eyes are like mine, warm and sweet, like oatmeal cookies. My mama is so beautiful, and she loves me so much.

I stab the miniature shovel into the dirt, watching a few ants dance around the soil. The sun beats down on us as birds chirp from a nearby tree. I love gardening with my mother. It's one of my favorite things to do. "Is this okay, Mama?" I ask, scooping out little piles of dirt.

"You're doing a great job, Oliver," she tells me, then throws a loving arm around my shoulders. "You just need to dig a little deeper..."

I open my eyes.

"What did you see, Oliver?"

Sitting up, heart thumping, I can't help the smile from blooming on my lips, much like my mother's precious garden. Memories of her trickle back in, wrapping me in a warm hug, a familiar smile, a comfort I have unknowingly missed for a very long time. Tears swell against my eyelids, a burning sense of loss mingling with the sweet memories.

Chasing butterflies, baking cookies, gardening, making crafts with Sydney at the kitchen table, watching *Winnie the Pooh* on that same living room sofa. Bedtime stories, tickle fights, board games, underdogs on the playground swings. Holidays and bonfires. Piggyback rides and sing-a-longs. Bubbles in the bathtub. Laughter.

Love.

My mother. My beautiful mother.

My God, how she must have missed me.

She'll never know that I'm okay.

She'll never, ever know.

Tears slide down my face as Dr. Malloy sits silently in the recliner across from me, her knees crossed, her smile wistful and knowing. It takes a few moments for me to collect myself, gather my bearings, and bring myself back to the present moment. Inhaling a grief-ridden sigh, I swallow, scrubbing a palm down my damp face. "I remember her," I whisper softly.

Dr. Malloy nods, discarding her notebook beside her on a small table. "Your mother."

"Yes." My throat feels tight and ragged, stinging with remorse. "I... I think I'm done here. With these sessions, I mean."

She nods again.

"I'm not certain I desire anymore answers. I feel at peace with the memories I've recovered," I explain, licking my lips and tasting the salty tears that gathered there. "The hole I felt has been filled—she was all I was looking for."

As I collect my jacket and thank Dr. Malloy for her services, she reaches out to shake my hand. "I'm glad I could help you, Oliver. I very much admire your strength."

Strength.

I used to think strength was rooted in the fight.

Prevailing. Surviving the things determined to tear us down.

But true strength isn't necessarily *overcoming* the fight—it is *how* we fight. It is not within the sword itself, but in how we wield it.

And sometimes, it's not about survival at all. It's about *living through* the worst possible loss, heartache and pain, regardless of whether or not we make it to the other side. My mother lived through an unimaginable tragedy. A devastating loss.

In the end, she did not survive.

But while she did not survive the battle itself, I am certain she wielded her sword with grace, dignity, and love.

And that is true strength.

After my appointment, I take the liberty of visiting Sydney. It's been three days since our argument, and I am not faring well. She wanted space, and I promised myself I would give her anything she needed, but I don't think what she *truly* requires is space—it's reassurance. It's the promise that I won't leave her again. It's the confirmation that I return her love, which, I thought had been overtly obvious. But I didn't want to communicate such a significant sentiment through electronic message, nor did I want to infringe on her desire for privacy.

However, it's been *three days...* I cannot go another moment without relieving her of her worries, regardless of her misguided request for space.

Of course, I love her. I love her more than I love fresh air.

And, well, it's Christmas Eve and I have a gift for her.

Sydney opens the door looking disheveled, dabbled in paint smears. Her glasses are crooked, her hair wild, clothes wrinkled and worn.

She's perfect.

"Merry Christmas," I tell her, one hand in my pocket and the other tucking her gift under my arm. "May I come in?"

Watery eyes drift to the wrapped present, a hint of a smile lifting. She nods. "Of course." Sydney steps aside, allowing me entry, her fingertips tapping together in front of her. "Merry Christmas."

My own smile greets her, lingering, showcasing just how much I've missed her over the last few days. The fact that I was able to touch her, taste her, *have* her, only to be abruptly cut off, is a feeling I can't quite describe. It's a loss that makes my soul ache. "I realize you asked for space, but..." I dip my eyes, locating the correct words. "Well, I don't agree it's in the best interest of either of us. We spent far too many years apart. There is no gain in purposely avoiding one another."

Sydney looks like a tightly wound coil of emotion, waiting to combust. She presses her lips together, fidgeting on both feet as she picks at her shirt sleeve. "I don't want space either, Oliver. But if it's going to be forced on me, I need to pull back now. I'm already helplessly attached to you," she chokes out, tears visible, destined to fall. "If I sink any further, I'll never get out. I won't recover from losing you twice."

"Syd..." I shut the door and set the gift down beside my feet, moving in on her with outstretched palms. Cradling her face between them, I whisper, "This was never about losing me. This was about trying to become the best possible version of myself, even if that meant a temporary sacrifice. It was never permanent, and it was only considered out of my feelings for you."

She places her hands atop mine. "But what if we grow apart, or you meet someone else, or..."

"Shh, that's nonsense," I tell her firmly, thumbs dusting away her tears. "That's all in your mind. There is only you."

Chin ducking to her chest, Sydney inhales a fractured breath, slipping from my grasp. At first I fear she's pulling away, taking back her space, protecting her heart from a loss that doesn't exist—but she reaches for my hand instead, offering me a small smile. "Come with me. I was just finishing up your Christmas present."

I follow her up the staircase to her office, hand-in-hand, curiosity overriding my worry for the time being. Her paints are lined up on a side table, well-used, and Alexis is curled into a ball on Sydney's computer desk in the corner, warming the keyboard. A tiny Christmas tree sits atop the desk, the only festive flare given to the room.

Sydney releases my hand to step over to her easel, bending down to fetch the canvas perched beside it, facing away from me. "It's almost finished," she tells me. "There's a minor detail I want to add, but I think it's ready for you to see."

Beaming with anticipation, I pace forward, unable to hide my grin. "You made me a painting?"

"I did. I've been working on it for a long time," she nods, flustered. "There's an addition I included that I hope you like."

"I'll love it."

She appears nervous and frazzled—as if there's a chance I would dislike it. Sydney could paint me a custom portrait of Lorna Gibson and I'd hang it on my wall with pride.

Sydney fiddles with her hair, worrying her lip between her teeth before taking a deep breath. She blows it out hard. "Okay, here you go. Merry Christmas, Oliver."

I reach for it eagerly, catching her fearful eyes before flipping the canvas around and viewing the picture.

The air catches in my lungs, and I have to remind myself to breathe.

A pink lotus flower is painted along the bottom of the canvas, fading up into a fairytale scene: a little boy in overalls holding hands with a little girl with sunshine pigtails as they stand atop a grassy hill, watching fireworks light up the sky. Reds, blues, and violets are spattered across the top of the portrait, raining color and beauty down upon the storybook image.

And sitting next to the little girl is an orange tabby, while a raccoon rests beside the boy.

It's us.

Me, Sydney, Alexis, and Athena.

We are watching the fireworks together.

An innate fervency stabs through my heart, choking me. The feelings running rampant in my chest are almost more than I can bear.

Joy and gratitude for the exquisite, thoughtful gift. Melancholy remorse for all the years spent apart, in two separate worlds, lost without each other. Hope for a future I can envision more clearly than any memory stored inside my brain. Intense yearning for a life I never thought would come to be.

And above all, love.

Love for her.

I tear my gaze away from the artwork, finding a wide-eyed Sydney, tearful and anxious, watching me as I process the emotions coursing through my blood.

She swallows, nearly shaking with unease. "God, Oliver, say something..."

My eyes close for a few heartbeats in an effort to prevent my own tears from flowing. "I love it. I love it so much, thank you..." Then I set the canvas down, leaning it against the desk, and pull her into my arms. I hug her, cling to her, cherish her, my fingers twining through her hair while my mouth presses a kiss to her temple. "I won't leave," I murmur softly, tightening my hold. "I can't... I can't leave you, Syd."

Her gasp is strained, cracked, a strangled cry of relief. Sydney buries her face into my chest, breathing me in, while her arms link behind my back. "We'll make it work, I promise. You're all I need, Oliver," she whimpers. "You're all I need."

We hold each other for a long time, Sydney's tears seeping through the cotton fabric of my shirt, while my mouth rains a flurry of kisses into her hair. When we pull back, I cup her face, smoothing back her flaxen locks, our eyes tied and tethered. I'm going to attempt to speak something profound, but I find myself distracted by a large smear of paint along her forehead.

A laugh escapes me instead.

Sydney frowns. "What? My hair?"

My grin widens. "No, you've got... some paint..." I gesture towards her forehead, and she quickly begins to swipe at it. More laughter floats between us when she smudges the bright crimson into her hairline.

"I'm making it worse, aren't I?"

"Worse is subjective. I think you make a brilliant canvas." I lick my thumb, using it to clear the dabs of paint from her skin, causing a sharp breath to release between her lips. I glance at those lips, momentarily distracted, when suddenly, I feel the back of her hand reach out and connect with the side of my face, leaving something cold and slimy in its wake. Her giggles fill me up, the mood turning playful.

251

"Orange looks good on you. Brings out your eyes," Sydney teases, smearing the paint down my jaw.

I can't help but retaliate by reaching around her and dipping two fingers into the paint tray, then coloring her in a vibrant shade of blue. It drips along her hair and neck, pulling a squeal from her throat.

She gives me a good-natured smack against the shoulder, then turns around to exact her revenge. Sydney's fingers are coated in orange and yellow when she returns, and we face each other with mischief in our eyes.

My insides are alight with a certain kind of giddiness as we stare one another down, our smiles big and bright. "I'm stronger than you," I tell her.

"I'm faster." She smears the paint on my neck, dragging her palm down the front of my shirt.

I reach for more paint as she flees, her laughter trailing behind her. My hands are covered in turquoise and purple, mixing into a dark, muddy shade. I catch her quickly, slinking my arms around her middle and pulling her to my chest, running my hands along the front of her body. Sydney laughs harder, her squeaks rising in pitch as she fights my grasp.

She pulls free, and I think she's going to run from the room.

I think she's going to bolt.

Instead, she kisses me.

Before I know it, Sydney's fingers are curled around the front of my t-shirt, yanking my lips to hers, familiar and sweet.

We both groan with equal parts surprise and desire when we collide, hard and swift. Crushing and claiming. I clasp her face between my paint-smeared palms, pulling her even closer, tasting her deeper. Sydney gasps as she weaves her arms around my neck and walks us backwards. I bump into a chair, tipping it over as our tongues battle it out, then reach for the table to steady myself. But all I manage to do is knock the tray of paints to the ground, coating her hardwood floor in rainbow patterns.

I ignore the mess, too far gone, and tug her t-shirt up and over her head, tossing it into the chaos near our feet. I reach around to unclasp her bra, our mouths still connected, while Sydney fingers the button on my jeans. She pulls down the zipper just as her bra is discarded and her breasts are exposed. I break the kiss to meld our foreheads together, my gaze drifting south to watch her push my pants down my waist, boxers following.

Sydney's gaze settles on my erection. Her eyes widen with dilated pupils, her swollen lips parting with a sharp breath. I pull back only to remove my own shirt before capturing her mouth again.

There is no hesitation. We simply react, we give in, we *take*.

Just as my tongue finds hers, Sydney steps closer to me and slips on the wet paint. I move to catch her, but my footing is hindered by the pants around my knees, and we both topple over, my arms spinning her around, so she falls on top of me. We start kissing again through our grins, and I roll us until I'm hovering over her, our limbs and skin sliding over the paint.

Kicking off my bottoms, I yank down her leggings until we're both bare, exposed, and vulnerable. I kneel between her legs, gazing down at this woman, dabbled in paint, her thighs and smile spread before me.

She is, by far, the greatest work of art.

I lower myself over her, holding my weight up on my arms on either side of her head. We are eye-to-eye, noses kissing, breath warm and heavy against our faces. Reaching down to line myself up at her core, her wet heat slicking my tip and making me shudder, I kiss her. I keep kissing her as I slide inside, groaning as our tongues dance together, reveling in the feel of her arms wrapping around my neck to hold me close.

My movements are slow, my rhythm seductive and sensual. I savor her, adore her, and when I lift my head to find her eyes, we are connected on a higher level. Pressing our foreheads together, gazes still locked, I whisper with ardency: "I love you, Syd. I loved you then, I love you now, and I'll love you until my dying day."

There was never a question, never a doubt.

I love this woman.

Sydney's hands grasp my face, a tear slipping from the corner of her eye. Her thoroughly kissed lips tip into a grin. "I've waited twenty-five years to hear you say that."

The back of my fingers sweep across her cheekbone. "No more waiting."

Our mouths collide, her legs curling around my waist, my fingers threaded through her hair as we move together in perfect time. We make love right there on her office floor, bestrewn in paint and sweat and kisses, our hearts finally at rest knowing that whatever comes our way, comes *our* way. We'll face the world together—as a team.

The Black Lotus finally has his queen.

"I think I have Ultramarine Blue in my cervix."

We are in the shower, cleaning ourselves up, watching the water run with the colors of the rainbow. I chuckle as I massage shampoo into her hair. "That sounds unpleasant."

"Well worth it," she sighs.

What was supposed to be a quick rinse turns into nearly an hour of laughter, soap fights, and holding each other beneath the jets, listening to each other's heartbeats. I tell her about Athena's return and how Gabe has allowed me to keep the raccoon for the time being—as long as she's consistently locked inside her crate when we aren't present.

And just when I think we're ready to get out, Sydney kneels down between my legs and takes me in her mouth... and I one-hundred percent understand the appeal.

My sexual recovery time seems to be remarkably quick when I'm with her.

Clean, satiated, and ready for a nap, we finally step out of the bathtub and dry ourselves off. While Sydney slips into a fresh t-shirt and Christmas pajama bottoms, awaiting her evening festivities with family, she suddenly leaps to her feet and rushes out of the bedroom. "My present!"

I follow with a chuckle, charmed by her enthusiasm, having a vague recollection of waking up on Christmas morning as a child and feeling a similar sensation. I make my way down the stairs, and Sydney is already dragging the large box to the sofa, tearing open the decorative paper. Sitting beside her, I watch with nervous energy as she punctures the tape with her long fingernails and rips the flaps open.

"Oh, my God..." When she pulls out the tissue paper and her eyes land on what's inside, she freezes for a moment, gaze fixed on the inner contents. "Are these...?"

"Yes," I say softly. "I picked them up from the police station a while back. I haven't even gone through all of them—it's a bit difficult to relive."

Sydney reaches in to pull out the enormous stack of comics I created while I was in captivity. The creative outlet was my only source of sanity, my only true cure for the boredom. This imaginary world gave me companionship and kept me from rotting away at the bottom of the earth. It truly saved my life.

"*The Lotus Chronicles*," she whispers, running her fingertips along the top page, enchanted and in a daze. "Whatever that word meant, or why it was significant... it gave you a purpose, Oliver." Sydney's tear-filled eyes latch onto mine as she squeezes the comics between her hands. "You want me to have these?"

I nod. "You're sprinkled into every single one of these stories, Syd. You were a part of me down there."

Her wistful smile blossoms with more tears, and we spend the rest of the afternoon skimming through the pages, getting lost in the tales. I can hardly remember creating some of them, as it was so long ago, but looking through them with Sydney by my side, holding my hand, eases the sting of recalling those harrowing, lonely years, locked away inside my head.

Sydney is looking through a very old comic, the pages tarnished and split along the edges, when all of a sudden, she freezes. I watch her body stiffen, her breath catching, and I furrow my brows with worry. "What is it?"

"Is this me?" she wonders, her voice laced with something that resembles... *horror*.

Leaning over her shoulder, I zone in on the image that has her rattled. It's difficult to decipher at first, as my artistic capabilities had not yet been polished, but it's clearly a depiction of the Faceless Man. He was the villain in all of my tales—a man with a blackened, shadowy blob where a face should be.

There is a little girl in the photo with blonde hair.

Sydney's grip tightens on the paper. "I had pigtails in every picture. Why don't I have pigtails?"

"I..." My eyes case the image further, confused. And when my gaze dips, I notice exactly what has Sydney so upset.

The little girl has her shorts down around her ankles.

And the Faceless Man has his hand in her underwear.

Dear God... why would I draw this?

Sydney cups a hand over her mouth, her cry muffled, and the sickening realization washes over us at the same time.

"Clem."

CHAPTER TWENTY-SIX

SYDNEY

AFTER RETCHING INTO THE KITCHEN GARBAGE CAN TWICE, I throw my coat and boots on, kiss Oliver goodbye, and hightail it over to my parents' house for Christmas Eve dinner with red-rimmed eyes and hot cheeks of shame, still wearing my holiday pajamas. My sobs almost force me to pull to the side of the road multiple times as the anguish attempts to suffocate me.

Anguish. Horror. Guilt.

Blinding disbelief.

I never knew. I never *fucking* knew.

I'm her sister and I failed her. I didn't see the signs. Clementine was always a quiet, moody child, and we teased her mercilessly about it. She was shy, insecure, aloof—Clem was always the odd one out in our little friendship circle.

Is this why? How long was my sister being molested right under our noses?

Oliver hovered behind me, unsure on how to help as his hand gently cased my spine. Hot tears streaked down my face, my mind reeling, my insides cracking to pieces.

"Sydney... I'm sorry. I don't remember drawing that," Oliver told me as I heaved into the trashcan—and when I glanced at him, I saw his own guilt reflecting back at me. A sense of responsibility. He held onto that truth, spilling it into the only outlet he had.

And then he forgot.

Everything faded away—a defense mechanism, a repressed memory, combined with years of psychological trauma, force-fed lies, and PTSD. Missing memories are common with PTSD victims, even more so if Oliver witnessed a traumatic event prior to the abduction.

It makes sense.

Scattered and broken, I did my best to quell his remorse. I held his face between my palms and kissed his forehead, whispering gently, "I'm sorry I have to go, but listen to me," I pleaded. "Do not hold yourself accountable for this. Whoever *is* accountable will pay the fucking price, and I swear to that."

He stared down at me, wordless.

"I love you, Oliver. Thank you for my beautiful gift."

His eyes glistened, his own words of love whispered from his lips as I left him standing in my kitchen, unprepared for the heart-wrenching conversation ahead of me.

As I pull into the familiar driveway, Clementine's car is already parked along the street. She's always early to family gatherings, eager to help our mother prepare the meal.

I accidentally set the kitchen on fire one time when I placed a potholder on top of a hot burner. It was Easter Brunch, and I was trying to help make a simple gravy, but that gravy turned into a visit from the fire station, thousands of dollars' worth of damages after I threw the potholder in a panic and it lit the curtains on fire, and a permanent ban from using my parents' stovetop. The memory only adds to my state of anxiety.

When I plow through the front door in my clunky snow boots and puffy eyes, Poppy is quick to greet me in her adorable holiday dress, which triggers an immediate breakdown before I even make it past the foyer.

"Auntie Syd, what's wrong? You don't like my dress?"

Poppy twirls twice, and I sob harder.

My dramatic entrance has my mother and sister rounding the corner from the kitchen wearing matching expressions and reindeer aprons.

Clementine eyes me with worry, and I realize this is the first time we've seen each other in person since her outburst in the car.

And now that outburst makes a hell of a lot more sense.

"I'm so sorry," I rasp out, nearing a hyperventilating state as I stare at my wide-eyed sister. "I didn't know. I didn't know..."

Her eyes flare, flashing with something sinister. "Let's go upstairs."

"What the hell is going on?" Mom demands, setting aside her turkey baster and crossing her arms, her troubled gaze floating between the two of us. "What happened? Is it Oliver?"

Clem is already heading up the staircase.

"Sydney, explain," she presses. "You look like death."

"I feel like death. We'll be down soon."

Trudging up the staircase like two ticking time bombs, we slip into the spare bedroom and Clem closes the door, taking a moment to collect her breath before slowly turning to face me. She stutters out her words, her body trembling. "Y-You know?"

My goddamn tears won't stop spilling out like rebellious little daggers, slicing their way down my cheeks, leaving scars. "Why didn't you tell me? How could you not tell me?"

"I couldn't. I..." Her head shakes with wild fervency, her own tears cutting her down. "I just *couldn't.*"

"Who was responsible? Who the fuck hurt my sister?"

Her throat bobs with a strained swallow, head still twisting side to side. "It doesn't matter."

"It *does* matter!" I shriek, throwing my arms up. "It fucking matters because I'm going to hunt him down and castrate the bastard."

"Stop, sis. Keep your voice down," she whispers harshly, eyeing the door over her shoulder. "It was a long time ago, okay? It happened, and it's done. Let it go."

"How can you say that? I'll never let this go. *Never.*"

"You have to. Please."

"Give me a goddamn name, Clementine."

"I can't!" She paces over to the guestroom bed, sitting at the edge and burying her face into her hands. "How did you find out?"

I follow, kneeling down between her legs. "Oliver got his comic books back from his time in captivity," I choke out. "We were looking through them together, and he drew a scene where a faceless man was... *touching* you."

I almost vomit when the word escapes me.

Clem licks away the tears gathered on her lips as she snaps her head up, staring down at me with a heavy expression. "W-What? Oliver... *saw?* He saw us together?"

A nod.

"Oh, my God... I had no idea." She weeps into her palms, sniffling and gasping for breath. "I was scared, Syd. I was fucking terrified. I was only ten-years-old."

My own sobs mingle with hers as I squeeze her kneecaps between my fingers. "Please tell me who hurt you. Please…"

"It doesn't matter. He won't hurt me anymore," she supplies, voice ragged.

"Who? Goddammit, Clem, *who?*"

Tempestuous cobalt blues scan my face, darting back and forth as her mind reels. Then she spits out a name: "Raymond Ford."

It takes a minute for the name to register. When it does, my eyes pop. "Oliver's kidnapper?"

She looks away.

Raymond Bradley Ford.

Bradford.

"What?" It's a whisper, a question, a desperate denial. I land back on my heels, my skin hot and my stomach sick.

Oliver saw them. That's why he took him. *My God*, that's why…

When my gaze finds its way back to my sister, she is still avoiding my stare, picking at the thread on the bed cover. "Clem…"

"Don't tell Mom and Dad," she begs. "Please, Syd, don't tell anyone."

"Dammit, why? We need to go to the police."

"No! He died, and my secret died with him, and I'd prefer to keep it that way. I've made peace with it."

"You deserve *justice.*"

"There is no justice."

"Clementine… fuck!" I rise to my feet, tugging my hair from the roots. How did I not know this was happening? How did I not see this stranger lurking around, molesting children? Nothing makes sense. *Nothing.* When my eyes land on her defeated form, hunched over on the bed, my insides coil. "You should have told me," I say softly.

Clem releases a sharp laugh. "You were seven-years-old, Sydney. *Seven.* The last thing I wanted to do was involve you," she tells me. "Then Oliver disappeared, and you were permanently gutted. There was no way I was going to hand you another burden."

"What about Mom and Dad? The police? *Anyone?*"

"I was scared, okay? Jesus, he threatened me. He said he'd hurt my family if I told anyone."

My throat burns with bile, my teeth clenching.

"I was just a fucking little kid, Sydney. I didn't … I didn't even understand what was happening."

The crack in her voice, the sickening fracture, has my emotions boiling over once again. Clem covers her mouth with a shaking palm, and

I find my way back to her, nearly tackling her in a bone-crushing embrace. My sister slips off the edge of the bed and we both collapse to the bedroom floor, arms clutching one another, tears flowing, bodies quaking with grief and anger and impossibility.

We remain wrapped up in each other for what feels like an eternity before we lean back against the bed, hollow and drained. My head drops to her shoulder as we stew in our own cacophony of demons.

"You had a fight with Oliver," Clem says, breaking our torturous silence. "You blamed me for it."

I glance at her through a frown. "What?"

She stares straight ahead, unblinking. "When Mom and Dad interrogate us, tell them you had a fight with Oliver. We came upstairs to work it out."

My eyes burn and water as I shake my head, not understanding her need to hold onto this secret for any longer than she already has. Why doesn't she want to tell our parents?

Clementine continues. "We're going to have a nice dinner. We're going to watch *It's a Wonderful Life* by the Christmas tree while Poppy falls asleep in my lap dreaming about fucking sugar plums. We'll laugh, we'll sing carols, and we'll gorge on pecan pie until our bellies ache." She finally spares me a glance before standing to unsteady feet. "And we're never going to speak of this again."

The following day, I'm still a mess of frazzled disbelief when I zombie my way to the kitchen to make a pot of coffee. It's Christmas morning, but it might as well be doomsday.

Alexis greets me with a friendly meow, and the little jingle collar I placed around her neck is the only thing that brings me a semblance of cheer.

While the coffee brews, I skim through my contact list to text Oliver, finding that he just messaged me a few minutes ago.

Oliver: *Good morning. It's me, Oliver.*

God, I love this man.

Oliver: *I've been worried about you, and I could hardly sleep. I'm hopeful we can visit each other today, as the only thing I wish for this Christmas is to hold you in my arms.*

He follows up the message with an assortment of Christmas tree emojis and little hearts, along with a blurry photo of Athena wearing a Santa hat. My smile is instant and organic, momentarily washing away the turmoil of yesterday. I didn't get home until after two A.M. and passed out from exhaustion on the living room couch, forgetting to let Oliver know I got home okay.

I'm spurred into action, typing back a quick reply before heading upstairs to shower and change.

Me: *I want the exact same thing this year. Be over soon. xoxo, Syd*

An hour later, we're curled up on the couch together watching *Garfield Christmas* after drowning my sorrows in French toast and mimosas. Gabe is still sleeping, so it gives me time to fill Oliver in on my devastating conversation with Clementine.

But when he asks me who was responsible for the assault, my tongue freezes up.

I have no idea why. Oliver has every right to know why Bradford kidnapped him, but I can't seem to get the name out. Not yet. It's Christmas, and this truth bomb will rip him to shreds.

So, I lie to him, and a tiny piece of me withers away with guilt: "She wouldn't tell me."

I can't say I entirely regret the decision because it's an incredible morning. We're able to push the traumatic ordeal aside in exchange for temporary peace, and we enjoy ourselves.

We enjoy our first Christmas together in over twenty-two years.

We're sitting on Oliver's bedroom carpet playing with Athena when there's a knock on the door. "Yo," Gabe calls out. "Merry Christmas, fuckers. Santa came."

Sharing a grin, we join Gabe in the living room for our modest gift exchange. Gabe and I get each other the exact same thing every year: alcohol.

"Shit, Syd. This is killer," he says, tearing apart the wrapping paper and holding out his Rémy Martin Cognac. He glances at me from the floor while Oliver and I snuggle on the couch. "Was this your grocery money? Are you on food stamps now?"

I toss a pillow at him. "Don't be an ass. It may have been an entire weekend of tips, but my boyfriend happens to be a mighty fine chef. I'll never starve again." Nudging Oliver with my elbow, I sneak him a grin.

His eyes widen with alarm. "Boyfriend?"

"Duh. We exchange orgasms and collective loyalty."

Gabe gags. "Dude. You're going to make me start drinking early."

"Orgasms," I repeat in my most sensual voice, my eyebrows wiggling with seduction.

The pillow finds its way back to my face.

Oliver intervenes, reaching for the gift near his feet and handing it off to Gabe, who is still sticking his finger down his throat with theatrics. "Well, I suppose now is an acceptable time to gift you with my own token of gratitude."

"Aw, shucks, man. You got me a present?"

"It's not overpriced liquor, but funds were a bit scarce. I hope you enjoy them."

Gabe plows through the meticulously wrapped gift with eager anticipation and pulls out...

Playboy magazines?

I snort-laugh, falling across Oliver's lap as I watch the look of confusion wash over Gabe's face while he stares at the magazines, turning them upside-down and inside out, just to confirm that he really did, indeed, receive nudie magazines from the nineties for Christmas.

Oliver tucks an arm around my waist as he fidgets, clearing his throat. "These were from my time in captivity. They were returned to me, along with my comics," he explains. "I discovered some files on your computer that contained explicit video footage, so I concluded that you would enjoy looking through these booklets. I recall the material being quite stimulating."

"Oliver!" I smack his thigh.

Gabe drops the magazines like they spontaneously caught on fire. "Jesus, if there are questionable stains, I swear to God I'm going to hurl..."

This only makes me laugh harder.

Oliver looks genuinely perplexed. "I assure you they are in good condition. There's a blonde female on page thirty-three that—"

I smack him again. "Oliver! Christ, I don't want to hear about this."

Gabe immediately flips to page thirty-three, his eyes popping. "Well..."

"Okay, I'm breaking up the boner-bonding. You can *enjoy* your gift later, Gabe."

He sends a thumbs up in Oliver's direction before leaning back on his palms and reaching for my gift beneath the tree. It's wrapped like a bottle of champagne, so I'm delighted to discover that it's a bottle of champagne.

"You rascal, this is my favorite brand!" Hugging the bottle of Bollinger to my chest, I flash him my pearly whites.

A wink floats my way, and then Gabe tosses Oliver the final present. He flounders to catch it, and it's adorable, and I swoon.

"This is very kind of you, Gabe," Oliver says thoughtfully, opening the gift with delicate care. When he reveals what's inside, his smile is as wide as mine. "Fantastic. Thank you."

"What is that?" I wonder, nose crinkling.

"I'm not certain, but it's very appreciated."

It looks some kind of harness. "A dog harness?"

"I do love dogs."

"Shit, it's for Athena," Gabe chuckles as he collects the wrapping paper and crushes it into a giant wad. "I don't know fuck-all about domesticated raccoons, but I figured you might want to take her for walks when the weather warms up."

I watch a twinkle spark to life in Oliver's eyes, brighter than the tree, lighting him up from the inside out. His expression is something akin to magical whimsy, a little contemplative, maybe even overwhelmed. He's lost for a prolonged moment, staring at the small purple harness, dusting his thumbs over the nylon fabric.

My fingers curl around his knee, squeezing gently, causing him to blink as he returns to the living room. "Where did you go?"

Oliver gathers a breath, nodding a tearful smile in Gabe's direction, then trails his attention to me. "Nowhere," he responds softly, his touch sweeping over the back of my knuckles. "Nowhere at all. I'm right here."

In true hot-mess fashion, we decide to throw together an impromptu Christmas feast, with Oliver taking the reins and me cheering him on from the sidelines.

I've had far too much champagne and start making up ridiculous cheerleading rhymes while I prance around the kitchen with two bountiful stalks of celery as makeshift pom-poms. I smack Oliver on the butt with the celery, and he startles with a laugh as he stirs the sauce on the stove.

This is why I start fires.

An hour later, we're eating together in a three-way circle on the living room floor, buzzed on laughter and liquor, quoting *Christmas Vacation*, and reminiscing about the 'good old days' from when we were kids. While Christmas Eve was always spent with relatives, Christmas day was for Santa presents and each other. I would head next door after brunch to explore our new toys with Oliver. Gabe was an irritating preschooler at the time, but he'd usually find his way into Oliver's bedroom and we'd make art, watch new movies, and play with the Lite-Brite or make-believe kitchen set.

A knock on the front door has Gabe hopping to his feet, groaning as he rubs his stomach. "Fuck, I ate too much. Props to the chef tonight."

"It was my pleasure," Oliver replies through his last bite of lasagna. He sends a sweet smile my way, setting down his plate.

My champagne buzz forces my face into a lazy, goofy grin as I drop my chin to his shoulder. "This might be the best night of my whole life," I blurt. "Christmas with my two best friends, a home-cooked meal, a sexy boyfriend on my arm." I link my arm through his for effect. "The only thing that would make it better is—"

"Intercourse?"

Oliver announces this just as Travis Wellington walks up the stairs with Gabe, and my already flushed cheeks redden further. Clearing my throat and raising my pitch an octave higher than what sounds natural, I babble, "No! How dare you imply... such a sinful abomination. We are all pure and virginal, unwedded... churchgoers." A cough. "Hi, Mr. Wellington."

He falters for a moment, gaze assessing me. Surely, he thinks I'm crazy. "Miss Neville. I wasn't aware I'd be seeing you tonight."

Gabe intercedes. "Sorry, Pops. Totally blanked that you were stopping by for dessert."

"I do every year."

I stand, slightly wobbling, and brush the garlic bread crumbs off my thighs. I'm so goddamn classy. "It's great to see you again, sir. It's been a long time."

He eyes me from my fuzzy slipper socks to my light-up Christmas tree headband. I swear there is a disapproving glare gleaming in his dark brown eyes as he stands there in his Burberry sweater vest.

And when Oliver rises beside me, wrapping his arm around my waist, I'm certain I was not mistaken. Travis Wellington doesn't think I'm good enough for Oliver.

Bah-humbug.

"Yes, well, I'm a busy man," Travis says in a clipped tone. He nods toward Oliver. "Merry Christmas, son. You look well."

"I'm very well, thank you." Oliver's grip tightens along my middle, pulling me closer. "Sydney and I are having intimate relations now, so I'll have to respectfully decline your offer of residency. It was much appreciated, though."

My eyes flare, heat traveling down my neck.

Oy.

Gabe slaps his father on the back with a hearty guffaw. "Yeah, so, pie. Made fresh, straight from the Walmart bakery."

Travis slips his hands in his front pockets as Gabe leads him into the kitchen, sighing in a way that a condescending rich person might. I don't know any other rich people, so I can only assume.

I remember Travis being so much cooler when I was a kid.

Facing Oliver, I pull out the pouty lip. "Your stepdad hates me."

"Surely not. That's impossible." A frown appears, and his hands clutch my hipbones with a possessive urgency. "You're exquisite in every way."

Exquisite.

In all of my almost thirty-years of life, that adjective has never once been used to describe me.

Messy. Complicated. Sarcastic. Blasphemous.

Those words I'm familiar with, but *exquisite?* I melt into him, my lips grazing the center of his chest as Oliver's fingers dig into my waist. His proximity, his masculine scent, his heat, his adoration radiating into me… it's intoxicating.

I love him.

And I really want him to be naked.

Hands trailing up his dress shirt and landing on his shoulders, I lean in and whisper, "I want your mouth on me."

Oliver audibly gulps, his eyes darkening. "Where, specifically?" he asks with a hitch.

"Two words…" I hold back my giggles and try to sound like the world's most come-hither sexpot. Eyebrow arched, boobs jutted out, I breathe against his neck, "Moist. Muffin."

A processing pause, and then Oliver breaks out into laughter, his forehead falling to mine as his shoulders shake. "Vixen."

"A very moist vixen. Let's go." Snatching his hand, I drag him towards the staircase, shouting my goodbyes to Gabe and Travis. "Merry Christmas! We're taking off."

Travis lifts a halfhearted wave from his perch against the kitchen counter. "Good to see you, Sydney."

"Shit, hold up." Gabe trots over to us, smacking a piece of gum between his teeth. He gives Oliver's shoulder a squeeze before tugging me to him by the Rudolph nose on my ugly Christmas sweater. "Thanks for the badass gift, Syd. You know you're welcome over for a drink anytime."

"Oh, you know I'll—"

Something in me goes still and my feet stick to the carpet as I lean into Gabe for a goodbye hug. There's a snap inside of me, like a tree branch breaking beneath my boot.

And then I'm frozen, chilled to the bone.

I'm in my bedroom, pressed into my mattress by a hard body, a knee jammed between my thighs to hold me in place. I'm fighting, I'm flailing, I'm writhing, I'm *helpless*.

He's looming over me, dark and determined.

"You just had to do this the hard way."

No, no, no.

The stranger is snarling, spitting, overpowering me with terrifying ease.

He's breathing on me.

He's breathing on me, and his breath smells strange, like... *eucalyptus*.

Gabe's chewing gum.

My hands plant on his chest, shoving him backwards with alarming strength until he stumbles back against the wall, his face a mask of utter confusion. Oliver's hand curls around my upper arm, pulling me away, and everyone is staring at me. Gabe is pissed, hurt, breathing heavily, wondering what the hell just happened.

No, no, no.

"You," I mutter, a tiny croak of betrayal.

Gabe just gapes at me, head shaking. "What the fuck, Syd?"

"Sydney, what's wrong? What happened?"

Oliver tries to steal my focus, but all I can focus on is the fact that my best friend attacked me.

A sob breaks free as my knees go weak. Oliver catches me before I collapse, and I cry out, my heart smashed into tiny splinters: "It was you."

CHAPTER TWENTY-SEVEN

SYDNEY

ABE PULLS HIMSELF UPRIGHT FROM THE WALL, eyes wide and indignant, brimming with absolute bewilderment. "Care to explain what in the *goddamn fuck* is going on?" he bites out, arms raised at his sides. Travis steps forward, a scowl thrown in my direction.

Oliver keeps me from tipping over, one hand on my shoulder and the other squeezing my hip as the tears fall hard. I stare at Gabe, dumbfounded. "It was you," I accuse, each word slicing him harder than the last, stabbing him with razor sharp fury. "Y-You were there that night."

Stab.

"You were *there*."

Slice.

"You attacked me."

Kill.

Gabe nearly crumbles where he stands, nostrils flaring, face flushed, lips parted as a gasp of disbelief breaks through and carries over to me. The look in his eyes is horror, pure *horror*, as if he can't even process what I'm saying. "Are you kidding?" He half-whispers the words, too heartbroken to say them any louder.

I'm still buckling and shaking, my back pressed against Oliver's chest as he holds me tighter.

The look on Gabe's face.

That look will haunt me forever.

God, no, it can't be true. He's gutted—*paralyzed* with incredulity.

Oliver attempts to be a mediator, muttering neutralizing words near my ear. "Perhaps we should discuss this rationally. There must be some sort of misunderstanding."

"Misunderstanding?" Gabe repeats scathingly, wounds still bleeding out at our feet. Travis presses a palm to his son's shoulder, loyalty lines drawn. "My best friend just branded me a fucking monster in my own house, in front of my family, on Christmas Day."

The same knife I used on him twists within my own gut. Averting my eyes, I rasp, "Where were you, Gabe?" *I can't look at him, I can't look at him, I can't look at him.* "Oliver heard me screaming. Where were you?"

Licking the tears from my lips, I finally spare him a glance.

Gabe's tongue presses against his cheek, his gaze beyond wounded. "I can't believe I even need to defend myself right now," he hisses, head shaking side to side. "But I was listening to music with my earbuds in, as I do every fucking night, as you *already know*."

I flinch back.

"And how do you know that, Syd?" he continues, stalking forward ever so slowly, balled-up fists at his sides. "Maybe it's because we've been best friends for two goddamn decades and you *know* I listen to music every night, just like you *know* how I take my coffee, and you *know* my favorite beer, and you *know* my first car, my shoe size, my ridiculous fear of monkeys, and that I despise ranch dressing almost as much as I despise country music."

The bile lodged in my throat almost chokes me, and I drag my fingernails through my hair, lowering my chin, confusion tearing me in half. What have I done?

What the hell was I thinking?

"And I'd like to think that someone who doesn't know me even a *fraction* as much as you do, would know with one-hundred percent fucking certainty, that I would never, *ever*, break into my best friend's house, terrify her, and physically *attack* her."

He's right. He's so right.

Oh, *God*, he's absolutely right.

A cry rips from my throat, a gut-wrenching, guilty sob, and I cup my hand over my mouth to keep more from spilling out. My eyes drift from Gabe to Travis, both faces etched with disappointment, before I twist around to find Oliver. He's watching me, silent and worried, trying to piece together something I can't even begin to understand.

I turn back to Gabe. "I'm so fucking sorry," I whimper. A pathetic apology for a fatal error. "The gum... your chewing gum, I-I thought... Oh, my God." Heaving in a breaking breath, I stumble forward, reaching for him. Gabe jumps away, disgusted. "Gabe, please, understand. Your gum is the exact same smell as the man who attacked me... eucalyptus. The scent has been carved into me since that night, and it just... *triggered* me."

Gabe's eyes dart across my face, his forehead taut with anger, his lips pressed together in a thin line. He doesn't reply.

"I just *reacted*. I didn't think, I just..."

There's nothing I can say. The damage is done.

I see it scrawled across his face, burned into his flaming jade eyes— eyes that have only ever twinkled with humor and affection around me... *until now.*

Yes, the damage is done, and I'll be sifting through the rubble, desperate to latch onto a tarnished piece of what we had for the rest of my life.

"The gum was in a kitchen drawer," Gabe finally says, his tone now deadly calm. "I thought it was Oliver's, but it was probably leftover from one of my parties. Now, get out of my house, Sydney. I can't fucking look at you."

I swallow. "Please—"

"Get the hell out!"

Travis steps forward, pointing his index finger towards the front door like I'm a scolded child. "You heard my son. You need to go."

Startled, I inch back, bumping into Oliver. I can hardly make out his expression through the blur of tears, but his arms are crossed, his body stiff. He probably feels just as betrayed as his brother, wondering when I'll turn on him next. "I'm sorry," I say, a small, mortified squeak. Then I race past him, down the stairs, not even bothering to grab my shoes or coat.

I just need to get out, I need air, I need to *disappear*.

I'm trudging through the snow in my slipper socks, the burning ball of shame inside me deflecting the icy wind that tries to knock me down. He's jogging towards me, appearing by my side as soon as I reach my porch, dropping my shoes and coat beside us on the stoop.

"Sydney..."

Oliver takes me in his arms as I fall against him, a painful howl snuffed out by his chest as I shatter and wilt, the verity of my crime sinking its teeth all the way in. I weep into the buttons of his shirt, fisting the material between my fingers as I cling to him. Oliver wraps me up and holds me tight, kissing my hair, resting his cheek on top of my head while I break.

He says nothing, and I prefer it that way. He just lets me cry, and it's an ugly cry, an ugly purge of ugly things.

With Oliver's hands stroking my hair, his whispered hushes a soothing soundtrack to my grief, and the moon and stars our only witnesses, I mutter softly, "Thank you."

Thank you for coming back for me.

Thank you for forgiving me.

Thank you for loving me, ugly parts and all.

The mood is solemn and quiet as we lie curled up on my couch, Alexis purring contentedly in Oliver's lap, oblivious to the turmoil enveloping us. I'm exhausted, defeated, and I have no tears left to cry. It's just the whooshes of wind outside my window, swollen eyes, and Oliver's heartbeat pressed into my ear. His arm hasn't left me since we stumbled in from the cold over an hour ago, a comforting promise that he's still with me; he won't let go. His fingers graze along my upper arm, his warm breath teasing my hair.

Nuzzling in closer, I reach inside to find my voice and finally break our silence. "There was no logic or reason or lucid thought in what I said back there," I murmur, my throat dry and cracked. "It's like I was taken over, possessed, living through that nightmare all over again, and I just spewed out careless words as my body reacted to the trigger."

"You can't attempt to find reason in trauma, Sydney." Oliver squeezes my waist with a knowing grip. "Trauma is like poison. It seeps in when you least expect it to, and it lingers long after the initial dust has settled, inflicting more damage, more destruction. It's a vicious cycle."

"How do you cope so well?" I wonder.

"I don't cope any better than you, Syd... just differently, I suppose. I spent twenty-two years fighting my battles alone inside my head, so that's what I'm accustomed to. I'm wired that way. You react with external emotion."

I nod against him in understanding, my eyes closing with a shaky inhale.

"I'd like to tell you there's an expiration date on your pain, but I will never lie to you," Oliver tells me, tender and kind. He places a kiss along my temple. "There will always be moments that take you by surprise and steal your breath. The fireworks, for instance—logically, I knew I was not in harm's way, just as you knew Gabe would never hurt you."

I sniffle. "He'll never forgive me."

"I'll talk to him. It will take time, but if I know anything, I know that hope is never lost."

"He hates me."

"No, Sydney, he loves you. That's why it hurts."

I'm forced to bite down on my bottom lip to keep it from quivering as I replay the look on Gabe's face over and over and *over*. All I want to do is pass out and dream away the wreckage I've caused. "I think I should get some sleep. I'm emotionally drained."

"I'm fatigued as well," Oliver agrees with a sigh, standing from the couch when I slide off of him. "I'm going to take a shower. I'll have to run home and tend to Athena, but then I'll join you in bed."

A smile lifts at the thought of spending the night with him. "Okay."

Oliver leans down to place a sweet kiss against my lips, lingering long enough that I feel the adoration, the emotion, his unconditional love for me. He moves a delicate wisp of hair from my forehead, his lips trailing up as his hands cradle my face. "You'll get through this, Syd," he whispers to my hairline, adamancy lacing his words. "You can survive anything. You're the Queen of the Lotus."

When he pulls back, his smile matches mine, his eyes showing me just how much he means that. I'm filled with a semblance of hope.

We file up the stairs, Oliver heading into the bathroom, and me lighting a few candles in my bedroom for ambiance, then collapsing onto my bed and burying myself beneath the sheets. I stare at the ceiling for a few minutes as the showerhead turns on, a calming backdrop to my turbulent mind. Tears and nostalgia mingle inside me, and I roll over, opening my nightstand drawer and pulling out the photographs from Lorna.

I focus on the ones of Gabe, trailing a finger along his happy, goofy grin, always the comedian—always the life of the party, even as a little kid. And then there's poor Clem with no smile at all, her light snuffed out by the hands of an evil man.

It still doesn't make any sense. How did I never notice Bradford hanging around the neighborhood, let alone assaulting my sister? And how did the police not uncover a single piece of evidence that tied him to our families?

God, I need to tell Oliver. I need to tell him tonight. The day is already ruined… might as well go out with a bang.

As my eyes scan the photographs, new tears sprouting to the surface, something unsettling catches my focus. I zero in on Clementine in the group photo, the day we played *Capture the Flag* in the front yard. I study her stiff posture, her sullen expression… the man standing behind her with his hand curled around her bony hip.

I flip through more photos.

Oliver and I are blowing bubbles. In the background, Clem is sitting on his lap.

Flip, flip, flip.

He's holding her hand.

He's sitting beside her.

He's standing beside her.

"You're on my team, Clementine."

She pouts, glancing my way. "Why can't I be on your team, Syd?"

"Because Oliver and Sydney are always on the same team. You know this," he tells her.

"Because I like him more than you!" I shout back, oblivious.

Oh, *fuck.*

Vomit climbs up my throat, and I roll off the bed, hurling into my bedside garbage can. "Oliver!" I shriek, crawling on my knees to grab the scattered photos between trembling fingers. He can't hear me over the shower running, so I pull myself up, tripping as I race from the bedroom. "Oh, God…" I whimper as I approach the bathroom door. My fist raised, ready to start pounding, I cry out, "It's Tra—"

A firm palm clamps around my mouth in a sickeningly familiar grip, yanking me to his chest and away from the bathroom. My eyes pop as terror courses through me, and I kick my leg out, just barely grazing the door with my toes as he drags me backwards toward my room. Screaming bloody murder against his hand, the sounds are muffled to almost nothing as I scratch at his arm and dig my heels into the carpet.

Heart pounding, blood pumping, thoughts scattered, he spins me around when we reach the bedroom, his large hand still held tightly over my mouth.

Our eyes lock, and I've never been more scared.

"You've always been a spirited one, *Syd*," he sneers, his spit misting my face as my futile sobs meet his enclosed palm.

Travis kicks the door shut with his foot, and before I know what hit me, everything goes black.

CHAPTER TWENTY-EIGHT

BRADFORD

July 2, 1998

THE KNOCK AT MY FRONT DOOR interrupts my *King of the Hill* marathon, and I grumble a few curses as I slam my fifth beer down beside me, the contents splashing over the rim of the bottle. "Hell, I'm coming," I slur, half-drunk but mostly irritated by the intrusion.

Storming towards the entryway of my secluded farmhouse, I whip the door open with a scowl.

"Ray Ford?"

My eyes narrow at the well-dressed stranger standing a few feet back from the stoop. Aggravated, I prop my shoulder against the frame and stare him down. "Who's asking?"

"Who I am doesn't matter much."

"It matters to me because I've got shit to do, and you're an inconvenience."

The cartoon blares behind me, giving away my plans for the evening.

"Yes, well, I'll try to make it worth your while. Can I come in?"

The man stands before me in his overpriced dress pants and V-neck tee. He looks like a goddamn kid—upper twenties at most. His blondish hair is slicked back with fancy styling gel, and a gold chain rims his slender neck. This asshole screams new money, and he smells like one of those cologne advertisements from the JCPenney catalog. "Make it quick."

Allowing him inside, his dark eyes case the modest living area, tipping his nose up to the mess of dirty dishes and miscellaneous piles of mail and junk. "Nice place."

"Fuck off. What do you want?"

A grin tips on his mouth. "I need a favor."

"I don't do favors."

"I heard you do *well-compensated* favors," the man breezes, studying his meticulously groomed fingernails. "I got your name from a guy."

My jaw ticks as I cross my arms over my chest. "What guy?"

"Earl Hubbard."

Well, this son-of-a-bitch certainly has connections. My face remains indifferent. "Fuck Earl. I haven't talked to that asshole since college."

"He still talks about you."

Dammit. *Goddammit.* I massage the nape of my neck with my palm, turning away from the dickhead in front of me as I attempt to prematurely talk myself out of whatever hit he wants to hire me for. "I don't do that shit anymore," I mutter, facing a stack of bills piled high on my dining room table.

"Everyone has their price."

I whirl back around, stalking towards him, my finger wagging in his cocky face. "I paid the price, and I'm *still* paying the price. Get the fuck out of my house, kid."

He's rigid, still, ramrod straight. The bastard doesn't flinch, and his smile doesn't waver. "I have a problem and I'm told that you're the man who can make my problem go away."

"I'm not that man anymore."

"Ah, yes," he drawls, head tilting to the left, almost condescending. "I heard about the unfortunate home invasion that cost you dearly. My deepest condolences."

He's shoved up against my wall before he can catch his next breath, my fingers curling around his ridiculous designer shirt. "Don't you *ever* speak another word about my family, or I'll leave a hole in that pretty boy face of yours, do you understand?" I seethe, hissing through my teeth. "Get the hell out."

A laugh travels over to me, the man seemingly unruffled by my threat. "See, I like this side of you. It's exactly what I'm looking for."

Indignation burns me, but I step back, releasing his polyester tee with a sharp withdrawal and watching as he stumbles to regain his balance. A sigh filters through my lips as one hand plants around my hip and the other scrubs down my jaw. I can't help but assess my living conditions—the mildew, the water leaks, the layers of filth that inhabit every room in this godforsaken house.

House.

It's not a home—it hasn't been a home since the day they were stolen from me. One wrong deal and my life was taken by the barrel of some anonymous prick's forty-five revolver.

My wife. My son. Even my fucking parakeet.

I told myself I was done—hell, I was more than done. I was one shot of Jim Beam away from taking my own pistol to the back of my throat. Some days I regret being such a goddamn coward.

Shaking my head, I signal him towards the exit. "I won't do it. Take your offer and shove it up your pretentious ass."

He puckers his lips through a smirk, mutely judging me from top to bottom. "You think I'm young and stupid."

"That, amongst other things. Mostly, I think you're barking up the wrong tree."

"I like this tree."

"This tree can't be bought."

A long sigh filters over to me. "How much did you get for your last hit?"

"You mean, how much did I *lose?*" I shoot back. "Fuck you. Go."

"Ten, twenty, thirty?"

My jaw clenches. "Twenty-five."

"That's a lot of money," he nods, pacing my dirty floors in his shiny shoes. He slips his hands into his pockets, quiet for a few beats, deliberating his next move. "I heard your wife was the primary breadwinner. I'm sure her death left quite the financial burden on you."

"I get by," I bite out, unimpressed.

"Their funerals probably set you back, yes?"

I'm about to lunge at him, but he steps away, hands up, palms forward. "Whoa, hey, I'm just trying to work through this with you. It looks like times are tough. I want to help."

"You want to help yourself."

A flippant shrug. "I'm a huge fan of mutually beneficial arrangements. It's the businessman in me."

"Can't be that great of a businessman if you're standing in front of me right now."

His lips twitch as he scratches at his lightly stubbled cheek. "I have my shortcomings. Someone saw something they shouldn't have."

"And now you're asking me to fix your problem."

"I'm *paying* you to fix my problem."

Blowing out a slow breath, I dip my chin to my chest and pinch the bridge of my nose, my heartbeat accelerating at the prospect of a hit. I used to live for this shit—the hunt, the adrenaline rush, the cash. I lived for it until it put my family in the ground.

But *fuck*, what the hell have I got to lose now? They're gone. I'm broke, bored off my ass, and I don't really give a shit if I get thrown in jail or wind up dead. The prospect of both sends a tingle of anticipation up my spine.

With a swift shake of my head, a reluctant compliance, I turn to face the stranger who greets me with a smug grin and eyes glittering with secrets. "Give me a number."

"Fifty," he answers with the upmost nonchalance.

Jesus Christ.

I don't need to weigh my options—he knows I'm in. "Details."

"See, that's where things get a bit controversial," he states as he resumes his pacing, plucking a cigar from his back pocket and offering me one. At my acceptance, he lights us both up and mumbles through the fermented tobacco. "My stepson."

Oh, fuck no. "A kid? Absolutely not. I'm out."

"I have a plan."

"Fuck you, fuck your plan, fuck your smarmy fuckin' face. *Leave.*"

"One-hundred."

The number steals the rebuttal from my lips, and I hesitate. I fucking *hesitate* over taking out a little kid. My hits have always been clean and fairly guilt-free—drug dealers, shady corporate assholes, cheating scumbags. I'm able to separate business from morals, compartmentalizing my work from my conscience.

But this is a different level of monster.

That number, though.

Fuck, fuck, fuck.

It would change my life.

I could start over, get the hell out of this shithole, meet someone, create a new family.

One kid.

One. Kid.

Goddammit, I'm going straight to Hell. My voice cracking, eyes on the floor, I croak out through a puff of thick smoke, "Details."

July 4, 1998

Fireworks begin to paint the sky as I arrive at the designated location. It's a neighborhood playground, bustling with a few children and parents as they watch the display from the bottom of a tall hill.

Perched in the driver's seat of my Dodge Intrepid, I glance at the photograph between my fingers, a line of sweat casing my brow. I'm fucking nervous and it's really goddamn irritating. I'm *never* nervous when I'm about to do a job.

But this is different.

This is the kind of job that changes everything. There's no coming back from this.

I study the Polaroid in my unsteady hand, fingernails dirty from working in the crops today. I've decided that's where I'll get rid of the body. My property is secluded, and the hole I dug is nearly five-hundred yards into the crop field. I have no connection to this kid, so I'm feeling confident he'll stay missing for a good long time.

Oliver Lynch. He's a cute little guy—reminds me of my boy, Tommy, with the shaggy brown hair and bangs that nearly cover his smiling eyes, a spattering of freckles along the bridge of his nose, and two perfectly placed dimples. There's a young girl in the picture, happy and pig-tailed, and they lick their respective popsicles on a set of swings.

Tommy loved purple popsicles.

A rattled sigh leaves me in a long breath, and I tuck the photograph into my shirt pocket. I have a clear image of the boy, along with a description of what he'll be wearing tonight: a red and white plaid button-down with denim overalls and *Ninja Turtle* light-up sneakers. I was told he'd likely be attached to the hip of the girl from the photograph. And when I peek through the slow-dancing leaves of a giant Sycamore tree, that's exactly what I find—Oliver lying beside the little blonde girl, shoulder to shoulder, at the top of the grassy hill. I'm a good distance away, but they look alone up there, staring at the explosions as a backpack rests beside them.

A sharp crack has me jumping in my seat, and I internally slap myself for acting like a pussy. I've done dozens of jobs, and this is a *kid*. Kids are trusting. Kids don't put up a fight.

It'll be a piece of cake.

Pulling myself together, I hop out of the car and close the door, assessing my surroundings to make sure there are no potential witnesses. I'm parked along a dead end cul-de-sac that backs up to the lake, and the hill looms overhead, two small voices barely penetrating the fireworks. Leaves and stones crunch beneath my boots as I try to get a better look through the trees.

"... for the man who grants our wishes. He lives in the sky."

It's all I can make out before another boom strikes, sheathing the treetops in a violet glow. The little girl starts rummaging through her backpack, pulling out art supplies, when I notice Wellington approach the two children from the left, his voice shrill over the firework display.

"Sydney, your parents want you home now," he hollers over to them, and I can't make out what they're doing when the wind steals the leaves again, hindering my view.

I pace along the side of the gravel road, inching towards the end of the tree line.

"One second, almost done!" a sweet voice responds. "Okay, coming. Bye, Oliver!"

My eyes find her running down the hill, slinging her rainbow backpack over one shoulder as she waves behind her, nearly tripping. Her pigtails bounce with every clumsy step.

I hear him then, calling back, "Bye, Syd. See you tomorrow."

Guilt punctures my gut and I feel sick inside.

Fucking hell, this is going to suck.

Wellington bellows over to Oliver once the girl has disappeared down the street, running towards her house. "Oliver, time to go. I'll take you home."

"Yeah, yeah, I'm coming," he says.

I watch him slide down the hill on his butt, causing Wellington to grow impatient. "Now, Oliver."

Oliver stands and skips the rest of the way. "Can we get ice cream now?"

"No. Let's go, troublemaker."

Troublemaker. That's my cue.

Insides curdling with unease, anxiety higher than ever, I walk backwards until I'm shrouded in brush, my face peering around a thick tree trunk. Wellington and the boy amble over to me, and just when they're a few feet away, Wellington curses under his breath.

"Damn, I forgot my wallet at the playground. You stay right here, Oliver," he orders. Dark eyes meet with mine through the black of night with a quick glance—*an execution.* "I'll be right back."

"Yeah, okay." Oliver kicks at a rock, sighing as he glances around the darkened side street. Moments tick by, matching my racing fucking heart, when Oliver begins to hum the tune to *Puff the Magic Dragon.* That same heart, cold and dead, clenches with memories of Tommy and me reading his board book by the fireplace together while the song drifted from our cassette player.

That song always teared me the fuck up, and I would dread the day Tommy grew up, forgoing his Lego blocks for Nintendo games and action figures for skateboarding with his buddies.

Now... I'd give anything to watch him grow.

I'm sweating profusely, the humid July air stale and thick as it strangles my lungs like a noose. I swipe at my forehead with the back of my dirt-stained hand, swallowing down my indecision and breaking into action.

Oliver's chin jerks up when a branch cracks, his aimless hum carried away with another gust of hot air. "Hello?"

I act fast, catching the startled look in his burgundy eyes before I pounce on him, one arm slinking around his middle and the other stifling his yell with my palm. "Shh, you're okay. Stay quiet and stop squirming." Dragging him to my car, his feet skimming the rocks and dirt, I heave us both into the backseat and shut the door, securing the childproof locks and reaching to the floor for my bag of rope. "I'll make it quick, kid. You'll be okay."

"Who are you? Where's my stepdad?"

"He wanted me to take you somewhere very special. But you need to be a good boy, yeah?"

Another round of fireworks burst to life outside the dusty windows, illuminating the look of terror in the little boy's eyes. "I-I'm scared, mister. I don't think I want to go."

"You gotta go. It's a real nice surprise." Pocketknife between my teeth, I work to secure the kid's hands behind his back, rope tight and unforgiving against his delicate skin. Droplets of sweat drip down, landing on his fingers. "You can't make any noise, or I'll have to gag you," I tell him firmly. "You just sit back and watch the fireworks until we get there, okay?"

He agrees with a timid nod as I crawl into the driver's seat and shuffle around my pockets for my keys, preparing for the thirty-mile commute back to my farmhouse.

It's a long, painful drive.

The kid is quiet, just like he was told, and I *hate* that he is.

Why couldn't he disobey? Why couldn't he be a little shit and try to claw my goddamn eyes out? This would be a hell of a lot easier.

"It's all right, kid. It's gonna be all right," I mutter, more to myself as my fingers curl around the steering wheel in a deathlike grip. I twist the dial on the radio to increase the volume, desperate for a distraction, and I'm grateful when a breezy sixties tune bursts to life.

Gaze lifting to the rearview mirror, I watch as Oliver stares out the window with big, confused eyes, rimmed with tears. He's silent but trembling, and I'm starting to doubt everything.

But how can I turn back now? I'm already *in this*. I've been paid half the money, the kid has seen my face, and Wellington's threat is not far from my mind…

"Earl told me you were clean and quiet, so I have no doubt you'll come through for me. But just so we're clear—if my stepson escapes, I assure you the consequences will be unfortunate for you. I am not clean, and I am not quiet," Wellington said before leaving my house two days ago. He paused in the doorway with narrowed eyes and an ugly sneer. *"And the boy will die regardless, so don't go pulling out any hero cards, understood?"*

I nodded, slow and certain. "You don't need to worry about that."

"Good." A sniff. "There's nothing I detest more in life than loose ends."

We pull into my long, winding drive a while later, and I kill the headlights, rubbing my palms up and down my damp face through a disheveled breath. I'm frazzled, jittery, and nauseated.

I look back at Oliver, who is perfectly still and silent as he glances around the unlit property. "You okay, kid?"

A small nod. He fixates on something outside the window, barely visible through the dark night. His body seems to relax, his gaze brightening with a spark of relief. "Is that the surprise?"

I follow his line of vision and my stomach drops.

Tommy's bicycle.

It still sits in the front yard, shiny and red, the tires lightly worn and caked with dried mud. I never had the heart to move it, let alone get rid of it.

The seconds go by, long and slow, until a thoughtful minute has passed.

It's only a minute, but it's a powerful minute. A life-changing minute—just like the minute I sat helpless, tied to a kitchen chair, as I watched my wife and child get their heads blown off.

A hell of a lot can happen in one minute, and I know that better than anyone.

Pulling the blindfold out of my pocket, I exit the car and round the hood to the backseat. Oliver climbs out when I order him to, and I carefully secure the piece of cloth around his eyes. His body tenses up again, limbs starting to quiver. "You're all right, I promise."

Oliver begins to cry, his tears absorbing into the fabric of the blindfold. "Can Syd come with us?"

"No. Syd can't come."

Another whimper as I pull him forward by the wrist. "But how will the man in the sky grant our wish?"

Instead of guiding the boy behind the house, toward his grave, I pull him through the yard, and we head for the front door. My own misty eyes land on the deserted bicycle as we pass, and I reply, "The only man granting wishes tonight is me, kid."

CHAPTER TWENTY-NINE

OLIVER

THE POUNDING IN MY HEAD is a peculiar thing to wake up to, and I can't for the life of me recall even going to bed.

I remember being in the shower.

There was an odd noise—a clattering of some sort.

Did Sydney hurt herself?

I clothed myself in my boxers and a clean t-shirt, drying my hair with a towel as I investigated the disturbance.

And then... *darkness.*

Groaning, I lift my head from my shoulder, noting a sticky fluid coating my tongue when I wet my lips—something tangy and metallic, like copper pennies.

Blood?

A noise pierces through the dull ache pulsing in my temple, causing my eyes to flutter, the small action nearly paralyzing me with pain.

Sydney?

I think I hear her calling for me, but she sounds muffled and far away. Instinctually, I attempt to move my arms, my will to reach for her hindered by the restraints digging into my wrists.

Rope?

"Syd..." Her name escapes as an anguished gasp, hardly comprehendible as I sputter on the liquid still dribbling into my mouth. It's most certainly blood and it must be directly correlated to the throbbing in my temporal lobe. *Dear God, what happened?* I give my hands another tug, meeting firm resistance as my eyelids finally blink open all the way.

I'm greeted with the blurry barrel of a handgun merely two inches from my face.

"Welcome back," says the man holding the weapon, his voice and image still obscured in shadow as reality slowly begins to solidify. "Again."

"Sydney."

She's my prime concern.

Pain radiates through me, from the roots of my hair all the way down to my fastened feet, but I manage to twist my head to the right and discover Sydney lying beside me, her own hands tethered to the bedpost behind her back. Her mouth is obstructed by a *Nirvana* bandana, her mascara streaking down cherry red cheeks, a throaty, screeching sound stifled by the fabric.

We're in her room, bound to the bedframe.

My body reacts on instinct, and I repel the gruff twine wrapped snuggly around my wrists and ankles, legs kicking, torso struggling against the headboard through a grunt.

"Don't hurt yourself now, Oliver."

I whip my head towards the assailant, his voice and features finally assembling into something familiar. The mask dissolves, the shadowy blob for a face disintegrating into a man I've come to trust.

The Faceless Man has been unveiled.

"Travis," I whisper hoarsely. My mouth is not wrapped in cloth, and I'm certain it's because the double-barrel revolver aimed between my eyes is intended to keep me quiet. "What is this?"

Travis releases a prolonged sigh of vexation as he sits perched on the edge of the mattress beside my legs. "This," he reiterates, gesturing his arms to the chaos he's created. "This is what I like to call loose ends."

Spitting a mouthful of blood to my left, my insides knotted much like my limbs, I find his hard gaze fixed on me as he holds the gun with a steady grip. Confusion bleeds with betrayal, but those things are overridden by the heart-rending worry I feel for the woman I love lying helpless beside me.

Sydney is writhing in place, her entire body tremoring with tears and terror as she unsuccessfully tries to escape. "I'm going to get us out of this," I tell her, holding her stare with mine. The tinseled sparks I normally see reflecting back at me have perished into ash. "I'll save you. I always save you."

Cold metal kisses my chin, pulling my attention back to him. Amused laughter follows as Travis taps the side of my jaw with the barrel of the gun. "Ah, yes," he says easily, smirk in place. "Your comic books. You always had a very vivid imagination, Oliver."

"Please don't hurt her," I beg, tugging at the ropes. "God, please, let her go."

"I respect the noble request, but I'm afraid I'll have to decline."

A surge of protective anger courses through me, culminating in a savage growl that tears through my lips. I try to lunge at him, but Travis flips the gun in his hand so the butt collides with my jaw, sending a mist of blood across the linens.

Sydney erupts with more repressed screams, the bed shaking violently beneath her ministrations. She's shouting my name through the wadded-up bandana in her mouth, and my God, I want nothing more than to quell her fear, ease her pain, and kiss away the tear stains that glisten her cheekbones.

Travis stands from the bed, the gun still pointed at me. "I assure you, this is not the festive celebration I had in mind when I woke up this morning," he drawls, holding one hand up in mock defense. "In fact, I was hoping it wouldn't come to this at all."

"What is this about? Why are you attacking us?" I demand through clenched teeth, chest heaving.

His weary sigh travels over to us as he scratches his head with the weapon. "You're not supposed to be here, Oliver," Travis replies. "And I wish I could bring that cowardly son-of-a-bitch back to life, just so I could bash his brains in again for leaving me with this mess."

"Bradford."

"Yes, *Bradford*. Ray Ford, the man I foolishly trusted to take care of my problem."

I shake my head, drowning in confusion. "I don't understand."

"I suppose you wouldn't," he says with a halfhearted chuckle. "Imagine my surprise when my son informs me that your memories were wiped clean. I thought for damn *sure* you were going to spill my secrets to your little girlfriend about what you saw that day. I thought I was done for. Hell, I even had my suitcases packed, ready to start over in Belize under a shiny, new alias."

Travis stalks over to me, forcing the butt of the gun against the side of my head. I wince through a hiss of contempt. "You attacked her."

His shoulders shrug with indifference before he pulls back, chomping on a piece of chewing gum. "It wasn't my intention. I avoid getting my hands dirty whenever possible, but I *had* to be sure she didn't know anything before I uprooted my life."

"So, you decided to beat the answers out of her?"

Travis paces the bedroom, cool and collected. "I was only there to bug her computer—I was in the middle of installing a listening device when she had to stick her nose where it didn't belong. She forced my hand, much like she's doing right now."

"My God, listen to yourself," I spit out, his crass words causing a lump of dread to fester in my gut. "No secret or indiscretion is worth *this*."

"You're so naïve, son," he quips.

"I'm not your son." Absorbing his tirade, the pieces begin to fall into place, and for as intelligent as I consider myself to be, I cannot believe I never picked up on any of the signs. "Gabe told me you'd been spending more time with him recently. You were keeping tabs on me, using your own son for information."

His snide leer is my response.

"You wanted me to live with you so you could keep an eye on me... so I would be under your thumb and you could monitor my memory recall."

Travis replies with a grating chuckle, confirming my suspicions. And when he saunters back towards me, I react instinctively, throwing my tethered legs over the side of bed and kicking the nightstand, watching as it crashes into his knees. Unfortunately, it doesn't do much in terms of injuring him—it merely slows him down long enough to incite a new wave of rage against me. With my bottom half hanging off the bed, I brace myself as Travis charges at me, jabbing the gun into my abdomen so hard, bruising is imminent. Sydney's muted cries intertwine with Travis' words:

"You always were a troublemaker."

"You're a troublemaker, Oliver."

Flashes of memories barrage me, open fire on my neurons.

"You're on my team, Clementine."

Flash.

"They're taking a really long time to hide the flag."

"Maybe you should go spy on them. I'll stay here with my teddy."

I squeeze my eyes shut, blinded and buried by the onslaught.

I tiptoe around the side of the house, following the sound of my stepfather's voice. They are hiding behind a garden trellis.

"It's okay, babygirl. I won't hurt you."

Clementine responds, sounding sad and frightened. "It feels weird. I want my mom."

"Shh. You know we can't tell anybody about this. You do know that, right? That would be very, very bad."

"I know."

Her shorts are pulled down to her ankles. He's touching her in bad places.

"Good job, babygirl. That's what I like to hear."

More flashes. More lights. More sounds. More horror.

Travis spots me over Clementine's shoulder.

The look in his eyes—oh no, oh no, oh no.

I'm in big trouble.

I run.

Flash.

I'm in the kitchen, hysterical, and my mother is so worried about me.

"I'm scared," I cry.

I'm weeping, screaming, frantic.

He's so mad at me. He's going to punish me. I won't be able to play with Sydney for a long, long time. Weeks, maybe.

"Sweetheart, tell me what's wrong. Tell me what happened."

My mother.

She's trying to console me.

And then he's there, behind me, his hand clamping around my shoulder, squeezing so hard he freezes the words in my throat.

"You're a troublemaker, Oliver." He addresses my mother, tone scolding. "I discovered Oliver cheating during our game of Capture the Flag. He knows better."

"Oh, honey, you know that takes the fun out of the game."

"It's unacceptable," Travis says, his grip tightening on my trembling shoulder.

He's lying. He wants me to lie, too. Maybe I won't be punished if I lie.

"I-I'm sorry. I won't do it again."

Another flash, and I'm in my bedroom.

I feel him there, standing in the shadows, looming over me as I stare up at the glow-in-the-dark stars on my ceiling.

Travis whispers in my ear, a deadly command, "If you ever tell anyone what you saw today, I will send Sydney away forever and you'll never see her again. Do you understand?"

No, no, no.

Not her. Not Syd.

I nod, tears leaking from my eyes. "I understand."

Flash.

He saw me. He saw me. He saw me.

But I can never tell...

My eyes pop open, my breaths ragged and unhinged as the last two decades culminate into a sickening pinnacle. Travis is centimeters from my face, a smile curling on his chafed lips. Sweat mixes with blood as I run my tongue along my own upper lip. "I never would have told anyone," I tell him, and it's true... *it's true.*

He knew Sydney was my weakness.

She still is.

His eye twitches. "I couldn't risk it. My life, my future, everything I was building for myself would have been snuffed out by a loud-mouthed kid," he says flippantly. "Don't underestimate the gravity of your situation, Oliver. There are no lengths I wouldn't go to in order to keep myself out of prison—not then, not now. I'm fully aware of what would happen to me there."

"You're a monster."

"I prefer *self-preservationist*," he counters.

I growl at him, a deep rumbling in my throat, laced with fuel and white-hot anger. "She was just a child. You ruined her."

Travis shrugs like it's the most casual thing in the world. "Trust me, I debated getting rid of her, too, but I'm not an idiot. Two children who live right next door to each other going missing at the same time? I couldn't risk the whispers and suspicion. Suspicion brings questions and digging and poking around—*obnoxious*," he says, his tone glib. "Besides, Clementine was my favorite toy. I trained her well, and I *knew* she would never speak a word of it to anyone."

"You're sick," I seethe.

A wicked grin stares back at me. "I'm a survivalist, and I'll do whatever it takes to protect myself." Travis straightens his stance, removing the gun from my side and stuffing it into the hem of his blue jeans. Cold gray eyes drift between me and Sydney before he begins to pace the room once again. "The biggest mistake I ever made was trusting that bastard, Earl, when he told me the deed was done. Ford must have paid him off. *Stupid.*" And then he plucks a lighter from his front pocket, flicking the little wheel until a flame sparks to life. "But I won't make the same mistake twice. This time, I plan to watch you burn with my own eyes."

His implication is not lost on either of us, and I turn to look at Sydney, eyes brimming with apology and love and remorse and so many things left undone. Our dreams will soon be nothing but ashes and decay, buried right along with Travis Wellington's secrets.

Travis saunters over to the window, muttering under his breath as he continues to flick the metal wheel. "No witnesses, no fingerprints, no motive..."

His words fade out as I focus on Sydney.

Her tears spill hard and fast, collapsing into the fabric of the bandana, her eyes locked on mine. Sydney tips her head back, just marginally, and I drag my gaze to her wrists while Travis is distracted across the room, talking himself through his plan.

She's chafing the rope along a piece of splintered wood, the bristles breaking, her restraints loosening. My breath catches as her eyes dance with frantic hope while she works the binds in a silent frenzy.

Sydney told me Alexis had been clawing at the bedposts in the recent weeks—her pesky misbehavior may now be our only chance of getting out of here alive.

Travis is still preoccupied as he peruses our burial grounds, casing the room, stepping from one end to the other. He starts humming a buoyant tune, the prospect of our painful deaths doing little to upset him.

Evil. Travis Wellington is pure evil.

And I realize in that moment that Bradford didn't take me because I reminded him of his son.

He *spared* me because I reminded him of his son.

Bradford knew that Travis would stop at nothing to keep his secrets safe—my life would always be in jeopardy, I would forever be in danger, unless I was kept hidden... unless *I* became the secret.

But I don't have time to mull over this revelation because Travis is ambling back over to my side of the bed, and just before he reaches me, I hear a tiny snap to my right, a thread breaking.

It sounds like hope.

It sounds like a fighting chance.

Thank you, Alexis. You're a wonderful sidekick.

Keeping my sights straight ahead to avoid giving us away, I inhale an emotion-laced breath as he approaches me. "You don't have to do this," I attempt in vain to reason. "You've frightened us enough—we won't speak a word of this to anyone."

"Loose ends, Oliver," he breezes. "Don't like them."

"Please..."

"What, don't you have superpowers or something?" Travis mocks, climbing over me on the bed, straddling my waist as he adds a second spool of rope to my wrists, securing me tighter to the bedpost. There's a faint movement in my peripheral, but Travis doesn't notice. "The Black

Lotus, right? Scary…." He laughs. "Shouldn't you be saving the damsel in distress?"

I swallow. "I've come to learn that Sydney isn't the damsel I always envisioned."

Sydney goes deadly still when Travis spares her a sneering glance. "I'll agree with you there. She's a firecracker, that one."

"Yes… and I am not without superpowers, Travis." Pulling his attention back to me, I lift my knees to his groin, causing him to buckle on top of me with a howl of pain.

"You stupid son-of-a-bitch," he barks through gritted teeth. Long fingers slink around my throat, hindering my airflow. "What's your superpower, Oliver? Huh? Unless it's magically escaping from this rope, I'd say you're in pretty deep shit right now."

"I'm fairly…" *Cough.* "…good at…" *Wheeze.* "…predicting the future."

Travis loosens his grip, curiosity flaring. "And what exactly do you predict is going to happen, aside from the fire department sifting through your ashes come sunrise?"

My expression remains stoic, eyes pinned on his. "I predict you're about to be hit in the head with a table lamp."

Confusion wrinkles his brow for a quick second before his eyes flash with realization.

But it's too late.

Thwap.

Sydney nails him in the back of the head with the lamp, and this time, her aim is impeccable. I think she even surprises herself when she freezes, mouth agape, watching in stunned silence as Travis topples off the bed and hits the floor, unconscious. She glances my way, kneeling beside me on the mattress. "Holy shit."

Despite the circumstances, a smile tugs at my lips as our eyes hold. "Would it be a burden to untie me?"

She blinks away the haze, tossing the lamp aside and jumping into action. "Fuck, sorry."

Sydney mounts me, hands quivering as she attempts to release the restraints. Our faces are close together, her warm breath on my cheek the greatest solace I've ever known. That breath hitches with tiny gasps of disbelief as tears well and fall upon my skin, her body shaking above me. "I'm trying t-to… God, it's so tight…" she stammers, glancing over to Travis' motionless body every so often.

"Just call the police, Syd. He won't be out long."

Her fingers continue to work. "He took our phones."

"Go get help," I insist. "Run next door and fetch my brother. Don't worry about me."

Sydney's eyes ping open, meeting with mine, but she ignores the request and keeps tinkering with the ropes. "I'm not leaving unless you leave with me."

"That's absur—"

My words are cut short when Travis tackles Sydney onto the mattress with a punishing growl, her scream also curtailed when his hand clamps over her mouth.

"You're a firecracker, Syd," he hisses, his words hitting the air like toxic waste as I continue to struggle out of my binds. "Firecrackers are designed to go up in flames."

Travis rolls them off the foot of bed, and I start shouting for help, pulling and tugging with every aching ounce of strength inside me, calling for Sydney, *desperate* and *sick* and *petrified*. They are scuffling, gasping and growling, back on their feet and toppling into Sydney's dresser where her candles sit above it on a ledge wall. A candle tips as Travis throws Sydney back to the ground and climbs on top of her.

And then I see it, I watch it unfold in slow motion—a small orange spark dancing to life in the corner of the bedroom, latching onto Sydney's window coverings and blooming into a tangerine tragedy.

Her pillar candle caught the fabric.

Oh, no.

No, no, no.

Everything seems to fade away for one impossible minute.

It's only a minute, but it's a powerful minute. A life-changing minute— just like the minute I sat helpless, tied up in the backseat of a stranger's vehicle, staring at the fireworks outside the window and wondering if Sydney was watching those same ones. I knew in that minute that everything would change. Life, as I knew it, was over... and I missed her immensely.

That same feeling of heartbreaking disintegration digs its claws into me.

As the flames flicker and climb, an inferno threatening to burn down the life I've rebuilt, I close my eyes and make a wish. I wish on fireworks, on every shooting star, on birthday candles and dandelion seeds. I wish to the man in the sky with all my heart, with each tumbling tear...

"One second, almost done!" Sydney calls back, finalizing her wish. She smiles at me as she packs her bookbag, glancing over her shoulder. "I have to go now."

"Yeah..." I murmur through my disappointment. "What did you wish for?"

Sydney's baby blue eyes twinkle brighter than all the stars in the sky. "Us."
Before I can question her further, she is already skipping down the hill.
"Okay, coming," she says to Travis, who is waiting at the bottom. She sends
me a final WAVE *goodbye. "Bye, Oliver!"*
I wave back as the fireworks blast above me. "Bye, Syd. See you tomorrow."
I wish for tomorrow and the tomorrow after that.
I wish for all the tomorrows... *with her.*

SYDNEY

His fingers wrap around my neck, his lower body pressing me into the carpet like I'm a ragdoll. My wrists are cut and stained with blood from the rope, there are stars in my eyes as my oxygen depletes, and my throat is burning from screeching through my gag.

Wait.

Burning.

My skin warms with a wave of heat right as Travis loosens his grip, his focus shifting to just over my shoulder across the room. I smell the smoke then, and all I can think about is Oliver.

He's still tied.

He's fucking trapped.

Choking through a sob, I watch the confliction cross Travis' face as he decides whether or not to bolt or finish what he started. He's a self-proclaimed survivalist, but he also hates loose ends.

Will he stick around to kill me and risk his life? Or will he run, giving us the chance to escape and spill his secrets?

His fingers squeeze tighter around my esophagus, eyes narrowing at me with disdain, and I think he's made up his mind—*kill*. I'm scratching at his arms, nails ripping through his vile flesh and drawing blood, yet he doesn't waver. He doesn't pull back or soften his hold.

It's over.

But as soon as the thought crosses my mind, there's relief.

I can breathe.

And I think he's changed his mind, decided to play it safe and make a break for it, but no... he slumps over on top of me, passed out cold.

I almost lose consciousness myself when I see Lorna Gibson standing above me with her cane held high, a noble weapon.

No fucking way.

"Never underestimate a nosy neighbor," she proclaims, holding out her hand to me. "The police are on their way."

I push Travis off me like the piece of trash he is and take her outstretched palm, rising to my feet. My brief moment of reprieve is snuffed out fast when I see how fast the flames are spreading, encasing the walls, nearly blocking us in. I turn to Lorna, my eyes pleading. "Find my cat and bring her to safety. I need to help Oliver."

Lorna falters, coughing as the smoke infiltrates our clean air. "Oh, child…"

"Please, save Alexis. *Go.*" Sirens sound in the distance, sending a whoosh of hope through me. I watch as she issues me a tearful nod, a possible goodbye, and then I race towards the bed where Oliver is lying with his eyes closed. "Oliver…" I call to him, choking on the smoke that grows denser by the second. I climb on top of him, shaking his shoulders.

"I'm making a wish," he says softly, eyes fluttering open with a smile.

I start to sob.

I can't help it—I need to concentrate, I need to focus, I need to be *strong* and get us the hell out of here.

I need to be a fucking hero.

But I'm crying and breaking and falling apart, my thighs squeezing his torso, my hands gliding up his arms and violently trembling as I pull at the knots. "I-I'm getting you out of here, Oliver," I whimper, weep, wither and wilt.

Oliver seems to snap back to reality—he returns from wherever he was, from whatever magical place he went to that was far away from here. Maybe the moon, maybe the salty sea, maybe that grassy hill beneath the fireworks on a fateful summer night.

Or maybe his bedroom last Sunday where we made love for the first time and ate room-temperature, heart-shaped omelets, laughing with blissful disregard for anything but us, wrapped in blankets and promises and each other.

His face changes then, our dire reality sinking in deep. "Syd…"

"I'm trying. I'm trying," I sob, hysterics imminent.

Fucking rope!

"Sydney, what are you doing? Get out of here."

Oliver is distraught, trying to push me off of him with his hips. I squeeze my thighs tighter. "I'm not going anywhere without you."

"No… no." His eyes case the room, the flames reflecting in his golden-brown orbs, making them look like an *actual* sunset. "Sydney, get off me. Now."

"No."

"Go, please… God, *please*."

"No!" I shriek, my fingernails bending backwards, grains of rope slicing my skin. I keep pulling, tugging, loosening, *repeat*.

Oliver's face is stricken with panic, with pure horror, his lower body trying in vain to shove me off of him. "Don't you dare do this. Don't you *dare*."

Tears crease the corners of his eyes, slipping down flushed cheeks, and a strangled, painful moan of dissolution ruptures through the ring of fire.

We cry together, we plead together, we wish together…

We'll die together.

"Sydney… I can't let you do this," he insists, his body twisting, turning, tirelessly hoping I'll release my hold and leave him here to die alone.

Not in a million fucking years.

"I'm not going anywhere."

"Goddammit, Syd… you have your whole life ahead of you. Fall in love again, have children, create, thrive, laugh," he implores, a desperate final plea. "Don't do this. I'm *begging* you."

Our sobs intertwine, and I don't know whose is whose.

I sniffle through the storm of tears, my attempts to loosen his ropes weakening as the smoke inhabits me, making me dizzy. "I'm exactly where I want to be."

He arches against the bed, his head thrown back in agony. "No, no, no…"

I clasp his face between my palms, already knowing I won't be able to free him. There's not enough time, I don't have the tools, and my mind is spinning, turning to fog. Coughing and sputtering, I lean in, pressing a kiss to his tear-glazed lips. "I love you, Oliver Lynch," I squeak out, breathing the words of adoration against his mouth and reveling in the way he finally gives in, stops fighting me, and kisses me back.

"I love you, Syd."

My wish came true, and I don't care that we only had ten months together—they were the best ten months of my life, and I wouldn't change a thing.

I wished for *us*… and here we are.

I hold him, I hold him, I just *hold* him, while everything around us burns.

There's no better way to go.

But as soon as I've made peace with my end, two strong arms encircle my waist, and at first I think it's Travis ruining our final, beautiful moment together. I resist, I scream, I cling to Oliver with my thighs around his hips and my nails clawing his shoulders.

"No!"

The arms pull tighter, much too strong for me to withstand, and I'm yanked free from the love of my life. I'm dragged away through the wall of flames, my skin scorching, my arms outstretched and reaching for him, my heart turning to cinders inside that room. I kick and fight and curse and cry at the top of my lungs. "Oliver! No! Let me go! *Let me go!*"

I sound like a banshee, a madwoman, utterly out of control.

Oliver still struggles on the bed, trying to break free, and I can hardly see him now as tears and smoke blur my eyes and we retreat farther and farther away.

"Fuck you!" I scream, legs flailing, nails scratching. "I hate you! I *hate* you! Let me go! *Oliver!*" His name comes out as a dozen heartbreaking syllables, my cry echoing as I'm carried down the staircase and through the living room.

"Go, Syd. Get the fuck out of here."

Gabe.

It's Gabe.

He shoves me out the front door until I fall backwards, landing on the cement stoop and watching in astoundment as Gabe turns around and heads back inside.

Oh, my God.

Oh, my *God.*

Firetrucks approach the scene, the red and blue lights reminiscent of a day that will never be far from my mind. My arms are puckered and bright pink, part of my hair is singed straight off, and the side of my face feels like it's melting. But I don't care, I don't even care, because my two favorite people are trapped inside a burning building and I'm out here.

"Oh, *God,*" I mourn, collapsing back against the cement, staring up at the starry sky. "Please, I beg you. Just one more wish. Please, please, *please.*"

I wait.

It's a slow-motion movie reel as neighbors run from their houses for a front-row seat and Lorna Gibson crouches beside me with Alexis tucked inside her arms. Firetrucks and police cruisers come to a halt along the side of the street, men in uniform filtering out of the vehicles with hoses and heat-protectant suits and mouths moving with mute words I can't even begin to process. Everything sounds far away; underwater.

All I can see is the stars.

All I can hear is my wish repeating inside of my head, over and over and over.

"Oh, Sydney... look."

Lorna's voice causes me to blink myself back to the present moment, and I pull myself up on my elbows, letting out an ugly fucking cry of joy when both Oliver and Gabe come stumbling out my front door, layered in ashes and soot with burns on their skin.

They're alive.

My body is too weak to stand, so I just lie there and wail, my soul sobbing with overwhelming, unparalleled relief. My boys fall beside me on the concrete walkway, Gabe at my side and Oliver in my arms. I roll us over until I'm holding them both, squeezing them with everything I have left. Our tears mingle together—a hymn, a song, a miraculous melody.

The medics approach while firefighters swoop past us into the house, but I can't let these men go, and I can't stop crying.

"Thank you," I croak, my face buried between the two men's chests. Oliver kisses my hair, his fingers tangled in the knotted strands, while Gabe reaches for my hand and holds tight. I look up to the sky. "Thank you, thank you, *thank you.*"

CHAPTER THIRTY

OLIVER

T HE FAMILIAR SOUND OF ZIPPER AND PLASTIC *pulls my chin from my chest as I set aside my comic sketches and face the man in front of me. Bradford takes his mask off, peering down at me sitting in the corner with my knees drawn up. "Are you fetching more supplies today?" I wonder aloud, rising to my feet and observing the subtle luster of sweat dampening his hairline.*

Bradford is older now, like me, and his forehead showcases faint age lines, while his dark hair reveals traces of silvers and grays. He ruffles a large palm through that hair, advancing on me, mask tucked beneath his arm. "Yeah, kid. I'll try to find some ingredients for a nice cake—it's your birthday, after all."

This morning I awoke, and I was eighteen. I'm officially a man.

"I would appreciate that greatly," I tell him, excitement revving through me, pulse quickening. I can hardly recall the taste of birthday cake, but my tastebuds still water at the thought of it. Pacing a few steps towards my guardian, another query tickles my tongue. "Bradford, I... I think, perhaps, I should come with you on your journey today. Seeing as I'm an adult now, I'm more apt to be of service to you."

My rapid heartbeats meet the pained look in his umber eyes. "Oliver, you know I can't let you out into the world. It's not safe. You wouldn't even recognize it anymore."

"I'm a fast learner," I insist, pressing further. I close in on him, a hint of desperation seeping into my tone. "Please, give me the chance to prove I am capable."

"It's not..." Bradford averts his gaze to the corner of the room, illuminated by my Vitamin D lamp lighting up the cement walls decorated in magazine clippings and comic book illustrations. Two potted plants adorn the space, along with stacks of books and video tapes. He sighs, strained and weary. "You don't understand. I can't protect you up there."

"I'm quite strong, Bradford. I've been focusing on my exercises. Please, lend me your protective gear and I'll make you proud."

"I can't do that, kid," he shakes his head, struggling through a mask of confliction. "You're all I've got. Keeping you out of harm's way is the only thing I'm good for anymore..."

His words pinch my heart. "I'll come back. You know I wouldn't leave you. You're all I have as well."

"Maybe one day, Oliver. Maybe one day it will be safe for you out there, but today is not that day," Bradford explains, his expression taut. "You're like a son to me, kid. You're special... you're important."

"Like the Black Lotus?"

"Yeah," he swallows, head nodding slowly. "Like the Black Lotus."

He's right. I have no idea how the world works anymore, let alone where I'd go or how I'd navigate through the threats and unknowns. If something happened to me, Bradford would be all alone and I couldn't do that to him. My shoulders sag with resignation, my lips thinning. "Yes. I suppose you're right."

"It's for the best," he whispers, gaze now lowered to the green rug beneath his boots. "But I'll bring you back that birthday cake, yeah?"

I clear the disappointment from my throat. "Thank you. I would enjoy that."

"And hey, one more thing..." Bradford pulls the zipper of his suit down a bit farther, then plucks two brown cigars from his pocket. Contemplation settles along his fine lines and wrinkles as he studies them and hands one over to me. "You know, I always looked forward to the day I could share a cigar with my boy, Tommy. I told myself I'd allow him one the day he turned eighteen."

A resounding grief fills the space between the stone walls as I pinch the rolled paper between my fingers, eyeing the offering with curiosity.

"Will you smoke a cigar with me, Oliver?"

I smile with an air of sadness. "Yes, of course. Thank you, Bradford." I'm uncertain what to expect as he lights up the end of my cigar, embers glowing, smoke billowing, but when I inhale a deep drag, I sputter. I choke and gag, the taste making me feel nauseated.

Bradford lets out a sympathetic chuckle, puffing on his own cigar with ease. "It's not so bad once you get the hang of it."

"I will take your word for it," I rasp out in between coughs, handing it back to him.

A watery grin spreads across his broad face as he murmurs around the roll of tobacco. "Happy birthday, kid."

The smoke from Bradford's cigar funnels around us, encasing us in the dense fog. It becomes so condensed, I can hardly see him, I can hardly catch my breath. My coughing fit turns into a frenzied need for air, a fight for oxygen as heat singes my skin and everything begins to fade.

I'm in Sydney's bedroom again, fettered to the bed posts, hopelessly trapped. She is kissing me, and loving me, and refusing to let me go.

She is dying with me.

God, I can't let her do this. I can't let her go this way.

Sydney calls my name through the haze of smoke, the wall of death, and my name on her tongue is the only semblance of sweetness I can salvage amongst the debris.

"Oliver..."

"Oliver!"

I startle awake beside her, realizing that Sydney is *actually* calling my name. She is searching for me through the darkened bedroom, her panic heightening when her hand doesn't immediately grasp me. Catching my breath and moving closer, I slink my arm around her middle and pull her flush to my bare chest. "I'm right here, Syd," I breathe against the soft lobe of her ear, finding solace in the way she relaxes in my embrace. Her body heat soaks into my skin like early morning rays of sunshine.

All I've wanted to do is hold her.

All she's wanted to do is hold me.

It's been over two weeks since Sydney and I faced the flames together, and we have been inseparable since our release from the hospital. We were treated for second-degree burns and smoke inhalation, but the physical scars left behind from that night are far less dire than the emotional ones that are cut and branded into our very essence.

I thought I had experienced the worst out of life, being brainwashed and held captive in a stranger's basement for over two-thirds of my life... but *my God*, how wrong I was.

The worst moment was the look in Sydney's eyes when she made the choice to end her life because she couldn't bear the thought of living without me again. She made a conscious decision to die that night. To burn.

For me.

It's a heavy, heavy weight—a boulder to my heart and a hammer to my lungs. It's a knife in my gut and a fist around my throat. It's hard not to sink in these dark waters with an anchor tied to every piece of me.

So, I hold her.

Every chance I get, I hold her, and I manage to stay afloat a little longer.

Spooning her tight, I curl a piece of her shorter hair around my fingertips, baring her neck to me. I lean in to kiss her favorite spot, right in between her shoulder and her jawline. It's a magnificent arch cased in silken skin and a speckling of freckles that resemble the Milky Way.

Sydney doesn't know this, but every time I kiss those tiny stars, I make a wish.

"Did you have a nightmare?" I whisper, splaying my fingers over her nude stomach, pressing her further into me.

She backs her rear into my groin when my tongue sweeps over the sensitive skin along her neck. "Mmm-hmm," she murmurs, a moan following.

My hand travels higher, cupping her breast, and she wriggles, abutting my erection in return.

It's fair to say we've been insatiable since we arrived back home. We made a promise to take things slow, to let our bodies and minds heal, and it was a promise we broke within seven minutes of walking through my front door, promptly christening the dining room table.

I hope it's the only promise we ever break to one another.

Ever since, we haven't been able to keep our hands off each other. It's always a desperate, primal sort of lovemaking, a frenzy of heartbeats and breaths and touches and warm flesh. It feels like life or death every single time, and I wonder how long it will be like this—this voracious need to crawl inside the other's bones and cling to the marrow, to the evidence of our living, breathing bodies.

It's beyond sexual.

It's *primitive*.

"I need you," Sydney tells me in a heated whisper, rolling around to face me.

We're always face-to-face, eye-to-eye, replacing that harrowing moment in her burning bedroom with something sweeter.

I move down her body, pulling her underwear with me and trailing my open mouth along her skin. And then my face is buried between her thighs, and she's gripping my hair, arching her spine, moaning, writhing, as I hungrily feast on her. Both of my hands glide up her body to palm her breasts, my eyes raised, watching every erotic quake and tremor that carries her toward ecstasy. I lower one hand to pump my fingers into her, curling them just the way she likes as I tease and torment her.

Sydney gasps. "Oh, God... Oliver..."

I know when she's close to climaxing by the way her thighs clamp around my face and her hands tug my hair, her noises temporarily ceasing like a dramatic prelude to her crescendo.

She breaks against my tongue, our mutual groans aligning, and I linger between her legs, savoring her release. I've realized we both reach orgasm rather quickly lately—almost as if we're in a reckless hurry to *feel*. To feel things we never expected to feel again.

Sydney comes down slowly, her tears beckoning me to crawl up her body and kiss them clean. "It's all right. I'm here, Syd." I pepper words of love across her face, chasing away the memories that are trying to steal her from me.

"Make love to me. Please."

I don't hesitate, pulling myself free from my boxers and pushing inside. Foreheads pressed together and eyes locked, I move with hard, deliberate strokes, needing to feel the deepest parts of her. "Are you with me?"

She nods, cupping my cheeks. "I'm with you."

It's imperative I know she's here and not... *there*.

Kissing her with starved lips, our tongues duel and dance as our bodies move together in perfect rhythm, our intimacy unmatched. I crave these moments when we're so expertly entwined and lost in one another, nothing else seems to exist.

It doesn't take long before pleasure overtakes me and I groan into her mouth, releasing inside of her, then collapse atop her and sprinkle kisses along her Milky Way freckles. I nibble her lobe, whispering softly, "I loved you then, I love you now, and I'll love you until my dying day."

I roll beside her, pulling her to me as the hurried beats of our hearts settle into something more content. Sydney falls asleep instantly, tangled up in me, and I place a final kiss to the freckled curve of her neck, making my wish.

She is every wish.

Today is the day Gabe returns home from his treatment at a burn unit in the city. My brother suffered more extensive trauma than me and Sydney, and just the thought of him running into a burning bedroom *twice* with little thought to his own safety, to save two people he cares about, inundates me with awe.

We have made regular trips to visit him over the last few weeks as he received a skin graft for a particularly ugly third-degree burn along his upper right arm. He's been in good spirits because that's just Gabe.

The betrayal from his father is the true trauma that wreaks havoc through his heart.

The firefighters managed to pull Travis out of the bedroom in time to spare his life, as Gabe hadn't even seen him through the thick veil of smoke, but Travis did suffer severe burns and is still in intensive care. If he makes it through, he'll be going to prison for a very long time.

A fitting end for him, indeed.

"He's here!"

Sydney skips down the hallway with an extra bounce in her step today. Her hair is now shoulder-length, styled into an adorable bob after the flames seared a noticeable chunk out of her light tresses. She obtained fairly extensive burns on both arms and the left side of her face, but they were only second-degree, thank goodness, and are healing nicely.

As for myself, I came out of the ordeal with burns along both thighs, as well as my left hand and arm. But I consider them nothing more than a pesky scratch, considering the dreadful alternative.

"You look lovely," I say to Sydney as an authentic smile lights up her face. Her glasses are perched upon her nose, a nose that wrinkles with playful animation when she saunters over to me in an oversized charcoal sweater and tight leggings. She's perky today. Lively.

She's Sydney again.

"You're sweet." Sydney props herself up on her tiptoes to gift me with a tender kiss. "I look like Freddie Krueger."

I blink. "I am not familiar, but I can only assume he's delightful. Especially if he looks this good in stretchy pants."

A snort reaches my ears as her forehead drops to my chest, fingers gripping the fabric of my t-shirt. A sigh escapes, and her voice kisses the front of my chest. "I feel better."

"You do?" My hands smooth her hair back, chin resting atop her head. "Mentally?"

A nod. "He's home. We're all home."

Home.

Sydney and Alexis have temporarily moved in with us while her own house acquires renovations. It's a lengthy process, due to the fact that the master bedroom was resorted to ruin and ash. Luckily, the fire was snuffed out before the flames spread too far and caused more damage throughout the rest of the interior.

And I have no complaints having Sydney in my bed every night.

Even Athena has taken to her, and to Alexis as well.

Alexis, on the other hand, tends to avoid the mischievous raccoon as often as possible. She can usually be found hiding in Gabe's room beneath his bed or behind the sofa. I'm hopeful the two animals can form a bond one day, seeing as they will be lifelong roommates.

Gabe pushes through the front door, Tabitha trailing behind him, and Sydney fidgets beside me as her breath hitches at the sight of him.

He's our hero.

Lorna, too. The neighbor woman ran next door to fetch Gabe, alerting him of the near-fatal circumstances. My brother didn't think twice before grabbing his pocketknife and jumping into the flames to rescue us. Neither of us would be here right now if it weren't for their quick thinking and courage.

"Thanks again for everything," Gabe murmurs to Tabitha hovering in the doorway, her coat long and black like her hair. She has a lovestruck look in her eyes as Gabe cups her face between his palms and leans in close, kissing her forehead, nose, and landing on her pink lips. "You've been my rock."

Tabitha closes her eyes, her fingers curling around his wrists while her smile blooms brighter. "I'm just so glad you're okay."

It's an intimate moment we have witness to, and it's a familiar intimacy—the kind I've grown to yearn and crave. It's a once-in-a-lifetime treasure, a true gift, a falling star breaking away from all the others and flying free. I smile right along with them.

"Give Hope a fist-bump for me," Gabe teases, planting a final kiss to her hairline and pulling back with a wink. "I'll call you tonight."

A charmed nod is her reply. Tabitha gives us a friendly wave as we gaze down at them over the railing before she turns leave and Gabe closes the front door behind her, hesitating with his hand pressed to the khaki-painted steel. Head bowed, stance tight with emotion, we wait for him to face us. He's collecting his thoughts—reining in the assortment of feelings that are surely running rampant through him.

Sydney looks dizzy, nearly about to tumble right over the metal railing, so I place a steadying touch upon her shoulder, giving her a reassuring squeeze.

Gabe finally spins in place, letting out a hard breath. And when his eyes dance between us, unreadable at first, a grin breaks free and those eyes twinkle with affection. "You assholes owe me *big time*."

I feel Sydney's sigh of relief before I hear it. She runs toward him as he stalks up the staircase, allowing him to scoop her up into a one-armed, elevated hug when he reaches the top.

"I'm thinking free taco dip for life," Gabe says, shooting me a wink over her shoulder when the soles of her feet finally touch back down. "I'd add to that menu, but I'm pretty sure that's the only thing you can make."

Sydney swipes at her falling tears, a laugh slipping. "You can't pretend you didn't love my nipple cakes."

"Pleading the fifth on that one." Gabe releases her, still smiling, and moves over to me. "And *you*, big brother. I'm thinking maybe you could draw me into one of your comics as this super powerful demigod who radiates molten good looks and sexual mastery."

His ensuing eyebrow waggle has me pulling him into a hug, and I'm uncertain if I want to laugh or cry, but I suppose that's the point. I'm careful not to make contact with his injured arm, where healing wounds poke through the neck of his t-shirt, traveling upward and fading as they reach his jaw. "I'm relieved that you're all right, Gabe. I'll spend a lifetime thanking you for your bravery."

He chuckles against my shoulder. "Considering you have more lives than Sydney's cat, you'll be a busy guy."

Alexis mews from the armrest of the sofa as if she knows we're talking about her, and I move back from the embrace. "Alexis has faced numerous deaths?"

"There's been a consistent curiosity with moving vehicles." Sydney clears her throat. "And an incident with a snow blower."

"Oh."

Another knowing mewl.

The three of us make our way into the living area and spend a great deal of time just sitting in the comfortable silence—the profound evidence of our survival. Sydney brings out taco dip at one point and our conversation transitions from laughter and jokes to tears and disbelief, then reverts back to the effervescent atmosphere. Sydney sits between us on the sofa, her hand in mine and her head perched on Gabe's healthy shoulder as we reminisce and commiserate together.

As the afternoon rolls in, Sydney pulls out her cellular phone and types out an electronic message. "There's one more person who needs to be here," she tells us softly.

That person is Clementine, who arrives an hour later, and I realize it's the first time since I've returned that we are all in the same room together at once. It's a fitting moment for our childhood reunion, despite the grave circumstances that still hover over us like a gray cloud.

We sit around the living room, Gabe's back to the front of the sofa, Clementine seated upon it with her knees drawn up, and Sydney resting between my legs in the middle of the area rug. We order pizza as our conversation turns heavy.

Clementine releases a jagged sigh, twisting her sock around her ankle to distract herself from the pain. "I feel responsible for everything," she mutters at one point, setting aside the pizza she didn't even touch. "I knew he was a sick freak, but I had no idea he was capable of…"

We all avert our eyes, and my arms give Sydney a tender hug.

"He was my fuckin' *father*," Gabe laments, scrubbing both palms over his face. "I still haven't wrapped my mind around any of this."

"It's no one's fault but *his*," Sydney says, pressing her back to me and cinching my hand in hers.

Clementine brushes back a tear. "Deep down I know that, but it doesn't take away the guilt. I can't explain the hold he had on me, or the sickening grip of my secret. I felt so much shame, so much humiliation and self-loathing." Her breaths are ragged, her words barbed, puncturing us all with their gravity. "The more time that went by, the worse I felt. The harder it got. Travis always told me that no one would ever believe me, and I believed *him*."

Sydney gives my hand a quick squeeze before rising to her feet and running to the sofa, wrapping her arms around her sister. "Sis, I love you so much," she weeps, head dropping to Clementine's shoulder. "Why did you tell me it was Bradford?"

Clementine shifts, glancing my way, irises shimmering with apology. "It was easier to blame it on a dead man," she confesses, a haunting whisper. "I guess I was still trying to protect our secret… *my* secret. I can't explain it, Syd, but those feelings of shame are so powerful. Even talking about it right now feels like I'm betraying some twisted, deep-seated part of me."

"Do you want to talk in private?" Sydney sniffs.

She shakes her head after a thoughtful moment. "No. Everyone in this room has paid a dark price for my years of silence. You all deserve to know why."

Leaning back on my hands, I try to put myself in Clementine's shoes. She feels accountable. She's carried a sense of responsibility for what happened to her for many long years, and now more grave repercussions have been added to that weight. My abduction, Sydney's attack, the fire, the scars, both emotional and physical. I can only imagine the demons that are hounding her, trying to drag her down and drown her.

I clear my throat through a swallow. "You are not to blame," I tell her quietly, garnering looks from all three. "Travis' power ends here, right now, in this room."

Six eyes stare back at me, soaking up my words, and I think for a brief moment we are all taken back in time to simpler days, innocent days, days of sunshine and popsicles and endless summer nights. Before Travis. Before my disappearance. Before a man dug his heinous claws into one little girl and molded a hundred different futures.

Clementine, Sydney, Gabe, myself.

My mother.

Bradford.

There's no telling how many lives were altered, tainted, snuffed out. His talons ran deep, but we sever them now.

We cannot change the past, but we can certainly shape our future, and Travis will have no part of it. We'll rise from the ashes with smoke in our lungs and scars on our skin, but we will persevere. We will *thrive*.

Those six eyes soften, as if we have all broken through an invisible barrier together—a force unseen yet felt with every tarnished piece of our souls.

We wield our swords together, finding true strength in one another.

We will fight.

We will live.

After hours of deep discussion and even some laughs, Clementine departs and Gabe settles into his room for the evening, while Sydney and I retreat into the solitude of our own bedroom. We let Athena out of her cage when the door is properly secured, and we laugh and engage with the playful critter as she explores her surroundings. We feed her the nuts and fresh fruit we carried in, watching as she holds a strawberry between her little hands and nibbles away. I smile, amazed by her.

A short while later, Sydney climbs onto the bed and beckons me to follow. "Want to watch a movie?" she suggests, bouncing lightly on the mattress.

I brought a television into the room for entertainment... that is, when we aren't participating in other forms of *entertainment*, which is decidedly often.

Joining her on the bed and nuzzling in close, I nod. "It's been a trying day. A movie sounds wonderful."

We get comfortable and Sydney turns on a film about a high school reunion with two blonde women who act strangely and get themselves into absurd situations. The picture pulls an abundance of giggles from Sydney's lips, which, in turn, makes it my new favorite movie.

Deciding to multitask as we sit shoulder to shoulder against the headboard, I lean over to my nightstand and retrieve my sketchpad from the drawer. I've been detailing a new scene for my comic strip. Armed with a handful of markers, I add pops of color to the fireworks lighting up the night sky within the picture.

Sydney peers over my left shoulder, curious. "Is that our hill?"

"Yes. You made a wish on the fireworks."

A soft sigh kisses the bare stretch of my upper arm. "You remember?"

"The images are still a bit jumbled, but more details have breached the surface since my hypnotherapy sessions. I try to put the pictures to paper whenever I receive a clearer vision." I add streaks of dark purple to one of the fireworks, recalling treetops sheathed in violet. "You wished for us."

"You told me to write it down so it would come true."

I don't recall that particular part. "Did you?"

"Of course," she grins, her voice cracking with nostalgic whimsy. "That's why it came true."

Smiling, I continue my picture, reveling in the feel of her warm breath dusting my skin. As I add more veins of color, Sydney reaches over and plucks the marker from between my fingers. There's a playful light in her eyes, and I decide that I'll color one of the fireworks that exact same shade of blue. If the color doesn't exist, I'll simply have to create it.

"Hold still," she says.

I fidget when the felt tip of the marker glides along the inside of my forearm. "That tickles," I say through a laugh. "What are you writing?"

"My wish."

I sift amusedly through the assortment of markers and colored pencils with my opposite hand, trying to find the perfect color blue to match the stars in her eyes.

"There," she whispers. "All done."

The pop of the marker cap brings my attention back to her. I chuckle as I glance down at my arm, muttering, "Syd, you—"

Time freezes, and I go still. My words are eclipsed, my skin tingling. Sydney is speaking to me, but I can hardly hear her over my thunderous heartbeats.

My eyes dart to her confused face. "Why did you write that?"

"What?" She blinks, her smile dimming. "What's wrong?"

A swallow grips my throat when I look down at my arm, the familiar word staring back at me:

l o t u s

"Syd, please tell me why you wrote this," I plead, nearly choking on my words. "Why 'lotus'? What does it mean?"

I feel frantic, utterly perplexed, my gaze shifting wildly between the woman I love and the word that has haunted me, *guided* me, for over two long decades.

It was her.

All this time, *she* had written it on my arm.

But why on earth didn't she tell me?

And why is she looking at me like she has no idea what I'm even talking about?

"Oliver, I-I didn't..." Sydney shakes her head, a frown pinching her brow. "I didn't write 'lotus'. I wrote..."

She gasps then, or maybe it's a sob, a choked cry of wondrous disbelief muffled by her palm that shoots up and cups her mouth as her eyes widen with realization.

Sydney climbs over me, then gazes down at the letters from the opposite direction.

"Oh, my God..." she rasps out. "Oliver... I didn't write 'lotus'. You were looking at it upside-down."

"What?" The word nearly catches in my throat as I blink, staring at the same scribbling I etched into a stone wall, knowing it meant *something*, knowing it was important somehow, but I didn't understand it then.

And I only understand it now when Sydney picks up the marker from the mattress and rewrites it with a trembling hand, right-side-up.

She inhales a choppy breath, her tears spilling onto the ink. "It's our initials, Oliver. I wished for *us*."

There it is, in plain sight, gazing up at me:

sn + ol

"What's your wish?" I ask her.

"I should write it down. Then it will definitely come true."

"So write it down."

Sydney sits up and reaches for her backpack, unzipping it and pulling a black Crayola marker out of the box. "Give me your arm," she says.

I hold up my arm and watch as she etches the letters into my skin.

"Sydney, your parents want you home now."

My stepfather's booming voice interrupts us from the bottom of the hill.

Sydney pouts, her tongue poking out in concentration as she finishes her wish. "One second, almost done!" she calls back. She smiles at me as she pops the cap back on the marker and rezips her bookbag. "I have to go now."

"Yeah..." Disappointed, I glance at the strange word written on my arm. "What did you wish for?"

"Us."

Before I can question her further, she is already skipping down the hill, waving goodbye. "Bye, Syd. See you tomorrow."

I sound the letters out in my head: l-o-t-u-s.

Lotus?

"Oliver, time to go. I'll take you home," Travis orders.

I don't want to go with him, but he did promise me ice cream.

Frowning at the unfamiliar word illuminated in purple when the fireworks burst to life, I call back, "Yeah, yeah, I'm coming."

Lotus.

What does it mean?

I'll have to ask Sydney tomorrow.

Sydney is in my lap, holding me, weeping into the front of my chest.

All this time, it had been her.

She was with me in that basement for twenty-two years in the form of a childhood wish.

Written on my arm in black ink, misconstrued and upside-down, those letters manifested into the only true friend I had down in that hole. It created pages upon pages of stories and adventures, keeping me company, keeping me sane, keeping me *alive* for so many years.

It was her.

It's always been *her*.

With our initials on my arm and branded in my heart, I squeeze her tight, peppering kisses into her hair as I whisper words of love against her ear.

Sydney Neville + Oliver Lynch

It's always been us.

CHAPTER THIRTY-ONE

SYDNEY

Six Months Later
July 4th

"**K**NOCK-KNOCK!"

I'm leaning out my office window, my eyes trailing Oliver as he jogs through the front lawn with Athena harnessed to the end of a short leash. He's quite the sight around the neighborhood, his title transitioning recently from "that missing boy" to "resident raccoon walker". The children flock to them, and I think Oliver has started enjoying the attention just as much as Athena does.

The sun beats down on the man I love, illuminating the light sheen of sweat coasting down his chiseled face, as well as the smile that unfolds at the sight of me. The authentic joy I see in that smile never wanes, not once, whenever his eyes land on me.

Oliver looks up at the window, slightly winded. "Who's there?"

"Athena."

An adorable, dimpled grin answers back. "Athena who?"

"Athena very sexy man wandering around these streets, and I'm desperate for him to make sweet love to me." I throw him my most seductive series of winks, but I'm certain I look like I'm having a seizure, so I change it to a finger-waggle. "Now, please."

His mouth falls open, a hard swallow following. "Oh. All right."

Sensing Oliver's distraction, Athena seizes the opportunity to book it, pulling free from Oliver's grip and making a beeline towards the brand new bird feeder we installed the prior week. Wings flapping, feathers flying, the birds flee to safety as Athena climbs the feeder at an impressive momentum and knocks the whole thing over, bird seed spilling everywhere.

Oliver chases her, admonishing the animal as he approaches the wreckage. "Athena, no! Bad raccoon." She dodges him by nose-diving into the garden bed and digging up our freshly-planted vegetables. "Athena!"

I decide to offer my assistance in capturing our furry troublemaker, forgetting I'm only wearing a t-shirt and no pants, and bolt out the front door just as Oliver fails to catch her and trips, falling into the dirt.

Wincing, I run to him, accidentally leaving the door open for Alexis to scurry free and head straight for the moving vehicles. "Alexis, get back here!" My pants-less legs carry me towards the street, and I zoom past Lorna Gibson who is clutching her rosary, surely praying for God to save my soul from eternal damnation. I shoot her a quick wave just as a black Mustang comes careening to a stop.

It's Evan, the writer. *Awesome.* "Jesus, Sydney, you okay?" His eyes lower to my bare legs with a frown. "Missing something?"

"My cat."

Alexis makes it to the other side of the road, and I breathe a sigh of relief.

"I need to start writing this shit down," he jokes, attention lifting to where Oliver is chasing Athena into the bushes. "You guys make for some pretty epic book material."

"Please make me cool and good at cooking." I throw a wave to Summer, who is grinning from the backseat. "Gotta go catch my suicidal cat."

Ugh. She's wandering into someone's garage.

Running across the road with my bare feet, doing an awkward tiptoe dance as the pebbles and stones dig into the soles, I skip up the driveway and start yell-hissing. "Alexis! You absolute miscreant. No catnip for at least a week." She dips underneath a vehicle and the car alarm starts going off.

Fuck my life.

Ass in the air, head stuck beneath a Toyota Corolla as my heathen cat gets comfortable a few inches out of reach, the homeowner appears with a baseball bat, looking like he just stepped off the set of *Sons of Anarchy.*

I glance up, shame-faced, my *Dinosaurs* underwear with the quote *"Not the mama!"* on full display. "I-I'm so sorry," I squeak out, crawling backwards on the pavement. "My cat got loose and chose your... super cozy garage with the..." My gaze inspects my surroundings, panic surging when I regard the weapons and taxidermy lining the interior walls. "... axes a-and decapitated heads to make herself at home..."

Oliver jogs up the driveway then, Athena clasped between his arms and dirt smudging his face, saving me from this future episode of *Forensic Files*. "Syd... are you all right?"

"Oliver! My boyfriend. My very manly, strong, and protective boyfriend." The smile I offer is strained and most definitely psychotic. "We're very sorry to intrude."

The beefy biker props himself up on his baseball bat, an amused smile curling the scar along his jaw. "I loved that show."

I blink. *"Forensic Files?"*

Wait, no, that was an internal thought.

"Dinosaurs," the neighbor replies, his chuckle gruff. "That fuckin' baby was a riot."

My nerves begin to dissipate just as my cat sneaks out from beneath the vehicle, slithering around each ankle and begging for forgiveness. *Not today, Satan.* I scoop her up and traipse over to Oliver, who is standing at the edge of the garage looking like a deer in headlights. My cheeks fill with air and I blow out a breath. "Ready?"

Oliver purses his lips with a short nod. "Thoroughly."

We collect our zoo and make our way across the street and back home, me with my ass hanging out and Oliver looking like he participated in the pig races and lost. Athena and Alexis both squirm in our respective embraces, and I swear they are attempting to high-five each other for a job well done.

"Fun morning," I deadpan as we break the threshold and release the animals. Alexis and Athena chase each other up the stairs, pulling a grin from my lips. Despite the chaos, I can't help but feel enamored by the bond they have created over the past six months. I never thought Alexis would warm up to the mischievous raccoon, but somehow, they have found a friend within each other.

Raising my eyes to Oliver, I realize that sometimes the most beautiful friendships come from the most unlikely pair.

Oliver slides a palm down his face, smearing the mud as he hefts out a frazzled sigh. His gaze shifts to me, settling on my very unclothed legs. "Syd, you're nearly naked. That ruffian was most certainly having impure visualizations."

There is no mistaking the little frown that appears between his eyebrows, causing an audible swoon to escape me. "Oliver Lynch, are you getting all territorial on me?"

So hot.

"Yes, a bit." His arms extend, hands clasping my hips and pulling me flush against him. They slip beneath the hem of my t-shirt, cupping my backside. "I don't enjoy when other men put their eyes on you. It gives me violent thoughts."

"Mmm." He smells like sweat and cedar, mingling with a trace of Miracle Grow. Ours groins collide as my fingers disappear underneath his running tank and skim the planks of his deliciously defined abs. "You're extra sexy when you're jealous."

Inching up on the tips of my toes, I crush our mouths together, my tongue instantly seeking his. He grips me tighter from behind, his arousal digging into my belly and triggering a frisson of heat to shoot south.

Holy hell, I can't get enough of this man.

We can't get enough of *each other.*

Oliver moved in with me after the renovations were completed on my bedroom, leaving zero trace of the damage that was caused that fateful Christmas night. Of course, the damage to the plaster walls was an easy fix—the damage that still lingers in our bones will never fully heal.

Travis Wellington survived the fire. After multiple skin grafts and extensive surgeries, he was eventually arrested and charged with arson, attempted murder, murder-for-hire, and the sexual assaults to my sister. There's always a spark of elation that tickles me when I think about his fate. Not only is he physically marred, nearly beyond recognition, but he'll likely spend the rest of his pathetic days behind bars... and we all know what happens to pedophiles in prison.

The events of that evening changed us, irrevocably, but our insatiable lust for life and each other is the greatest gift we pulled from the ashes and we count our blessings daily.

We also have a lot of sex.

Oliver's mouth finds the sensitive stretch of skin along my neck, the place where he gives me "Milky Way kisses", and my knees turn to jelly as I collapse against him. "Need you inside me..." I whimper into his shoulder, breathing in the earthy scent of him.

"Right here?" *Nibble.* "By the front door?" *Nip.* "All sweaty and dirty?" *Lick.*

"God, yes."

Fingers curling around the waistline of his jogging shorts, I tug them down his thighs until his erection is free and my palm is wrapped around him, stroking and tugging.

Oliver's moan caresses my ear, sending a shockwave of shivers through my poor, sex-starved body. It's only been five hours, but I'm ravenous.

I fall to my knees in front of him just as the front door whips open behind me.

"Holy fuckin' hell no, Jesus, God, *fuck.*"

The spew of profanities comes from Gabe, and I jump back up, barking at him. "Dammit, Gabe!" Helping Oliver pull his shorts up, I growl through the flush of humiliation staining my cheeks. "Can't you knock for once? God!"

Gabe stands there, pale and frozen. "I have never resented my twenty-twenty vision more than I do in this moment."

Oliver fumbles for his cell phone, frantically pressing buttons as he holds it upside-down. "Goodness, I have a great deal of notifications to sort through. I'll be right back."

A snigger slips through my exasperation as Oliver makes a hurried retreat out of the room. "What the hell is going on today?"

"Not sure, but I'm requesting a redo. I came over to grab the beer for the party tonight and stumbled into some perverted level of Hell I can't unsee. And do you *ever* wear pants?"

A huff. "Beer is in the kitchen. My grave is out back, dug and ready to go."

"I might just join you," he laughs.

We share an amused grin, heads shaking with a collective sigh.

My repaired friendship with Gabe has been another blessing to come out of the rubble and ruin. I still feel horrible about my ridiculous accusations against him, and I know it's something I'll never truly forgive myself for. But if we've learned anything at all, it's that life is far too fleeting, too precious, to take a single second for granted—*we* are too precious.

Travis had a wicked hold on every single one of us. He was a master of manipulation, bearer of destruction. None of us came out unscathed, but we all came out better. Stronger.

Together.

Gabe slings an arm around me—the same arm that has healed remarkably well over the past six months, despite leaving behind scar tissue and harrowing memories that will always be a physical reminder of that night. He calls it his epic battle wound.

I call it love.

Gabe smiles, sensing my momentary drift in thought. "Anywhere I want to be?"

Leaning into my friend, head dropping to the side of his chest, I smile back, exhaling a thankful breath. "Nah. We're good right here."

Our traditional Fourth of July party rages around us, while Clementine and I slurp Jell-O out of tiny plastic shot glasses with our tongues. She giggles through a blue smile that matches her hair. "These are the moments I love having a bartender for a sister," she states with a wink.

Clem looks amazing, healthy and glowing, having made incredible healing strides over the last few months. She's been in extensive therapy, as well as speaking out at local schools and functions, and has even been featured in various media broadcasts. I know my sister will never completely recover from the trauma she endured, a trauma that stemmed from six years of sexual abuse and manifested into a decades-long domino effect of subsequent grief, but her progress is already inspiring. She's my hero.

I have a lot of heroes in my life.

Speaking of one of them, Gabe slips into our Jell-O shot bonding session and clinks his beer bottle to my plastic cup. He gives Clem a wink and a fist-bump, and I smile at the gesture. I'm glad they have managed to rekindle their friendship after the tension between them.

It all makes sense now—why my sister panicked and bolted at the "babygirl" nickname and why she wasn't able to progress any further with Gabe, despite her feelings for him. While Gabe is nothing, *nothing*, like his sorry excuse for a father, that correlation will never wane.

Besides, it all worked out. Gabe and Tabitha are happier than ever, and Clementine is content with the single mom life for now. She's focusing on herself, her journey to healing, and her incredible daughter.

"Where's your wifey?" I ask Gabe, stealing his beer and taking a sip. I call Tabitha his wife, even though they aren't at that level of commitment yet. But it's one-hundred percent happening.

He snags the beer back, swatting at me. "She couldn't find a sitter for Hope, but we're meeting up later."

Hope. Dear Lord, if my ovaries weren't already kicking into overdrive with Oliver's sweet kisses, words of adoration, and the magic that dwells inside his pants, watching Gabe go from an eternal bachelor to a doting father figure to little Hope will most certainly get me pregnant.

The baby fever is real.

"By the way, your better half is looking for you," Gabe adds, his eyebrows dancing over the spout of the bottle.

"*Better* half?" I glare at him before my shoulders sag with defeat. "True and fair."

Clem slings back another alcohol-infused gelatin concoction and stands from her chair. "Oliver's been MIA for a while," she breezes. "I think I saw him leave with a sexy mystery girl."

I blanche. "What?"

"Jeez, kidding," she snorts. "The man wouldn't notice another woman if she fell from Heaven, butt-naked, face-first into his lap. He's in the guest room drawing."

Slugging her in the arm, my heart rate returns to a less concerning pace. "Skank."

"Hoochy." She blows me a kiss and disappears into the kitchen.

Rude.

I issue Gabe a quick goodbye and make my way down the hallway to Oliver's old bedroom. He's looking mighty scrumptious in his red and white striped collared shirt, and I debate locking us in the room for the remainder of the evening for... *reasons.*

But he's crouched over, zipping up a little backpack, looking at me standing in the doorway with the sweetest, most eager smile, and I honestly wouldn't change these plans for anything. Even multiple orgasms.

Maybe.

"Is it time?" I grin, my smile gleaming.

"It appears so. They'll be starting shortly." Oliver slings the black backpack over his shoulder and reaches for my hand. "Let's go."

The walk to our secret hill is full of giggles and hand-holding, sticky air and clumsy feet, reminiscent of our childhood treks to this same location. And when we climb up the familiar ravine, I can't help but think about how far we've come.

Two years ago, I sat here all alone, wishing on the fireworks, begging for something I thought would never come to be.

One year ago, I had my wish, but he was still so fragile, so full of missing pieces. But I *had* him, he returned to me, and I've spent every waking moment since thanking the stars.

And this year...

This year is just the beginning of an entire lifetime of fireworks, promises, and starry-eyed wishes.

We lie side-by-side beneath the vibrant glow of the night sky as it bursts to life with radiant colors. I reach for Oliver's hand, the fireworks muddling into painted blurs when my eyes well with the intensity of the moment. "You should make a wish," I tell him in a hushed tone, my voice cracking in time with the sky. Turning my head, I find him already staring at me.

"All right."

His gaze holds me in a striking clinch as reds and yellows and blues reflect within his sunset eyes. "You should write it down. Then it will definitely come true."

Oliver smiles, and I swear I see nerves glittering in the upturn of his lips. With a small nod, he rolls to his opposite side and fetches his backpack, unzipping it and pulling out a sketchpad. He trails his index finger over the top page, and there's a noticeable hitch when he inhales. "I did," he responds, handing the pad of paper over to me.

We both sit up straight while butterflies dance to life inside my belly, their wings in a tizzy. I take the outstretched paper and cut him a quick glance, brimming with curiosity before flipping it open.

"I was working on a new scene for the comic and thought this particular part might interest you."

Eyes casing over the images with the firework display as my nightlight, I absorb his beautifully crafted sketches. The first box is a picture of us holding hands as we walk down a familiar street. The second is us climbing this very hill. The third is a photo of fireworks overhead, while we lie beneath them, just as we are now.

The fourth is Oliver reaching into his backpack.

The fifth is me, looking through a comic strip—*this* comic strip. He's captured this exact moment, right down to the fantastical twinkle in my bright blue eyes.

And the sixth box...

The sixth box.

A sob breaks loose, my hand flying to my mouth and catching the rebel tears that slip free.

"Syd..."

My eyes are squeezed shut, my whole body tremoring. I force a gulp of air into my lungs and turn to face him, pink-cheeked and stupefied. "Oliver," I squeak out.

There he sits with a ring in his hand, the diamonds in the shape of a lotus flower.

Oliver resituates, propping himself up on one knee as the colors rain down, sheathing the diamond in dazzling hues, while illuminating the look of awestruck whimsy on his face. "Sydney," he says, linking my fingers through his unoccupied hand as he holds up the ring. Oliver finds my eyes, my weeping, lovesick eyes, and holds tight. "I loved you then, I love you now, and I'll love you until my dying day. You're my best friend. You're my queen," he whispers, words spilling out like poetry. "Will you be my wife?"

I tackle him. I throw my arms around him and nearly steal the air from his lungs as we both topple backwards, and I pepper his face in a thousand tiny *yeses*. "I love you. I love you so much. Yes, yes, yes. Please marry the shit out of me."

Oliver grins through my kiss attack, then rolls us over until he's hovering above me. He takes my hand and places the lotus diamond around my ring finger, wiping away my tears. "I'm very relieved you said yes," he whispers, our foreheads touching.

"Who else would I marry?" My nose scrunches up in a teasing way, my words echoing his response to me from many years ago, window to window.

A smile stretches. "It also would have been a bit awkward for the people waiting at the bottom of the hill."

What?

I turn then, looking down below us, my gaze landing on the crowd that has gathered. Our friends and family erupt into cheers, sparklers bursting to life, Gabe whistling up at us with an arm around Tabitha who is moving Hope's little hand in an enthusiastic wave, Clem clapping through her tears, and even Lorna Gibson nodding with a knowing grin. Familiar neighbors, some who participated in Oliver's original search and rescue, whoop and holler in celebration, and my tears fall as hard as my heart did on Oliver's front stoop twenty-five years ago.

Oliver pulls me to my feet and circles his strong arms around my middle, crushing me to his chest. We slow dance to the music of fireworks, the cheers from down below, and the beautiful beats of our hearts.

As we hold each other beneath the starry sky, I stretch out my hand, watching as the lotus diamond sparkles and gleams with every burst from above. I think about its meaning and how it represents our love story in the most exquisite way.

*The **Lotus** will bloom into the most magnificent flower, even when its roots are in the murkiest of waters.*

I wrap my arms around Oliver Lynch, my forever best friend, burying my face against the comforting warmth of his chest.

And it's there upon our secret hill that we dance, we cry, and we fall in love all over again.

It's there we bloom.

EPILOGUE

OLIVER

Two Years Later

"I S THAT A HEAD? Is it supposed to be a head?"

Yes. Of course it is. I know this because all I've done is research childbirth for the past thirty-nine weeks and five days.

It's a head.

My daughter's head, adorned with tuffs of dark blonde curls.

There's also a fair amount of blood and unidentifiable fluid that has me teetering on both feet, dizzy little stars flickering behind my eyes.

Oh, dear.

"Are you about to pass out? Oliver! Don't you dar—" Sydney's battle cry interrupts her demands as she continues to push the tiny human from her womb. She cinches my hand, nails digging in like talons.

The head is crowning.

Along with more blood and fluid.

So much fluid.

I sputter, still feeling exceptionally woozy. "How will the shoulders breach? How on earth will they fit?" This is concerning to me. My chest feels tight, my legs like fluctuant jellyfish. All of my research turns to dust as I squeeze my wife's hand harder than she squeezes mine.

Her huffing and puffing has me equally concerned, so I blink away the stars and attempt to focus on her. I lean down, my fingers brushing the sweat-soaked hair from her forehead while the medical staff coax her through the birth. "Are you all right?"

Sydney glares in my direction. "It feels like I'm pushing a goddamn freight train out of a pinhole." *Another wail.* "My insides are on the outside." *Another push.* "And my vagina is literally ripping in half like Moses is parting the Red Sea."

I make the grave error of glancing back down at the *red sea* in that moment, instantly regretting the decision.

The stars win, and I go down.

"I still can't believe you fainted."

Three days later we are home, sitting side-by-side on the living room sofa while we watch *The Parent Trap* together. Our daughter is sound asleep against my chest, her little lips in the shape of an 'O' as her cheek molds into me. A dribble of drool stains the front of my shirt and squeaky sighs bathe me in fulfillment.

After a climactic labor and delivery, I was properly resuscitated, unconscious for only thirty seconds. Nevertheless, the memory causes my skin to heat with embarrassment. "I will never stop apologizing for my grossly inconvenient timing," I mutter, my wife's head propped up on my shoulder, our hands interlaced. I turn to see her smiling at me in amusement. "No amount of books could prepare me for the… well, the…" I gulp. "There was a great deal of fluid."

Sydney snickers, nuzzling into me, her fingers dancing along my arm and trailing to our little bundle. She snakes a soft curl around her index finger.

Despite my momentary disruption, the true highlight of that day was my superhero wife delivering the most extraordinary gift. The memory takes my breath away as I gaze down at the woman I chose. The woman I *choose*, every single day. "God, Syd, you were incredible."

She quirks another smile, lifting her chin. "Way better than you."

"Yes, much better." I kiss the top of her head, inhaling her floral shampoo as I process the fact that I'm a father. We are *parents*. "It feels surreal… we have a baby."

Our eyes hold, a thousand wordless sentiments passing between us before we shift our gaze to the little treasure lying in my arms.

Charlene.

We named our daughter after my late mother.

Sydney painted a stunning mural of me and my mother planting vegetables in her precious garden that we've hung in the nursery—a tribute to the woman I miss every day. I know she is looking down on her new granddaughter, watching her grow, just as she would watch her springtime blooms.

"I think she's out..." Sydney murmurs softly, eyeing the adjacent bassinet. "We should put her down."

I nod in agreement, carefully rising and placing the swaddled newborn into her sleeping chambers. A sigh of relief escapes us both when Charlene remains still, despite the transition. Then my eyebrow arches with mischief when I glance at Sydney, casing her from head to toe. *Goodness,* she's lovelier than ever, standing before me with tired eyes and baggy clothing, a burp cloth protruding from the top of her blouse, three days post-partum. "She's asleep," I tell her with a wink. "You know what this means, yes?"

A wicked gleam meets my own. "We have about thirty minutes to pig out on oatmeal cookies and binge *Rugrats* episodes."

"I was thinking we could finally indulge in one of the seventeen casseroles Lorna made for us, but I'll settle for cookies," I reply in jest.

We make our way into the kitchen, Alexis trailing our ankles, and we let her outside to join Athena in the outdoor playpen we had custom built. It's been a lifesaver as we take time to acclimate the raccoon to our new baby.

The animals chase each other in circles as I gather two plates for our cookies.

Sydney holds a finger up. "Wait, one more thing."

A moment later, the kitchen is flooded with the musical soundings of *The Barenaked Ladies.* I have yet to memorize this song, but I find great entertainment in the fact that Sydney has. She snatches up my arms and starts parading us around the kitchen, echoing the onslaught of ridiculous rhymes, making us both laugh until our stomachs ache. We step on each other's toes, and I spin her into a terribly clumsy circle, and she sprawls against my chest, winded and wondrous.

When the song falls silent, we still hold each other, swaying gently to the sounds of our pets fighting over a toy mouse and Charlene startling awake with a cry that resembles a squealing elephant. We share a humored glance.

I'm about to break away to fetch our daughter when Sydney pulls me back. "Just give me one more minute," she whispers, a delicate plea muffled into my shirt. I squeeze her tight, fingers threading through her hair. "You're a dad, Oliver. I always knew you'd change the world someday."

The corner of my mouth quirks up, touched. "We both have, Syd. We make quite a good team."

We certainly do.

Sydney still creates custom websites for authors, along with pursuing her true love of painting. She's designed numerous pieces of artwork for high-profile clients after our love story became national news due to Gabe posting pages of my comic strips on social media. His post went viral, and so did our story.

While I never ended up selling my original comic books, I did sign a deal with a publisher to release a new edition of *The Lotus Chronicles*. The payment advance I received has been a great relief, allowing me to purchase my first vehicle and provide for my growing family.

The stories feature familiar faces, such as a super powerful demigod who radiates molten good looks, as well as his snow queen bride. There is a blue-haired sorceress with a mystical frog and clairvoyant daughter, a meddlesome old woman with a magical cane, and an oddball scientist who lives beneath the earth with his young son.

Then there's me, The Black Lotus, fighting the good fight with a quirky orange tabby cat for a sidekick and a devious raccoon who tries to foil our plans. There is magic and adventure and friendship and grand love.

The only thing that's changed is Sydney's role—The Queen of the Lotus.

She is still my queen, but she's no longer a damsel in distress.

Syd is a hero, like me, and we defeat the villains side-by-side, hand-in-hand. She is my partner, my companion, my equal... the other half of my heart.

We save the world together.

I press a tender kiss to her forehead and hold out my arm, my gaze dancing between hers and mine.

Our matching tattoos smile back at us:

sn + ol

The End

ACKNOWLEDGMENTS

Late one night as I was attempting to fall asleep, the word "Lotus" popped into my mind—and for some reason, I was convinced it was the title of my next book.

How? No clue whatsoever. I had barely plotted anything out at that point. All I knew was that the book was going to be about a man who escapes captivity after twenty-two years, along with his childhood best friend who tries to heal him. When I researched the meaning of the flower, I was even more convinced... but it still wasn't enough.

So, I started toying with the idea of it being some kind of code or misconstrued word. Upside-down, backwards, all mixed up. Nothing really worked, but I shot a text message to my husband with my thought process. A few minutes later he comes upstairs and says, "If you're willing to change their names, I have an idea."

Originally, Oliver and Sydney had different names. But when my husband told me his idea about flipping the word upside-down and having it be their FREAKIN' INITIALS, I almost fainted. Then I hunkered down to write this thing because I was pathetically excited for the big reveal.

This brings me to my first acknowledgement, as per usual: my husband, Jake.

You guys, I may write the words, but this author stuff is a joint effort. My husband is my partner in crime, my sounding board, and my better half. (*True and fair.*)

He's a superhero.

Another overwhelming, gigantic shoutout goes to my three initial readers: E. R. Whyte, Chelley Schultz, and Vanessa Sheets. Honestly, I don't know where this book would be without you ladies. Probably burned. Hopefully not, but maybe. Thank you for holding my hand through the complicated plot points, giving me sage wisdom and suggestions, encouraging and inspiring me, and for helping me with edits.

So much goes into making a story the best it can possibly be, and I'm very grateful you are such a big part of that process.

Thank you to all of my beta readers for your lovely feedback and kind words: Jillian Cunningham, Stephanie Goodrich, Ashley Sartorius, Amber Kristyn, Laura Christine, and Amy Waayers. And huge thanks to my ARC readers for the early reviews that have brought me to tears.

Thank you to my sensitivity reader who will remain anonymous. Tackling sensitive subjects is difficult, and my continuous goal is to bring as much truth and realism as possible to these situations. And hope. Always hope.

Thank you, Steve Holland, for *The Lotus Chronicles* comic sketch! I'm over-the-moon happy with how it turned out. It brings my heart so much joy. Go follow Steve's movie musings here: http://nerdlistsand horrormovies.blogspot.com

Big thanks to Athena Southern (AHEM) for the invaluable raccoon knowledge! You are now immortalized between these pages, represented as Oliver's mischievous furry friend. I appreciate all of your support and kindness. Thank you as well to Antoinette Naber for the additional insight into domesticated raccoons. While I did take the liberty of pushing the boundaries of what may be realistic, I felt it was acceptable with this particular story. There is an overall sense of magic and imagination, I think. Raccoons aren't generally *that* sweet and cuddly. Sadly.

Thank you to my incredible group of queens in my reader's group and promo team for cheering me on with my writing journey and with life in general. I love my growing community of fans, friends, and readers, and I wouldn't be where I am without all of you. Thank you for the messages, the recommendations, the tags, the comments, and the sweet, encouraging words.

Lastly, all the thanks in the world to my amazing children and family for always pushing me, cheering me on, and keeping me inspired. I love you all so much.

Oh, and also lastly, thank you to Lord Huron for being my muse. Anytime I think of this story, I will think of *Strange Trails*. I'm pretty sure I had "Louisa" on constant loop for two months straight.

No regrets.

PLAYLIST

Listen to the playlist HERE

"Someone Tonight" — Kevin Griffin
"Blinding Lights (Acoustic Cover)" — Nick Fradiani
"Miles" — Phillip Phillips
"Louisa" — Lord Huron
"Hallelujah" — Kate Voegele
"Into the Wild" — Lewis Watson
"Guiding Light" — Mumford & Sons
"Bloom" — Paper Kites
"If You Could Only See" — Boyce Avenue
"Something Just Like This" — Coldplay
"Frozen Pines" — Lord Huron
"Cancion De La Noche" — Matthew Perryman Jones
"I'll Be" — Edwin McCain
"One Week" — Barenaked Ladies

ABOUT THE AUTHOR

If you enjoyed this story and would like to chat more about it, check out
the *Lotus Discussion Group* on Facebook: http://www.facebook.com/
groups/442744946995331
And feel free to join my reader's group!
http://www.facebook.com/groups/145154332790534
Follow me and stuff:
Facebook: @jenhartmannauthor
Twitter: @authorjhartmann
Instagram: @author.jenniferhartmann
TikTok: @jenniferhartmannauthor

No pressure, but my heart explodes when I see a nice review.
Leave your thoughts on Amazon, Goodreads, and Bookbub!

♡

www.jenniferhartmannauthor.com

ALSO BY JENNIFER HARTMANN

Duet Series: Aria & Coda

Still Beating

The Wrong Heart

June First

Claws and Feathers

Co-Writes

The Thorns Remain

Entropy

ABOUT THE AUTHOR

Jennifer Hartmann resides in northern Illinois with her devoted husband, Jake, and three children, Willow, Liam, and Violet. When she is not writing angsty love stories, she is likely thinking about writing them. She enjoys sunsets (because mornings are hard), bike riding, traveling anywhere out of Illinois, binging Buffy the Vampire Slayer reruns, and that time of day when coffee gets replaced by wine. Jennifer is a wedding photographer with her husband and a self-love enthusiast. She is excellent at making puns and finding inappropriate humor in mundane situations. She loves tacos. She also really, really wants to pet your dog.
Xoxo.

Made in the USA
Monee, IL
30 July 2022

10580766R00193